Praise for

FIERY EDGE OF STEEL

"Archer delves deeper into the enticing and magical world of *Dark Light of Day* in this original and clever urban fantasy . . . Excitement and action leap from the pages as Archer's skill with description pulls readers fully into her magical world."

—*Publishers Weekly*

"An astounding adventure tale. Archer's unique world, where Lucifer's army triumphed at Armageddon, is filled with adherence to strict laws that keep an uneasy peace between races . . . A really fresh and fascinating series!" —*RT Book Reviews* (4 stars)

"Archer has a great ability to keep the story moving along through characters' dialogue and through her imaginative and unique world . . . World-building is incredibly detailed and consistent."

—*Rabid Reads*

DARK LIGHT OF DAY

"A spectacular debut novel."

—Faith Hunter, *USA Today* bestselling author

"There is a fresh new voice in urban fantasy, and she has a unique take on Armageddon . . . With her unusual heroine, Noon Onyx, Archer has created a brilliant character who struggles against fate to find her place in the world. Set against the backdrop of university life, there is an abundance of adventure, mystery, and passion!" —*RT Book Reviews* (4 stars)

"A great debut from the urban fantasy world. Ms. Archer is now down on my 'never miss' author list." —*Night Owl Reviews*

"Very original and enjoyable." —*Rabid Reads*

"A fascinating story line . . . Archer has created a dark world that will grab your attention from the very start." —*The Reading Cafe*

"Coming of age/new adult set in a dark world where demons have won . . . An interesting and unique take on demons and angels . . . A lively and engaging fantasy which twisted some elements in a refreshing way!" —*The Book Pushers*

WHITE HEART
OF JUSTICE

JILL ARCHER

ACE BOOKS, NEW YORK

THE BERKLEY PUBLISHING GROUP
Published by the Penguin Group
Penguin Group (USA) LLC
375 Hudson Street, New York, New York 10014

USA • Canada • UK • Ireland • Australia • New Zealand • India • South Africa • China

penguin.com

A Penguin Random House Company

WHITE HEART OF JUSTICE

An Ace Book / published by arrangement with Black Willow, LLC

Ace Books are published by The Berkley Publishing Group.
ACE and the "A" design are trademarks of Penguin Group (USA) LLC.

For information, address: The Berkley Publishing Group,
a division of Penguin Group (USA) LLC,
375 Hudson Street, New York, New York 10014.

ISBN: 978-0-425-25717-3

PUBLISHING HISTORY
Ace mass-market edition / June 2014

PRINTED IN THE UNITED STATES OF AMERICA

10 9 8 7 6 5 4 3 2 1

Cover art by Jason Chan.
Cover design by Lesley Worrell.
Interior text design by Laura K. Corless.

Acknowledgments

Many thanks and much gratitude to:

Lois Winston, my agent, who excels at both pep talks and plain speaking.

The team at Ace who helped make this book happen: Jessica Wade, senior editor; Michelle Kasper, senior production editor; Mary Pell, copy editor; Isabel Farhi, editorial assistant; Lesley Worrell, art director; and Jason Chan, the cover artist.

Joan Havens, for helping with the Latin. As with *Fiery Edge of Steel*, I took some liberties with the translations, so any errors are entirely my fault.

Roxanne Rhoads, owner of Bewitching Book Tours, who helped with promotion and publicity for the first two Noon Onyx books and will hopefully do so again for this third.

All of the bloggers who interviewed me, allowed me to guest blog, spotlighted the series, participated in cover reveals, reviewed the books, and/or helped to spread the word in other ways—you are all amazing! Your enthusiasm and support is more appreciated than you could ever know.

My family and friends, for their endless encouragement and understanding. (Writers working under deadline pressure have been known to be cranky or sometimes simply absent.)

Marion L., Lonnie M., Matt A., Monica H., Jen S., Dianne T., Kate C., and everyone else who bought extra copies of the books to share with others—you are awesome!

My readers: Without you, the world, the character, her stories, and this series would only exist in my imagination. Authors need an audience for their work to be complete. We write to entertain, to provoke thought and emotion, to create something that can be shared. We write for *you*.

If you like *White Heart of Justice*, please consider reviewing the book wherever you hang out online. These days, writing a review is one of the most effective ways you can help an author whose work you like and want to see more of. Even a sentence or two can make a big difference in whether or not the book is discovered by someone else who might like it.

For a glossary, discussion questions, and other extras, please visit my website at jillarcher.com.

Prologue

❦

I can't be with you anymore. *That's what she'd said. Six words that had become sixty then six hundred then six* thousand ... *sixty thousand* ... *six* million ... *reverberating in his head, bouncing around inside his brain, driving him absolutely mad. There were no other words. No other memories. Only that last one of* her. *Standing at the edge of the oozy stew of the destroyed keep's moat, flanked by two Angels, one preternaturally beautiful, the other full of purpose. The same purpose* he'd *had until those six words stripped him of it.*

Flying out, he'd barely cleared the wreckage of the keep. His heart beat against the walls of his massive chest, and his monstrous wings beat against the infinite, empty sky, but the beats were slow and grew slower still. Slower. Until finally ...

Stop.

He made it across the river and then dropped like a ten-ton stone, crashing into the brush, breaking tree limbs and a wing. He lay there amongst the blackening scrub refusing to shift back into human form.

Man's thoughts were unwelcome.

In time, the rogares *came. Water wraiths. He killed them all. And then sickened by the smell of blood and meat he couldn't—*wouldn't—*consume, he left his nesting place. By then, the wing had healed, but unnaturally, so that flying straight was impossible. For days, he traveled in circles, never getting far. It wasn't just the wing. The yearning to return to her was nearly unbearable. The emptiness inside of him an abyss.*

Was she still in the Shallows? If he could just . . .

But then he remembered the Angels. And the look on her face when she'd said the six words. And the feelings in her signature. She'd need more than mere weeks for them to abate. She might need months. Hopefully, not years. Years meant nothing to him, but they did to her. And then the reminder that her time was more precious than his drove his yearning to a new level of ferocity. Ruthlessly, he tamped it down. He realized then that it might be best to return to man's thoughts. After all, she was a woman.

And he wanted her back.

I

T'was so, he stroke me with a slender dart,
Tis cruell love turmoyles my captive hart.

—OVID, *AMORES* 1.2,

as translated by Christopher Marlowe

Chapter 1

§

"G lashia calls Noon the ballista." Waldron Seknecus' low voice rumbled through the Gridiron, a deep, cavernous underground space used by the upper years at St. Lucifer's for sparring. "Because of how she fights now. Watch."

He was speaking to three other spectators: my father, Karanos Onyx, executive of the Demon Council and the man who would ultimately employ all of the magic users who trained here at St. Luck's; Friedrich Vanderlin, an Archangel who was the dean of Guardians over at the Joshua School, the Angel academy we shared a campus with; and a woman who looked unsettlingly familiar to me, though I couldn't remember when we'd met or who she was. I cleared my mind and concentrated on my opponent, Ludovicus Mischmetal, who preferred the moniker "Vicious" for short. He was a second year Maegester-in-Training at Euryale University. We were competing against one another in the New Babylon MIT rank matches, which St. Luck's was hosting this year.

All second-year MITs were required to compete. The top-ranked MITs from each school would then be eligible to compete in the Laurel Crown Race. The object of the race was to bring back an assigned target. Targets were either *rogare* demons or priceless artifacts that needed to be recovered. Participation in the Laurel Crown Race was voluntary, but the MIT who returned to New Babylon with his (or in my case, her) target before any of the others, won the coveted Laurel Crown. Winning the Laurel Crown often set a future Maegester up for life because winners could choose where they wanted to spend their fourth-semester residency. And ofttimes, those residencies turned into permanent positions. Everyone else would receive offers, but it would be the Council that decided which of those residency positions they accepted.

Last semester, we'd been given our first field assignment. It was an assignment that had been full of *rogare* demon attacks and other lethal situations. That assignment had lasted a mere three months and I'd barely survived it. My residency would last for twice as long, so I was well aware of how important the residency venue would be. Winning the right to choose *where* I spent next semester, not to mention *who* I would be working for, would go far in preserving not just my happiness, but also my life. The Maegester who was judging the match, a middle-aged man with thinning, ginger-colored hair and a near-permanent frown, called out for us to begin.

I'd watched Vicious spar with other MITs. He was smart. His infliction of pain would be very calculated, very precise. There was nothing personal about his desire to beat me. He just wanted to win the match so that he could retain his current *Primoris* ranking at Euryale and compete for the Laurel Crown. Of course, I was similarly motivated.

Vicious gave me a curt bow, his long, black, razor-cut bangs briefly falling forward before he shook them back and used his waning magic to fire up a weapon, a flaming broadsword. It hissed and spit with fury in the damp air of the Gridiron as Vicious raised it toward me in an opening invitation to spar.

As a sparring partner, Vicious looked fairly intimidating. His front teeth were shiny, silver, and sharply pointed (likely, his real ones had been knocked out in fights) and he was much larger than me. He wore the usual black leather training pants and vest, but he'd elected to go shirtless underneath the vest. I guessed it was an intentional show of muscle, literally. He flexed his forearms and grinned at me, his message clear: I might be a woman playing a man's game, but he wasn't going to spare me any blows.

That suited me fine. Sparing me blows wouldn't win me the match.

I unhooked the cloak I'd worn to keep warm until the match started and let it drop to the floor. I faced Vicious in similar black leather training pants, but I wore a black leather bustier instead of a vest. Since my hair had been singed to shoulder length, my demon mark—that splotchy, dark, discolored spot of skin above my heart—was now prominently displayed. Like Vicious' muscle flexing, my decision to bare my mark was calculated. Last year at this time only my parents had ever seen the mark. Now I exposed it intentionally. It never failed. Even though my opponents knew I had waning magic, the sight of a demon mark on a woman's bosom always gave them pause. And a single second was all it took for the judge to award a point to me for their hesitation. Of course, most of them realized their mistake soon after and then redoubled their efforts and aggression toward me, but no matter. As expected, Vicious' gaze swept to my left breast and his eyes widened. *Score: Onyx, one.* He narrowed his eyes and advanced, clenching the end of his broadsword. The judge wouldn't take away points, but Vicious wasn't going to win any by gripping his weapon so tightly. It was made of fire and magic and points were awarded to students who exhibited magic mastery by wielding their weapons effortlessly, with finesse and style.

I fired up my own weapon, a poleax. Shaping the weapon with magic took less than a second, but really it had taken over a year. When I first came to St. Luck's I'd been conflicted, inexperienced, and—let's face it—completely inept. But over the last twelve months I'd gone from the girl who had never met a demon before, didn't know how to fight or use her magic, to a woman who had battled countless *rogare* demons, meted out punishment to a select few, and even executed one in cold blood. That had been exceedingly difficult, but I hadn't shied away from what had to be done. The demon had killed innocent Hyrkes—humans with no magic—and would have continued doing so if I hadn't executed him. So when I coolly shaped a fiery poleax out of thin air and twirled it around in my hand as if it were no more than a kid's baton, it looked impressively easy only because for so long it hadn't been.

I kept my eyes averted from my weapon. In the dark underground space of the Gridiron, fire was blinding. Surrounding me were three stories of blackness, interspersed with an occasional stone column. Two thousand years ago, St. Lucifer's used to be a fort. Not many of the original buildings remained, but this lower level had survived. The Gridiron that we fought in now had likely been used for the same purpose for millennia—training Maegesters to fight. It looked like a miniature coliseum, one that had been buried by time. The light from our weapons flickered against the stone columns and our breath puffed out in small gray bursts as Vicious and I circled each other.

Our signatures—the magical aura that waning magic users have and can sense in one another—flared with *expectation*. It was a battle response I was used to.

I waited for Vicious to make the first move. I almost always let my opponent make the first move. I knew from my training that smaller fighters could sometimes make up for their lack of size through speed, but I'd been born touched by Luck's heavy hand. I didn't need speed; I had strength—the strength of my magic.

Vicious made the first move, but instead of stepping toward me or slashing at my neck as I'd anticipated, he waved his sword in front of my face. Instinctively my gaze locked on it for the briefest moment, but a second was all it took. Blinded to anything but Vicious' magic, I was unaware of where his left hand was until I felt the ringing slap of his palm on my right cheek. My head snapped toward my shoulder. That side of my face now stung as if a hundred hornets had landed there. But anger quickly displaced pain. *He'd slapped me.* Not punched me, as he would have done with every other opponent he'd been paired with, but slapped me, like the girl he obviously thought I still was. My signature flared. Damn, I'd misjudged Vicious. I'd thought he wouldn't spare me any blows but he had. And now he was likely at least two points ahead because he'd managed to briefly blind and stun me. Livid, I threw a spray of blistery waning magic at his face. He easily deflected it and laughed, the low rumble infinitely irritating due to the almost never-ending echo down here.

"I heard you're St. Luck's *Primoris*," Vicious said. "You know you wouldn't have advanced this far with your ranking if Ari Carmine were still a student here. Pity he *disappeared* during your last assignment."

Vicious' emphasis on the word *disappeared* was because he, and mostly everyone else, thought that Ari had been killed during our last assignment, and Vicious, like many of the other MITs, had heard that Ari and I were close. He just didn't know how close. His words were an attempt to unsettle me emotionally. Unfortunately, his wide unaimed verbal shot was working. *Score: Vicious, three; Onyx, one.*

Everything Vicious said was true. I probably couldn't have beaten Ari in a sparring match, and he *had* disappeared during our last assignment. But what Vicious didn't know was that Ari hadn't disappeared because he was dead; he'd disappeared because he'd been hiding a bigger secret than I'd been when we'd first enrolled at St. Luck's. Ari didn't just have a drop of demon blood like the rest of us future Maegesters, he had an entire body full of it. He'd been a demon masquerading as a human with waning magic. Lamentably, Ari Carmine had also been my lover—and the man I'd loved with all my demon-marked heart. So even the mention of his name still hurt . . . and infuriated me.

I gritted my teeth and hurled the poleax directly at Vicious' head. *Onyx, two.* I knew Vicious' reflexes were good enough to avoid a direct hit. Sure enough, he dodged the shot by lunging to his right and falling to the floor while swinging his broadsword in an arc toward my middle as he fell. By the time he landed, the sword would have slashed through both my ankles—*Vicious, four*—if I hadn't leapt to avoid the amputating burn. My poleax exploded in a shower of sparks as it collided with one of the columns on the far side of the room and Vicious let go of his sword. It lay harmlessly spitting on the Gridiron's stone floor until it went out, plunging us into darkness.

Both Vicious and I, and every other Maegester in this room, could easily have lit a fire to restore our sight. But no one did. Vicious and I didn't need light to "see" one another. We could sense each other through our signatures. Vicious' signature felt like some sort of rock aggregate. There were some hard bits like nickel and then there was a whole lot of what felt like sand and grit to me. Dense filler. Formidable, but something I could probably withstand, even if he came at me directly from the front. I stood still, waiting. Vicious could feel me too, but signatures just gave us a sense of where the other was, like heat coming from a fire pit.

Vicious threw a volley of fireballs toward me. One after the other their fiery blasts lit up the room in increasingly shallow arcs, culminating in two final, furious, straight shots directed right at my head and chest. I blocked them all almost without thinking and redirected them into the darkness beyond the stone pillars surrounding us. After that, Vicious charged. It was inevitable. They all did. It was what we were here for after all. He rushed toward me, the fiery broadsword reformed. This time I fired up a similar weapon and we began the match in earnest, circling each other, dodging, lunging, thrusting, pivoting, feigning near misses so that the next moves would be direct hits. In a matter of minutes we were both winded, injured, and burned. Vicious had dislocated my kneecap and given me a black eye, and my sword had cut a two-inch gash on his forehead, a ten-inch slash down his inner thigh, and a slight nick on his neck. If I'd pressed harder with my blade or if I hadn't allowed my magic to cauterize the cuts, it was possible that Vicious would be dead by now. He knew it and I could feel in his signature that it pissed him off. *Probable score: Vicious, seven; Onyx, ten.* The match was far from over.

"Let's have a go without fire, Onyx," he said.

I barked out a laugh. "Why would I agree to that? I'm winning."

Without warning, Vicious punched me. I should have seen it coming, what with his request to do away with our magic and start scrapping like beasts. Problem was I'd expected it earlier and my reflexes were a fraction too slow. His fist connected with my mouth, knocked my head backward, leaving a sharp, searing pain in my upper lip that quickly morphed into a mind-numbing ache. I tasted blood and spit something hard onto the stone floor of the Gridiron.

My tooth. No wonder Vicious wanted to "have a go without fire." He knocked my tooth out and he hadn't even used his magic to do it. My signature heated up. Had this been last year, I would have started getting scared. Scared that I couldn't control my magic. Scared that my fire might burn something unintended. Scared I'd be bullied, lose, hurt someone . . . or worse. No more. Now my rising temper only meant this match would soon be over.

I looked up at Vicious and grinned at him. In my current condition, my smile was likely the ghastliest and bloodiest it had ever been. Vicious shook his head in mock sympathy and tsked.

"Don't worry," he said. "I know a good Hyrke dentist I can recommend." He clicked a nail against his sharp, silvery teeth and formed a new weapon, a huge glowing fireball. He held it delicately with his right hand and deftly tossed it in the air, catching it easily. He then wound up as if to pitch it. As he stepped forward, his left hand moved toward my cheek. This time I was ready. I caught it before it could connect. Drawing inspiration from his horrible moniker, I viciously wrenched his wrist, twisting it in an intentionally unnatural angle. I put all of my weight and magic into the move and jerked until I felt a sickening crunch. At the same time I blocked his fireball with a waning magic ball of my own, but mine wasn't fiery—it was *dark*. My dark magic blast hit Vicious, knocking him off his feet and into the air. He collided with the nearest stone pillar and slid to the floor, barely conscious.

I walked over to him. I wanted to tell him I was sorry. That I hoped I hadn't broken his wrist and that I always tried to win the matches with a minimum amount of magic.

But this was the Gridiron. Apologies were unnecessary and unwanted.

So all I said was, "Don't worry, I know a good Mederi."

Vicious looked up at me from the floor. His voice was slurred and thick. "*You* should have been a Mederi, Onyx. You're an abomination. A woman with waning magic?" He made a sound of disgust as he tried to get up. I didn't offer to help. "At least *my* injuries can be healed by a Mederi." He made a sound that was part laugh, part cough and hauled himself to his feet. "No Mederi can grow your tooth back," he said, pointing at my now-battered face.

I raised my eyebrows. "Huh," I said, my swollen lips likely producing an ugly grimace. "Well, you've obviously never met my brother, Nightshade."

I gave the judge a perfunctory bow, picked up my tooth and cloak, put the former in my pocket and the latter around my shoulders, and limped over to the stone bench where Seknecus and the others sat.

Seknecus' signature was as hard as ever. But not in a harsh, hostile kind of way. Rather, to me, it felt strong and supportive. Karanos' signature was well cloaked and his face was expressionless. Friedrich looked pleased, although I couldn't figure out why. He and I didn't get along. Last semester I'd lost control of my magic and had accidentally destroyed an irreplaceable statue of Justica, the Demon Patron of Judgment, Punishment, and Mercy, which had been in the Joshua School's possession for centuries. (I'd also told Friedrich and the Joshua School to *shove it*, that I didn't need *or want* a Guardian Angel, *thank you very much*, so we were still battling over whether I should be allowed one now that I wanted one and, if so, who it should be.)

"How did everyone else do today?" I mumbled, not out of meekness but because it was hard to enunciate with a fat lip. Seknecus knew what I was really asking. *Was I still ranked* Primoris? *Would I be competing in the Laurel Crown Race?*

So far, I'd beaten all but one of the MITs I'd sparred with. The matches hadn't been easy, especially the ones with the other MITs from St. Luck's. Sasha (a distant cousin of mine who had only contempt for me) had burned off the end of my hair. Brunus (a cruel, repulsive MIT whose signature always reminded me of rotten cabbage) had broken my nose. Unfortunately it hadn't stopped me from experiencing the noxious stink of his signature during the rest of our match. Tosca I could have easily killed—if I had the stomach for it, which I didn't. But I'd become very adept at hiding my revulsion to violence. In the Gridiron, posturing and presentation were part of the ranking system. If you *looked* weak, the judge assumed you *were* weak.

Brunus was the one MIT out of all of the second year MITs in New Babylon who had bested me. This year, his hatred of me had only increased. His naked animosity toward me had propelled him into a fighting form he might never have achieved otherwise. He'd been so aggressive and brutal during the rank matches leading up to ours that he'd actually killed one of his opponents, an MIT from Gremory Tower—Martius Einion, the only child of a poor, elderly Host couple who lived on the outskirts of Etincelle. Then, after trying and failing no less than seven times during *our* rank match to kill *me*, he'd passionately (and madly) declared that he'd rather *die* than watch me win the Laurel Crown. It was revolting to know that he had scored enough points throughout his matches to possibly overtake me today.

"Congratulations, Onyx. Brunus lost his match. You're still St. Luck's second year *Primoris*. If you elect to compete, you'll be starting with the rest of the racers a week from today."

I nodded, hiding my relief and satisfaction, and glanced at the rest of my audience. Karanos was contemplating Vicious with narrowed eyes. He was likely still assessing

Vicious' capabilities and trying to figure out where to best place him.

Friedrich's head was bent close to the vaguely familiar woman. They finished speaking and met my gaze. Friedrich positively beamed. *Had he forgiven me for destroying Justica's statue already?* Since destroying it, I'd tried to meet with him at least half a dozen times to discuss how I could make amends, but each time I was told, "When suitable reparations have been determined, you will be notified."

The woman simply stared. It was unnerving—and not just because most stares are. It was unnerving because her taupe-eyed contemplative stare was one I'd been subjected to many times before. My Guardian Angel from last semester, Raphael Sinclair, had the same eyes. Suddenly I knew who she was and where I'd seen her before.

This was Rafe's mother, Valda Sinclair.

She rose from the bench and walked over to me. Even after having sent a man who was nearly twice my size crashing into a stone pillar not two minutes prior, my instinct was to stay alert. I suddenly felt as if the match wasn't over.

Karanos' gaze shifted to Valda and he frowned.

"I want to ask her a question, Karanos," she said dismissively, which spoke volumes about her position in the Divinity. "If you win the Laurel Crown Race, where do you want to serve your residency?"

I paused. Not because I was thinking about my answer. I knew exactly where I'd choose to work next semester if I won. For years, all I'd wanted was to become a Mederi—a woman whose magic was waxing instead of waning; a woman who could grow and heal with her magic instead of burn and destroy. But I'd learned to accept my waning magic. And while I didn't love it, I was proud of my achievements and I no longer longed to be something I wasn't. I had a new dream. One that was much more compatible with my waning magic than my last dream, but one which was not typically held by Laureates—Laurel Crown winners. I fought not to clear my throat. Glashia's Artifice class had taught me better than that. Laureates didn't worry what anyone else thought of their ambitions. They pursued their goals without reservation.

"I want to serve as a sentry on board the *Alliance*," I said.

Valda's eyebrows arched. Seknecus and Friedrich looked up. Even my father turned toward me. For once, he wasn't expressionless. In fact, a number of emotions played across his face: surprise, disappointment, and then derision . . . or possibly bemusement. The *Alliance* was my roommate Ivy's family flagship. It was a big double-decked vessel that took supplies, equipment, and passengers up and down the Lethe to the various outposts. Currently, the ship's captain was making do with cannons and worn-out spells as a defense. I knew for a fact from speaking with Ivy that he could benefit from having a Maegester on board. Problem was Maegesters, especially Laureates, didn't work for Hyrkes. They worked for demons.

"You want to win the Laurel Crown so you can work for a Hyrke riverboat captain?" Friedrich asked, clearly perplexed.

"That's right," I said, keeping my chin up and meeting their stares.

Karanos harrumphed (another remarkable show of emotion) and pulled two sealed envelopes out of his pocket. He handed them to me.

"Your residency offers. Neither is conditioned upon your winning the Laurel Crown. So, if you don't win, or choose not to race, you'll likely be placed in one of these positions."

I looked down at the envelopes. One was the color of clotted cream with crisp corners and a leaden seal bearing the image of a gaol. The other was a dirtier, more tattered version of the first with a crimson seal bearing the image of a waterfall.

The one with the gaol seal looked like it might be from the Office of the New Babylon Gaol. Its demon patron was Adikia. In Halja, once sinners were tried and convicted, they no longer had any rights. They were either executed or sent to gaol to serve out their sentences under the patronage of Adikia, who was also known as the Patron Demon of Abuse, Injustice, and Oppression. I repressed a shudder. And who knew where the envelope with the waterfall seal was from? Likely some outpost lord who thought a female Maegester might make a good sheriff.

"And if you do win," Karanos continued dryly, "you might change your mind and accept one of these offers voluntarily." He cleared his throat. For once, what Karanos thought was abundantly clear. He found the idea of a Laureate working for a Hyrke riverboat captain wasteful and self-indulgent.

It smarted just a bit that there were only two envelopes. I couldn't help remembering that last year's Laureate had received over twenty offers from various patrons.

All the more reason to win the race. Because if I didn't, the Demon Council would be able to place me in either of these residencies whether I wanted to go or not.

Or somewhere even worse.

Chapter 2

ક

Climbing up out of the bowels of Rickard Building where the Gridiron and our other dungeon-like training areas were took time. The only exits were high, twisty, ancient iron staircases, anchored solely at the top and bottom, which circled in tight, dark loops for four stories or more. I alternately limped and hopped, step by step, clutching the railing with my right hand while holding a lit fireball in my left. By the time I made it to the top, I was sweating and exhausted. I immediately doused the fireball and headed straight for the outer door with one goal in mind: find Raphael Sinclair. Angels weren't quite as good at healing as Mederies were, but Rafe would easily be able to heal all of my injuries except the lost tooth.

I shoved the heavy steel door of Rickard open and let it bang against the building's stone wall as I stepped gratefully into the clear, crisp evening air of Timothy's Square. I stood there for a moment, panting and surveying the square, looking for Rafe.

St. Luck's shared a campus with the Joshua School, an

Angel academy. Timothy's Square was in the center of both
schools and was often the site of various outdoor social
events. Tonight was Friday and it was the Festival of Frivolity. To one side of the square was a giant bonfire, all glowing
red and crackling. A group of students stood around it,
drinking, talking, eating, and laughing. Ashes from the fire
rose into the air like reverse confetti combining with the
myriad stars splashed across the dark, indigo sky.

In the center of the square was a gathering of booths,
tents, and kiosks—a collection of vendors granted a temporary license to sell their wares, confections, and libations for
the next twenty-four hours. And on the other side of them
were the snow demons. They weren't real—although plenty
of demons in Halja were. They were *made* out of snow; they
weren't *patrons* of snow. There were dozens of them. Immediately, I recognized several: Lilith (Luck's mate—even
carved out of snow she appeared fiery and defiant as she
charged two-thousand-year-old enemies astride a huge barghest brandishing a sabre made out of ice); Estes (Patron
Demon of the Lethe, the mighty river that cut Halja west to
east, depicted as a giant merman complete with a trident as
large as Luck's lance must have been); Ionys (Patron Demon
of Wine, carrying no less than half a dozen liquid peace offerings in his clawed hands); and Cliodna (Patron Demon of
Waves and Waterbirds, portrayed as a long, lithe, snowy
white swan). Each of them had been sculpted out of snow
earlier today by St. Luck's and Joshua School students eager
to compete for some ludicrous prize like an icicle or a snow-
flake.

But even I had to admit that a contest for something so
trivial sounded pretty good right now. I limped through the
crowd, keeping my hood up and my face averted. Everyone
at school knew I had waning magic now—and that I knew
how to use it, which meant I often came to class bruised and
sometimes bloodied, but the lost tooth was new. Call it vanity but I just didn't feel like talking to anyone until I found
Rafe. He'd said he would meet me here after the sparring

session. We weren't allowed Guardian Angels for the rank matches, and even if we were, the Joshua School still hadn't okayed our partnership. Truth was, after I'd destroyed that priceless statue of Justica, Rafe had remade it, but in *my* image, not Justica's. I grinned remembering, but my lip split anew so I stopped.

Buffered from the slight wind by the crowd, I passed the booth where the Angels were selling hot apple cider. I'd wander over later to see if it was ensorcelled or not, and if so what the spell did to the drinker. Some of the Angels' ensorcelled drinks were fun and some . . . were not. I was just about to check the inside of one of the larger tents when someone grabbed my shoulder. Still jumpy from my earlier fight, I dropped my hood and pivoted, my hand held at waist level, palm side up, ready to hold an instantly forged fiery weapon. Luckily I stopped short of actually shaping the weapon because my "attacker" turned out to be Ivy Jaynes, my Hyrke roommate.

The look on her face told me how bad mine must look.

"Vicious was more vicious than I anticipated," I said grimacing, which caused Ivy to gasp.

"Your tooth!"

I pulled it out of my pocket and showed it to her. She stared at it and then met my gaze. "You need a Mederi."

"For now, I just need Rafe. Have you seen him?"

She shook her head. "Why don't you wait inside," she said, gesturing to the tent I'd been about to enter, "I'll go find him. Fitz is in there. He was picked to be St. Luck's 'Lord Lawless'—can you believe it?" She shook her head, clearly amazed at her cousin's unerring ability to find the gravitational center of any gathering of lunatics, dilettantes, or dramatists.

Unlike the snow demons, Lord Lawless wasn't based on anyone—or anything—that had actually lived. He was a character, which made Fitz the perfect choice to play him. Fitz was Ivy's fun-loving cousin. He was also a Hyrke. When I wasn't getting beat up and learning how to fight with fiery weapons, I spent all of my time with them. So when Ivy offered to go find Rafe while I hung out inside Lord Lawless' tent, I gratefully accepted and stepped inside.

There was a long line of supplicants. I took my place at the end and glanced around Fitz's "castle" for the night. It was opulently furnished with emerald and amethyst silks adorned with thick gold rope and peacock- and ostrich-feather tassels. Toward the back of the tent, Fitz lounged on an overstuffed settee, which had been placed on a raised dais. In front of me, fellow students waited in varying states of inebriation to speak to Lord Lawless. Ordinarily I would have bitten my cheek to keep from laughing—a more apt scenario for Fitz's Friday night pleasure could not have been scripted by Luck himself—but my mouth was too sore.

The Festival of Frivolity is nearly as old as the Apocalypse. Two thousand years ago, Lucifer's army trumped the Savior's in the last great battle, Armageddon. New Babylon—Halja's only city, and the city within which St. Luck's was located—was built on top of that ancient battlefield. In fact, St. Luck's used to be Fort Babylon and we were now standing where portions of Luck's army used to practice marching.

Both Lucifer and the Savior were killed at Armageddon. But their armies survived. Lucifer's army, the Host, evolved. His warlords, those with mixed demon and human blood, had children. Along with their blood, Luck's warlords also passed down their magic. The daughters (usually) became Mederies, or healers, and the sons (usually) became Maegesters, or modern-day knights. Since we aren't at war anymore, and haven't been for millennia, being a modern-day knight really meant knowing the law, and how to uphold it, as much as knowing how to fight. That's why we trained at St. Lucifer's, a school of demon law. When we graduated, those of us with Host blood would become Maegesters. We would be given jobs where we counseled, judged, and/or executed demons who disobeyed the law. Hunting down and persecuting Hyrke criminals would be left to the Hyrke barristers.

One night of every year, however, shortly after midwinter,

everyone got a night off from following our country's strict rules. Sacrifices weren't serious, promises weren't kept, and laws did not have to be obeyed. We called it the Festival of Frivolity. (Although a more appropriate name might have been the Festival of the Drunk and Disorderly. Thankfully some of the more bloody and debauched aspects of the holiday had disappeared during the third century.) As with all Haljan holidays, the festival had a patron, but in keeping with the spirit of the holiday, the patron of the Festival of Frivolity wasn't a demon. In fact, the patron never had magic, which meant it was always a Hyrke. That patron presided over the festivities, granted boons, heard confessions (whether they were true or not is anyone's guess), gave out dispensations, and took liberties. In short, there could be no better choice than Fitz to serve as our school's festival patron, Lord Lawless.

The line moved fast and before long I was next to present myself to him. The student in front of me offered Fitz a broken pencil stub, asked for an A in Amnesty and Absolution, and received the completely fallacious reassurance that not only would he ace that class, he would be forgiven for all of his future sins in perpetuity. When it was my turn, I removed my cloak in a dramatic flourish and bowed, sincerely regretting that my dislocated kneecap prevented me from kneeling. Fitz would have loved it.

"Lord Lawless," I said in a somber voice while keeping my head bowed, "I am Nouiomo Onyx of Etincelle, second year Maegester-in-Training here at St. Lucifer's school of demon law, daughter of Karanos Onyx, executive of the Demon Council, daughter of Aurelia Onyx nee Ferrum of the Hawthorn Tribe, and sister to Nocturo Onyx, the Mederi who goes by the name Nightshade."

About midway through my introduction Fitz yawned exaggeratedly.

"Such a long *and boring* introduction, Ms. Onyx," Fitz said, grinning in mock jest. "You know I can't grant boons to members of the Host. Tonight is for those of us without mag—"

I looked up and Fitz saw my face. Though he was outlandishly dressed in the most ornate king's cloak I'd ever seen, his expression rapidly changed from farcical to angry to sympathetic.

"Nouiomo Onyx," he said in a quieter voice, "come forward."

I stepped up to the bottom of the dais. Fitz leaned down from his makeshift throne until he was close enough to speak to me without anyone overhearing. There were so many other people packed in the tent, most of them talking to others, and nearly all of them heavily intoxicated, that our brief tête-à-tête went largely unnoticed.

"Please tell me Vicious looks worse," he said, reaching for my hand and giving it a light squeeze. He and Ivy had the same coloring: fiery red hair, a ruddy complexion, and eyes as bright as malachite.

"No, but I won," I said, giving Fitz my toothless grin. "Which means that I'll be the MIT that St. Luck sends to the Laurel Crown Races."

Fitz looked dubious. "Congratulations? I think . . . Are you really going to race? Over a third of the racers are never heard from again?"

I thought of the two letters in my pocket. The unopened invitations from patron demons who wanted me to come work for them next year. And I thought of all the worse places the Council might send me if I didn't win the race and the ability to choose my own place of residency.

"Yeah, I'm racing," I said. My voice already sounded tired. I hoped it was because I still needed to be healed after my fight and not because Fitz had just reminded me how dangerous the Laurel Crown Race was.

Fitz studied my bruised face. He looked as troubled as I felt, but opted to complain about the unfairness of the successfully completed rank match instead of dwelling on the lethality of the upcoming race.

"Well, I think it's ridiculous that they won't let Rafe cast some protective spells over you prior to a match. How is that realistic? Maegesters are always paired with a Guardian Angel in the field. Why shouldn't the rank matches reflect that?"

During Armageddon, the Angels had been our enemy. But two thousand years had taught (most of) us how to get along. Now, the descendants of Armageddon's warring sides worked together all the time. We'd learned that our magic was complimentary. While a Maegester's magic was inherited, an Angel's magic came from their faith, as well as their constant study and rigorous discipline. Angels were Halja's spellcasters. They had to memorize myriad spells in order to practice their magic.

I shrugged. "They want to assess *our* magic, not our Guardian's."

Fitz laughed. "Besides, who could beat you and Rafe together, right?"

"Right," I said slowly, looking around the tent. I knew who I was looking for. I'd said I'd come here looking for Rafe, but I was also looking for someone else. It was the same person I looked for on campus nearly every hour of every day—Ari.

Why? Because I was still in love with him, that's why.

Rochester, my former professor and sparring coach, had once told me I had a "soft spot" for demons. At the time he'd only meant that I shouldn't be so reluctant to kill the law-breaking ones. But now the memory of those words taunted me. Forget about a request to ace one of my classes—or even a request to beat every other MIT in the Laurel Crown Race—what I really wanted was for someone to knock my "soft spot" out the way Vicious had knocked my tooth out. But I was careful not to let my emotions show. Not only had the Gridiron taught me not to, but I didn't want to ruin Fitz's good night. After all, it wasn't every night that Fitz got to play Lord Lawless. In lieu of the Hyrke trade of making a frivolous offering in return for a fictitious boon, I granted Fitz a liberty. He said he wanted a kiss from me—on the cheek—but I was in no condition to honor his request, so I'd have to pay up later. Then, with a wink, he dismissed me from court.

I limped back to the tent's opening. A few other students offered to help me, but they'd had so much spiked cider I thought it more likely they would fall than me so I declined. After waiting a few more minutes I decided Ivy and Rafe must have gotten stuck somewhere and I slipped out, leaving Lord Lawless to dispense unjustice alone.

I opted to explore the cold side of the square first—the side with the snow demons instead of the bonfire—and hobbled around toward them. Up close, I not only recognized which demons had been carved but what frivolous offerings had been left to them. I was happy to see that no one had left anything truly offensive. Tonight might be the Festival of Frivolity, but tomorrow would be just another day. Some demons didn't take kindly to being the butt of a joke. (In fact, some demons didn't take kindly to anything. But thankfully no one had carved *those* demons out of the snow.)

Instead of the usual bowl of blood, the offering in front of the snow carving of Lilith was a bowl full of miniature sugar lilies. Estes had been given a pile of fish bones and Cliodna, assorted paper birds: avocets, sheathbills, and snipes, jacanas, plovers, and lapwings. Ionys just had a pile of empty cider and wine cups in front of his snow carving.

I walked over to the bowl of sugar lilies, stole one out of the dish and popped it into my mouth. In return I left my bloody tooth, perversely pleased at how disgusting it looked against the sugar lilies. Ironically, Lilith would probably appreciate my gift. The tooth had been a true sacrifice after all—and what demon would quibble about whether they received blood, bone, or tooth?

I turned toward the fire, thinking I would look there next for Ivy and Rafe when I saw him—not the Angel I was looking for, but the Angel I'd avoided all last semester. *Peter Aster.*

He looked the same. Long, bone white hair tied back with a black leather strap. An angular, almost beautiful face—and that grim, disapproving look.

"Hello, Peter."

"What happened to your hair?"

Was he taking lessons from my father? No *hey, how have*

you been for the last six months? No *sorry I almost let your boyfriend (now ex-boyfriend) die.* Honestly, his asking me about my hair after the way our friendship had ended made Karanos' insistence on avoiding small talk look positively cheerful.

"Sasha de Rocca burned off the end of it."

"And your face? What happened?"

Unfortunately his tone conveyed more horror than concern. Peter Aster had once been my best friend. We'd grown up in Etincelle, the small village across the Lethe from New Babylon where all the rich kids with magic grow up. Peter's estate abutted ours. A long time ago, I'd even dreamed of marrying him. No more. Even though I wasn't with Ari anymore—and even if Ari *was* a demon (and, truth be told, he wasn't just a demon; he was a drakon, a rare subset of winged demons born to human mothers)—I could never forgive Peter for almost letting him die.

But that was six months ago and Peter had broken no laws and he'd kept his distance from me since. Until now.

"Ludovicus Mischmetal happened," I said.

"Vicious," Peter spat out the name.

We stood on the dark side of the square, eyeing each other up. Finally, I asked him what I'd been thinking.

"What do you want, Peter?"

At one time, it had been me. But not really. He hadn't wanted Noon, the woman with waning magic; he'd wanted Nouiomo Onyx, as she should have been born, with the waxing magic of a Mederi. For years, we'd searched for a way to reverse my magic. But last year I'd elected to live my life as Luck had intended, with the magic I'd been born with. Peter hadn't taken my decision very well. And if it weren't for the fact that he'd almost let Ari die, I would have tried to make amends.

"Actually," Peter said, "I came to ask you what you want."

I frowned at him. "What do you mean *what I want*? I want what I've always wanted—to survive being a student here."

Peter's face softened and he stepped toward me. "And who could blame you? This whole"—he waved his hand around in a sweeping motion indicating all of St. Luck's—"experience has likely been horrible for you."

My frown deepened. No doubt, parts of it had been. But I could not say that, as a whole, my *entire* experience here at St. Luck's had been horrible.

"Noon, last year you came to St. Lucifer's to hide while I searched for a way to reverse your magic. Now, this year, you're on your way to becoming the second year *Primoris*. Forget about your hair or your face, what happened to *you*?"

I barked out a laugh. Last year I would have stared back, mouth agape, perplexed about why Peter couldn't understand my coping strategies. This year I was just irritated that he was wasting my time. I was becoming impatient to find Rafe. As the night progressed, my jaw was getting sorer and my headache was getting worse.

"I decided I wanted something different, Peter."

"You want to be a demon executioner? Noon, you hate to kill."

It wasn't just what he said; it was the way he said it. Peter had always been slightly egotistical and more than ambitious, but until six months ago, those traits had always seemed harmless, charming even. Last year, Peter and I had shared a single goal: find an ancient, mythical, powerful spell, which could, in theory, reverse my magic. We had different reasons for wanting it, but each of us had desperately desired that I become what I should have been in the first place—a waxing magic user instead of a waning magic user. I'd wanted magic that could grow and heal, not destroy and kill.

So Peter was right. I did hate killing things. And I didn't want to be a demon executioner. But he was also wrong. Because, though what he said was accurate, his tone implied that I still hated what I was. And that wasn't true. Not anymore.

"There are plenty of Maegester positions that don't involve killing, Peter."

His eyebrows rose. "Really? How many? One? Two?"

"Actually, there are six."

"And you're hoping the Demon Council will place you in one of those positions, *when you've fought your way to the top*?"

"I don't need to hope. I'm not on my way to *becoming* the second year *Primoris*, Peter. I *am* the second year *Primoris*. And when I win the Laurel Crown Race, *I'll* get to choose where I work next semester."

I turned on my heels but he grabbed my arm. I felt my signature expand. I tried to shake him off but instead he stepped closer. I didn't want to—*couldn't*—fight with him. Physical sparring between waning magic users and Angel spellcasters was *highly* discouraged.

"*Win* the Laurel Crown Race? Become this year's Laureate?" Peter's expression was equal parts astonished and angry. "Noon, you can't be serious."

I willed my expanding signature to slow. Emotionally, Peter was a tougher opponent than Vicious, but I knew how to control my magic now.

"I am," I said simply, a few moments later, after I'd calmed down. But Peter wasn't going to leave off.

"So which demon would you spend your residency with? Which demon out of the six will get the benefit of your services next year if you win?"

"Actually, I won't be working for a demon next year, Peter. I'll be working for a Hyrke. I plan on offering my services to the Jaynes family. I hope to secure a position on the *Alliance*."

Peter looked less surprised than the group at the Gridiron had looked when I'd told them that I wanted to work for the Jayneses next year. He nodded his head in an ambiguous gesture, considering.

"And you'll be satisfied sitting second chair to a Hyrke riverboat captain?"

I shrugged and twisted free from his grip. "Why wouldn't I be?"

Peter grimaced. "Because you're an Onyx; that's why. And you're a Ferrum."

"What are you saying, Peter? That just because I'm Karanos and Aurelia's daughter that I'm blood bound to adopt my ancestors' patrician arrogance?"

"Non procul a proprio stipite poma cadunt." The apple *doesn't fall far from the tree.*

I scoffed. "Yeah? Well I prefer '*vitibus uvae dulces veniunt a fortibus.*'" *From strong vines come sweet grapes.*

"Noon, have you looked in the mirror lately? You don't look sweet. You look . . . terrifying."

My signature bubbled and roiled. My palm itched to fire up a weapon. But I kept it all tightly under my control.

"See you around, Peter," I said, stepping back. *I hoped I didn't.*

I turned to go, and put about three feet between us, when his voice stopped me.

"There are other ways to reverse your magic than the one we were first pursuing," he called to me.

"We went down that road," I said slowly, turning around. "It was a dead end."

"No, it wasn't. You just got . . . sidetracked." I knew he was talking about Ari. "With your blood, Noon, you deserve a greater role in Halja's future than the one you'll have if you work on the river."

I blew out my breath and glanced around the square. Somewhere nearer to the fire a pack of students were singing. I looked over at the bowl of sugar lilies that had been left for Lilith and remembered my tooth—and all the other sacrifices I'd made.

If I became this year's Laureate, would I really choose to work for the Jayneses?

I sighed. The only thing I knew for sure was that I didn't want to continue talking to Peter.

"Defending Hyrkes from *rogare* demon attacks sounds like honorable work to me, Peter." I turned around a second time, determined to walk away, but Peter's rushed words stopped me.

"Halja has magic that's more powerful than waning or waxing," he said to my back. "More powerful even than faith magic."

I frowned, but didn't turn back toward him. His words made me uncomfortable.

My tongue worried the hollow spot left in my gum by my missing tooth. The wind whistled in my ears as if my whole body was hollow, not just that one spot.

Finally, I stopped worrying over the hollow spot. I gritted my remaining teeth, raised my hood, and walked away.

Chapter 3

ઽ

After leaving Peter it didn't take long to find Rafe. He was coming out of Lord Lawless' tent looking for me. His face brightened when he saw me—and then immediately fell.

"Why didn't you come over to the fire when you first came up?" Rafe asked, taking me by the elbow and leading me over to an empty bench. His face held all of the concern that had been lacking in Peter's. We sat facing one another and I lowered my hood so that Rafe could get a better look at the injuries I wanted him to heal. Gently, he took my chin in his hand and turned my face toward the fire. I gave him a smile, intentionally poking my tongue through the gap in my teeth. His eyes widened and then narrowed.

"You let Vicious knock your tooth out?"

"Let him?" I said jerking my chin away from Rafe's fingers. "Hardly," I growled. And then in a lower voice I admitted, "He surprised me." I looked up and met Rafe's taupe-eyed gaze. So like his mother's gaze earlier this evening—and yet so different. Rafe's gaze was as warm as the bonfire we sat next to, whereas Valda's had been as cold as the Gridiron. I told him I'd won the match and that I'd be racing for the Laurel Crown starting next Friday.

"What do you think your target will be?"

I shrugged. "Who knows? Something difficult to retrieve, that's for sure. Know any good tracking spells?"

"Why?" he said, quirking his mouth. "Am I going to be your Guardian? Did Friedrich relent and agree that we could work together again?"

I frowned. He hadn't. Yet. Rafe's questions made me realize my biggest priority for tomorrow would be to visit the office of the dean of Guardians and start groveling. Rafe was considering me carefully. He always did that. It used to make me uncomfortable. Now, I was used to it, although I did often wonder what he was wondering about. After a while he said:

"You know I can't cast a spell that will actually grow your tooth back, right?"

"I know."

"But I can cast an illusion so that people won't be able to tell."

"No," I said. "Leave it."

Rafe arched a brow at me. "Another intimidation tactic for your opponents? I'm not sure it makes you look tough, Noon."

"What does it make me look like?" I asked, remembering Peter's comment that I looked terrifying. Rafe's gaze dropped from my eyes to my swollen lips.

"Like someone who's going to have trouble chewing."

I rolled my eyes. "Get on with the healing, spellcaster." I scooted closer. Rafe had told me that he didn't necessarily have to touch me to heal me, but that it made it a whole lot easier.

"Close your eyes," he said.

I gave him a puzzled look. He'd never asked me to do that before. But my head was pounding, and arguing with my unofficial maverick Guardian Angel wasn't something I had the energy for.

I closed my eyes.

I felt his fingers settle beneath my jaw as he held my face in place.

"I met your mother earlier tonight," I murmured. Almost imperceptibly his fingers tightened their grip.

"Oh?"

I remembered where I'd seen Valda Sinclair before—at Rafe's brother's funeral, twenty years ago or more. I hadn't been there (and even if I had been, I would have been too young to remember). I "remembered" now only because there'd been an accident involving magic during my assignment last semester. We'd each been given a piece of someone else's memory. I'd been given Rafe's memory of his infant brother's funeral. He'd drowned when Rafe was six years old. Even now the memory made my throat ache and my eyes tear.

Rafe had been given a memory of Ari's, but he'd refused to tell me which one, even though I was in it. The only thing Rafe would share (after much coaxing and not a small amount of threatening) was that, in the memory, I was fully clothed. I hadn't brought up the subject again.

"What did she want?" Rafe asked, pulling me back into the present.

I shrugged. "To observe me?"

My chin, jaw, and inside of my mouth now felt agreeably warm whereas my swollen lips and aching head felt soothingly cool. *Magic,* I sighed pleasurably. Every now and then, it had its perks. I opened my eyes. Rafe was staring back at me.

He had the most beautiful eyes I'd ever seen. Not that I'd tell him that. It would be awkward and, besides, he'd only say something inane in return like *I eat a lot of carrots.* But they were. Yellow tourmaline flecked with gold. A most unusual color.

I blinked and scooted back, raising my hand to my jaw. The blood, swelling, and soreness were gone.

"What does your mother do for the Divinity?" I said instead.

"She's one of the Amanita," he said.

My gaze met Rafe's again. I was suddenly glad I hadn't known that earlier. The Amanita were an old, powerful order of Angels. There were only four of them at any given time and each of them was more dedicated to the order than to anything else, even their own families. No one knew what the exact requirements were for entry into the Amanita but there were rumors of secrecy pacts sealed with an Angel's equivalent of sacrifice, tales of initiation rites that some did not survive, and myths of mysterious magical practices. I suddenly wondered if that's what Peter might have meant when he'd said *Halja has magic that's more powerful than waning or waxing . . . More powerful even than faith magic.*

"Rafe," I said, sitting up straighter, "do the Amanita practice faith magic like the rest of the Angels?"

"Of course."

"But that's not all they practice, is it?"

He looked at me keenly.

"No . . . they also practice perennial magic."

"I didn't think anyone *could* practice perennial magic."

I didn't know much about it, other than it was more ancient than the Amanita, but I'd always thought of perennial magic as magic that was associated with a place or a thing, rather than magic that could be wielded by a person.

Rafe made some noncommittal sound. I thought that would be the end of the discussion—that he wouldn't want to say anything more—but then he said:

"The Amanita are sworn to *eradicate* the practice of perennial magic. They claim it's blasphemous. The order was founded in medieval times as a response to Metatron and his magical experiments. The Amanita loathed Metatron. They believed he was the worst thing to ever happen to the Divinity."

My eyebrows shot up. I'd never heard this side of Metatron's history before. All I knew was the history that every-

one knew: Metatron, a medieval Angel scribe, had supposedly
fallen in love with Justica. He'd spent the better part of his
life traveling around Halja in a rickety old oxcart bringing
news from outpost to outpost and adjudicating small disputes
along the way. That his judgment was illegal and highly un-
enforceable is often glossed over in the histories because
Metatron had been such an extraordinary Angel. The Host
viewed him as an inscrutable inventor, whose magical devices had varying degrees of success. His most famous creations were supposedly made for Justica. He made numerous
sets of ensorcelled Sanguine Scales (which he no doubt sold
for exorbitant sums of money to outposts desperate for an
"easy" way to dispense justice; their judgment was rumored
to be less fair than a coin toss and their punishment to be
cruel and extreme). He is also said to have made at least one
sword for Justica, which Metatron claimed was his *magnum
opus*. He was nothing if not a consummate showman and
salesman. I knew some Angels viewed his legacy with a gim-
let eye, but I hadn't realized an entire order had sprung up to
fight against it.

"The Amanita believe that Metatron's work defied everything an Angel stood for, because he practiced perennial
magic more than faith magic."

I nodded. That made sense. The Angels' identities and
magic was tied with their faith. *If Metatron hadn't put his
faith first, could he even be called an Angel?* But Rafe
scoffed when he saw my nod.

"The Amanita practice perennial magic though. When
they are infrequently asked to justify their hypocritical practices they respond with platitudes like *similia similibus cu-
rantur.*"

"Fight fire with fire," I murmured.

Rafe grunted. "An Angel would probably say *like cures
like.*"

"And what do you say?"

"Valda has her own vision of how the world should work
and that vision isn't always in sync with the more main-

stream Divinity's vision. Or mine. All Angels have faith. But each of us practices it in a different way."

I knew then that Rafe would say no more, but it was enough. The fact that Valda Sinclair was one of the Amanita went a long way in explaining the chilliness I'd sensed from her this morning and in the memory that I now had of Rafe's brother's funeral. I squeezed his arm in sympathy as a thought suddenly occurred to me.

"Remember how we destroyed Justica last semester?"

"We?" Rafe cocked a brow at me.

"Well, I mean *I* did. But then you recast her . . ."

"In your image," he said, laughing now. "How could I forget?"

"Want a chance to make amends?"

"Absolutely not," he said.

"Come on," I said, dragging him to his feet. Now that my injuries were healed I was full of energy. "I'm not talking about carving anything from stone or casting anything with magic. Let's make her out of snow. No one has yet."

"What will we win?"

I shrugged. "A rusty ax? A paper ice pick? Who cares? The fun is carving them, right?"

Two hours later we'd recast Justica out of snow. Our snow carving was three times as big as anyone else's and we'd added something that no one else had—an Angel. There, in the center of St. Luck's and the Joshua School, we'd carved Justica and Metatron in a wintery clinch. Justica had Metatron bent back over her arm. Her snow white hair seemed to writhe in the wind as she lowered her face to his. In our frozen tableau, her love for him was irrefutable.

We would either win the Festival of Frivolity's snow carving contest or we'd both be kicked out of school.

Tired as I was later that night, I forced myself to read the two residency offers that Karanos had handed to me after my rank match with Vicious. I opened the crisp, white enve-

lope with the gaol seal on it first, unsurprised to see that it was
from the Office of the New Babylon Gaol.

OFFICE OF THE NEW BABYLON GAOL
ADIKIA, PATRON DEMON OF ABUSE,
INJUSTICE, AND OPPRESSION

Dear Ms. Onyx,

*Our patron has been following your academic career
with interest and would like to extend an invitation to you
to spend your fourth semester residency working for her
at the New Babylon Gaol. A job description and brief list
of duties is included within this letter.*

*It is our understanding that you may become a con-
tender for the Laurel Crown. Please note that while
Adikia has employed several Laureates in the past, winning the Laurel Crown is not a prerequisite for the position. You are our patron's top choice and the residency
offer will be open to you regardless of your final class
rank or race placement.*

*Working at the New Babylon Gaol is challenging, but
fulfilling. Adikia only employs Maegesters who have
proven, measurable, powerful magic. There are only a
dozen or so demon prisoners at the gaol. (As you are
aware, most rogares are summarily executed after trial
and conviction.)*

*Your primary job would be to assist the other Mae-
gesters by keeping the rogare prisoners restrained and
contained. Resident MITs may also be called upon to
search prisoners, supervise hard labor assignments, en-
force rules and regulations, and mete out punishment to
rule breakers. The specific form of punishment is at the
enforcer's discretion but may include boiling, burning,
and flaying. If you accept the offer, you would also have
an opportunity to perfect your combat techniques, weapons skills, and use of personal restraints on the rogare
prisoners.*

Thank you for your consideration. We look forward to hearing from you.

Adikia's humble and obedient servant,
Volero Travertine, Warden

Toward the end of Traverine's letter, I'd started clutching my stomach. Yes, I'd come to terms with who and what I was, my role in Haljan society, and the need for the magical services I could provide. I was a waning magic user. My magic was deadly and my purpose was to be a demon peace-keeper, which sometimes meant I needed to execute *rogare* demons. I didn't like killing, but I was capable of doing it. Especially if it was to protect innocent people from harm. Torture, however, was another matter entirely. I knew that some sins were so heinous death would be too kind for the perpetrator. But I honestly didn't think that torture was the answer. I didn't know what the *rogares* at the New Babylon gaol had done, but I did know that I wanted no part in torturing them.

OFFICE OF THE PATRON DEMON
OF ROCKTHORN GORGE

Dear Ms. Onyx,

As you may know, the Demon Council recently decided to build a hydroelectric dam at Rockthorn Gorge, which will supply water from the Acheron to the New Babylon power plant via an underground conduit. Construction was expected to be complete by the end of this year, but the project has suffered numerous setbacks, including several rogare *attacks and one workforce mutiny. The outpost lord believes you may be in a unique position to lend assistance and would like to extend an invitation to you to spend your fourth semester residency at Rock-thorn Gorge.*

He is aware that you may be a contender for the Lau-

rel Crown. He has never employed any Laureates, but would welcome the chance to do so. While he cannot offer the salary, honor, or accommodations that Laureates typically receive, he is hoping you might accept the Rockthorn Gorge residency on a pro bono basis.

Once the dam is complete, the New Babylon power plant will be able to provide electricity to an additional 10,000 Haljan residents, which will directly and positively impact their standard of living by providing a renewable, reliable, cost-effective energy source for their lighting, heating, and refrigeration needs.

The outpost lord would like to meet with you before you accept his offer so that he can outline the project particulars, the workforce challenges, the rogare threat, and discuss other matters that may affect your desire to accept his offer.

Please let us know if you would be interested in speaking with the patron demon of Rockthorn Gorge about a fourth semester residency with us. I look forward to hearing from you.

Nephemiah Zeffre
Foreman

Luck below! The patron demon of Rockthorn Gorge's foreman sounded as if he were auditioning for a radio commercial for NBSE—New Babylon Steam & Electric. I certainly didn't begrudge those residents who didn't yet have electricity their right and desire to have it, but the cynical side of me was highly suspicious of the outpost lord's motives. Reading between the lines (and knowing that Rockthorn Gorge had been a place of historic unrest), it sounded to me like this demon lord had bitten off more than he could chew with his pointy teeth or massive jaw and now he was worried about losing not just his investment, but the shirt off his back and his demon-marked skin as well.

I had to admit, though, that despite the lack of salary, honor, or accommodations, the Rockthorn Gorge offer was more appealing than the New Babylon gaol one—but not by much. *Of course* I didn't want to accept a residency where torture was part of the job description, but the Rockthorn Gorge residency was in . . . well, *Rockthorn Gorge*. A bolder, brasher, more savage place I could scarcely imagine. And helping a demon lord recoup his ill-invested savings didn't sound like a very good "pro bono" matter to take on to me. Surely there was a more direct way to help Halja's magicless masses. Like picking a few of them to watch over as they sailed the river on vessels like the *Alliance*.

Chapter 4

ॐ

By Monday, all of the snow demons had melted. The weekend had been unseasonably warm and the only evidence of Friday night's frivolity was a black spot where the bonfire had been. (Rafe and I didn't win, nor were we expelled for our provocative entry. Ionys' carver won, perhaps in part because by the time the festival ended the pile of empty cider and wine cups in front of his masterpiece had grown into a mountain.) All the tents had been taken down, the booths and kiosks dismantled, Saturday hangovers nursed, and Sunday studies attended to. I felt sufficiently prepared for a new week.

The cases we were studying in Artifice class were all bailiff and bounty hunter cases: how to protect artifacts entrusted to us by a demon client; how to recover said artifacts if they were stolen; how to track down reluctant witnesses and "encourage" them to testify; how to collect tithes, sacrifices, and offerings; when to accept collateral against future payments; how to remit holdings to an absent demon lord, etc., etc., *ad infinitum*. At least the bailiff and bounty hunter cases were less grisly than the execution and murder cases had been.

W hat's got you so full of light, O Dark One?"
Gordianus "Gordy" Sphalerite was one of the other MITs in Artifice with me—and my new tablemate now that Ari wasn't a student here anymore. Upper-year students took classes with both second and third years at St. Luck's. Gordy would be graduating at the end of this year. His signature felt like snakeskin. During class he would send out wispy tendrils that would wrap around unsuspecting students and start constricting. I don't even think he meant to do it. Fact was, Gordy's attention often wandered, and with it, so did his magic control. So I was left to divide my own classroom focus between Glashia's lectures and fencing with Gordy's wayward serpentine signature. I beamed a smile at him, pinched one of his tendrils that was trying to climb up my leg, and slipped into my seat.

"I missed you over the weekend, Gordy."

He gave me a nonplussed look. "You did?"

"Uh-huh," I said, nodding my head emphatically. I pinched another tendril back that had started creeping up my arm and winked. Gordy scowled and turned his back to me.

Artifice class was on the same floor as Manipulation (our first year "Intro to Demon Law" class) but it was farther down the hallway. The fourth floor of Rickard Building was semi-abandoned. Only MITs, our Maegester professors, and a demon or two came up here. We assumed the lack of maintenance and modernization was meant to create a more welcoming environment for our ofttimes centuries-old clients but who really knew? Maybe Waldron Seknecus, our dean of demon affairs, just preferred vintage aesthetics. In any case, once students stepped out of the winder lift at the end of the hall, they stepped back in time.

Wooden worktables on this floor were old and scarred. As were the floors. In this classroom there was even old bead board on the lower portion of the walls. On the upper stone walls, there was only one tiny square window, very high up, with iron bars. A holdover from St. Luck's Fort Babylon days. No doubt our Artifice classroom had once housed high-rank prisoners. Little had they known how appropriate and appreciated their jailhouse graffiti would one day become. Singed into the bead board with waning magic or real fire were several oft quoted laments, with *libera me ex hoc purgatorio* (deliver me from this purgatory) being the most popular among students. With a quick pruning slash across another errant strand of Gordy's signature that had crept too close to my neck for comfort, I focused my attention on the row of students in front of us.

There were five other MITs taking Artifice with me: Gordy and another third year named Benvolio "Ben" Nyssa and Mercator, Sasha, and Brunus, who were all second years like me. I sat across from Ben.

Mettius Glashia paced up and down the aisle separating our tables. I took out my casebook, notepad, and an ink pen, nodded at Ben and gave Mercator a small wave. Brunus and Sasha I ignored. Although Sasha was my cousin, we weren't close. Sometimes I wished I could get along with more people, but then I reminded myself it wasn't *my* fault if *they* couldn't accept the fact that I was a woman who'd been born with waning magic.

Brunus ignored me too, but I could feel his hatred for me in his signature. It felt even worse today than usual, which I imagined was because the question of which one of us would compete in the Laurel Crown Race had now been decided.

And that person would be me, not him.

"Congratulations, Ms. Onyx," Glashia said. "I hear you beat your opponent in Friday's rank match." I tensed inwardly but tried not to let it show. Glashia, and the rest of the St. Luck's faculty, excelled at provoking students. Glashia's words were mostly testing Brunus, but they were also testing me. "So you'll be St. Luck's contender for the Laurel Crown starting this Friday."

I gave a curt nod of acknowledgement and murmured my assent and thanks, careful all the while not to sound too boastful or too modest. Brunus, however, was incapable of feigning good grace over my win. He glowered at me as a single nova-like burst of naked animosity pulsed from his signature. Glashia cleared his throat, redirecting attention back to class.

"Does anyone know who the first bounty hunter was?" he asked, returning to his lectern at the end of the aisle. Mercator raised his hand.

"Anyone besides Mr. Palladium?"

No one else responded. I could almost see Glashia's inward sigh.

"Ms. Onyx, I couldn't help but notice your contest carving at Friday night's festival."

I met Glashia's stare, making sure to keep both my signature and expression light and easy. It wouldn't do to look guilty. Besides, I hadn't done anything wrong, and no one had complained.

"We didn't win."

"So I was told," Glashia said, his voice pitched low with disappointment. He cleared his throat. "*I* would have voted for you. Your interpretation of Justica was very . . . assured."

It took every ounce of willpower I had to keep the surprise off my face. I gave Glashia a winsome smile and shrugged. *"Quandoque bonus dormitat discipulus,"* I said. *Even the good student sleeps* or, more loosely translated, *Win some, lose some.*

Glashia frowned and waved his hand dismissively. If Glashia had a motto it would surely be: *Speak not of losing.*

"My point is that you seem to have an affinity for the Patron Demon of Judgment, Punishment, and Mercy, Ms. Onyx. Which is why I thought *you* might know who the very first bounty hunter was and what they were after." I shook my head and he tsked disapprovingly. "Mr. Palladium?"

Mercator gave me an apologetic smile. (I honestly don't know how Mercator found the time to read all that he did, what with the Gridiron rank matches, our other law classes, the endless cases, code sections, and hypothetical fact patterns we were supposed to read and memorize, not to mention our need to brief, outline, and discuss all of it with other students *outside* of class in the hopes that we could understand and retain at least half of the information we were exposed to.)

"The first bounty hunter was a Maegester named Antonius Graemite, who was tasked with finding and retrieving the sword that Metatron made for Justica, *Album Cor Iustitiae*, or the White Heart of Justice."

Like every other kid in Halja, I'd heard of the White Heart. It was Metatron's *magnum opus*, a near-mythical artifact that Metatron supposedly carved out of a giant opal and then ensorcelled for Justica. These days, most people believe that Metatron carved a white sword out of *something* (possibly ivory from the tooth of a defeated demon) and that he probably ensorcelled the sword in some way, but almost no one believes the rest of the legend—that the White Heart was some sort of doomsday weapon or philosopher's stone.

Mercator repeated what most of us knew. According to medieval lore (no doubt spread by other Angel heralds and scribes who hoped to follow in Metatron's entrepreneurial footsteps), Metatron traveled extensively throughout Halja during the middle ages "searching for Justica." Some believe Metatron found her and the two reigned together for a time in a traveling circuit court over the far-off outposts. Others believe Metatron died on the road, lost and lonely. Many others—including me—believe that Metatron's love for Justica was merely symbolic. That he revered what she stood for, not the demoness herself.

"In any case," Mercator said, "the route of the first 'House of Metatron'—the covered wagon that Metatron rode around in with Justica's statue and the White Heart enshrined in the back—was the route of the Old Justice Circuit."

"Which was abolished in 1305," Brunus cut in, apparently anxious to show that he too was capable of contributing to the classroom discussion, "after a group of Maegesters and their Guardians were ambushed and killed by *rogare* demons somewhere along the southern part of the route."

"True," Glashia said. "But let's get back to the first bounty hunter case." Brunus scowled and Glashia continued uncaring that he'd just told Brunus his contribution was factually correct but irrelevant. "So Gaemite was the first bounty hunter and the White Heart was his first target. Did he find it?"

We all shook our heads. The White Heart was legendary in part because it was still missing. So no one could compare fact with fiction. *Had it really been carved from an opal? Was it truly ensorcelled with unimaginably powerful magic?*

"The White Heart is still missing," Glashia continued. "Different theories have surfaced from time to time on its possible whereabouts, but no one has yet recovered it." He looked at me when he said that last bit. Considering I would be entering a race to find and retrieve a difficult target starting this Friday, his look caused a small pinprick of alarm to pierce my belly.

There was no way the race coordinators would pick the White Heart as my target. Right?

It was too big, too mythical, too . . . irretrievable. It had been missing for hundreds of years. Greater minds with stronger bodies and more powerful magic had searched for it and failed. I bit my lip (violating my own policy of never looking nervous in Artifice class) and refocused on Glashia, who'd just asked if anyone knew who had hired Graemite to find the sword for them.

"Astraea?" Sasha volunteered. Astraea was the young demoness who had inherited Justica's followers, but apparently not her sword. Glashia shook his head.

"The Divinity?" Ben suggested.

Glashia looked thoughtful. "Be more specific, Mr. Nyssa."

"The Ophanim?" But it was clear from Ben's tone that he wasn't at all sure of his answer. The Ophanim were a more militaristic branch of the Divinity. They were modern-day knights—similar to Maegesters in a way—but their sole client was the Divinity. It was a good guess, but I was pretty sure it was incorrect.

"No," Glashia said, confirming my hunch.

"The Amanita," I said quietly. I too might have phrased it as a question, but for the fact that Glashia admired confidence above all else. But my answer was as wild a guess as the others, based only upon my earlier discussion with Rafe when he'd told me that the Amanita believed that Metatron's work defied everything an Angel stood for.

I could tell I'd surprised Glashia with my answer. Apparently, he hadn't been expecting anyone to know. He seemed both pleased and annoyed.

"Correct, Ms. Onyx. Metatron died without issue so the Angels inherited his possessions. When the Amanita discovered that the White Heart was missing they hired Graemite to find and retrieve it for them. You seem remarkably well informed. Do you know why they wanted it?"

Again, that stare. The one that made me nervous about the upcoming race. The one that made me think Glashia knew more than he was saying. It also looked the least little bit like a warning.

Did I know why the Amanita wanted to find the White Heart?

Other than the fact that most people generally wanted what was theirs, not really. But I could guess. Most likely the White Heart had been created using perennial magic, which would explain some of the more outlandish suppositions about its capabilities. And since Metatron had created the White Heart, and the Amanita believed his magical "experiments" were blasphemous, my guess was the Amanita wanted the White Heart so they could destroy it.

But then I remembered that Rafe had said the Amanita were hypocrites. That they practiced perennial magic in order to "fight fire with fire." So maybe the Amanita wanted the White Heart in order to use it.

I shrugged. Glashia narrowed his eyes at me, perhaps guessing I knew more than I was willing to say. But he moved on.

"Last question about the first bounty hunter case before we move on to the more modern ones . . . Where was the White Heart last seen?"

"In Metatron's grave?" Ben said.

Glashia shook his head. No one else volunteered. "Ms. Onyx?" Glashia prompted. "Your thoughts?"

"In Metatron's oxcart? The first 'House of Metatron'?" I was way too unsure of my answer this time to state it with any sort of confidence. Glashia didn't even acknowledge that it was incorrect. He just frowned and looked around the room for other volunteers. Gordy's magic tendrils were getting so bad, it was starting to feel like I'd fallen into a nest of vipers. *He was anxious,* I thought. Well, so was I. But at least I was able to keep my magic in check now.

"Metatron's squire was the last person seen with the White Heart," Glashia finally said. "There was a footnote," he said grumpily, shuffling through the papers on top of his lectern. He located the reference and held up the paper snapping it between his hands before lowering it to the lectern again. He peered down at it, squinting. "Here it is. Footnote two hundred and eighty-seven." He looked up at us again and motioned impatiently when he saw that we still hadn't located it. To a person, we all scrambled to comply. After flipping through three of the chapters that had been assigned for today, I finally located the footnote:

> **287. Kaspar Bialas**: Chosen by Metatron to be his squire because Bialas had several unusual Hyrke characteristics, one of which was Bialas' immunity to magic. Legend says Bialas was marked by Luck's hand in the same way that Luck marks his waning magic users, but that Bialas' mark was as light as a waning magic user's is dark. It is no longer known what the mark was.

Class continued in similar fashion for over an hour. We discussed all the modern bounty hunter cases next—in extraordinary, excruciating, mind-numbing detail. Finally, *thankfully*, the class came to an end. I packed up my books and was just about to leave when Glashia called me back to his lectern.

"If you win the Laurel Crown, what will you choose to do for your residency?"

I could have just told him—*I'm going to become a river-*

boat sentry and work for the Jayneses—but instead I said, *"Aut laborare aut pugnare parata sum." To work or fight; I am ready.*

Glashia peered at me, his gaze steady. After an uncomfortable moment, he nodded.

"I hope you chose to do both, Ms. Onyx," he said finally, handing me an oversized thick white envelope.

"Friedrich Vanderlin had this delivered for you here just before class."

I smiled and thanked Glashia. Hopefully, this envelope contained a letter from Friedrich Vanderlin accepting my apology for destroying the Justica statue—and a positive response to my petition for a Guardian. I waited until I was downstairs in the lobby of Rickard Building before opening the envelope. Inside it was a single sheet of thick white linen paper embossed with black ink. It wasn't a letter accepting my apology and it wasn't a positive response to my petition for a Guardian. Instead, it was an invitation.

ARCHANGEL FRIEDRICH VANDERLIN
REQUESTS THE PLEASURE OF YOUR COMPANY
AT AN OATH CEREMONY
EMPYR
8:00 P.M.

Chapter 5

ਠ

I couldn't ignore the invitation, nor did I want to. I had no idea who was going to be taking what oath, but this could be my chance to set things straight with Friedrich and the Divinity. So in between my remaining classes that day, I decided on my outfit. Under ordinary circumstances, agonizing over clothing choices would have seemed like sartorial silliness at best and appalling vanity at worst, but no one—especially someone who wanted a chance to offer the Angels an olive branch—would make the mistake of showing up underdressed for an Angel event.

In the end, I opted to dress in white and silver (my nod to the Angels; they loved white and bright), but other aspects of my appearance were a nod to the Host. I wore a bustier, as I had in the Gridiron, but this one was made of delicate silver chainmail. I'd found it in a vintage arms shop in Northbrook over the break. The lustrous patina proclaimed its age, which was easily ten times mine. To counter the idea that I was showing up in battle gear, however, I paired it with a silver satin skirt, which had a train long enough to pool at my ankles, and a shimmering wrap. Since Angels loved ornamentation, I fastened the wrap at my throat with a starshaped diamond cloak pin.

That night, I stood in front of my dorm room mirror, assessing. Ivy, who'd had no small part in helping me select my attire for the night, was sprawled across her bed. I couldn't help but remember the last time I'd dressed for an event at Empyr—the Barrister's Ball, our first semester. It was the night I'd rejected Peter's plan to use the Reversal Spell to reverse my magic. The night I'd first told Ari I loved him.

Something sharp pricked my finger and I looked down to see that I'd managed to stab myself with one of the pins from Ivy's hairpin box. A small drop of blood welled. *Damn,* I thought, grabbing a tissue. I fight every day with weapons forged from fire and magic and it's the prick from a small metal pin that makes me want to cry. I viciously pinched the tip of my finger with the tissue.

"Do you think Peter will be there?" Ivy asked.

"I hope not," I said, tossing the tissue in the trash can.

"Do you think Rafe will be?"

"I'm not sure. I haven't seen him since the festival Friday night and he never said anything about it."

"Do you miss—" Ivy stopped suddenly and I stilled. I knew what she'd been about to ask.

Did I miss Ari?

Yes. I did. Every day. Still.

But it wasn't as if I wasn't getting on with my life.

"Do you think it's a mistake?" Ivy said instead. "The headband? I mean, on you, it almost looks like a crown."

But not the crown I want, I thought, smiling at my reflection. It was true. The white sapphire headband I'd found in Ivy's hairpin box did look vaguely crown-like when combined with the rest of my outfit. Even I had to admit, I looked impressively regal. And the best part? Amongst all the white satin, sparkling gemstones, and shimmering silver, my demon mark looked even darker.

Who could refuse the woman in the mirror? If dressing for a ceremonial oath had been an Artifice assignment,

Glashia would have given me an A. The only thing marring my appearance was my lost tooth. Maybe I should have taken Rafe up on his offer of an illusion. *Too late now.*

I turned to Ivy, wanting to leave on a profound note, with some sort of proclamation befitting the woman in the mirror, but all I could think of was *don't wait up* and *make sure you lock the door behind me.* I squeezed Ivy's hand and she wished me Luck's presence.

Empyr was a restaurant. But calling Empyr a restaurant was like calling the Gridiron a playground. Empyr was a showcase. In it, the Angels exhibited their flair for the dramatic, their love of the refined, and their superb taste in decor, food, and wine. Unlike St. Luck's campus, which had no less than eight buildings sprawled across three city blocks, the Joshua School housed everything (dormitories, administration offices, classrooms, libraries, archives, their eatery, and more) in a thirty-three story skyscraper. It was one of the tallest in New Babylon. Empyr was located at the top. It was said the Angels had heaven in mind when they'd built it.

I entered the Joshua School and was about to hand over my invitation to the lobby clerk when he motioned me toward the winder lift. Either my outfit was already working or I was expected. I pressed the button for the lift and nervously waited for it to arrive. The ride up was solo and silent. Unlike the winder lift in Rickard Building, the Joshua School lift didn't have an operator. (My guess was the Angels thought winder lift operators were old-fashioned throwbacks; Angels were all about modern aesthetics.) When the lift finally reached the top, I stepped out.

I hadn't been to Empyr since the month of Blostm, eight months ago. The decor was unchanged, but the murmur of voices and the tinkling of glasses I'd heard here on my two previous visits were completely lacking. I walked down the hallway toward the main dining room, taking care to keep my train off the ground and my head held high. After all, I didn't want it to look like I was coming to Friedrich with my head down (or my tail between my legs). I wanted to make up for the loss of the statue and be allowed a Guardian of my own choosing. But I also knew the best negotiation strategy was to start from a position of strength.

Since there was no hostess or seraphim at the door, I walked right in.

And stopped short.

The invitation had been a setup.

Unsurprisingly, the room had been arranged for a ceremony instead of dining. So instead of white linen draped round tables laid with china, silver, and crystal, there were rows of seats with an aisle up the center. The candles that the Angels were so fond of lined the aisle in abundance. At the end of the aisle was an altar, upon which were more candles. Not a single electric light lit Empyr tonight. The room was full of Angels who were seated in the rows. Seated on the altar were Friedrich Vanderlin, Valda Sinclair, my father, and—this was the surprising part—Peter Aster.

When I stopped at the entrance everyone turned toward me and stared.

"Welcome, Ms. Onyx," said Friedrich from the front, his voice loud and clear. "We're glad you could join us. Please . . . come forward."

Did I have a choice? My desire to offer the Angels an olive branch faded. If Peter were a part of this ceremony, I wanted no part of it. In fact, I now began to worry in earnest over who was taking what oath tonight. *Had Friedrich finally capitulated on allowing me the services of a Guardian? Was* Peter *the Angel everyone in here expected me to work with?*

I walked slowly up the aisle, outwardly maintaining my regal bearing, hoping I looked calm and in control. I kept a tight hold on my magic. *Now* would not be the time to repeat past magical meltdowns. But inwardly I was starting to panic. As unobtrusively as possible, I searched the audience for Rafe. Even if he was here, I didn't know how he could help, but I couldn't help wondering if he'd been aware of any of this or if he knew what Friedrich was planning.

My father's involvement was puzzling. His presence seemed to suggest that he approved of Friedrich's intentions. But Karanos had never been fond of Peter and since the altercation at Lucifer's tomb (the night that Peter had used Ari's near death to force me to make promises I'd never have made otherwise), Karanos had shunned Peter as I had.

I reached the altar and met Karanos' stare. As usual, his face was expressionless and his signature was cloaked. He appeared as outwardly calm as I did. Maybe he'd capitulated as well and had decided that Peter was a better Guardian for me than no Guardian.

My gaze switched to Friedrich and then Valda. Their expressions were nearly identical to those they'd had the day they'd observed my Gridiron match with Vicious (Friedrich looked almost happy; Valda looked contemplative). I nodded my head to each of them in turn. Anything more would look like a bow and concede too much. I then turned my gaze to Peter and smiled, intentionally baring my teeth—and lack thereof.

The look on Peter's face was worth it. I was quite certain, in that moment, that Peter Aster never would have thought he would see Nouiomo Onyx standing before a crowd of over forty people, included among them an Archangel, one of the Amanita, and the executive of the Demon Council, looking as beautifully savage and self-assured as I did just then. Peter's eyes widened and his jaw hardened as his gaze zeroed in on my unmistakably dark mark amongst all the white. He'd always hated my mark. I turned back to Friedrich. If Glashia were awarding points during this ceremony I'd have taken the first one. I'd given no ground and I'd already caused Peter some discomfort. *Score: Onyx, one; Angels, zero.*

"Nouiomo Onyx of Etincelle," Friedrich began, "daughter of Karanos Onyx, the current executive of the Demon Council, and Aurelia Onyx nee Ferrum of the Hawthorn Tribe, you have petitioned the Joshua School for a Guardian Angel."

I stiffened and my signature pooled with *expectancy*—a battle preparation response. Luckily, no one but Karanos would be able to sense it and he would simply see it as good practice.

"In the past," Friedrich continued, "I've denied your petition for two reasons. One, prior to your petition you told me in no uncertain terms that you did not desire a Guardian, and two, reparations have not yet been made for your destruction of Metatron's Justica, the irreplaceable Angel artifact you destroyed last summer."

Friedrich waited for my reaction. When I didn't react (none seemed appropriate or advisable; I wanted a Guardian, but not the one who was sitting on the altar), he said, "It is my understanding that you now wish to have a Guardian formally assigned to you and that you wish to make reparations for the ruined statue."

He paused again, waiting for my response.

"That is correct."

"Then I'm prepared to grant your petition. The Divinity will provide you with a Guardian Angel and you will make 'suitable reparations.'"

It was exactly what I'd hoped for, except . . .

"Will I be able to choose the Guardian?"

Friedrich laughed. "Aren't you the one who petitioned us?" he asked. "The practice of allowing Host to pick the Angels that guard them is a boon. The practice could just as easily go the other way, with Angels choosing who *they* wish to watch over. You lost your right to choose when you walked out—"

"Surely, Friedrich, you don't expect her to work with just anyone," Valda cut in, her voice as brittle as a thin sheet of ice. She turned toward me. "Peter Aster told us that he knows where the White Heart is."

"The White Heart," I repeated slowly and somewhat dumbly.

"Yes, Noon," Valda continued calmly, as if she were describing the cut of pork she wanted me to pick up at the butcher rather than a near-mythical, magical sword that hadn't been seen in centuries, "*Album Cor Iustitiae?* The sword that Metatron made for Justica? You see, we've worked everything out with Karanos and the Demon Council. Your target for the Laurel Crown Race can be the White Heart. If you retrieve it for us, we will consider it as suitable reparations for the statue you destroyed."

Oh, boy. Glashia had suspected, although I'm not sure how, and he'd done his best to warn and prepare me. Even so, despite all the strides I'd made since last year and the training I'd received, I was still finding it hard to breathe right now. In hindsight, a chainmail bustier probably hadn't been the best idea.

I glanced up at Peter. His blond hair was tied back and he wore a white cloak lined in black. He sat in his chair as if it were a throne and he were a tyrant. I assumed from his hostile expression that he'd guessed I wasn't going to work with him willingly.

"There are lots of theories floating around about where the White Heart might be," I said finally. "How do we know Peter's is correct?"

"Because I have the thief's journal," he said, holding up a small leather-bound book. "And it says, in his own hand, that he took the sword to—"

With a flick of her wrist, Valda silenced Peter. *Whoa.* I'd known Rafe could cast spells using hand gestures, but it was an Angel trick few knew. Most Angels only cast verbal spells. They were supreme orators. Angel culture was wrapped up in their love of languages. Their spellcasting abilities came from their voices. So seeing an Angel silenced so easily, so effectively . . . well, it was almost chilling. *Was it an Amanita trick that Rafe had "borrowed" from his mother?* Rafe had an unfortunate habit of pilfering other Angels' spells.

On stage, Friedrich looked uncomfortable. Valda smiled. Her smile was very unreassuring.

"Ms. Onyx has not yet agreed to work for us. Details will be provided only if and when she does."

"I won't work with Peter," I said quickly. Best to get that on the table and deal with it now. It was a showstopper, as they say. I'd rather take my chances up in Rockthorn Gorge with the demon who was failing at building the dam before I'd work with Peter again.

"Who said anything about working with Peter?" Valda said.

Peter leapt out of his chair, livid, and obviously eager to respond. He turned toward Friedrich, who also looked surprised. Apparently Friedrich also thought the reparations deal included me working with Peter.

"Valda . . ." Friedrich said, his voice holding a warning tone. Under ordinary circumstances I might have enjoyed watching a power struggle between Valda Sinclair and Friedrich Vanderlin. (I wondered if Friedrich had any tricks up his sleeve like Valda's silencing spell.) But all this talk of Peter and the White Heart was beside the point. I'd come here tonight for two, albeit related, purposes: to determine how to make amends for destroying the Joshua School's statue of Justica and to secure Friedrich's acquiescence that I be allowed to have a Guardian for the Laurel Crown Race. And, come demons or death, that Guardian was going to be Raphael Sinclair, not Peter Aster.

Up on the altar, Peter had been given his voice back and he was loudly proclaiming his right to search for the White Heart. Peter was nothing if not consistent. He loved searching for ancient spells and artifacts more than *anything* else.

Behind me, the Angel audience started murmuring among themselves. I knew the Angels weren't finished with me, and that the night was far from over, but I wanted it to be. I already knew my decision.

"I'll do it," I called out. Valda turned around to face me and, suddenly, all eyes were on me again. The room grew quiet.

"I'll search for the White Heart," I continued in a lower voice. "I'll follow whatever clues Peter Aster thinks are important. But I get to choose my own Guardian."

Valda and Friedrich exchanged a look. They then glanced at Karanos, who was staring at me. It was impossible to tell what he was thinking, as usual. After a moment, during which Karanos could have frowned slightly, he gave an almost imperceptible nod. After that, Peter slumped in his chair, looking defeated.

"Done," said Valda, smiling. "Tell her where she's headed, Peter," she commanded.

"Tartarus," he said in a dead voice.

I wanted to say something witty in return. Something like *only fools searched for something halfway between Hell and back* but I couldn't. Jokes like that became tougher with each assignment. If I accepted this one, and agreed to go after the White Heart as my target for the Laurel Crown Race, it might be the last assignment I ever accepted, the last contest I ever entered.

A trip to Tartarus would make last semester's trip to the Shallows look like a luxury cruise.

Chapter 6

‽

"Tartarus?" My voice echoed throughout Empyr. "I don't think so."

"But you've already agreed," Valda said. "You can't renege on your promise."

"It's not reneging if the other side omits a material term from the offering. I said I'd search for the White Heart. But if it's located in Tartarus, even if I found it, I'd never make it back alive. So you wouldn't get the sword anyway."

A thousand years ago, Tartarus had been Halja's southernmost outpost. In Metatron's time, Halja's southern Verge was populated with half a dozen or more outposts, all of them mining and blast furnace towns. Tartarus was located on the northern face of Halja's tallest southern mountain, Mount Iron. Its lord had been Orcus, Patron Demon of the Verge, a berserker who'd ruled his lands with a fist as hard as the metal he'd mined. At the height of its productivity, the Verge had been home to almost ten thousand Hyrkes. But that was before the permafrost crept north and the iron ore ran out. That was before the Old Justice Circuit was abolished and the people left and Orcus—thank Luck—died.

But the fact that the Verge's former patron was now dead didn't mean the trip to Tartarus would be any easier. The Verge was now infested with *rogares*. The land was much more inhospitable than the eastern Lethe (or even Rockthorn Gorge up north) could ever hope to be. And Tartarus itself had a reputation as an impenetrable fortress, an abysmal pit from which escape would be damn near impossible.

"The assignment *is* dangerous," Valda said. "We're not going to argue about that. But I think you underestimate your own abilities. We didn't choose the White Heart as your 'suitable reparations' on a whim. We've been watching you and we think you're the one who can do it. *You* can bring the White Heart back to New Babylon."

Flattering as Valda's words were, I didn't believe them. No one had ever come back from Tartarus.

"No," I said, shaking my head. "What you're asking me to do goes well beyond 'suitable reparations' for a destroyed statue, even an irreplaceable one."

Valda's expression darkened.

"I appreciate the offer," I said, "but, upon further reflection and after having considered terms you failed to mention previously, I'm declining."

The situation wasn't ideal. Even if the Demon Council assigned me a different target for my Laurel Crown Race, there was no guarantee it wouldn't be located somewhere just as perilous as Tartarus. And the likelihood that I could finish the race, let alone win it, without the aid of a Guardian was as likely as the snow demons from the Festival of Frivolity surviving until summer without the aid of great and powerful magic.

"Nouiomo," my father said quietly, instantly causing my attention to shift to him. "You did destroy the statue."

That's all he said. But it was enough. His words were a warning. I could tell Karanos thought I was making a mistake.

"And I regret that destruction," I said. "But killing myself won't bring the statue back. And, as reparations go, suicide seems excessive for a sin involving destruction of property."

After a long moment, Karanos simply sat back in his chair. I had no idea if he agreed with what I'd said or not.

"Before you reject our offer completely," Friedrich said, "you should hear the rest of the 'material terms' of our deal. I've spoken to the St. Lucifer's faculty and to the executive here. If you'd rather not search for the White Heart, then as punishment for your sin of destroying Metatron's Justica you will be stripped of your ranking and have no further right to a Guardian. *All* Angels will be forbidden to work with you."

Suddenly, I felt like I'd been gut punched. Friedrich's alternative was almost as bad as his initial offer. No one in their right mind would want to go to Tartarus. But to know I would never again, no matter the circumstances, be able to work with another Angel . . . well, it was a lot to consider. I couldn't imagine *never* working with Rafe again. Or being strictly forbidden to work with Fara, Friedrich's daughter (who was one of my closest friends despite my prickly relationship with her father).

Friedrich sensed my indecision and made his final offer.

"On the other hand," he said, "if you agree to pursue the White Heart as your Laurel Crown Race target, you'll finish your third semester at St. Lucifer's with your *Primoris* ranking still intact and you'll be allowed to choose your own Guardian for your fourth semester residency position, *even if you don't become the Laureate.*"

Ah, the Angels. I should have known. I might have been one of the top-ranked students at St. Luck's, but I was still a student. My arguing and debating skills might have improved dramatically since I'd first enrolled here, but I was still a babe in the woods compared to the Angels. What hope had I ever had of convincing them to let me make reparations on my own terms? How naive I'd been to think that a fancy looking bustier, a pretty looking skirt, some diamonds, and a missing tooth would somehow bolster my negotiating power. I might just as well have come to them dressed in my leather battle gear or the canvas pants and tunics I wore to class for all the difference my dress had made. Tonight's outcome had been a foregone conclusion. *I* was the only one who hadn't realized it.

But instead of sighing or deflating, I kept my head held high (Glashia would have been proud) and asked, "Is there anything else you haven't told me?"

"The details," Valda said, as if the many ways I might perish while in pursuit of a near-mythological sword in an inhospitable land were mere trifles. "So, do we have a deal?"

"And I can choose my own Guardian?" I asked Friedrich. After a moment, he nodded.

Valda smiled brightly at me, baring *all* of her teeth. "Then let's proceed with the oaths. You'll be taking the Bounty Hunter's Oath and your Guardian will be taking the Guardian's Oath."

"The Bounty Hunter's Oath?"

"It's not that we don't trust you, Noon. But an oath will assure us of your loyalty. After all, we don't want you changing your mind halfway through the trip."

"Halfway through the trip I'll be in Tartarus," I grumbled. (Glashia would not have been proud of my mumbling, but if a miracle happened and I survived, I'd be all too happy to take extra elocution lessons from him upon my return.)

"So Nouiomo Onyx, who will accompany you to Tartarus as Guardian?" Valda asked.

I cleared my throat, wondering what Valda would think of my choosing her son as Guardian. She knew Rafe had accompanied me to the Shallows last semester, but did she know we were still friends? I suffered a brief pang of regret for getting Rafe into this, but then reminded myself that he didn't have to accept.

"Raphael Sinclair," I said, my voice easily carrying throughout Empyr. There were some murmurs in the crowd and Peter groaned. Friedrich looked resigned and Valda looked . . . pleased. As if she'd planned this outcome all along. She walked over to one of the Angels in the front row and whispered to her. The Angel left and came back a few minutes later with Rafe in tow.

I almost laughed. He'd either not expected to be summoned to attend a formal oath ceremony or he was intentionally rebelling against it through his clothing choices. Then again, knowing Rafe, he could have been put on notice and simply decided dressing for the occasion was too much effort. His outfit—ripped cargo pants paired with a ratty, threadbare pullover—could not have contrasted more sharply with mine. I knew then that Rafe was still playing the part of academic slacker and all-around unenthusiastic Angel.

No matter. I didn't care what Rafe looked like. I only cared about whether he wanted to work with me. Formally. Temporarily. For a short jaunt to Hell and back.

The Angel who had escorted Rafe into Empyr's main dining room took her seat again and Rafe walked over to where I was standing. He didn't give the crowd or anyone else on stage—including Valda—a second glance. How could he when his gaze never left mine?

He stopped about a foot or so from where I stood and said:

"You sure do like dramatic clothing, Noon."

I blinked.

And then he grinned. And I grinned back.

"Let me guess," he said in a mock whisper. "You're getting a Guardian after all."

I nodded.

"So who'd you choose?"

"Raphael Sinclair." I paused then, suddenly nervous. "Do you think he wants the job?"

Rafe's grin turned into a simple smile. It was *much* more reassuring than Valda's smiles had been.

"Do you really have to ask?"

"Don't you want to know where we're going?"

He shrugged. "Not really, but I'm sure you'll tell me."

"Tartarus," I said.

He barked out a laugh and then shook his head. "That's

one of my favorite things about you, Noon. You don't do things by halves."

Later that night, standing on the Angel's altar amid hundreds, perhaps thousands, of candles, with me dressed in silver and satin and diamonds and Rafe dressed in clothes that were one step away from the rag pile, we took our vows. I solemnly, sincerely, and truthfully swore and affirmed that I would use best efforts to find, retrieve, and deliver the White Heart into the hands of its rightful owner and Rafe solemnly, sincerely, and truthfully swore and affirmed that he would do whatever was necessary to preserve and protect the life of his ward, Nouiomo Onyx, daughter of Karanos Onyx, the current executive of the Demon Council, and Aurelia Onyx nee Ferrum of the Hawthorn Tribe. I caused a slight stir when I added a codicil to Rafe's oath swearing and affirming to do the same for him.

Afterward, Rafe walked me back to my dorm room. I was more than capable of taking care of myself around campus, but I let him. Neither of us spoke about the race. I think we both sensed this would be our last night (possibly ever) to act like regular students. What had I said to myself not twelve hours ago? *At least the bailiff and bounty hunter cases were less grisly than the execution and murder cases had been.* Well, we'd see about that.

Vicious must have knocked more than my tooth out. Obviously, he'd knocked my sense out as well.

Chapter 7

༒

Rafe and I were told to gear up at Kalisto's Crystal Palace. Kalisto was a minor demon who spent summer in the deep south of Halja and winter at her New Babylon palace. The word "palace" was a misnomer; it was really a bazaar, although the building that housed all of Kalisto's merchants was as big as a palace. It was made of cast iron and plate glass and inside it was a maelstrom of vendors, wind, and ice. It was the place where rich Haljan hunters outfitted themselves for southern hunting trips.

Rafe and I had been given leaves of absence to compete in the Laurel Crown Race so we'd decided to meet Tuesday morning to catch a cabriolet to the palace. The race would begin at noon on Friday, so we had three days to prepare. There was no official starting line (although racers weren't allowed to enter Halja's hinterlands until the start of the race), but there was an official finish line: Timothy's Square at St. Luck's.

Every year, the finish line was held at a different demon law school. Since St. Luck's had hosted the rank matches, we'd also been given the honor of creating this year's Laurel

Crown and placing it at a finish line of our choosing. The St. Luck's faculty had opted for a crown made of gold leaf, which they planned to hang on one of the lampposts at the start of the race. The first *Primoris* to make it back to Timothy's Square would exchange their target for the crown and win. It was that simple. (Or rather, it was that simple on paper. In practice, the race was often lethal.)

A sampling of other racer's targets included:

† *EIDOLON'S ALTERNATE ENDING*

Commissioned by the demon lord Nickolai as a bride gift for his inamorata, the painting is purportedly "enhanced" by the Angel artist's botched spell. The scene in the painting changes for each viewer so no one knows what the original subject was. Anyone who gazes upon it is ever after incapable of feeling love. The painting was stolen sometime around the turn of the century by the Graeae, the trio of demonesses who were spawned from the ground together and who are now bound by their shared flesh and formidable magic.

† 623 BARS OF GOLD BULLION

This weighty amount was the grand total stolen from the New Babylon Mint over the last three months. The thieves are reputed to be hiding somewhere around Rockthorn Gorge. Liberating the gold and returning it to the mint will take not only a Guardian but a small army of magic users prepared to battle the outlaws and then protect the heavy cargo on its way back through a dizzying array of steep, narrow mountain passes full of argopelters and hidebehinds.

† GOU NAN JOUNEN AN

A.K.A. Rasha Pearl, a Hyrke courtesan and spy. Employed by the Office of the Executive since the age of

*eighteen, no woman is as well educated or as well trav-
eled. She speaks almost as many demon languages as an
Angel, she knows hundreds of exotic and erotic dances,
and she's been to nearly every* regulare *outpost—and
not a few* rogare *hotspots. Problem? She acted as a
double agent while doing so. Since the early 1990s, she
passed all sorts of supersensitive Council information on
to her* rogare *contacts. In 1997, she was arrested. But
she escaped from her Maegester captors shortly thereafter and has been on the Council's "Most Wanted" list
ever since.*

† 1 OZ. EACH OF BLITHE AND BITTERS

*Two fabled spices highly prized by the Mederi. One is a
powerful aphrodisiac, nearly a love potion for those who
use it, and the other is a sedative, one strong enough to
keep someone asleep for a hundred years or more. Both
spices are harvested from the same legendary tree, the
Saeculi Spinae, which only grows in Halja's western vol-
canic mountains—an area protected by the fierce, fiery
djinn. The djinn's price for just a pinch of blithe or bitters? Helping with the harvest.*

† LILITH'S LAST RESTING PLACE

*I'd found Lucifer's tomb two semesters ago, but the loca-
tion of Luck's lover's gravesite was still unknown. History is clear that she survived Armageddon and lived for
another two centuries or so. But the stories surrounding
her death are wildly inconsistent. Some say she went
north, beyond Rockthorn Gorge, toward Warja hoping
to start another fight. Others say she went west and
made a deal with the djinn to be sealed away in a room
full of blithe and bitters forever. Still others say she
went east and sailed off toward the Morning Star. So it
would take far more than Luck's blessing to find her*

*remains. Or any of the other targets we racers were
being asked to retrieve.*

Friedrich had given me a race file, which was much thinner than the case file I'd received before heading off to the Shallows last semester. Inside it were only two things: a map and some route notes. Valda had to practically pry the thief's journal out of Peter's hands in order to give it to me, but the Angels had finally handed that over as well. The thief turned out to be none other than Kaspar Bialas, Metatron's squire. According to the Divinity, Bialas stole the White Heart shortly after Metatron's death and the Divinity has been looking for it ever since. I couldn't honestly say that it gave me any confidence to have my name included among the bounty hunters who'd searched for (and failed to find) the White Heart before me: the little known Graemite and the illustrious Percevalus and Jacindus. And yet I couldn't honestly say that it didn't.

If not them, why not me?

The weather, while we waited for our cab, was typical of Eis, our first month. The mercury in the thermometer was barely visible and the wind was punishing. The thing is, the temperature and wind gusts were going to be just as bad inside Kalisto's Crystal Palace as out. She paid an Angel to keep it that way because, as her off-season marketing campaign often reminded New Babylonians, *anyone who geared up for a blizzard in less than blizzard-like conditions deserved to die.*

So, with that optimistic thought in mind, we piled gratefully into the cab's warm interior. On the way, I discussed our traveling plans with Rafe.

"I booked us tickets on the North-South Express for Thursday afternoon. You'll need to be at the train station by twelve thirty. We should arrive in Maize an hour or two before nightfall. We'll stay the night—"

"I guess you're going to ask your brother to regrow your tooth, huh?"

I worried the gap in my teeth with my tongue. *Undoubtedly.* I gave Rafe a lopsided smile and continued.

"The Mederies in Maize will supply the food, the barghests, and the sledge we'll need for the trip."

Rafe grinned. "Barghests! Do we get to ride them like the legends say Lilith did?"

I snorted. "Only if you want to get yourself killed before we even make it to Corterra."

Corterra was one of the old, abandoned outposts in the Verge. South of Maize, there were no more inhabited outposts. But the Old Trail continued, in greater or lesser states of repair, past the railroad's terminus in Maize. The land between Maize and Mount Iron was a huge, frozen steppe, full of formerly occupied outposts like Ironworks, First Forge, Furnace Town, and East and West Blast. Corterra sat in the very heart of the Verge. In fact, one could almost draw a straight line from Maize to Corterra to Tartarus at Mount Iron. Since speed was a priority, we'd take the shortest, straightest route, even though there were other, safer ones.

Rafe whistled. "I'll bet even Ivy's never been to Corterra."

"She hasn't," I said, wanting to move on. Frankly, Ivy had turned so pale when I'd told her we were headed to Corterra that I hadn't had the heart to tell her our real destination—Tartarus, which was even farther south.

"After Corterra, we'll continue south using the map and route notes Friedrich gave me, Kaspar Bialas' journal, celestial navigation, and Luck's guiding hand." I cleared my throat. Except for my trip to the Shallows and back, I hadn't spent much time out-of-doors. Still, I was trying hard to keep my spirits up so it wouldn't appear as if our mission was hopeless. "Before Thursday, I need you to find the spells Sigma Octantis and Joule and add those to your spellcasting repertoire." Sigma Octantis was a spell that boosted celestial navigation skills and Joule was a jumped-up spell of warmth.

"Already done," Rafe murmured, gazing out of the cab at the immense hilltop structure that slowly came into view.

I paid the cabdriver his fare, and we climbed out. In front of us, on a high windswept hill on the outskirts of north New

Babylon, was the Crystal Palace. We made our way up the steep stone steps that led to its entrance and I imagined how enticing this building might look during spring. With its great glass dome full of wintery winds nestled atop a hill full of grass and flowers, it would, no doubt, look like an enormous snow globe set on a colorful perch, a veritable beacon to would-be adventurers, Haljan hunters, and other wannabe travelers dreaming of something different. Today, however, there was little difference between the gray sky behind the building and the gray atmosphere within it.

Just outside the entrance was a fountain, but instead of water, this one sprayed snow. At its base was a sign:

> *Winter either bites with its teeth*
> *or lashes with its tail.*
>
> *Make a wish and swish.*
> *All proceeds benefit*
> *Kalisto's Hunters' Widows' and Children's Fund*

Beneath the sign was a cup for offerings. I looked up and suddenly my pulse and signature skyrocketed with the snow. High above the fountain was the wispy outline of a yeti—a snow beast. Its face materialized from the snow with black eyes the size of the cab we'd just climbed out of and an open jaw at least half the size of Timothy's Square. It swooped toward us, teeth gnashing, just as Rafe dropped a coin in the cup. He waved his hand in the air and the snow yeti slowly dissolved. A mist of cold, wet snow rained down on us.

"Did you wish for an umbrella?" I said, wiping my cheek with the hem of my cloak.

"Nope, I made a *serious* wish."

I gave him a dubious look. "Uh-huh. Let me guess. You wished that Kalisto would have a nose warmer with whiskers inside?"

He shook his head.

"Levitating snowshoes?"

Same response.

"Hot chocolate, at least?"

Rafe didn't answer. Instead he locked his arm with mine and led me toward the iron-doored entrance. On the way, he sang softly:

"I wished I could kiss your gap-toothed smile."

When he saw my reaction, he stifled a laugh.

"It would be bliss to do so awhile."

He stopped abruptly and turned me toward him, keeping a hold on my shoulders.

"But you're fierce and you're fiery and oh so wisery."

He lowered his head close to mine and then said *sotto voce*:

"So it's certain you'd yell, 'Go straight to hell!'"

The wind buffeted us from every direction as the snow continued to fall from above. Suddenly, I was acutely aware that Rafe was holding on to me. He stared at me and for a single second I wondered if he'd meant it when he'd said he wished for something serious.

"Wisery?" I said finally, stepping back. "Only you could come up with a word like that, Rafe."

Inside Kalisto's Crystal Palace, I immediately sensed the presence of two very different waning magic users. The first felt like a she-bear. Her signature was grizzly and rough, strong, capable of great violence, but not malevolent. The second, however, fell over me like a pall. It felt like the shadow of a signature, like a signature that had been cloaked by a gifted and powerful Angel. A waning magic user with less sensitivity than me probably wouldn't have been able to feel it. But I did, and the personal animosity I felt within it was like a punch to my gut. I stumbled and would have sprawled headlong onto the floor if Rafe hadn't caught me and cast a simple shielding spell over me.

"Sorry," he said quietly, looking around for the offending magic user. "I should have cast you up before we came inside."

I regained my balance and my magical equilibrium and shook him off, angrier with myself than him. I should be used to feeling malignant waning magic signatures by now. But, even I had to admit, I'd never felt one like this. There was something vaguely familiar about it, but because it was cloaked, I couldn't tell if the signature belonged to a demon, Maegester, or fellow MIT. All I could feel was a whisper of it, lingering around the edges of Rafe's shielding spell. It had felt my signature too. I could feel its interest. But it stayed away. Because the other one was coming closer.

Before the she-bear signature arrived, I took a moment to check out the Crystal Palace. We'd entered on an upper level that circled the perimeter of the lower level bazaar. Rafe and I walked over to the railing and peered down at the vendors below. It was like looking at a miniature snow village—one that was combating a blizzard. The snow and winds were just as fierce here, under the glass dome, as they had been outside. In fact, the iron cast work that held the glass together was barely visible against the sky. Below us were hundreds of log cabins, timber huts, leather tents, and ice igloos. Firelight made the tents and igloos glow in various shades of yellow, gold, and amber.

In the center of everything was a sparring ring and an archery range. I supposed they were there so customers could try out the weapons they were considering buying. Two brawny men circled each other in the ring. It looked a bit like a rank match except their weapons didn't glow with fire and they seemed like they were having fun. There were more archers at the range. At least twenty of them. I imagined that was because Hyrke hunters could use arrows to shoot down winged ice basilisks.

"How will we know which vendor has what supplies?" Rafe said, his voice raised against the wind. "I don't see any signs. It'll take us all day and into tomorrow to visit all those tents and huts."

I turned away from the rail and started looking for a floor map or vendor list, finally spotting one near a set of iron stairs that led to the floor below—the same set of stairs the she-bear was ascending. Except it wasn't a she-bear. Or at least she didn't look like a she-bear. She looked human, although that didn't mean the woman looked ordinary. In fact, I suspected she was a demon.

"Come on," I said, pulling on Rafe's cloak and pointing toward the stairs. "Something tells me that's Kalisto."

The three of us reached the top of the stairs at the same time. I stared at the woman in front of us, somewhat awe-struck. Everything about her was extreme—her size, her coloring, her clothing, her bearing. If I hadn't known she was a waning magic user, I might have thought she had giant's blood. She was big, but well proportioned, and from the way she carried herself, I was betting she was agile despite her size. Her hair looked like the pelt of a winter fox, all silvery gray and tawny brown with streaks of black, and her eyes were the color of ice with just the slightest hint of blue. She wore a fur-lined dappled leather cape paired with copper-colored leggings and snow boots. She carried no weapon. But then again waning magic users usually didn't. Our fire was our weapon. And, looking at her, I had no doubt that Kalisto was a master at shaping her magic. In short, Glashia would have *loved* her.

As my Guardian Angel, it fell to Rafe to initiate the intro-ductions. He did, referencing our full names, family connec-tions, and places of birth. Kalisto smiled then, her teeth gleaming and her eyes bright, and said in a booming voice that was easily heard above the wind:

"And I am Kalisto, Patron Demon of Bears, Hunters, and the Old Trail. I know your father well, Nouiomo. He told me you were coming—and where you're headed." She grinned even more fiercely. "I've never outfitted anyone headed to Tar-tarus before. It is an honor and a pleasure to do so. Come." She motioned, turning toward the stairs. Just before following her down, I glanced over at the vendor directory. Next to it was a larger sign with letters as big as my fist. It read:

STOP!

The southern Verge is one of the most dangerous and forbidding places in all of Halja. One out of every two hunters who follow the Old Trail will not return. Read the risks below. If you are unprepared to face these dangers, turn back now.

Under the warning was a long list of dangers hunters would face: freezing to death, starving to death, exposure, exhaustion, dehydration, getting lost, falling into a crevasse, losing a limb to frostbite, natural beasts, ice basilisks, as well as "other miscellaneous atrocities made of blood, bone, metal, and/or magic."

I shivered. *One out of every two?* I glanced over at Rafe, feeling guilty again for getting him involved. I opened my mouth to tell him—

"Don't," he said in a firm, serious voice that cut right through the wind. "*Don't* insult me or the vow I took by suggesting that I don't have to come with you."

My eyebrows shot up. I wasn't used to seeing Rafe with his ruff up. "I wasn't going to say anything of the kind," I said quickly. "I was merely going to point out that Kalisto forgot to include in her list of dangers snow blindness and scurvy."

"Scurvy?" Rafe laughed. "Noon, you are such a bad liar."

Throughout the morning, Rafe did his best to pay attention. But he'd always been the sort to learn on his own so it didn't surprise me when he wandered off during one of Kalisto's lengthy lectures about how to use the gear she was selling us. There'd been countless instructions: how to pitch a tent, pack the sledge, restring snowshoes; how to tie knots, repair ripped clothing, keep our goggles from fogging; how to keep our sleeping bags dry and our spirits up during the single most challenging thing I'd ever do in my life (and, yes, Kalisto was aware of some of the things I'd done already).

Kalisto managed to pack a semester's worth of outdoor training into a single morning. The only things she didn't teach me were how to build a fire (we'd both had a good laugh over that one) and how to use the metal weapons and tools I'd be bringing. Kalisto knew both Rochester and Glashia and was well versed in what my St. Luck's education had already taught me. There was nothing she could tell me about swords, knives, daggers, pickaxes, and poles that I didn't already know. She knew a lot about barghests too, she said, but the Demeter Tribe knew just as much and since that's who we would be getting the beasts from, the Mederies in Maize could tell us all about them.

Around midday I started to feel the other waning magic signature I'd first felt when I'd entered the Crystal Palace—the shadowy, whispery, cloaked one. At first, I didn't recognize what it was. The feeling started out as ordinary hunger, which quickly morphed into exhaustion. *Small wonder,* I thought, *considering the sixty pounds of gear I'd been carrying around all morning.* I looked around for a place to rest, but all I saw was unbroken snow. We were near the edge of the palace's frosted glass wall, which was about as far away from the spectator seats and stands lining the sparring ring and archery range as one could get. I gazed at the palace wall, my neck craning from floor to ceiling, my gaze following the black skeleton frame as it zigzagged its way across numerous irregularly shaped frosted-glass panels. Against the dull, leaden afternoon light, the black frame's jagged spread made it seem as if the sky itself was cracking.

My limbs became numb. I couldn't tell if it was the cold—or something else. And then my hearing faded. The vendors' voices behind me grew dim and I heard only the high-pitched sound of the wind. It sounded like the squeal of an animal in a trap. I turned around. I wasn't much for premonitions, but I could feel something coming . . .

Something ancient and powerful. Something that was as dark and cold as fire was light and hot.

Pfft! Searing pain shot through my left shoulder. The impact of it made me stagger backward and I dropped my gear in the snow. *Had my left arm just been torn off by a fireball? Even Nightshade wouldn't be able to regrow an arm,* I thought crazily. My upper chest *burned* as if it were on fire, but when I turned my head, I saw something redder than fire. I saw blood. My own and lots of it, leaking from the hole in my chest made by the arrow sticking out of it. I stared down at the gear I'd been holding, which was now scattered around me in the snow. My right hand clutched the shaft of the arrow. The only thing I seemed capable of comprehending right then was how tightly it was wedged in my chest. My grip on the arrow loosened and I stumbled backward, falling into the snow.

Above me Kalisto shifted into a bear and roared. She stood up on her hind legs and her pelt puffed out like a por-cupine while she gazed around the lower level of her winter bazaar looking for the erring archer. On the ground, I wheezed as Kalisto bared her teeth and then snapped them shut. She fell down on four legs, causing a minor explosion of snow at her feet and then turned and ran toward the direc-tion the arrow had come from.

Less than a second later, Rafe was at my side. His expres-sion scared me so I turned my head and focused on the snow, hiccupping because I couldn't breathe right. The snow's lack of color was calming. Peaceful. The cold and the numbness returned. Rafe knelt beside me and pressed his cheek to mine. My breath hitched. And then I stopped breathing.

I passed out to the quiet murmur of Rafe's voice whisper-ing spells in my ear.

Chapter 8

ॐ

When I woke up, we were on a train, but all around us was darkness. My head was in Rafe's lap and we were in a railcar alone. From the sway of the seat beneath me, I figured we'd pulled out of the station long ago. Above me, Rafe slept. His cheeks were hollow and his skin had a grayish green cast to it. I'd seen other Angels run out of *potentia*, but never Rafe. Until now, his power to cast spells had seemed limitless. I knew then, without a doubt, that the only thing keeping me alive was Rafe's *potentia*. I wanted to tell him not to worry if he failed. That my dying wouldn't be his fault. I knew, because of the memory I'd been given of his brother's funeral, how guilty he still felt over *that* death. I couldn't stand the thought of mine being another weight that he would have to bear.

Without thinking, I tried to raise my hand to grab his sleeve so that I could tell him that but pain immediately arced across my chest. I groaned and coughed and tried to talk, but couldn't. There was a thick, bubbly feeling in my

throat, like I'd been gurgling with salty syrup and had accidentally swallowed some. But I knew it wasn't syrup. I
looked down. The arrow shaft had been sawed off, but its tip
was still in my chest. I could feel it. Rafe woke and looked
down at me, his eyes bloodshot and wild. He swiped his arm
across his face, rubbing at his eyes and cheeks with his
sleeve. He then reached down and put his palm on my forehead and started feverishly murmuring the words to a spell
again.

When I woke again, the train was still. Rafe was lifting
me off the seat and into his arms. The pain was excruciating.
I tried to tell Rafe to *leave me be*. I didn't want to move, even
if I died on the train. I didn't have the strength to put my
arms around his neck so I just lay there like a rag doll, my
cheek pressed against his chest, my mouth opened in this
horrible scream I didn't have enough breath to complete.
Leave me! was my only thought. But there was no way to tell
Rafe that's what I wanted. I didn't have enough energy to grit
my teeth or move my fingers, let alone talk or grab Rafe's
arm to make him listen.

And that's when I felt the other waning magic signature.
But this one wasn't dark and malignant like the one I'd felt
just before the arrow pierced my heart at Kalisto's palace.
This one was white-hot and felt like the sun. It was Ari. Or
rather, it was an echo of Ari. It was my dying memory of him
because it faded as soon as Rafe started whispering the
words of his healing spell in my ear again.

Rafe walked down the aisle of the train and descended a
short set of steps, trying—and failing—to keep my bleeding
body still. It was an agony I thought I'd never survive. When
Rafe's foot hit the ground, the impact jolted me. Instantly it
felt like my bones had just been pulverized and turned to
dust. If felt like the simple act of moving me off the train had
reduced me to nothing more than a sack of skin that Rafe
was going to drop in a grave somewhere. My eyes rolled up
in my head and I let the darkness take me. My last thought
was that Rafe was saying the wrong prayer. Instead of a heal-

ing spell, he should have been saying the Final Blessing: *breath to ember, ember to flame, flame to fire, fire to ember, ember to ashes* . . .

W hen I woke for the third time, I knew I wasn't dead and likely wouldn't be anytime soon. But then, the very next moment, I almost wished I was. It hurt *that much*.

I lay in bed, in a darkened room with log walls, a vaulted ceiling, and a large glass window that overlooked ice-covered evergreens and a blanket of unbroken moonlit snow. Inside, an oil lamp flickered on a small bedside table and beside me, in a large armchair, Rafe slept. For a single moment I wondered if maybe I *had* died. If maybe, in death, I was caught in some vicious never-ending cycle where I would relive the last moments of my life by waking and sleeping and waking again next to the man who'd tried to save me.

"Rafe," I said. My voice was a scary surprise even to me. It sounded as if someone had shot an arrow down my throat, not into my heart.

Instantly, Rafe was awake. He bolted out of the chair and over to the bed. His eyes weren't quite as wild as the last time I'd seen them, but they were pretty close. But as soon as his gaze met mine, his expression softened and some of my fear fled. His shoulder-length, straw-colored hair was tangled and clumpy and he had the beginnings of a beard, but he smiled when he saw me.

"For a while there I was worried you might follow in Crae Ibeimorth's footsteps."

Crae Ibeimorth had been a minor demon, but she was firmly entrenched in the public's affection. She was the Patron Demon of Sleep. It was said when her lover first kissed her, she swooned and fell into a deep sleep for days. Her lover had finally revived her in a most ungentlemanly way, by throwing a bucket of ice-cold water on her.

"Were you tempted to throw a bucket of water on me?" I said. I laughed then but the pain in my chest brought tears to my eyes and I stopped.

"As a matter of fact, I do know a spell called Bucket of Ice-Cold Water," he said softly, "but I think you've had enough of my spellcasting for now."

"What happened?" I asked, my voice croaking like a frog's.

"You were shot in the chest with an arrow."

I wanted to scoff at him but didn't have the energy. "I know *that*," I said, coughing. But it came out as a sick-sounding bark. Rafe got up and walked over to a dresser. He poured some water into a glass and came back over. Thankfully, the glass had a straw because sitting up to drink it suddenly seemed like it would be as difficult as hiking to the moon. While I drank, Rafe brought me up to speed.

Apparently, the arrow had lodged in my chest right next to my heart. There hadn't been a lot of time to decide what to do, but Rafe, Karanos, and Aurelia had all thought heading straight for Maize was best, so my brother Night could heal me. Karanos contacted Demeter's monarch via the tribe's one electro-harmonic machine and then arranged for our unscheduled train trip south.

During surgery, Night had been able to remove most of the arrow, but he was forced to leave its tiny, barbed tip inside my chest. He suspected the arrow might have been ensorcelled. My brother then stabilized me with waxing magic and I'd been resting ever since. Night was also resting, in the other room, and I'd been here—at Demeter's springhouse—for a day and a half.

I breathed an inward sigh of relief. A day and a half meant it was only Wednesday night. I could still compete in the race. We could leave from here on Friday just like I'd originally planned. That is, we could if I could make it out of bed by then. And what had Rafe meant when he'd said Night thought the arrow tip may have been ensorcelled? That didn't sound good. But I had all day tomorrow to worry about me. Right now, I wanted to know how Rafe was doing.

"And you?" I said to him. "Are *you* okay?"

"*Me?*"

"Yes, you. I know you almost ran out of *potentia*." Just

because I hadn't died didn't mean I didn't still want to tell him what I'd wanted to tell him on the train.

"Rafe," I said slowly. "If I die during the race . . . promise me you won't feel responsible."

He gave me a sardonic look. "I'm your Guardian, Noon," he said in a dry voice. "Of course I'm going to feel responsible." He frowned and bent down to open one of the drawers in the bedside table. The table and the bed frame were both made of white enameled cast iron. The furniture and the slightly antiseptic smell were the only indications that I was in a convalescent house.

I wanted to tell Rafe that's not exactly what I'd meant. That Luck, and Luck alone, was responsible for when someone died. But maybe Rafe didn't believe that and wouldn't appreciate hearing it. And he *had* managed to keep me alive against all odds during the trip down here. Whether it was Luck, faith, *potentia*, or simply Raphael Sinclair's sheer will that I remain alive, who was I to argue?

I handed Rafe the empty glass of water and was just about to close my eyes again when he held up a pack of gauze, tape, and some sort of ointment.

"What's that?" I said warily.

"I think you know," he said. "Hold still."

Rafe peeled back the covers and, with no warning, started to untie the strings that held my tunic together.

"Wait!" I cried (although my voice was so weak, it sounded more like a squeak). "What are you doing?"

"Changing your bandage," he said patiently. "It might be uncomfortable, but it won't hurt."

"Have you done it before?"

No one worries about being seen naked when they're near death. Holding on to life (or wishing you were dead if the pain's that bad) is all anyone thinks about. But now that I wasn't in agonizing pain or hovering near death, my natural modesty returned. Baring my demon mark during a fight was one thing. Baring anything lower than that—for any reason— was quite another.

Rafe laughed. "No, one of the Mederies has been. But it's not like it's complicated and—"

He interrupted himself as something occurred to him. "Are you *shy*, Noon? About me . . . undressing you?"

He grinned.

I felt the blood rush to my face. It betrayed emotions I'd rather Rafe not have seen. If I didn't think about him in *that way*, I wouldn't be shy, right? And I didn't. Think about him in that way.

Except that I just had.

I tried to clear my throat, but the sound came out as a hic-cupy grunt. *I'd probably best shut up now,* I thought and leaned back on the pillow.

I tried to relax.

But it was hard when Rafe started to untie my laces again.

In the end, however, it was much less awkward than I thought it would be. Nothing untoward was revealed. Rafe untied the laces at the top of my tunic and then peeled the shirt down just low enough to see the bandage he'd be chang-ing. My chest was unbelievably sore too, so once Rafe got to work, there was nothing suggestive about anything he did. And when I got a look at the arrow's entry point, it was off-putting to say the least.

My demon mark was gone, obliterated by a thick, nasty looking, dark slash that was crisscrossed with stitches.

"And they say '*X* marks the spot,'" I said. "Looks more like *X*s mark the spot."

"It'll heal," Rafe said offhandedly. Once he'd started changing the bandage, he was all business.

"I know," I said, gazing up at the ceiling as Rafe worked. "Did I ever tell you about the time I tried to cut my demon mark off?"

Rafe paused and our gazes met briefly.

"No," he said, his tone indicating the information was ei-ther surprising, unsettling, or both.

"Oh yeah," I said matter-of-factly. "I tried to gouge it out with a kitchen knife."

Again Rafe paused, but this time he didn't meet my gaze. "You must've really hated your mark."

"I hated my magic," I clarified. "But it didn't matter. The mark grew back, darker than before—with no scarring."

Rafe looked at my wound with a doubtful expression. "I'm not sure even Nightshade could prevent scarring this time."

I shrugged. I didn't really care. And then something occurred to me. I ran my tongue across my teeth, feeling the gap where Vicious had knocked my tooth out.

"Night didn't grow my tooth back," I said.

Rafe put the last piece of tape in place and started tying the strings of my tunic.

"He said your body had had enough of stuff being pulled out of it with waxing magic. He said that healing can be more violent than people realize. Sometimes bones need to be rebroken in order to be set properly. Fevers can ravage a body for days before finally burning off a deadly infection. Even learning how to move—how to fight—after an injury like yours can be . . . painful. He said the tooth could wait."

He tied the last strings together and then placed his hands gently on my shoulders.

"Better?" he asked softly.

I nodded. I hadn't heard him casting any spells—and he'd said I'd had enough of his spellcasting for a while—but whatever he'd done had taken away the burn and eased the ache. I had a feeling my wound would be throbbing again by morning, but for now, it felt wonderfully numb.

For a long moment, Rafe didn't move. I could see the outline of his face in the moonlight. He had a strong chin, which was now covered in stubble, and high cheekbones. His taupe-colored eyes looked like granite in the low light. He looked absolutely serious, but suddenly I remembered the silly wish he'd made at Kalisto's fountain two days ago. *I wished I could kiss your gap-toothed smile.*

Did he still want to? Would he now?

Is that what *I* wanted?

I stared at Rafe in the dark next to my bed, wondering

when exactly I'd started to think of him as a rival for my affections. And then I immediately scolded myself. Rival? Against what? The *memory* of Ari? The ex-boyfriend who lied to me about being a demon? I kept telling myself I was moving on. Living my life. But clearly there was one area where I was still holding back.

I'd never been much for dating. I'd had casual relationships with a few Hyrkes in college, but I'd never really gotten close to anyone romantically until Ari. Which was probably why I'd taken the whole my-boyfriend-is-really-a-demon revelation pretty hard. I'd opened up to Ari about who and what I was, but he hadn't trusted me in the same way. Without thinking, I asked Rafe:

"Have *you* ever had your heart broken?"

He stared down at me with those impossibly large, mercurial eyes.

"Not yet."

He lowered his face toward mine. He was close enough so that I could see his eyelashes now, his scratchy looking whiskers, and the outline of his full lips.

"You know you never talk about him," he said in a near whisper.

"Who?"

He raised an eyebrow. We both knew who he meant. *Ari.*

I shrugged. "What's there to say?" I shifted my gaze from Rafe to the silver-coated pines outside. "He lied to me, Rafe. Lied to me about being a demon. How do you forgive someone for that?"

Rafe didn't answer at first. I peered into the darkness. *Was there anything out there worth finding? Or was all of it just deadly and dangerous and eager to kill us?*

"I don't know," Rafe said finally. "*Forgiveness* isn't my specialty."

I turned back toward him. There was something about the way he'd answered that made me think there was more to it than that.

"What *is* your specialty, Rafe?" I said, asking a question I'd asked him half a dozen times already. Every Angel had a declared specialty, or a focused course of study. Peter's had been power polarities. Other Angels I'd known had specialized in things like adjudication, enforcement, tracking, extracting confessions, and retribution. But Rafe had either never declared one or he was reluctant to share it with me. (Although he'd once joked that "taking care of me" was his specialty.)

"Grace," he said quietly. And then it was his turn to draw inspiration from the moonlit night. He turned away and stared out at the cold, frozen landscape. It was an environment that could easily kill a man if he went into it unprepared.

"Grace?" I whispered. "And you said *I* didn't do things by halves."

Grace was the heaviest of the heavies. It went way beyond forgiveness. It was forgiveness and redemption, suffering and salvation all rolled into one elusive concept. Grace was a process, not a state. Angels who studied it didn't believe they'd ever actually achieve it.

Rafe shrugged and made some vaguely affirmative sound.

He quickly moved back into his former position though and leaned over me, bracing himself with his hands on either side of my head. He lowered his face to mine. His expression told me he preferred to focus on someone other than himself.

"So, now that I've saved your life *again* do I get to kiss you now?" His words were the barest whisper, but the feel of his breath on my lips made them tingle. My eyes widened and I suddenly wondered how large *my* eyes appeared in the dark.

"Come on, Noon," Rafe said, deliberately blowing on my lips. "Don't you think we've chased each other around the school yard long enough?" This time, I didn't imagine it. My lips felt as if I'd rubbed them with crushed mint and camphor. Rafe was using magic on me.

"And don't *you* think you've cast enough spells over me for a while?"

Rafe grinned, but stopped. The tingling faded.

"Face it, Noon, you've been wondering what it would be like too."

But that was as far as he pushed things. He leaned back and sat on the edge of my bed, waiting. Waiting for me to reply. Or for me to make the next move. He looked very patient and I remembered that he was. I remembered how many times Virtus, Fara's tiger, had hissed and spit at him before they'd finally become friends. I remembered how irritating he'd been to me when I'd first met him. And how I'd sworn I'd *never* pick him as a Guardian. And I remembered how Rafe's seemingly endless *potentia* had almost run out last night. But he hadn't let it. And I didn't remember, but I *knew*, that he'd been by my side ever since. Ever since last night . . . and maybe from the day we'd first met.

What could I say?

Part of me wished he hadn't said anything. That he hadn't brought up this feeling that was starting to develop between us. Then we could go on forever without acknowledging anything. Because acknowledging our feelings, however nascent, meant changing the dynamic between us. Instead of potential, now there was risk.

"I don't want to hurt you, Rafe."

He gave a faint laugh and said, "Onyx, you couldn't hurt a dragonfly right now."

"I meant—

"I know what you meant," Rafe said sighing, serious once again. "I saw you and Ari together. I traveled with you for weeks. You think I didn't know how it was between you? Only a blind fool wouldn't have seen how you felt about each other."

There was a pregnant pause. We both knew what the next part of the story was. It was the black moment of every story, the part where it all goes to hell. And, as Rafe had said, he'd been there when it all went down. He and Fara had been the ones who helped me pick up the pieces of myself after Ari's lie had crawled inside me, exploded, and then blown me to bits. Which meant I wanted to make sure if I kissed Rafe, it was for the right reasons. I didn't want to kiss him because I was on the rebound or out of gratitude because he'd saved my life. I was grateful, of course. But I didn't think that—*and that alone*—was a good basis for starting a new relationship.

He saw the hesitation in my face. But he didn't look upset.

"No worries, firestarter," Rafe said, kissing my forehead instead of my lips. "I told you I knew the spell Bucket of Ice-Cold Water. And it doesn't have anything to do with Crae Ibeimorth."

Chapter 9

ತಿ

The smell of pork frying, the brightness of the morning sun on the snow outside, and several people talking at once assaulted my senses. I stood at the end of the hallway I'd just shuffled down, peering into what seemed to be the great room for Demeter's springhouse. My brother, Nightshade, was standing behind a wooden bar with his back to me. He held a three-tined fork in one hand and the handle of an iron pan in the other. Rafe was kneeling in front of a large, fieldstone fireplace. A woman I'd never seen before stood in front of a huge lead glass window sipping something out of a crockery mug. She turned as I entered.

"Nouiomo Onyx," she said, putting her mug on the table in front of her and walking toward me, "I was beginning to think I might never see you awake. You know the first time I saw you, you were almost as injured as you were when your Guardian brought you here just two nights ago."

"You must be Linnaea Saphir," I said, smiling. My brother had told me lots about her. I could tell when he talked about her that she impressed him. *Who wouldn't be impressed?* At twenty-four Linnaea had been voted in as Demeter's new monarch. Now, three years later, she was still leading the tribe—a group made up of a hundred or so actively practicing on-site Mederies and hundreds of alumni healers who practiced up in New Babylon. She supervised Maize's hospital, greenhouse, gardens, fields, and this springhouse, which I knew from talking with Night, was Demeter's guest house for waning magic users.

Night put his fork down, walked over and gently put his hands on my shoulders.

"How's your heart?" he said.

"Still pumping, thanks to you," I said, turning my smile into a full-fledged grin.

Nightshade had been born as Nocturo, a Maegester's name if ever there was one. He looked the part too, with hair that was darker, straighter, and thicker than mine. He wore it long and tied back with a simple strip of leather. He had a widow's peak, light skin, and piercingly dark eyes. I wondered briefly if his looks were ever a problem in the hospital. Did patients wake thinking a Maegester was at their side? That might be frightening for some of them. But when Night smiled, his natural warmth lit up all the dark parts of his looks.

Part of me wished I could tour the whole of Maize with him and Linnaea, meet the other women Night worked alongside, and see with my own eyes what he was creating down here in southern Halja. But no one knew more than I how deadly my touch could be. Rafe might be able to cast a powerful spell over me to protect Demeter's patients and crops, but why take the chance? Far better to stay sequestered near this springhouse.

Since I was likely to collapse if I kept standing there, I moved over to the table and slumped gratefully into a chair. Linnaea sat down across from me and Night went back to the stove. Rafe walked over to the table, bringing with him a steaming mug of something that smelled like hazelnut, sweet cream, and coffee. He handed me the mug and sat down beside me. I gave him a sidelong glance, wondering if he felt awkward about last night's almost-kiss. But he caught me staring and winked. So much for thinking Rafe would ever feel awkward.

"Something tells me you still want a chance to race for the Laurel Crown," Linnaea said. I remembered that my brother had said Linnaea's healing focus was more on mind than body. As a Mederi, her magic could mend broken bones or purge disease, but her true talent was assessing a patient's mental state and helping them heal their head and heart. *Well, good luck with me,* I thought. But the last thing I wanted was to appear sullen. I was grateful to Linnaea for all that she'd done for Night and me, and thankful to finally have a chance to meet and speak with her.

"I'm not doing it for honor or glory," I said quickly. It suddenly seemed important that Linnaea not think I was some vainglorious treasure hunter. She was the monarch of Night's tribe, my current host, and the one who would be supplying the food, sledge, and barghests we'd need for the race. "I don't care about the Laurel Crown itself. I care about the right that it gives me."

Linnaea's eyebrows rose. "Which is?"

"The right to direct my own future. Laureates are allowed to choose where they spend their fourth semester residency."

Linnaea nodded slowly, looking contemplative. She was quite pretty, I realized, in an earthy sort of way, with slate blue eyes, thick, wheat-colored hair, and a smattering of freckles across the bridge of her nose and high cheekbones.

"Mederies go where they are needed most," she said. "But then I'm sure it's the same with Maegesters, even Laureates. I'm betting your residency will be well matched to your skills regardless of whether you win the race or not."

I thought about the offer from Adikia, the Patron Demon of Abuse, Injustice, and Oppression. *How would my skills match her needs?* And the offer from the Patron Demon of Rockthorn Gorge? What would an MIT know about hydroelectric dams? (In fact, what would a *demon* know about those things? The Patron Demon of Rockthorn Gorge's followers would likely go the way of Orcus' former followers before long. And since Rockthorn Gorge had always been a place of historic unrest, riots, revolts, and general lawlessness, it was probably for the best. Surely, the Demon Council could come up with a safer way to secure electricity for those ten thousand New Babylonians who needed it.)

"I also want to race because I need to bring my target back to the Joshua School's dean of Guardians. I owe him a debt because I accidentally destroyed something of his last year. He told me my debt would be repaid if I brought my target back to him." I fiddled with my mug, wondering how revealing my next statement would be to someone as intuitive as Linnaea. "He also told me, if I didn't race and at least attempt to bring my target back to him, I'd be stripped of my rank and never be allowed to work with another Angel again."

This time Linnaea nodded without reservation. "And being stripped of your rank would bother you?" she asked.

I looked surprised. *Wouldn't it bother anyone?* But then maybe Night had told her what a reluctant student I'd been in the beginning, or maybe she'd heard on her own.

"It would," I said. Hopefully, the tone of my voice and my expression conveyed my sincerity. With absolutely no hint of boastfulness, I said simply, "I've worked hard to accept, master, and control my magic. I don't know what it's been like for Night here, but training to be a Maegester has been . . . tough at times. I don't want to go backward."

Linnaea smiled and glanced over at Night, who was walking over to the table with a platter of ham, biscuits, butter, and a jar of marmalade. The cheerful plate of food was so at odds with the grave look on his face that my hunger vanished.

"Has it been hard for you, Night? Training to be a Mederi?" I said.

He gave me a reassuring smile, but it was just the slightest bit pitying too, which of course made me frown, grip my mug too tightly, and nearly boil the coffee inside of it. I guess his grave look had been for *me*.

Night's gaze switched to Linnaea. "It hasn't been too

bad," he said, his mouth quirking at the corners. He grabbed plates, napkins, knives, and forks from the counter and passed them out. "On the whole, Demeter has been very welcoming."

Night's and Linnaea's gazes held for just a moment longer than necessary, causing me to wonder whether there might be more to their relationship than just monarch and mentee. She was five years older than Night so it seemed unlikely . . . But then Rafe was six years older than me . . . . I blinked and shook my head, wondering why my thoughts had suddenly become so scattered.

"And never being allowed to work with another Angel again," Linnaea said smoothly, as if following the direction of my thoughts, "well, avoiding *that* makes sense. You have a very skilled and devoted Guardian, Noon. Better watch out," she said, grinning widely now, "Demeter might try and recruit him."

Rafe had been silent up to now. He often was in group settings. But I'd learned that even when he looked disinterested or disengaged, he wasn't. He stabbed two pieces of ham and a biscuit with his fork and put them on his plate. He turned toward me, his eyes bright. "If Friedrich forbids us from working together after this, we could become mercenaries." I rolled my eyes.

"Think about it," he said in a serious voice, although I knew he wasn't. "You and me, Onyx. Hiring ourselves out to the highest bidder. Only beholden to ourselves and the black market. No more answering to the Divinity or the Council. We could take our show on the road. Visit all of the outposts. Live like Metatron and Justica."

I laughed. "Metatron and Justica? They didn't even know each other."

"The Angels believe they were in love," Rafe said dismissively, cutting into his meat.

"Do *you* believe that, Rafe?"

He held his fork and knife in the air for a moment, staring at nothing in particular, and then shrugged. "It's a good story." He started cutting again and said in between bites,

"What I do know is that I'm oath bound to you. So, even if you don't race, *you'll* be the one deciding whether we work together in the future, not him."

I reached up and squeezed his hand briefly, glancing over at Night and Linnaea to see their reactions to Rafe's seditious declarations. Linnaea looked equal parts charmed and admiring. Night looked concerned. Little wonder. Night was one of the least rebellious people I knew. He always did the right thing. I wish I could assure him that Rafe's outrageous statements were mere bluster.

Problem was, I'd be lying. But while Rafe's loyalty touched me deeply, I wasn't going to let either of us live in violation of the law. His statement made me more determined than ever to race so that he wouldn't have to contemplate verboten actions I couldn't allow him to perform.

After breakfast Linnaea left for Demeter's main hospital. She invited Rafe to accompany her, both because she thought his spellcasting might be useful on a few of her patients and because he expressed an interest in meeting some of the other Mederi healers and learning some of their nonmagical techniques. Night suggested I rest, but breakfast had given me some energy and I had some questions for him. So I followed him into the springhouse's small surgery room, both eager and reluctant to see the place where Night had operated on me just two nights ago.

My first impression was that it was very bright and very clean. The room smelled faintly of lemon and it was a few degrees colder than the rest of the house.

"This room was built above a natural spring with healing properties," Night explained, walking over to an old, wooden cupboard on the far side of the room. Its shelves were full of bottles in all sorts of colors and shapes, small wooden boxes, and leather-bound books. He pulled one of the books out, flipped it open, reached for an ink pen, and began jotting some notes in it. My guess was that he was probably writing notes about my recovery. I could only imagine what they said:

1. Appetite unaffected by life-threatening injury. (Make sure to slaughter another pig, churn more butter, and make more marmalade!)
2. Doggedly refuses to give up on Laurel Crown Race . . . What is the matter with her?!
3. Don't ask about Ari Carmine. It's clear she doesn't want to talk about him because she hasn't mentioned him *once* since he "disappeared" in the Shallows.
4. Don't ask about her Guardian either. She refuses to see that she could be happy with anyone else and instead prefers to focus on impossible tasks like winning the Laurel Crown Race.
5. Her heart? She said it's still beating . . .

In the center of the room was a wooden operating table. In fact, nearly everything in the room was made of wood, including the floors and the few other tables scattered around the perimeter. All of it shined with the smoothness of age and frequent polishings. There was absolutely no sign of blood anywhere, which was a relief. Above the operating table was a modern electric light. (I was suddenly grateful for it. I couldn't imagine how difficult it would be to perform surgery by candlelight. Patients couldn't always wait until daylight, as my own case had more than adequately demonstrated.)

"Rafe said you weren't able to completely remove the arrow tip," I said. "He said you thought it might be ensorcelled."

"It is ensorcelled," Night said in a tone that was both distracted and matter-of-fact. He finished making his last note and closed the book. "Likely with a curse." He looked up at me. "But I don't know which one—or what kind—and that makes it even more difficult and dangerous to remove."

"So I'll need to live with it inside me forever?"

Night frowned. "No . . . it will come out one way or another. But I wanted some time to try to figure out the safest way to remove it. When Rafe brought you down here on Tuesday night . . ." His gaze was sharp, but then his features softened and he cleared his throat. "I'm not sure you realize, Noon . . . Anyone else with that injury would have died."

We stared at each other. And then I frowned at him, easily turning it into a scowl.

I should be used to almost dying by now, I thought.

I switched my gaze to the operating table, wondering for a moment if coming in here was such a good idea after all. The last thing I needed was to suffer a crisis of confidence just when I needed my courage the most. The Laurel Crown wouldn't be won by someone who was afraid of dying.

"Maybe the arrow tip isn't cursed," I said. "Maybe it's blessed. Maybe the archer's shots routinely go astray and so he pays an Angel to bless his tips, just in case. Maybe my getting shot was an accident and it was the tip that saved me."

But Night scoffed at this suggestion. "It's not blessed," he said simply. "It feels malignant. And if you haven't felt that yet from it, you will." He placed the book he was writing in back on the shelf. "No, it wasn't the arrow tip that saved you, it was your Guardian." Night may not have approved of Rafe's rebellious breakfast talk, but it was clear he admired his spellcasting skills. "Even Linnaea says she's never seen anything like it. She thinks he's in love with you and that was the reason he was able to keep you alive for so long."

I'm sure my face registered the surprise I felt upon hearing Night's words. Rafe had great affection for me, as I did him. But love? *True* love? I doubted it.

"Well, Linnaea's young," I said, trying to put Night's statement in perspective. "There are probably lots of things she hasn't seen yet."

But Night was shaking his head. "She may be a young monarch, but unlike me, she's spent her whole life around Mederi hospitals and healing wards. In any case, while I can say for certain that the arrow tip is harmful, I can't say for certain that it was meant to kill you. Kalisto said it was shot from a very great distance. Under the environmental conditions of the Crystal Palace it would have taken an archer of consummate skill to have successfully hit anywhere near your heart if you were the intended mark."

I walked around the room, only half focusing on the items in front of me—a chalkboard, empty ceramic bowls and pitchers, shelves full of linens, anatomical drawings, clay models of various body parts, an old scale, a stainless steel sink—as I digested what Night had just told me.

"So Kalisto wasn't able to find the archer who shot the arrow?"

Night shook his head. "She questioned each and every one of the archers who were on the floor that day." I grimaced. The way Night said the word *questioned* led me to believe that Kalisto had done more than just interrogate the archers. *Did bear-force "encouragement" to provide information make someone's credibility more or less suspect?* Probably more, but since no such information had been provided it was a nonissue.

"It was most likely one of the other racers," I said. "One of them must have asked his Guardian to cast a curse into the arrow tip. Who else would want to curse or possibly kill me?"

Night's forbidding look was back. "Do you really *need* to win the Laurel Crown, Noon? Your best option now would be to decline your race invitation and stay here until I can find a way to remove the arrow tip."

Which was exactly what the archer who'd shot me wanted me to do—bow out of the race, whether due to death, inability to compete, or just fear of going forward.

I picked up the model of a human heart and held it in my hand, marveling at the complexity of the human body. All my life, until relatively recently, I'd said I wanted to be a healer, and yet, I had no idea what any of the parts of the heart were called. I wouldn't know the first thing about how to fix one that was broken. Or how to purge one of a curse. If I'd been so hell-bent on being a healer, why hadn't I read more anatomy books or studied more herbal lore while I was growing up?

The answer seemed simple. Standing here now in Demeter's springhouse surgery room holding a clay replica of a human organ I knew nothing about, surrounded by mysterious bottles full of liquids and powders I knew even less about, it occurred to me that my choice to become a Maegester hadn't been made only a year ago. I'd been unconsciously making it all my life.

I *wanted* to be a Maegester.

But I also wanted to work with people I knew, liked, and trusted.

"What if *you* made a mistake," I asked Night, "and as a result of that mistake you were threatened with never being able to work with Linnaea again? How far would you go to prevent that from happening? What would *you* risk to be able to continue working with her?"

I could tell by the expression on Night's face that my words affected him. Night infrequently made mistakes. But my hypothetical helped him to understand one of my biggest motives for wanting to race. Finally, he nodded.

"All right then," he said. "Let's get you healed up and ready to go. I know just the place, and the person to take you there."

Chapter 10

&

I hadn't realized my mother was in Maize and her presence underscored anew how perilous my grasp on life really had been. In the last year or so my mother had been increasing the number of trips she took into New Babylon, but as far as I knew, this was her first trip south of Etincelle in over twenty years. She likely hadn't stepped foot in a Mederi tribe outpost since before Night and I were born. Aurelia had spent Tuesday night at Demeter's springhouse, but last night at the hospital. Night explained that, while Aurelia hadn't started using her magic again, she would want to see me now that I was awake and would be more than willing to accompany me to Maize's other, larger, outdoor healing spring. So, after a short rest at the springhouse, I awoke to find my mother already dressed for a winter hike in doeskin pants, thick tunic, and mohair vest. She'd brought suitable clothes for me too: soft leather leggings, underclothes, a heavy wool sweater, fur-lined cloak, and snow boots. After one brief, fierce, heartfelt embrace and some initial bland pleasantries, my mother and I laced up our boots and left the cozy confines of the springhouse.

Since I'd spent the last forty-eight hours inside, the air felt extra sharp, almost like a splash of ice-cold water. But it wasn't unwelcome. We set off along a snowy path that was lined with a split rail fence through woods with trees so spindly and bare they looked like they'd been drawn onto the opalescent landscape with a pointy piece of charcoal. My breath puffed in front of me in small white clouds. If Rafe were here, no doubt he would have shaped them into something. A rabbit or a shooting star or even toasted marshmallows.

I kept my signature open, to detect any unannounced waning magic users, but felt nothing during our hike. About an hour later, we stood at the lip of the spring, huffing and puffing from our exertions. For someone who didn't get out of the house much, Aurelia was in pretty good shape. Me, on the other hand— *Ugh.* It was like all of the training and conditioning I'd worked so hard at these past couple of months never happened. I was doubled over at the waist, hands on my knees, trying to catch my breath amidst the frozen beauty of the place.

The hot water from the spring bubbled up out of the snowy landscape and formed a rough oval before meandering off into the woods via a small, steaming stream. I imagined, to anyone with a bird's-eye view, that the spring would look like a giant beryl-colored balloon with a string attached. Some ways away, a dozen oak trees lined the spring. Their dark silhouettes were draped with icicles. Sunlight beamed from behind, casting long, jagged shadows across the expanse of white and, here and there, was a sparkling prism of refracted light. Inside the ring of sleeping oaks were orchard trees and topiaries. Tons of them. More than there had ever been in the Aster garden back home in Etincelle.

"Night said a spring. I didn't think there would be a garden too," I said, still panting.

Aurelia snorted delicately, tucking a stray strand of her dark hair back into the knot she'd tied it in earlier. "Maize is a Mederi outpost. Expecting an absence of gardens here would be like expecting an absence of fire at St. Lucifer's." She started walking the perimeter of the spring, as if she were looking for something. "Besides," she said almost absentmindedly, "you'd be hard-pressed to kill anything here. The spring waters have as much magic as we do."

Interesting that she'd used the word *we*. Aurelia hadn't practiced medicine in at least as many years as she'd been south. I followed in her wake, trying to identify the topiaries as I had the snow demons during the Festival of Frivolity.

Right away, I spotted the familiar shapes of Mephistopheles, Michael, and Mary. A few feet away from them were Lucifer and Lilith. Lucifer sat astride a large warhorse with his infamous triple-tipped lance in hand. Lilith rode a barghest. She was standing up in the saddle brandishing a sabre. During Armageddon their weapons would have been made of fire and waning magic, but here they were made of aged copper.

I don't know what made me look up. Instinct maybe. A prickling feeling that I was missing something. Something big. Suddenly I glanced up and saw the shape of a drakon. Even though it was only a drakon carved out of shrubs, my signature pulsed and my heart spasmed momentarily. The arrow tip in my chest burned as if it was made of fire. I stood rooted to the spot, my hand pressed against my heart, staring up at this garden's most glorious creation—Demeter astride a flying drakon. Instead of a weapon, she held a single branch. I took a deep breath and steadied my magic. When my heart was safely beating again, I walked closer.

And the illusion vanished.

There'd been no drakon topiary. Just my imagination.

"Did you see something, Noon?" my mother asked.

I turned to her. "Was I supposed to?"

She gave me a puzzled smile. "The only magic here"— she made a sweeping gesture with her hand that encompassed the entire clearing—"is in *there*"—she pointed at the spring—"and in *here*"—she thumped on her own chest with her fingertips—"inside of us."

Did my mother still have magic . . . inside of her? Was it sleeping like the sentinel oaks that lined this spring? Or had it withered and died from lack of use?

She walked over to where I was standing then and, almost as if she'd known what I was thinking, broke a branch off the tree. The same branch that I'd imagined the drakon-riding Demeter had held.

"It's a pear tree branch," she told me. In Halja, pears were often considered peace offerings because they could be served to a mixed gathering of Host and Angels without offending.

"Watch," she said.

And with that one-word warning, Aurelia reawakened that which had been dormant—the branch for a season, my mother's magic for a lifetime.

Watch I did as the branch sprouted buds and then white blossoms. She held the branch with one hand then and stripped it of its petals with the other. Cupping the petals in her hand, she then blew them onto the surface of the spring where they fell like snow. The pear blossoms then became water lilies and suddenly the entire surface of the spring was covered with lily pads and white star-shaped flowers.

She looked at me, her mouth quirking up at the corners. I couldn't be sure, because it was something I'd seen so rarely, but I think Aurelia was enjoying herself. I was too. Until she asked me to use *my* magic.

"*Here?* How?"

"Make a fire offering," she explained. "To Demeter. Demeter was the patron demon of a Mederi outpost, so the last thing she'd want is your spilled blood.

"Noon," she started, paused, and then continued more cautiously. "I'm sorry about your magic. I did what I did because I wanted you to live. Maybe it was wrong to pray to Micah, the Angel's Savior, as well as pleading to Luck that you and Night would be born healthy. And maybe it was wrong to promise Micah that, if he saved you, I wouldn't raise you to be a part of the Host. Because my promise denied you so many things. But it granted you *life*. And I'm glad you're here now—*as you are*.

"I want to see you shape your magic into something more than rough flames or crude fireballs. I never have before. I couldn't. Because I was too afraid it would be encouraging you and I couldn't break my promise. But my oath is no longer binding. You declared your magic without any interference from me.

"And now I want to see you use it," she repeated. It was a request, not a command, however.

How was I supposed to make a fire offering here? I thought. I doubted Demeter would appreciate my burning the trees or the topiaries, even if she had been a demon. And that would hardly be the elegant offering my mother was hoping for. But then I remembered a fiery peace offering I'd made last semester. Sailing on a dahabiya to the Shallows, I'd formed a fiery dove and offered it to Estes, the Patron Demon of the Lethe. That fiery dove had harmed nothing. I'd willed it to circle me and then had made it dive harmlessly into the Lethe. So . . . maybe I could create another animal out of fire . . . and simply will it into the spring.

I searched for inspiration and found it in the lily pads Aurelia had just created. I closed my eyes and centered myself. It wouldn't do to make a mistake here. I felt my waning magic surge, and then I combined it with other emotions—*gratefulness*, that I was alive; *joy*, at seeing my mother use her magic for the first time; and *compassion*. I forgave Aurelia for my mixed-up birth and my unhappy childhood. It was an absolution that I'd been working toward for a year now and, once I gave it, it was blissfully freeing. When I opened my eyes, fiery frogs leapt from lily pad to lily pad. Some went into the water, where they fizzled and "died" only to be reborn moments later a few lily pads away.

Who knew frogs could be a symbol of forgiveness?

My mother laughed, the sound of it like tiny silver bells echoing throughout the clearing. I wanted to laugh too, but the arrow tip in my chest was burning again. I knew then that something was wrong. That it *was* cursed. And that it was interfering with my magic. But I pushed those thoughts away. Because it was so much easier, and more pleasant, to simply enjoy the *now*. To save the memory of this moment for any dark days that may lie ahead.

Aurelia and I stood and watched until the waning magic I'd thrown petered out. When the surface of the spring was dotted with only lily pads and lilies once again, Aurelia continued wandering around the spring's perimeter.

"What are you looking for?" I asked her.

"A marker."

Interested, but somewhat wary (markers, signs, and symbols in Halja were not usually as innocuous as fiery frogs leaping across magically grown lily pads), I followed her and saw that she was uncovering stepping stones. A skeleton was carved onto each of them, although each was holding something different in its bony hand: a scythe, a sword, a shield, and a pickax. I realized they were death markers for Halja's four magic classifications: Mederies, Maegesters, Angels, and Hyrkes, respectively. The pickax, no doubt, was a reference to the Verge's southern magicless miners. A Haljan death marker for Hyrkes up in Bradbury, where everyone was a longshoreman or fisherman, would likely carry a filleting knife.

"Did Night ever tell you the history of Demeter?" my mother asked.

"Just that it was formed much later than Gaia or Hawthorn were. He said the tribe had a liberal reputation. And that they were more accepting of the unconventional."

Aurelia smiled thinly and then nodded conciliatorily. She'd been trained by Hawthorn and there was little doubt about what Hawthorn thought of Demeter and its liberal practices. But Aurelia wasn't on the best of terms with her tribe, and hadn't been for twenty-two years.

"Unlike Gaia and Hawthorn," she said, "both of which can trace their origins to pre-Apocalyptic times, Demeter wasn't founded until a few hundred years ago. In the middle ages, Maize was called Requiem. It's between New Babylon and Mount Iron so initially Requiem was built to feed, clothe, and outfit the settlers who were headed even farther south—"

"The miners and their families, who formed the Verge's mining and blast towns." I'd gotten the impression from my history classes that, in its heyday, the Verge had been like an ant mound that had been kicked by a frost giant, with settlers scattering every which way over land on its way to a permanent winter.

"Eventually, there was a need for a hospital," Aurelia said. "Which led to the need for a cemetery. Thus Maize's former name. Haljans have been resting here for one reason or another since people first ventured south after the Apocalypse."

"So what happened to the original Requiem settlers?" I asked. "Are there any Hyrkes here now?"

My mother shook her head. "They either died, left, or were cursed. Long before Demeter arrived."

"Cursed? Did Night tell you about my arrow tip? Let me guess, this hike up here has something to do with trying to purge the curse from it."

My mother gave me a sharp look. "Yes, but there's more to it than that. Karanos told me that your race target is *Album Cor Iustitiae*—the White Heart, right?"

"Yes . . ."

"This hike, and your introduction to the spring here, is really about teaching you everything I know about perennial magic."

"Perennial magic? *You practice perennial magic?*" I couldn't keep the surprise out of my voice. I didn't think my mother practiced any magic anymore, let alone magic that was as ethereal and mysterious as perennial magic.

"No," she corrected. "I'm not sure that anyone practices perennial magic, although the Amanita make a practice of trying to learn its secrets."

"If you don't practice it, how is it that you know about it?"

She met my gaze and made a face. I wasn't very good at interpreting my mother's expressions since heart-to-hearts like this were so out of the ordinary. But, if I had to guess, I would have said that she looked *somewhat* sheepish. Or *somewhat* guilty. As if whatever she'd done, she'd do again.

"I already told you how desperate I was when I was pregnant with you and Night and how I thought I might lose you," she said. I cleared my throat, not wanting to hear again about how she'd pleaded to Luck and prayed to Micah at the same time. It seemed wrong. And part of me couldn't help worrying about whether payment for such a choice would be limited to her children's magical birth defects . . . or if her "reparations" column was still in the red like mine. But at least I was only indebted to Friedrich Vanderlin. My mother had indebted herself to absent gods.

Aurelia grimaced. "Let's just say I explored a lot of options. Some were more . . . grounded than others." She bent down and brushed snow off another stone marker. "And one of the options I looked into was saving you by using perennial magic."

She looked up at me then. To gauge my reaction I suppose. To be honest, I was surprised but not shocked. My mother was an extreme person. Hearing that she'd considered using magic that was not generally practiced because of its unreliable, incomprehensible, and controversial nature was all too consistent with her personality. Sometimes I wondered how big a rule breaker she might have been if Aurelia Ferrum had not married the Maegester who would become the next executive of the Demon Council.

Okay . . .

So that was *how* my mother knew about perennial magic. But *what* exactly did she know? I asked her, and got an earful.

According to my mother, perennial magic was older than any other magic. And my gut feeling about its natural reservoirs had been right. Perennial magic mostly existed in places and things. It didn't need *people* in order for it to work. It was the magic of time and inanimate elements. If waning and waxing magic were all about life, death, and sacrifice, and faith magic was all about believing, discipline, and study, then perennial magic was all about other, more elusive, everlasting concepts.

Perennial magic caught and released the power behind abstract universal forces like chaos and peace, emptiness and fullness, absence and presence, dormancy and revival. A practitioner of perennial magic could easily be led astray by his, or her, own human perspective. The impersonal forces that generated peace and chaos could easily be misinterpreted as the moral forces of "good" and "evil." And one's own personal desire for things like revenge, forgiveness, the presence of an absent loved one, or the revival of youth could too easily cloud the otherwise objective perspective that is necessary when studying the absolutes of perennial magic. Which was why using perennial magic to achieve complicated aims or goals motivated by emotion was a tricky business that resulted in catastrophic failures just as often as it resulted in astonishing successes.

"Consider Metatron's most well-known magical monuments to his beloved Justica," my mother said.

"The Sanguine Scales and the White Heart."

She nodded. "The Sanguine Scales are an example of a perennial magic failure. Supposedly, Metatron made dozens of them. He sold them to every outpost who would buy one. But their judgment was a poor substitute for a Maegester's. Did St. Lucifer's teach you what happened to those who were judged guilty by the Sanguine Scales?"

I shook my head.

"They were cursed. But unlike an Angel's faith-based curse, a perennial spell will neither wear off nor last forever. Perennial spells work like a switch. The effect of an 'absence' spell will simply last until a 'presence' spell is cast. *And vice versa.*"

Suddenly it dawned on me why my mother hadn't wanted to use perennial magic to "save" Night and me.

"You were afraid if you used a perennial 'presence' spell to save our lives before we were born that Night and I would always be vulnerable to the counterspell—the 'absence' spell."

She nodded very slowly. "I didn't gain my knowledge of perennial magic in a vacuum. And the people I learned it from would have known that I'd used it on you. If I'd been successful—a huge if—you might have been born with waxing magic, but your life would have been theirs."

I knew then who—or what group of magic users—she was speaking of. The Amanita.

"Did Valda Sinclair teach you about perennial magic?" I asked, barely able to believe how interconnected we all were to one another. But then, that's how it always had been—and how it always would be. When you were one of the hundreds of magic users out of the magicless million, your life became so twisted up with the other magic users' lives you hardly knew where your life ended and theirs began.

Aurelia shrugged. "It no longer matters who taught me. Because I didn't use it, which is what I wanted to talk to you about. *Don't* try to manipulate perennial magic as you would waning magic. It resists being wielded like a weapon. When it occurs naturally in a place or thing, one can experience it, and the experiences will generally be the same with slight individual differences. But when it is artificially placed within something—*anything*—a person, place, or object, well . . . the consequences are unpredictable and"—she paused, as if she were either unsure of what she was about to say or maybe even afraid of it—"potentially more hazardous than any effect you could possibly achieve with even the largest blast of uncontrolled waning magic."

"Waning magic is the most destructive magic there is," I said, bending down to brush snow off another stone marker. It appeared the entire spring was lined with them and that my mother intended to uncover each and every one of them. "You've never missed an opportunity to tell me that."

"It *is* the most destructive magic there is. But what if there were nothing to destroy in the first place? Waning magic has the power to burn and destroy, but perennial magic has the power to make things never exist in the first place."

"I don't believe it!"

"Your belief isn't necessary. That's what makes it so . . . frightening. There's no need for faith or innate power. There's no need for discipline, study, practice, or control. The only restriction on the use of perennial magic is knowledge of its secrets."

"And you know its secrets?"

"Even if I did, do you think I'd tell them to you when the whole point of this discussion is to discourage you from wielding it?"

"So, in a nutshell, what you're saying is . . . don't use the White Heart if I find it because who knows what might happen?"

"Yes."

My mother bent down again and brushed snow off yet another marker. But instead of a skeleton, Aurelia uncovered the figure of a robed man standing in front of an oxcart.

Metatron.

I knew then that this spring wasn't just a healing spring because of its mineral content or soothing warmth.

"Let me guess," I said. "This spring has perennial magic in it. And now that you've spent the morning telling me not to use perennial magic because of how potentially hazardous the effects might be, you're going to suggest that I climb in there to try to heal myself if I still want to race."

Aurelia started unfastening the toggles on her cloak. "I said you shouldn't try to manipulate or wield perennial magic as you would waning magic. I didn't say you shouldn't experience it when it occurs in a place where its effects are well-known. Like this spring. Metatron laid these markers when Maize was still called Requiem. Local history says that he was searching for a way to reverse the curse that befell anyone judged guilty by his faulty Sanguine Scales.

"Many Mederies have successfully used this spring in the last few hundred years, although that doesn't mean our swim will be completely without risk."

"*Our* swim? *Swim?*"

I couldn't even imagine swimming feeling like I did now. It had taken nearly all my strength just to hike here on foot. But Aurelia nodded. "You need your strength back and the spring can give it to you. The only trick is getting out once you're in. Deep within the spring are underwater caves.

Water is pumped into the spring from some of the caves. And it's carried out by others. The spring is kind of like a giant beating heart. And its underground veins and arteries are marked with these stones. So long as we swim through the artery marked with Metatron's stone, we'll be fine. That passage will take us back to the spring underneath the Demeter springhouse's surgery room."

I eyed the steaming, glassy blue surface of the spring with mistrust. "I think I'd rather walk back."

"Since when are you a coward, Nouiomo?" Aurelia harrumphed.

Did she really not know me that well? These days, fear followed me more closely than my own shadow.

"Besides," she continued, shucking her cloak and dropping it to the ground, "if the arrow tip's curse was made with perennial magic, then swimming through the spring will remove it. Remember how I said perennial magic works like a switch? You turn it on; you turn it off. If there's a perennial magic curse inside of you, the spring's magic will act as an 'absence' spell and remove it."

"So why didn't it work for those afflicted with a curse from Metatron's Sanguine Scales?"

"I don't know *everything* about perennial magic, Nouiomo," she said, somewhat impatiently, bending down to unlace her boots. "Maybe their curse wasn't a 'presence' or 'absence' type of curse. Maybe it was a 'chaos' or 'peace' type of curse." She cleared her throat, stood up, and gazed pointedly at me. "Or maybe Metatron just couldn't get the afflicted to swim through the spring with him.

"Karanos is on his way down here," Aurelia finally said when, after a few more minutes, I still hadn't moved. "He asked if Night and I could have you healed and ready by nightfall." Her voice once again had that crisp, cold efficiency to it that I'd grown up hearing.

"Why's that?" I asked. My legs suddenly felt even weaker than before.

"Because he's bringing someone from Bradbury down

with him. They have additional information about the White Heart and they want to speak with you about it."

"Bradbury," I repeated, more to convince myself than because I thought I'd misheard her. Bradbury was where Ari was from. But surely Karanos wouldn't be—*couldn't be*—bringing Ari down to Maize. He would have said so, right? I mean, Karanos (and everyone but Rafe, Fara, and I) thought Ari was dead. His turning up alive would have been big news. Unless . . . Karanos was keeping Ari's secret now too. I clenched my fists and shook my head, staring at the spring.

Compared to being cursed, planning to storm the gates of Hell, and contemplating a meeting with my lying, hiding, drakon ex-boyfriend, how bad could a healing swim with my mother be?

Chapter 11

⪼

How wrong I was.

My mother explained that the markers were like the numbers on a clock face. All we had to do was shuck our cloaks, remove our boots, stand on the marker, and step backward into the spring. We could even hold hands and jump together, although Aurelia admitted this would be her first time jumping into the spring too. But if all went well, we should be able to swim right into the mouth of the cave in front of us. So long as I didn't open my eyes, get disoriented, turn around, panic or do anything stupid, the swim should be easy, even in my injured state. In fact, my mother assured me the healing effect of the waters would take effect right away. And that the spring's magic would allow us to swim the half mile or so back underwater.

Since Aurelia had never actually accomplished the feat she'd set for us, I was nervous *before* the jump. After . . . well . . . I panicked.

I lost Aurelia's hand almost immediately. The impact of

jumping in was a lot harder than I expected. Maybe it was the spring's magic, but it felt like I'd punched through a window. The spring's near-scalding temperature was more shocking than I'd been prepared for too. After standing in the cold for so long, the jump into hot water made me feel as if my skin had been flayed from my body. I opened my eyes and saw only vague, gray shapes. And not one of them was my mother.

Where was she? Had she swum ahead, thinking I was right behind her? Or had she been pulled into one of the other outgoing passageways?

I thrashed around underneath searching for her, realizing I'd managed to accomplish the first three things my mother warned me not to do in just as many seconds. I'd opened my eyes, become disoriented, and turned around. Now I had no idea which cave mouth I was supposed to swim into.

No matter, I thought. *I'll just go back up and jump in again from Metatron's stone.*

But when I swam up to the surface, it was frozen over. I hadn't recalled it being frozen, but maybe there had been a thin layer of ice I hadn't noticed before and that's why breaking through had been so jarring. Although that didn't make any sense. The spring water was hot. Seriously hot. Like burning, boil-me-to-death hot.

I swam back down to the center of the spring and studied each of the passageways, marveling that I didn't feel winded or out of breath. But that scrap of good fortune was clearly all I was going to get. Three of the passages were pumping water into the spring. I didn't think I could swim into them if I tried. The deepest, darkest one was bringing cold water in. *Freezing* cold water. The cold water seeping out of that bottom passage seemed to grow darker in color as well. It blended with the warmer waters of the spring the way spilled oil blended with water, which is to say: *not one bit.*

Slowly the dark water changed color and shape. It became redder and fierier as each ribbon-like swirl morphed into something more defined: a long snout, sharp teeth, claws, horns, and finally a long tail . . . and wings. It was a fiery drakon. Even though I knew it wasn't real (first of all, drakons weren't made of waning magic, they were made of blood and bone, same as the rest of us; second, real fire—even fire made from waning magic—couldn't burn underwater), I nearly sucked in a lungful of water when I realized what it was. But before I could adjust to seeing it, it swirled into a different shape and after that, the changing images came fast and furious. It was like watching a spinning zoetrope. I saw a cracked bell, a white sword, a set of scales, a bloody tooth, a crossroads, a jail cell, a bonfire, an arrow, an iron coin with a hole in it, a dam with lightning in the sky above it, and then a huge, slobbering, grinning beast with a star on its forehead and the most enormous canines I'd ever seen. The thing came rushing toward me and my signature redlined. My heart *burned* as if it were on fire and I kicked my legs in a blind panic to get away from the black water, hardly noticing which passageway I darted into. After a time, I realized I was still holding Aurelia's hand after all.

We were swimming together down a cool, dark passageway, but the cold, black water was gone. We emerged in a brick-lined pool in what I assumed was the rocky basement of the springhouse.

"Were you holding my hand the entire time?" I asked her.

She gave me a quizzical look. "Yes." Then she frowned. "You opened your eyes, didn't you?"

I shrugged, gave her a sheepish look, and then told her:

"I think I'd rather die than be healed by that hot spring again."

But the swim had healed me. I felt as strong as I had before taking that ill-fated trip to the Crystal Palace. The spot where the arrow had entered my chest was all healed up too, albeit in a surprising way. Instead of a darker demon mark (which was what I'd expected, based on my last experience with an injury there), mine was now lighter and nearly invisible against my new, prominent scar. More distressing than the partial loss of my mark, however, was the fact that I could now feel the arrow tip near my heart. It burned like a hot coal. I couldn't tell whether it was burrowing deeper or if my body was trying to expel it. But the effect was the same: overall, I felt strong, but just thinking about using my magic now gave me heart palpitations.

If using my magic before had hurt, what would it feel like now?

Aurelia looked down at my new scar, looking contemplative. "How do you feel?" she asked.

"Stronger."

It wasn't a lie. And what was the alternative? Tell my mother that our swim through the spring hadn't removed the curse? What would that accomplish other than worrying her? I wasn't going to bow out of the race so the last thing I wanted was to leave tomorrow with everyone trying to stop me. Using my magic during the race would be painful, but better to suck it up and deal with some temporary pain than to spend all next semester in a residency position that was absolutely unbearable.

I ran my tongue across my teeth and smiled. There was one thing the spring hadn't fixed—my missing tooth. Although I wasn't too surprised about that. Nightshade was the only Mederi I knew who might possibly be able to regrow it and, truth be told, it wasn't as if a missing tooth made me less strong or healthy.

Aurelia and I grabbed robes from the rack in the springhouse basement. Glancing around on my way up the stairs, I guessed that guests came down here for a soothing soak from time to time. Hereinafter, not me. I fervently hoped I'd never touch the waters of that spring again.

Upstairs Rafe and Night were waiting for us. Aurelia recounted the necessary details of our swim. But my focus was elsewhere—racing ahead to tonight. Was Karanos really bringing Ari with him? If so, I needed to get my thoughts (and my emotions) in order. Ari's habit had always been to press his suit without reservation. In the end, I'd loved him

without reservation—and look where it had gotten me. I'd
spent the last two months doing everything I could to forget
him. Now, tonight, I might have to face him again.

Of course, even if I did see him again, that didn't mean
Ari would still be pressing his suit with me. I'd told him in
no uncertain terms we were through. And I'd meant it. Truly.
I couldn't trust him. Wouldn't.

I ducked out of the springhouse's great room to get
dressed and mentally prepare. But I was in my room for
barely a second before Rafe came in. I closed the door and
leaned against it. Rafe leaned against the white dresser, arms
folded across his chest.

We stared at each other.

Finally he said, "You know Karanos is bringing someone
down with him tonight from Bradbury, right?"

I nodded.

He nodded.

But he didn't do anything else. Just kept leaning on the
dresser with his arms crossed. This time he stared at the
floor though, not me.

"Noon," he began slowly. "If it turns out to be Ari . . . and
the two of you have some sort of reconciliation, I just want
you to know that I'd understand."

I walked over to the bed and sat on its edge, facing Rafe.
I wasn't sure how to respond. It would be tough to see Ari,
because I had loved him so deeply and he'd hurt me so badly,
but I didn't want to start dating him again, regardless of how
any future meetings between us might go. The real question
was whether I'd healed enough emotionally to see Ari without still feeling betrayed. Whether I'd ever be able to take a
chance on getting close to someone new was a question I
wasn't yet ready for. I'd meant what I'd said last night about
not wanting to hurt Rafe. He was my friend, not to mention
my Guardian Angel. I didn't want to screw up a really great
relationship by adding romantic complications.

I sighed. "There's not going to be any reconciliation."

He nodded halfheartedly, as if he were humoring me. It
was irritating.

"Why would there be?" I snapped.

But instead of shrugging or grinning suggestively (two Rafe-like responses he might have made in the past), he stepped forward and crouched on the floor in front of me. He clasped my hands as if to underscore the significance of what he was going to say.

"There are a few things I haven't told you," he said. "About Ari. And about me." I tensed immediately and Rafe gently squeezed my hands.

"Please tell me you're not a demon in disguise," I growled.

Rafe chuckled softly. The sound of it was reassuring.

"No, I'm exactly who I said I was. But you should know the truth about a few things."

I pulled my hands away and stood up. How I *loathed* secrets.

But Rafe didn't seem the least bit agitated. Of course, I reminded myself that this was the man who'd perfected the carefully carefree look I'd seen so much of last semester. I hadn't missed that look, and seeing it again didn't make me any less wary of what Rafe was going to say next.

"Remember how last semester Ebony's Elbow took one memory from each of us and gave it to someone else?" He stood up and went back to leaning against the dresser.

I nodded. Part of me hadn't wanted to give Rafe's memory back to him because it was so painful, but I knew, because Rafe still wore a silver bracelet with his brother's name etched on it, that he'd have wanted the memory of his funeral back. So I'd told him about it.

Rafe, on the other hand, had been given a memory of Ari's. But he'd never told me which one. In the beginning of our friendship, it had almost been a game. I'd ask what the memory was and Rafe would wink or grin and refuse to tell me. Well, it seemed like Rafe wanted to tell me now, but suddenly, I wasn't sure I wanted to hear. Why did Rafe think *now* was the right time to reveal it?

He cleared his throat and mine felt instantly tighter.

"Do you remember seeing Ari on Bryde's Day last year?" Rafe asked.

I nodded, almost reluctantly. "We took our Sin and Sanction midterm together and then, later that night, we met our clinic clients for our first settlement attempt."

"But you saw Ari on campus before that meeting."

"I did," I said, remembering. "He brought me a candle from the Bryde's Day ceremony they'd held at Lekai." I smiled at the memory, because it was a happy one, even if our relationship hadn't ended that way.

"Ari loves you, Noon. I know some people think that demons don't have feelings like we do. But it isn't true. I felt his love for you in the memory. So drakons *can* love like us."

I blinked. *Change of heart much? Now Rafe was trying to convince me that I should be with Ari?*

"This from an Angel," I said dryly. "I wasn't aware that Angels had soft spots for demons." Rafe grimaced, but I continued. "I didn't break it off with Ari because he was a demon. I broke up with him because he didn't tell me the truth." (Although the fact that Ari was a demon would have been a major stumbling block in our relationship even if he had told me about it up front. But no need to worry about that *now*.)

"Well, that's even more reason to listen to what I have to say. Because I don't want anything unsaid between us."

"Okay . . ."

"It was Bryde's Day and they were handing out lit candles. He couldn't wait to give you one. Because Bryde's Day is the only day of the year that *fire* means *life*. And he knew how you felt about your magic. How much you hated it. He wanted to show you that fire could bring light and warmth. But there was another emotion it brought that Ari didn't anticipate. At least not as forcefully as he felt it then. *Love*. When Ari gave you that candle and saw the look in your face when you stared into the flame, he was lost. I know because it's my memory now."

We stared at each other for a few moments. I tried to digest what he'd just said.

"I'm not sure we have any chance, Noon. But if we do, I want to start off right. Tell you everything in the beginning. And . . . I felt I owed it to my brother's memory to tell you."

"Your brother?" I said, totally confused. "What does your brother have to do with this? Your lost memory has nothing to do with Ari's."

"I know that. And it doesn't. Not really." Rafe twisted his silver bracelet. "But . . ." He swallowed hard and looked away. Then he took a deep breath and turned back to me.

"Bhereg was a demon too. A drakon."

I don't know what my face looked like just then (likely it was full of bewilderment) but Rafe's face—oh!—it was *full* of pain. He'd always blamed himself for his brother's death. But, now that I knew his brother had been a demon and not an Angel, Rafe's grief took on new meaning.

Raphael Sinclair had to be the most astonishing, most sentimental, and most devoted Angel I'd ever met. As residents of Halja, all Angels are required to follow the law, which of course means not harming *regulare* demons. That said, Angels generally aren't in the habit of helping them either and, in fact, most Angels have only the barest, veiled tolerance for them. Rafe's anguish over causing the accidental death of a drakon "brother" he'd never really known showed that, even at six years old, his compassion for other living things had rivaled my own.

"They're not born knowing how to fly . . . or swim," he said dully.

And that's when I knew Rafe's admission tonight had as much to do with the fact that Ari might be arriving later as it did the fact that Rafe was still consumed with grief over Bhereg's drowning. I remembered that Rafe's specialty was grace. Rafe intended to spend the rest of his life paying for his brother's death. And this admission—telling me about Ari's memory and implying I should consider reconciling with him—was all part of that.

I walked over to Rafe and wrapped my arms around him. I laid my head on his shoulder and he rested his cheek against my head.

"I'm glad you told me," I said. "About both things. The memory and Bhereg. But it doesn't change how I feel about Ari. Or you."

I felt Rafe exhale softly—and then inhale sharply, as if he were about to say something else, when we heard a knock on the springhouse's outer door.

It had to be Karanos . . . and whoever he was bringing from Bradbury.

Rafe's face slipped back into his carefully carefree look.

"I'll let you finish getting dressed," he said. But he kept hold of the lapels on my robe and, for a moment, I thought he'd go ahead and say whatever it was he was going to say before the knock. But instead he let go, turned on his heel, and left.

Chapter 12

ॐ

I was pleasantly surprised to find a beautiful selection of clothes to choose from in the white dresser of the room I was staying in. (Unfortunately, finding myself in mortal peril and then waking up somewhere else without a wardrobe of my own was becoming a habit.) I donned a black dress tunic with long sleeves and a high neck. It had whorls stitched into the ends of the sleeves and down the middle in emerald and silver thread. I paired it with simple fur-lined leather leggings and tied my hair back. Luckily, someone had fetched my boots from the spring where I'd left them, so I wouldn't have to greet the new arrivals barefoot. I glanced in the mirror, thinking I may have overdone it. In my attempt to downplay femininity, I'd achieved severity. But I didn't want to put off emerging from my room any longer.

Walking down the hall I realized the mood and energy level in Demeter's springhouse had changed dramatically since Aurelia and I had returned from our swim. Loud voices—people talking, some even laughing—filled the great room. Darkness had fallen, but the nearly full moon had risen anew, so the scene on the other side of the lead glass window was as tranquilly pretty as the one from my bedroom window the night before. I realized I'd inadvertently chosen to wear colors that reflected the landscape. How fitting for a mostly Mederi gathering, which was what this was.

Inside the great room were thirty or so other women—Mederies. It made sense, I thought. Lots of tribe members would likely want to pay their respects to Karanos and meet Nightshade's sister. As soon as I walked out of the hallway, I was assailed by kindhearted, well-meaning women. I smiled and shook hands, exchanged hugs with strangers, answered all sorts of questions about the arrow's near miss at Kalisto's Crystal Palace, my recovery here, my swim through the spring, and my life at St. Luck's. All the while though, I kept an eye out for Karanos . . . and Ari. After an agonizing half hour that felt as if it had been a half century, I spotted my father at the far end of the room. He was speaking with Linnaea. Standing next to Linnaea was a woman I would have recognized anywhere. Her hair was as white as the snow and her eyes as pink as rose quartz. It wasn't Ari that Karanos had brought down from Bradbury.

It was Joy Carmine, his mother.

Once I spotted them, I politely excused myself from my current conversation and made my way through the crowd to them.

"Hello, Father," I said, greeting Karanos first, which was the expected and respectful thing to do. Throughout my childhood, my father had been a shadowy figure. Ever present, but often out of sight. Lately we'd begun to talk more, although it was mostly about Maegester matters.

He nodded at me. "Nouiomo, glad to see that Aurelia was able to get you healed up on such short notice."

"Me too. Hello, Linnaea," I said, giving Demeter's monarch a nod of acknowledgement. And then I turned to Joy. It was the first time I'd seen her since I'd found out Ari was a drakon. No need to wonder if she knew. She *had* to know. Which meant she'd deceived me as well.

The last time I'd seen her had been months ago (after one of the aforementioned times I'd been in mortal peril. My clinic client had tried to kill me and I'd recovered over Beltane Break at her house—Ari's house—or the house he grew up in). For the span of two heartbeats I tried to figure out if I was relieved or disappointed that it was Joy and not Ari who'd come, and then I decided it didn't matter.

"Joy," I said, nodding to her, "good to see you."

I'd forgotten how arresting she looked. I suddenly wondered if maybe *she* was a demon in disguise. Her chilly white coloring and pink eyes were certainly unusual. She'd told me she was *hveit*. Ari had assured me that she was a Hyrke, but he'd admitted Joy had an uncanny ability to read people. Joy herself had told me she had the ability to *see* things, but she'd never elaborated on that gift. Clearly she had other gifts as well. Like the ability to raise an adopted drakon child.

"What happened to your tooth?" she asked. I swear, I don't know how she did it, but she actually managed to sound like a concerned mother.

I frowned, because her concern made me uncomfortable, and waved my hand in the air to indicate that the who, how, and why of my tooth getting knocked out was unimportant. "A Gridiron ranking match," I said peremptorily and then turned to Linnaea.

"I was told that Demeter would be willing to supply the barghests we'll need for our trip south. Could we visit the pen tomorrow morning and make our selections?"

"I'm looking forward to it," Linnaea said. "And if the barghests knew you were coming, they would be too. If they had a motto it would be *paratus sum. I am ready.* Barghests scoff at being 'born ready.' They are *conceived* ready. Conception to birth in less than twenty-four hours."

I choked back a laugh, reminding myself that Mederies were never shy when discussing matters of breeding. But I soon became somber again. The truth was beastly sled dogs were the last thing on my mind. Linnaea glanced from face to face taking in our solemn expressions and made her excuses, leaving me alone with Karanos and Joy. Part of me wished Karanos would leave too, just so I could confront Joy about all the things she hadn't told me last year, but then I reminded myself that she'd been kind and generous when I'd stayed with her and it wasn't as if she owed *me* her loyalty. So I skipped the small talk (Karanos despised it anyway) and got right to the reason why she was here.

"I was told you have more information about the White Heart," I said.

"So you're really going to do it?" Joy asked me. "Storm the gates of Tartarus?"

"That's the plan," I said, refusing to let any of my fear or reservations about the race show.

"I heard you have a Guardian Angel now—Raphael Sinclair?"

I glanced at my father. Had Karanos told her about Rafe? Or had Ari? Had she been in touch with Ari since I'd last seen him in the Shallows? She *had* to have. I knew Ari loved her too much to let her wonder whether the rumors of his death were true. For a fleeting moment, I wanted to ask her where Ari was and if he was okay. She must have seen something in my face—a hint of emotion, an echo of my feelings, or perhaps even a glimpse of my future—because her expression softened.

"Your father told me about Mr. Sinclair," she said. "I'd like to meet him too, if he's around."

I searched the crowded room for Rafe. It was odd, after working with Ari on two previous assignments, not being able to sense Rafe's presence. I was just about to say I didn't know where he was when he appeared. I made a mental note to ask him later how he did that. Did Guardians cast spells over their wards that would alert them if they were needed?

He'd changed as well. It was one of the only times I'd ever seen Rafe wear anything that wasn't ripped, faded, or both. He wore a black high-necked tunic with a vest made out of the nastiest, fiercest looking fur I'd ever seen. He hooked his thumbs into the arm holes and grinned at me. "Barghest fur," he said in answer to my unspoken question. He turned to face Karanos and Joy.

He gave my father a short bow and acknowledged him formally, with my father's full name and title. He then turned to Joy.

"This is Joy Carmine. From Bradbury," I added, although it was likely unnecessary. Rafe was well aware of Ari's last name and had probably figured out that this was the person Karanos had brought down with him.

I turned to Joy and introduced her to Rafe.

They stared at each other and just before it might have become awkward, Rafe said, "You're Ari Carmine's mother." The emotions raced across his face nearly too fast to see: relief, confusion, and then—Rafe's default—nonchalance.

"Karanos told me you worked with Noon and Ari last semester during their trip to the Shallows," she said.

"I did." And then: "That trip turned out to be tougher than any of us anticipated it would be. I'm sorry . . . about Ari disappearing in the Shallows." He glanced briefly at me and then said to Joy, "Have you heard from him?"

My signature pulsed and I clamped down on it, hoping Karanos would chalk it up to the fact that we were discussing Ari, not because I knew Ari was still alive. And then I wondered once more why in all of Luck's lost land I was still keeping Ari's blasted secret for him. Why I didn't just tell everyone that Ari had been revealed as a demon in our midst, a drakon who'd been training to be a Maegester.

But one look at Joy and I knew I wouldn't. At least not now. I could tell she had truly come to help us.

"How did you, a Hyrke from Bradbury, come by information about *Album Cor Iustitiae*?" I asked.

Joy gave me an enigmatic smile. "You know me only as Ari's mother. But Carmine is my married name. My given name is Letizia Liberta Bialas—"

And then it hit me. Who Joy was. *What* Joy was.

"You're Kaspar Bialas' descendant," I said suddenly, almost breathlessly, remembering Glashia's lecture from Artifice class the day Rafe and I took our oaths. *What was that footnote Glashia had read?* Something about Metatron's squire being a Bialas and that he'd been chosen because he'd had several unusual Hyrke characteristics, the most notable of which was his resistance to all but the strongest magic. Well, I wasn't aware that Joy was immune to magic, but it would certainly explain how a magicless Hyrke had been able to raise (and presumably discipline) a drakon child like Ari. The footnote had also mentioned a legend. That Bialas had been marked by Luck's hand similar to the way Luck marks his waning magic users—but that Bialas' mark was as light as a waning magic user's is dark.

Looking at Joy, who had a complete absence of coloring, even in her eyes, I recognized her mark for what it was. It was unmistakable. She'd inherited Bialas blood as surely as I'd inherited Onyx blood.

"Let's step out to the patio," Karanos said.

The springhouse patio was a crisp change from the crowded, heated interior. The four of us stood under a raftered awning surrounded by tables, benches, and chairs that were draped with burlap to keep the snow off. A few feet away the snow-covered lawn started, and yards beyond that, the woods. Joy wasted no time getting back to our discussion.

"My many-times-great-grandfather was Metatron's squire, Kaspar Bialas. He's the one who hid the White Heart from the Divinity. I was told he hid it in Tartarus, Halja's southernmost dungeon."

For a moment, I was speechless. Joy had just casually admitted she was descended from a thief—and, apparently, a notorious one at that. Still, the fact that she'd done so without any sign of guilt and in front of the executive of the Demon Council, told me there was more in her closet than just a generations-old skeleton.

I turned toward Rafe to see how he'd taken Joy's admission. Standing beneath the shadowed rafters in his barghest fur vest, Rafe looked menacing.

"Why did Bialas want to hide the sword from the Divinity?" he asked.

"It was Metatron's dying wish that the sword be kept from the Amanita. He told Bialas to hide it in Tartarus."

Rafe's expression hardened at the mention of the Amanita but he said nothing else.

"Why Tartarus?" I asked. "And why didn't Metatron want the Amanita to have it?"

I had hunches about the answers to both questions, namely that if you had a strong, young squire who was immune to magic, asking him to hide something in Tartarus for you made some sense. And Metatron likely wanted to prevent the Amanita from doing whatever it was they wanted the White Heart for—to use or destroy it. But I wanted to hear which from Joy.

But instead of answering my questions, she fished in her cloak pocket for something. A tin box bound with string. The wind kicked up and suddenly Joy's hair reminded me of the way Justica's had looked when Rafe and I had carved her out of snow at the Festival of Frivolity—all snowy white and writhing in the wind.

"The journal you've been given by the Divinity to aid in your search will take you to a dead end. Bialas left it with Metatron's oxcart to throw off any future White Heart hunters."

Ah, I thought, *that would explain why all of the former White Heart hunters—Graemite, Percevalus, and Jacindus—had failed to find it.*

"This box contains three letters written by Bialas, which will help you to retrieve the White Heart, if that's truly what you intend to do."

"It is. But why do you want to help me? Sounds like the Bialases have been perfectly content to leave the White Heart in Tartarus all this time. If your ancestors didn't share these letters with the hunters that came before me, why me? Why now?"

"Because," Karanos said, his deep voice melting into our discussion the way waning magic sliced through snow, "after your accident at the Crystal Palace, Friedrich asked another bounty hunter to find and retrieve the White Heart for him."

I stood shell-shocked for a moment, considering the implications. I think it was only my training with Glashia that prevented me from clenching my fists or shouting my frustration. Instead, I said calmly:

"I assume, since you brought Joy down and she just handed me the box full of letters from Bialas that I won't be assigned another race target."

"That's correct."

I wasn't sure if that was good news or not. It would have been difficult to prepare to retrieve another target the night before the start of the race. But then again . . . my target was still *Album Cor Iustitiae*. Which had been famously missing for so long, finding it would be like finding Lucifer's tomb. (Of course, I *had* found Lucifer's tomb, first semester. With Peter's help.) But now I wouldn't just be racing the clock and other bounty hunter teams generally, I'd be racing against another team specifically for the same target.

Rafe must have been having similar thoughts because we both blurted out the question at the same time:

"Who's the other bounty hunter?"

"Brunus Olivine."

I made a face and Rafe's hand twitched. Probably some sort of hand-cast spell reflex. Luckily Rafe had never had the magical control issues I'd had.

"And, let me guess, Holden Pierce," I said, my voice leaden. Holden Pierce was the number one ranked Angel at the Joshua School. He was an amazing spellcaster. As in *amazingly ruthless*. His noteworthy spells (Painfall, Damage Cascade, and Hemorrhage) were ones I'd used and they were brutal. I'd predicted Brunus and Holden Pierce's pairing months ago. But Karanos' next words surprised me.

"Peter Aster will serve as Brunus' Guardian during his hunt for the White Heart," my father said. His stare was unblinking. Against the frozen, inhospitable landscape, Karanos' boxy frame looked like a battle tower waiting out a siege. He continued, his gaze resting briefly on Rafe before switching back to me.

"Friedrich heard grave news about your chances of recovery. Clearly, he underestimated both your Guardian's and the Demeter Mederies' skills, including your brother's. Brunus and Peter were given leaves of absence from St. Luck's and the Joshua School to accept their . . . *extracurricular assignment.*" It was clear from the way Karanos said it that he didn't approve, but had no authority to disallow the assignment. "Brunus, obviously, isn't a contender for the Laurel Crown, but he will be able to prevent *you* from winning it."

Karanos shifted his weight. It wasn't exactly shuffling his feet, but the movement made my father seem uncharacteristically restless.

"How important is it to you that you work for the Jayneses next year, Noon? Wouldn't it be better to go where you are most needed and trust the Council to place you in a position where you will do the most good for Halja? You don't have to race. Or hunt for the White Heart."

"What's important to me is that I have a choice in where I work. And that I be allowed to work with Angels of my own choosing."

"You could *choose* to go where you are most needed," Karanos said. "And trust that the Council would make other arrangements for your protection."

We stared at each other. It was the closest I'd ever come to openly defying my father. I wasn't, of course. The Laurel Crown Race was a Maegester tradition and had been for centuries. Laureates were well respected, even if every now and then they chose unconventional residencies. But it was the first time Karanos had ever articulated his wishes about my future so vocally. And, I had to admit, if only to myself, that if it weren't for the fact that lack of choice about the way we led our lives was one of my biggest problems with Halja's ruling magical elite, Karanos' words might have had more of an effect on me.

I glanced at Rafe and Joy, wondering what they thought of this polite, but public Onyx family wrestling match. I found their body positions telling. Rafe was standing as close to me as he could possibly get without touching me, while Joy stood apart from all of us, almost as if she were an observer.

I chose to quit squabbling with my father over my future choices and focus on something more immediate. Like following up with him about the arrow shot that had led to Brunus and Peter being tasked to find the White Heart.

"Father, do you know if any of the other racers have been shot with cursed arrows?"

He didn't answer immediately. Probably mulling over whatever sparse information Kalisto and others had managed to gather in the wake of my life-threatening injury. But finally he answered with one word that put what had happened into sharper perspective.

"No."

We both frowned, an amazing show of synchronized Onyx emotion. No doubt it occurred to Karanos at the same time as me: the arrow may not have been meant to kill me, but I'd been its sole target. The only remaining questions were who did it, why, and when I'd be able to remove the cursed tip from my chest. Almost involuntarily I reached up and rubbed the spot where my demon mark used to be.

After that, our moonlit meeting wrapped pretty quickly. Karanos inquired about Rafe's knowledge of a few spells that may be useful for our trip (all of which Rafe already knew; I was no longer surprised by Rafe's untouted yet vast cache of spellcasting skills). I thanked Joy for giving me the box full of Bialas' letters and Karanos bid us good night, telling Rafe and me he'd meet us at the barghest pen tomorrow to see us off.

We were all heading back inside when Joy pulled on my sleeve to indicate she wanted to talk to me alone. I stayed behind and the two of us faced each other in the chilled, semi-darkness.

Since no one else tonight had wasted time on irrelevant things, I immediately asked her:

"Why didn't you tell me?" Luckily, she didn't feign ignorance.

"It wasn't my place to tell you. It was Ari's. I thought he

was making a mistake by not telling you in the beginning, but he can be very determined."

I narrowed my eyes. "A demon trait, no doubt."

"He dated plenty of women before you," she said, ignoring my barbed words. "Mederies mostly." Joy glanced inside the springhouse. "Pretty ones, smart ones, kind ones. But not one of them affected him the way you did. I think he was worried about losing you before you even started dating."

I crossed my arms across my chest and turned away, instinctively looking toward the shadows instead of the snowy brightness. My breath came out in increasingly dense clouds. I waited until my magic settled and then said, "He told me it was your idea for him to train at St. Luck's. Why did you encourage him? If my father finds out that Ari's still alive—and that he's a drakon—he could declare him a *rogare*."

With Joy's coloring, it would be impossible to tell if she paled at my words. But they did seem to have a chilling effect on her. She finally swallowed and said tightly, "Ari is as far from a *rogare* demon as any full-blooded demon can get."

"Full-blooded?" I laughed. "Is there any other kind?"

She snorted. "All waning magic users have some demon blood, Nouiomo. You of all people should know that."

I glared at her but she didn't seem the least bit afraid that I might lose control of my magic. But then, why should she be? *Her* blood made her immune to it.

"What did you want to talk to me about?" I asked her. She was the one who'd wanted to speak to me in private. I had a feeling she had more to share than just her side of Ari's past deception.

"For most of Metatron's life," she said, jumping back into our earlier discussion, "he was obsessed with finding Justica. The Bialas family histories are a bit unclear, but the story I was told is that Justica died during Metatron's lifetime and he wanted to bring her back. All of his magical experiments were conducted in memory of her, or in the hopes that it would give him a greater understanding of the magic that might bring her back.

"In the years leading up to his death, however, Metatron began to regret some of his more extreme magical experiments—like the Sanguine Scales. What do you know of them, Noon?"

"Only that their judgment was often unfair and their punishment unusually cruel. A curse of some kind," I added, remembering the discussion I'd had with Aurelia earlier today.

Joy nodded.

"Those judged guilty by the Sanguine Scales were cursed to live forever as walking corpses. They're called the *mortem animae*. They have no memory of their past life except a great longing for it."

"You're speaking in the present tense. Are you saying they're still down there? The *mortem animae*?"

"Yes. That's another reason I wanted to meet with you. To make sure you understand just how dangerous this trip will be for you. Noon . . . I know you're not very experienced. You may have come a long way in learning how to use your magic, but do you have any idea what you're considering going up against? The *mortem animae* won't kill you. They simply touch you and make you one of them. We'd never see you again. You'd spend the rest of your life, and all of eternity, in Tartarus not remembering any of us. Instead of an arrow through the heart, the *mortem animae* curse removes it. That's what they're all searching for. Their hearts, their lives, their loved ones. Their souls, Noon, if they ever had them."

I frowned. Not many Haljans spoke of souls.

"Metatron worked tirelessly toward finding a cure for the *mortem animae* curse. It was his *magnum opus* or 'great work.' And we Bialases believe *Album Cor Iustitiae* was the result."

"Then why not use the sword to save them?" I cried, suddenly irritated that Joy had painted such a bleak picture when the solution for fixing it was right in front of her. "Instead of continuing to hide it, why not use the White Heart to free the *mortem animae* from their curse?"

"Because Metatron used all of the perennial magic tricks

he'd learned while trying to find a way to bring Justica back to make the White Heart. So that sword may be capable of far more than removing a curse. It may be able to make someone who is absent, present again. Think about what that means, Noon. If you had the power to bring someone back, would you?"

My fingers pressed against the left side of my chest, following the line of my recently made scar through the coarse linen of my dress tunic. *I guess it would depend on who was missing,* I thought. But Joy was continuing with a tone as serious as I had ever heard her use.

"*Should* someone be brought back? What would our world be like after? It's taken two thousand years for Armageddon's warring sides to learn to get along. Tip the balance and how long do you think it will take to relearn it? And how many people will die before then?"

Suddenly, I realized what she was talking about. It wasn't ex-lovers like Justica or Ari. It was absent lords, like Luck or Micah. Instantly the hairs on the back of my neck rose. The air felt like it did before an electric storm. All was quiet. Intense. Like the whole world was watching this conversation, although we were completely alone.

If I had the power to bring Luck back, would I? Should I? What would it mean for Halja? We'd learned to live with the Angels. We worked with them and sometimes we even married them. What if they were suddenly persecuted again? Or the opposite. What if we were? Those of us with Host blood? What if bringing someone back meant returning to the days of war?

Could the White Heart start Armageddon II?

But then I scoffed at the direction of my own thoughts. They were so melodramatic. I needed to focus on the task at hand. Not blow everything out of proportion. Things were actually very simple.

Find the sword. Win the race. Work for the Jayneses. Try and be happy as a sentry on board the Alliance. *And thank Luck I didn't have to make a decision about whether or not to bring him back from the dead.*

But I couldn't resist one last question.

"Who are you, Joy? For real?"

"A neutral party who sees farther into the future than you can possibly imagine."

I scoffed. "Well, that doesn't mean you've interpreted the past correctly. And I've never been one for signs, symbols, or visions. I have yet to experience one that wasn't capable of being twisted into at least two different 'truths.' Speaking of that, did you know I've also heard that the White Heart is just a yeti tusk that Metatron fashioned a handle for and then ensorcelled with a healing charm?"

But Joy appeared unconvinced by the alternate history I suggested.

"Just promise me, if you use Bialas' letters to retrieve the sword, you'll honor my request."

"Which is?"

"Don't give the White Heart to the Divinity. Return it to me."

"I swore an oath to return the sword to them."

"Your father told me the Bounty Hunter's Oath only requires that you return your target to its rightful owner. I think Bialas' letters will convince you of my claim."

"Do you realize what you're asking? If I find the White Heart and give it to you instead of Friedrich, I'll never be able to work with an Angel again."

"It will take more than Friedrich Vanderlin to prevent Rafe Sinclair from watching over you. No Angel is more devoted to the people he cares about than that man."

I frowned. I guess she'd *seen* something about Rafe too. I hoped it wasn't him defying the Divinity for me. But much as I thought Joy might be right about Rafe's character, I refused to believe that she could see the future. Nobody could. The most anyone could see was *possible* futures. And there were way too many of them for anyone to predict the one that would stick out of the millions that might.

"Are you also aware that Rafe's mother is one of the Amanita?"

"I didn't think you wanted to become the Laureate to please your Guardian's mother."

I barked out a laugh. "I don't. But then again I don't plan on *not* becoming the Laureate to please my *ex-boyfriend's* mother either."

Joy gave me a cryptic smile, but I doubted it was due to any oracle-type vision she was having. I think she was just glad I'd referred to her son as an ex-boyfriend instead of a *lying demon*.

"What would you do with the sword if you had it?" I asked. I wasn't going to promise her anything, but I was curious about her intentions.

"Nothing. If you are its hunter, I am its keeper. There's nothing more to it than that. And then eventually I'll pass on its keeping to my heir."

"Ari."

"Perhaps."

"He's hardly a neutral party."

Joy laughed. "No, *neutral*, *detached*, and *dispassionate* are not words I would ever use to describe Ari." She patted my arm and turned toward the door. "The Council and the Divinity aren't the only ones who believe in you, Noon. And not all the letters in the tin box I gave you are hundreds of years old. One of them is less than six months old."

I spent a considerable amount of time at the party after that. Despite the fact that Joy's words caused an alarming spike in my signature, I refused to rush off to my room to read Ari's letter. It would have been rude and inconsiderate. I'd already spent half the night on the patio. And I didn't want to miss my last chance to mingle with Night and the Mederies he worked with.

And a small part of me was worried about what the letter would say. But I tucked that thought, along with the box of letters, away until later.

In the meantime, I ate and drank and laughed and talked,

with no one (I hoped) being the wiser to my anxious thoughts. Toward the end of the night Rafe brought me a glass of wine. He said he'd been working with one of Empyr's sommeliers this semester and he offered to cast my choice of spells over it.

"What are my options?" I said, playing along. It was just like Rafe to learn how to ensorcell wine (a lauded Angel skill) and then use it purely for his own pleasure and his friends' recreational entertainment.

"I can offer you Chin Up, I've Got Your Back, or Good Night's Sleep."

"Hmm . . ." I said, smiling at him. "Tough choices. But I'm going to go with unensorcelled, okay?"

To his credit, Rafe didn't look one bit disappointed. He handed me the wine, careful not to touch me as he did. It was the only moment of awkwardness between us since our almost-kiss.

"Where's yours?" I asked him. He looked surprised for a moment and then went to retrieve a glass. He came back with a glass that matched mine.

"If not a spell, then at least a toast?" he said, raising his glass.

I thought for a moment and then said:

"To barghests and new beginnings."

We clinked glasses, took a sip, and then parted ways to talk with other people. Maize's Mederies gradually left in twos and threes, bundled against the cold for their walks home. My family stayed at the springhouse so that they could see us off the next day. Our plan was to leave from the barghest pen no later than midday tomorrow.

Around midnight I finally read Ari's letter.

Nouiomo—

I told you I would have told you the truth eventually. Now I'm not so sure. Letting you go and leaving you alone is the hardest thing I've ever had to do. But it's probably best this way, at least for a while. I never could decide whether to help you stand on your own two feet or sweep

*you off them. I realize now, it was never my choice to
make. Stay close to your Guardian. May both he and
Luck protect you.*

—*Aristos*

I crumpled Ari's letter up into a tiny ball and set it on top
of the tin box Joy had given me. Then I burned it. The arrow
tip in my chest burned too, but I ignored it. I watched as the
white paper and black words turned red, then orange, and
then white. Finally, when there was no further trace of the
letter—not even ashes or a black singe mark—I put the box
away.

Chapter 13

ɔ

The squeals, grunts, growling, and yowling coming from the corral made it sound as if it were a demon prison instead of a barghest-breeding pen. Linnaea had confided proudly to me that Demeter was the only tribe that raised barghests. I'd already been aware of some of Demeter's unorthodox practice methods (which of the other straightlaced Mederi tribes would have taken in a male Mederi like Night?) but seeing the barghests made me appreciate anew just how open-minded these southernmost of the southern women were.

The pen was a huge, fenced enclosure in a cleared area of the woods. The ground was full of dirty snow, rocks, and other debris that the barghests had dug up. A stone path circled the rough rectangular perimeter. I looked around carefully, as I always did, to make sure there were no gardens or greenery that I might accidentally kill. It was a precaution I was used to, but here in Maize it was even more necessary than elsewhere. But there was nothing close enough to worry about. My guess was that Demeter was so used to Kalisto visiting the pen and picking out sledge beasts for her hunters, that they kept the area intentionally clear.

In all, there were twenty barghests currently in the pen: a dozen pups, five females, and three males. Rafe and I had come down at dawn to meet Linnaea and to spend some time with the pack before making our selections. The rest of my family was meeting us here later. We'd risen in the early morning light, packed up what little belongings we had at the springhouse—which for me included my race file, Bialas' journal, and the tin box of letters—grabbed coffee and biscuits, and had trekked up here, happy to see that Linnaea was already waiting for us outside the pen. She stood next to the sledge we'd be taking, which was now packed with all the gear we'd bought at Kalisto's Crystal Palace before I'd been shot.

We watched Linnaea feed the barghests their morning rations: some hideous dried concoction made up of crow, vole, and lizard parts. We'd be taking a few bags of the stuff on the sledge, but the barghests would also be able to hunt for live food off the trail.

The barghests looked as horrible as their food. Only in the vaguest sense did they resemble dogs. They had four legs, a tail, claws, and jaws full of sharp canine teeth. But barghests are to dogs the way drakons are to bats. First off, they were huge. Everything about them was bigger and meaner. On four legs their faces were even with mine. Upon seeing them it became easy to imagine a demon like Lilith riding one. They had barrel chests and wolfish grins. Their teeth were as large as horns and their paws four times the size of Rafe's booted foot. And their fur . . . well, let's just say seeing it on the living creature didn't improve its appearance. It reminded me of long, thick, tangled rat fur. I shuddered and tried to reconcile myself to the fact that, so long as I didn't get eaten by one in the pen today, two of them would be under my care by midday.

"So which of you is first?" Linnaea said, motioning to the pen.

"Do we lasso them? Saddle them?" Rafe asked. Hands in

his pockets, he rocked back and forth on his heels surveying them. "Cast a spell over them?"

Linnaea snorted. "I wouldn't cast a spell over them at first. In time, as they get used to you, you might be able to cast something simple over them, but don't start that way. In the beginning, all you're going to do is let them get used to you. They'll try to push you around. See what you're made of. They're as curious about you as you are about them. *Don't show any fear.*"

Like dogs and demons, I thought.

"I'll go first," I said, walking over to the gate. "What about waning magic? What's their response to that?"

Linnaea smiled, but it wasn't reassuring. "That depends on the user." She walked over to the gate and held it open for me.

"You're not coming in?" I asked, trying to ignore the growls coming from the beasts behind her.

"Nah, it's better if you go in alone," she said, winking at me.

Better for who? Her or me?

I took a deep breath and tried to steady my nerves by reminding myself that these were nonmagical beasts. As long as I kept my fear and my magic in control, I'd be fine. *Just like a Gridiron match,* I told myself. But instead of facing one Ludovicus Mischmetal, I was facing the equivalent of twenty tigers.

Well, Virtus, Fara's tiger, hadn't been that bad, right? In fact, he'd been extraordinarily helpful when we'd battled the *rogare* demons who'd attacked us last semester. But I knew I only felt that way because Virtus had been on my side. Now I just had to convince these barghests that they too should side with me, not against me.

Follow me, not attack me.

"Oh, I forgot to tell you," Linnaea called. "Don't let them knock you down."

I swallowed and nodded stiffly to her.

Thankfully, the barghests couldn't sense my signature. Because if they'd been able to, I surely would have spooked them. The beasts appeared to be clustered in three main groups. One group was a male and female with one small whelp who had a white star on her forehead. That gave me pause because the little whelp looked like a miniature version of the huge, slobbering, grinning beast I'd seen under the water at the spring yesterday morning with my mother.

The second group was a lone pair. They were two of the biggest beasts in the pen, which meant they were probably the other two males. They grappled with each other in a corner. When one of them butted the other, causing him to crash into the fence, I idly wondered if Linnaea ever worried about them getting loose. The third group was the closest with four females and eleven pups that ranged in size from large whelps to nearly full grown.

The moment I switched places with Linnaea and stepped into the pen, the closest group rushed me. I tried not to panic. Under different circumstances, it might have been humorous. Last year, I'd been completely green and untested as a fighter. I'd never engaged in hand-to-hand combat and had never killed so much as a house spider. This year . . . well, I couldn't say the same. And yet . . . I had no experience with animals. Virtus didn't count. He'd been Fara's tiger. We Onyxes had never had any pets. The very idea of four-footed creatures permissively trotting around our family's estate during my formative years was laughable. So I had no wellspring of furry-friend love to tap into when faced with these bizarre half-domestic, half-wild beasts.

Should I try to cluck my tongue? Snap my fingers? Whistle? What would make them listen and obey? What would make them stop rushing me?

Too late, I remembered Linnaea's warning not to let them topple me over.

All eleven of the pups immediately got tangled around my feet while two of the adults butted their noses against my chest. There was no way to prevent stepping back. Not only did instinct cry out for me to *get away* from their jaws, but the strength and weight of them pressing against me forced me to step back. I spared a second's glance behind me, trying to gauge where the whelps were so I wouldn't step on one of them, but the motion caused an awkward shift in balance and I started falling. I cried Rafe's name in alarm.

Odd, perhaps. What could he do? He was outside the pen. But Rafe had cast Impenetrable and other spells over me so many times during our last semester that calling out to him for help just came naturally to me. Luckily, he knew exactly who I wanted to protect. And it wasn't me.

Rafe's cast of Impenetrable over the whelps had to have been the fastest cast in history. I landed with a thump as the whelps twisted and struggled their way out from beneath me completely unharmed. But I realized—as I looked at the slobbering, slavering jaws of the full-sized adult barghests that now lunged toward me—that I'd gone and done exactly what Linnaea had warned me not to do. I'd let them knock me down. In a rush I gathered waning magic to me to use as a shield, but . . . fact was, if I used it on these beasts, they'd be dead.

I only had a split second to decide. Trust that they wouldn't hurt me or start blasting them into oblivion. I raised my arm to cover my eyes, and just before I shut them I took a good look at the creatures.

Would they really hurt me?

Linnaea started shouting from the side of the pen. I felt several spells slip into place over me. But the most unusual feeling of peace came over me. It was similar to the feeling that I felt when I'd been at Demeter's hot spring with my mother throwing the waning magic that I shaped into fiery frogs. Suddenly I knew these beasts weren't going to hurt me, even if I was sprawled on the ground in front of them like live meat for the taking. Or they wouldn't so long as I didn't lose my wits and act scared. So I flung my arm off my face and sat up. My signature still hummed with all the waning magic I'd gathered to me, but instead of shaping it into a shield and bladed weapon, I shaped it into fireballs that I rolled along the ground.

The barghests *loved* it. They chased after my waning magic fireballs with tails wagging as if lethal fire was a toy for them to play with. Each time one of them got close enough to actually catch one, I'd snuff it out just before they reached it so the fire wouldn't burn them. Time and time again I watched as barghest jaws opened wide to try and catch my fire, but then closed on nothing more than smoke. A few of the whelps sneezed and looked puzzled, but most growled and shook their heads and then immediately searched for a new one to attack. I knew then that these beasts were even fiercer than I'd first thought. They willingly chased fire *and* tried to eat it. *We'd get along just fine,* I thought.

After a while, when it seemed as if my rapport with the barghests was well established, Rafe came into the pen. Remembering how Virtus had hissed and spit at him when they'd first met, I was wary. It would make things difficult if Rafe and our sledge beasts didn't get along. But he was one step ahead of me. Instead of fire . . . he offered them bacon. They soon abandoned me and surrounded Rafe, who unsurprisingly looked like he was having the time of his life. I was quite sure, in that moment, that if Linnaea had allowed us to take the entire pack, Rafe would have happily agreed.

Instead, over the course of the next few hours, we selected the ones we would take. In the end, we picked the dam and sire of the smallest whelp with the star on her forehead. Telesto, her sire, had been the most fearless about chasing my fire, beating the other barghests to the ball nine times out of ten, while Brisaya, her dam, had been the first one to figure out if she got too close to it, the ball would disappear. Fast, fearless, and smart seemed like good traits for the animals who would be our only friendly company to have. And Linnaea assured us that the little whelp was more than ready to move to the larger group (*"Paratus sum,* remember?" she said).

By midday, when Karanos, Aurelia, and Nightshade arrived to see us off, I felt as if I knew enough about barghests to start breeding them myself. Linnaea's lessons had been thorough. Rafe and I now knew what they liked to eat (frost herons, graupel porcupines, and auster hares), what else they could eat (carrion, yeti entrails, and hiburnal grubs and maggots), what they couldn't (*any* demon meat, including ice basilisk or berserker carcasses), how to put them in the sledge harness (bacon helped, but would be in short supply), and the commands we'd likely use the most (whoa, hike, gee, haw, easy, and on by).

Since Telesto and Brisaya were already rigged and ready to go by the time my family arrived, our good-byes were short. Night and Linnaea gave us big hugs and Night promised to regrow my tooth when I stopped here on our way back to New Babylon. If I didn't know Night to be one of the most honest people in all of Halja I might have thought then that Night had lied to Rafe about the reason for not growing it back earlier—that Night had chosen not to regrow it so that, no matter what happened to me, he might always think I was on my way back up to Maize so that he could finish healing me.

But then I shook my head to clear it of such melancholic thoughts.

As she had for my last assignment, Aurelia brought parting gifts for me. This time her gifts came in a dirty burlap bag that she handed directly to me. I could tell immediately from its weight and shape that it was full of sharp pieces of metal. I gave Aurelia a puzzled look and untied the top. I pulled out something with a wooden handle and a flat, half-moon-shaped blade at the top. "An edging iron," my mother explained. My puzzled frown deepened as I sifted through the bag pulling out first a rusty pair of hedge trimmers, then several different-sized pruning hooks, a daisy gruber, hand hoe, and finally a scythe.

What exactly did Aurelia expect me to do with gardening tools?

She saw the confusion in my face and took pity on me, laughing. But when I glanced up from the bag to her, her smile was colder than the wind blowing in from the south. I knew her smile was for my enemies though, not me.

"Nightshade wasn't interested in my old gardening tools,"

she said, winking at Night. "I dug them up from the back garden before I came down. These tools are *naturally* imbued with perennial magic. I would only use them in the direst of circumstances though," she warned and then added: "It's the only thing I had that might be of any use to you where you're going."

For years, I'd known that the blackened garden outside of my bedroom window had mysterious magic in it, but I'd never known what kind until now. In light of what I knew about perennial magic and my mother's blackened garden, it now made perfect sense. I smiled and squeezed her back, whispering fiercely into her ear:

"It's not the only thing. I don't think I'll ever forget yesterday's swim—or the fiery frogs you coaxed me into offering."

We parted with tremulous smiles. I was determined not to cry. *Of course, I would see them all again!*

My father was less demonstrative with his good-bye, but it was more heartfelt than any farewell I'd yet received from him.

"Keep your signature open, Nouiomo. *Abundans cautio non nocet.*" *Abundant caution does no harm.* It was probably the closest Karanos had ever come to saying, *be careful.*

Ever the stickler for rules, Karanos consulted his pocket watch to make sure we weren't setting off prior to the designated start time. When the minute hand met the hour hand at the top of the watch face, we heard a faint boom from the direction of New Babylon. The waning magic version of a starting gun.

The day was so beautiful and clear, it was easy to pretend that Rafe and I were really just headed out for an overnight hunting trip. That we'd be back tomorrow—two days, tops. With sunny skies, a loaded sledge, fast, fearless beasts to pull it, and our own formidable magic and not insubstantial skills, it didn't seem as if what we were attempting was that impossible. Rafe and I climbed on the sledge and yelled *hike!* to Telesto and Brisaya and off we went.

Who said the road to Hell was paved with good intentions?

It isn't paved at all. It's a sunny, snowy, southern trail through wintery woods, with wagging tails at your front, waving hands at your back, wind in your hair, and naive optimism in the grin of the Guardian sitting beside you.

Chapter 14

ਠ

I had slept beside Rafe countless times in the field. All previous times, I'd given it little thought. Last semester, I'd been with Ari. Madly, head over heels in love with Ari. I wouldn't have noticed if a tiger had slept next to me (and of course, one had). And then in Maize, when I was recovering from the arrow shot, I was unconscious. Once I'd woken, and Rafe had declared his interest—made it clear his wish to kiss my gap-toothed smile was not just some silly joke he'd casually made at Kalisto's Crystal Palace—he'd ceased sleeping in the armchair next to my bed. So our first night together in a tent off the Old Trail felt strained and uneasy, at least it did to me. Maybe it *was* just me. Rafe, damn the man, never seemed uneasy about anything.

After making sure the barghests were squared away and the rest of the gear on the sledge was secure, we crawled gratefully into our two-man tent. The weather that first day had stayed crisp, clear, and blindingly bright. We'd worn dark spectacles to shade our eyes from the sun's snowy glare. Later that night, those spectacles were the easiest piece of

our gear to remove. Shucking the rest took a lot longer. We
each had fur-lined leather leggings that seemed to be glued
to our skin, wool sweaters with long necks that required endless tugging to get them off our heads, down-filled vests with
what seemed like dozens of toggles, hats with knotted chin
straps, not to mention the heavy, hooded cloaks we'd draped
over it all. The boots were the worst though. Their laces were
frozen solid under an inch-thick crust of snow and ice. Even
though we'd kept our hands warm with magic and mittens,
untying them was a major pain. I hadn't realized, until I sat
cross-legged on the floor of the tent undressing with my back
to Rafe's, how exhausted I was. It felt as if *I'd* pulled the
sledge all day. I positively *ached*. Every motion was slow and
clumsy.

That was, until Rafe took off his sweat soaked tunic to
change into a dry one at the same moment I did. Instantly, I
became acutely aware of his naked back against mine. I tensed
and in the darkness, my other senses sharpened. I heard the
whistle of the wind, the flapping of the tent walls. I smelled
the clean scent of moisture-laden air and the slightly more
pungent scent of sleeping beasts and one very awake man. I
felt biting cold on the tip of my nose and in my fingertips. And
I felt the smoothness of Rafe's back pressing against mine. For
one wild second, I wanted to turn around. To wrap my arms
around him. I wanted him to wrap his arms around me. I
wanted him to massage the ache out of my tired, sore muscles.
To possibly do more than that.

For the span of a few heartbeats, I wondered what it would
be like to share the warmth of my body with Raphael Sinclair. He was someone I cared about. Someone I'd laughed
with, shed tears in front of, and nearly died with. Many times.
But I didn't love him and I didn't want to ruin what we had
by leading us down an emotional road that would be more
treacherous than the Old Trail we were already traveling.

Rafe felt me tense. He also stilled. Waiting. When I slowly
straightened my back so that we were no longer touching, he
suddenly, *thankfully*, scooted away and crawled into his bedroll. "'Night, Noon," he said in a soft singsongy voice. I

couldn't tell if his jesting tone was to let me know his pun was intentional or if he was teasing me for feeling the way I did and not having the guts to do anything about it.

A moment later, his steady, quiet breathing told me he was asleep. Part of me wanted to poke him in the shoulder and demand that he cast Good Night's Sleep over me (*how was I supposed to sleep now?*), but the other part of me knew that waking him would be a mistake. That it would lead to actions I didn't yet want to take. So I slipped into my own bedroll and curled up beside him. Next to him, but not touching him. To help me sleep, I pulled out Kaspar Bialas' first letter.

2nd day of Ghrun, 991 AA
Requiem

To my successor—

The Mederies of Gaia supplied me with a fresh mount at Farro, but instead of the monarch's destrier, I am saddled on a mule. It is not vanity that causes me to resent it, but practicality. I ride with none other than the mighty Ophanim at my heels.

Metatron died a fortnight ago. Some say of angina, some say of a broken heart. Within the week, the Divinity seized all of his goods and chattel, including his oxcart and the carved statue of Justica. What they most wanted, however, they did not find: Album Cor Iustitiae.

I swore an oath to hide it from the Divinity. The Ophanim knights are honorable, but the clandestine Amanita's motives are suspect. They have infiltrated the ranks of the Divinity. No one is certain of who they are or what their plans may be.

I write in the hope that my words survive me. And that whomever should come to read this will want to keep the sword safe and in a suspended position.

Who still remembers the ancient, pre-Apocalyptic Sword of Damocles? The sword that hung over a lord's throne by a single horse hair? All else about that story has been lost, but Metatron believed—as do I—that the throne beneath it was empty. And that the people ruled and judged themselves, without blindfolds, based on their deeds, not their blood, beliefs, or birth affiliations.

So I ride for Tartarus, Halja's southernmost fortress, to bargain with Orcus, the Patron Demon of the Verge, to secure safe refuge for the White Heart.

KB

As we had last semester when we'd worked together during our first field assignment, Rafe and I quickly established a routine. We rose before dawn, roused the barghests and let them hunt for food. Sometimes they brought back freshly killed herons and hares, other times a mouthful of maggots (those days, I was even more insistent about my "no licking" policy; barghest breath was bad enough, saliva laced with chewed up bits of grubs was *not* to be borne). Around sunrise, Rafe and I would heat water for tea and washing up. After breakfast, we'd pack up our tent, poles, pots, pans, and plates, douse the fire, and harness the beasts. From then on, it would usually take us all day to travel just ten miles because all manner of mundane things seemed to impede us: rocks, stumps, and other debris getting caught on the sledge's runners, ice forming between the pads of Brisaya's or Telesto's paws, as well as soft patches of snow or crackling ice that had to be given a wide berth. Yet . . . despite the body-numbing coldness of the environment and the mind-numbing banality of the everyday hazards, those early barghest sledging days were almost fun.

Sure, we knew that greater dangers lay ahead. We'd only been warned a half dozen times or more about them. (Heck, I'd already survived one possible attempt on my life.) But last semester's assignment had taught us how short life could be. How one moment a person on your team could be alive and the next moment . . . not be. So we weren't going to waste a single second of the time we weren't under attack—from demons, beasts, the weather, our opponents, or Luck himself if he thought to end our lives earlier than we wanted him to—on feelings of fear, dread, or anxiety. *Carpe viam! Seize the road!* became our motto and our mantra. We headed for Corterra with near reckless abandon.

Our second night out, I pulled out my race file, Bialas' journal, and the tin box of letters that Joy had given me. Sitting cross-legged across from Rafe inside the tent with my cloak draped around my shoulders, I thumbed through the journal, ignoring the route notes since Joy had said that Bialas intentionally fabricated them to mislead future White Heart hunters. Which really meant the only information of value in the journal was the detailed description of how the Sanguine Scales worked. From a historical perspective, the account was fascinating. From a judicial perspective, horrifying.

I snapped the journal shut, shoved it back in my bag, and reached for the race file. I spread the map of Halja's southern Verge out in front of us. Immediately I spotted Corterra, which was smack-dab in the middle of everything. Directly to the north was Maize, where we'd come from. Around us, in a rough ellipse, were the remains of the former outposts. A few miles west of here was Briery Vale, where traces of gold had been found. And almost directly to the south was Mount Iron. In between here and Mount Iron, however, was a smaller mountain called Septembhel—the seventh bell. The map had a skull-and-crossbones symbol at Septembhel and another at Mount Iron. The one at Mount Iron had an "M+" after it.

Rafe peered at the map's legend, clearly looking for the skull-and-crossbones symbol.

"Mortem animae?" he asked, looking perplexed. "I thought our biggest concerns would be yetis, ice basilisks,

and possibly a berserker or two. What are the *mortem animae* and why are there more than a thousand of them where we're headed?"

I told him about the *mortem animae*, watching his expression change from interested to wary. He stopped short of looking mutinous though. I gathered, from the resolute look that finally settled on his face, that it would take more than the threat of a perennial curse to keep him from racing alongside me.

"I've never worked with perennial magic before," he said, his tone telling me he didn't like the idea.

"What about all those hand-cast spells? Those aren't a trick your mother taught you?"

His look hardened. "No. Those are faith-based spells, same as the rest of the spells I cast."

I frowned.

"Then how come all Angels don't cast spells using their hands?"

Rafe shrugged. "Why can't all waning magic users shape their magic into fiery doves?"

We stared at each other across the map of the land we might never return from. Underneath the paper, our knees touched. *All it would take is for me to lean forward . . .*

"I'm not sure," I said softly.

"You'll figure it out," he said in a voice as soft as mine. I had a feeling we weren't talking about magic anymore. But a few minutes later Rafe crawled into his bedroll leaving me with only Bialas' letters as company. I pulled out the second one and began to read:

7th day of Ghrun, 991 AA
Corterra

To my successor—

Corterra . . . The heartland. How appropriate. After a week on the Old Trail, sleeping in ditches with only my mule for company, I start to understand what is really meant by "heartland." No place could more test a man's heart, or commitment, than this one. The grasping ice, the starless skies, the hard ground. Nothing provides any comfort, security, or assurance that one's goal is the right one.

The only way to survive is to press on, push on, keep going, because what is the alternative? I must remember the reason I gave Metatron my oath if I am to accomplish such an impossible task. I didn't do it out of duty. I did it out of love. I have a wife and a young son back in New Babylon.

Will I see them again? Only Luck knows. Or Micah. Or possibly both and neither, which is why I ride . . . I ride . . . I ride . . .

I want my children and my children's children to rule themselves. And if that is a sin I will willingly burn for committing it.

Besides, any fire at this point would be welcome.

Forgive me . . . It is only the cold and hunger setting in. My mule and I ride for Septembhel in the morning.

KB

We reached Corterra's bailey gaol on our fifth day out. I knew about bailey gaols from all the bailiff cases and commentaries I'd read earlier this semester. The Old Trail we were traveling on had been part of the Old Justice Circuit that Metatron had traveled. It was hard to imagine an Angel traveling through this area in an oxcart with a stone statue of Justica in the back. But in the early middle ages, the Old Trail wasn't half as inhospitable as it is now. The permafrost hadn't crept this far north yet, nor had the *rogare* demons. Everyone was still finding their place in the postwar world. My understanding was that things were very catch-as-catch-can in those days, with everyone—man, demons, and even the ice—gearing up to stake their claim. Seven outposts were built in southern Halja from the first century through the turn of the first millennium. And each of those outposts had erected a bailey gaol.

Made of stone and petrified wood, they served as a court-house, post office, library, and gaol. In Metatron's day, he likely would have wheeled his oxcart right into the bailey, unveiled Justica's statue, and declared himself open for business. But when Metatron died (and his oxcart and statue went to the Divinity), the bailey gaols continued. And for the next three hundred years justice was meted out at them by a set of always-available, though deplorable Sanguine Scales and the more upstanding, but infrequently seen Maegesters who rode the Old Justice Circuit. At least until that fateful day in 1305 when the last group of traveling Maegesters were killed by *rogares* and the Old Justice Circuit was abolished. By then there were only a few outposts left anyway and by the fifteen hundreds those were gone too. Over the next few hundred years, the snow crept north and buried the outposts. Now, the exact locations of their other buildings, inhabitants, and individual histories have been all but forgotten.

When I saw the crossroads outside of Corterra's bailey gaol, I told Rafe I wanted to stop. Partly, it was because the winds were increasing, the temperature was dropping, and the sky was darkening with the threat of an oncoming storm. I figured, if a massive blizzard was headed our way, it would be better to take shelter in a building made of stone than a tent made of leather. But the other reason was that I'd seen this crossroads before. In the same place that I'd seen the larger version of the little white starred whelp—Demeter's perennial magic spring. Seeing the Old Trail fork in three different directions gave me goose bumps, but only because it felt so odd to recognize a place I'd never been to. I knew that the forks led to three of the other abandoned outposts: East Blast, West Blast, and Tartarus. But knowing this was just an ordinary crossroads didn't make seeing it any less eerie. It seemed to hum with dormant energy.

Was Corterra infused with perennial magic? And, if so, had it occurred here naturally or had Metatron artificially brought it here?

I yelled "Whoa!" to the barghests before we reached the crossroads but they weren't used to stopping when the sun was so high. It took more yelling, a few sharp pulls on the reins, and a warning fireball thrown into the snow in front of them to finally get them to listen. Telesto promptly plopped down in the snow, harness and all, while Brisaya tried to chew her way free. I jumped off the sledge to unbuckle her while Rafe rescued some of the gear that had come loose during our disorderly stop.

After unhitching both Brisaya and Telesto, I whistled to let them know I wanted them to follow me. We'd likely sense any *rogare* demons before they attacked, but yetis had no signature and Corterra's bailey gaol would probably be the perfect place for one to hide. Rafe cast a few spells over me and I shaped my magic into a throwing ax. With "abundant caution," as my father had advised, we approached the door. Above it, in letters faded with time, was the name of the abandoned outpost:

Corterra

Chapter 15

ꛯ

Inside, it was dark and there was a faint sound of something dripping in one of the back rooms. I hoped it was just melting ice. Telesto and Brisaya positioned themselves just outside the door. They were so large, I couldn't decide if their bulk would be a help or a hindrance if we were attacked in here. Rafe cast Angel light and I couldn't help feeling that, as we stepped forward, we stepped back in time.

The room had a raised platform in the middle with a desk and a high-backed bench on it. The walls were covered with shelves, cubbies, and drawers in all different sizes and shapes. Rotting books, shredding paper, and piles of dust filled every opening. I wondered what was in the drawers. Luck trinkets? Angel charms? Curse tablets? Or something more grisly like ears, fingers, or knuckle dice? I repressed a shudder. On the far wall was a fieldstone fireplace and a set of iron keys, which were hanging next to an open doorway. After hearing nothing but the sound of our breathing for the span of several minutes, I moved over toward the door.

It was a stairwell.

I glanced behind me and caught Rafe's gaze. I motioned to the stairs and he nodded. I increased the light output from my ax and we slowly descended. At the bottom was a short hallway and two iron doors.

Still unable to sense the presence of a demon—or even any magic beyond that faint hum I'd first felt—I gripped my fiery ax with one hand and reached for one of the door latches with my other. But Rafe beat me to it, as he did nearly every time there was a door to open. It was an Angel trait I was still getting used to. (Peter had certainly never acted that way when we were kids. But then again, there'd never been anything waiting on the other side of doors in Etincelle to kill me either.)

Behind the iron door was a circular set of stone steps that led down into darkness. Based on the magic I now strongly felt from below, I was betting there was a perennial magic spring at the bottom, similar to the one in Maize. I felt its odd magic swirling at the edges of mine, plucking at my signature, as if it were seeking a thread by which to unravel it. I waved my hand dismissively toward the stairs, shut the door, and then pointed at the next one. Rafe opened it as well. My flickering ax and Rafe's steady Angel light illuminated another hallway and two cramped enclosures with iron bars instead of a door.

Ah, I thought, *Corterra's dungeon, the* gaol *part of the bailey gaol.*

Unfortunately, there had still been prisoners here whenever Corterra had been attacked or abandoned. Both of the cells had skeletons in them. I swallowed tightly. Starving to death in a space you could barely turn around in would be a horrible way to die.

Had they known one another?

With how small the outposts had been, they'd had to have. Which then led me to wonder whether they'd been enemies. Maybe they'd been locked up for fighting. Or maybe they'd been friends. Locked up for drinking too much. Or maybe they'd been lovers. Forbidden for whatever reason to be together in life, yet bound together in death.

"Noon," Rafe's soft voice broke my macabre reverie. He reached out and gently rested his hand on my shoulder. "We should unload the sledge before the storm breaks."

I turned to him, my eyes meeting his. In the semi-darkness, his light-colored eyes reflected our light, giving him a preternatural look.

"Without their names, we can't give them a proper burial," I said. "But I can't leave them like this."

Especially if we were going to spend the night here, I thought. *How could anyone rest in peace upstairs knowing these two had died downstairs without it?*

After a moment, Rafe nodded. I walked over to the first cell.

"Breath to ember, ember to flame," I murmured softly. Rafe's voice joined mine. "Flame to fire . . ." In a tightly controlled burn I cremated the remains of the sinner or poor unfortunate person who had died here. "Fire to ember, ember to ashes." The skeleton turned first fiery red and then chalky white, finally disintegrating into ashes.

"Requiescat in pace," I whispered into the now dark and empty cell.

We did the same for the second skeleton and then I reached for Rafe's hand and dragged him upstairs, more determined than ever that we avoid a similar fate.

I t took us the better part of an hour to get everything inside that we wanted in when the storm hit. But in that hour I became more and more convinced that, even if we lost some time by unloading and making camp in Corterra's old bailey gaol, I'd made the right decision. By the time we lit a fire and got the barghests settled into a makeshift pen between one wall of the bailey gaol and the sledge, I could barely see the horizon. Tiny pellets of ice stung my cheeks and I had to squint to see anything at all (my dark spectacles were of no use in this weather; they made me completely blind). I slammed the wood-turned-to-stone door shut and leaned against it, marveling at how quiet it seemed inside compared to the roar of the wind outside.

Rafe was standing on the platform in the middle of the room examining something on the desk. I walked over to him and, with a sinking feeling in my stomach, saw that it was a set of Sanguine Scales.

"Whatever you do, don't weigh our chances with that," I warned, stepping up beside him. I was only half joking. We both knew that, though the bailey gaol gave us greater shelter against the storm, it also made us easy targets. We were, for all intents and purposes, trapped. Should any *rogare* demons find us, this building would first become a fortress from which to fight from and then, perhaps, our tomb. And there'd be no one to say the Final Blessing for us or grant us peace in our passing.

"I'm trying to figure out what the feathers are for," Rafe said, pointing toward the scales.

I peered at the scales more closely, amazed despite myself. Made entirely of copper, the apparatus was old, worn, and dented. It had two bowls, one much bigger than the other, and a set of weights in various sizes in a tray at the bottom. Alongside the weights were two wells. One well held a small knife and the other held one white feather and one black.

Rafe picked up the white feather and examined its end. "No ink," he said, frowning. He shook his head, clearly puzzled, and put the feather back in the empty well.

"It's not a writing quill," I said. "And these are no ordinary scales. I think, based on the description I read in Bialas' journal, that this is an old set of Sanguine Scales. The Corterra settlers—brave and hardy people, no doubt—used them to measure everyday things like salt, shot, and silver."

I placed the tiniest weight in the smaller bowl and turned toward him. I was only going to demonstrate how the weights worked—*not* the feathers.

"May I?" I asked, pointing to the silver bracelet Rafe always wore. On the outside, it looked like a smooth band of solid silver, but I knew that Bhereg's name and the date he'd died were etched on the inside. Rafe slipped it off and handed it to me. I placed it in the bigger bowl. It dipped lower than the small bowl. I rearranged the weights until I found one that very nearly matched the weight of the bracelet.

"Four hundred and eighty grains," I said, giving the bracelet back to Rafe.

"Lemme guess," he said in a dry voice. "The feathers are 'featherweights.'"

"Something like that," I said, considering the two feathers closely, wondering which I would choose if I were a medieval settler facing trial. "The black feather is a hawk's feather and the white feather is a dove's feather. In addition to everyday items, a set of Sanguine Scales was also used to measure the amount of honor in a man's heart—"

"Or a woman's," Rafe murmured. His gaze caught mine and I could see that his attention was split between the scales . . . and me.

"Of course," I said, my voice slightly higher than it needed to be. I cleared my throat, annoyed with myself. I didn't want there to be any awkwardness between Rafe and me. I'd grown far too fond of him for that. "Anyway, the accused used the knife to prick the tip of their ring finger—"

"Because the *vena amoris* runs from the tip of that finger directly to the heart."

"I thought you didn't know how the scales worked," I said, frowning at him.

He grinned. "Maybe I just like saying *vena amoris*."

I decided to try to ignore Rafe's comment about the vein of love and doggedly continued my explanation of how a set of Sanguine Scales worked.

"The drops of blood go in one bowl and then the confessor, or the accused, chooses whether they will be judged as a hawk or a dove by placing one of the feathers in the opposite bowl. If the bowl with the feather sinks lower than the bowl with the blood . . ."

"It's fire to ember, ember to ashes for them," Rafe said somberly, all traces of former humor gone.

I nodded slowly. With his long, thick, wavy, windblown hair and his full-grown beard, Rafe looked like one of the wild Hyrke hermits who shun city life, preferring instead to live a shortened life of solitude in Halja's hinterlands.

"And what about you, Nouiomo?" Rafe said, picking up the white feather again. "If you were being judged, which feather would you choose?" He reached for my hand and lightly traced my *vena amoris* with the tip of the feather.

"I told you not to call me that," I whispered. But this time, my voice lacked conviction. Rafe's ginger-colored gaze was soft and hazy, slightly smoldering. As if he were a banked fire that could easily be set alight with one poke or prod.

"Would *you* ever use one of these scales to determine someone's fate?" he asked.

"Of course not," I said, moving back. "Joy Carmine believes these scales were the cause of the epidemic *mortem animae* curse in southern Halja."

I plucked the black feather out of the well and looked up at him. Maybe it was seeing the two skeletons earlier that made me do it—the reminder that life is so fleeting. Or maybe it was the fact that we were once again discussing the *mortem animae* curse, which always made me grateful that I still had my memories of those I loved and cared about.

Or maybe it was just that I sensed it was finally time to apply my new motto *carpe viam!* to more than just the Old Trail.

I motioned to Rafe to hand over the white feather. He did and I placed it, along with the black feather I'd been holding, back in the well, so they stood side by side.

I swallowed.

"If the Sanguine Scales granted wishes instead of measuring silver and honor," I said, my voice hoarse with emotion, "would you still wish for what you wished for outside Kalisto's Crystal Palace?"

I hoped I wasn't making a mistake. That Rafe hadn't changed his mind. Then things really would be awkward between us. *He* might be incapable of feeling discomfort over bungled social situations, but I wasn't. Luckily, the look on his face told me his wish hadn't changed. If anything, it had only been wished for more fervently in the time since he'd first made it.

Still, old habits are hard to break because Rafe tried to act like the fact that I'd just agreed to let him kiss me was *no big deal*. I watched as his face transformed from *beaming* to *blasé*. If I didn't know him as well as I did, I might have been insulted. Instead I just smiled and upped the ante of this poker game he'd decided to play.

I stepped toward him and put my hands on his hips. Even under his beard, I could see his jaw harden. *Just how repressed* were *his feelings toward me?* I moved one of my hands from his hip to his cheek. Beneath my fingers and palm, his beard felt rough and prickly. I'd never kissed anyone with a full beard before. In fact, I hadn't kissed many men before at all. But now wasn't the time for doubts. Rafe could pretend nonchalance, but I wanted nothing more than to show him how serious I was.

Gently but firmly, I pulled him toward me.

The moment our lips touched, a feeling of exhilaration flared within me. It was somewhat similar to the feeling I'd had when Telesto and Brisaya had led the sledge out of Maize for the first time. There was a sense of anticipation, a snap of action, and then miles of feeling like we were flying. Rafe couldn't sense my signature, but it flared around me like a great, big fiery wind.

His beard and mustache tickled, but Rafe's lips were soft and full as they pressed against mine. It didn't take long for me to open more completely to him. I felt a rumbling in his chest as he ran his tongue across my teeth.

He broke off the kiss abruptly. I met his gaze. At least the kiss had blasted his blasé look into oblivion.

"Onyx, remind me to *never* make a wish at Kalisto's Crystal Palace again." I narrowed my eyes at him. "They take *far* too long to be granted." And then he slid his arms around me and settled his mouth on mine for a deeper kiss.

Chapter 16

&

If I'd had qualms about kissing Rafe, they were completely
dashed by the experience of it. I'd been worried that it
wouldn't feel right, that I wouldn't be capable of enjoying
kissing anyone else but Ari. I'd been worried that, if the kiss
felt "off" somehow, our friendship would never be the same.
I'd been worried that, because I'd viewed Rafe as only a
friend for so long, it would be impossible—beyond a theoretical *what if?*—to consider taking my feelings to the next
level. But when Rafe moved one of his hands to the middle
of my back, splaying his fingers and pressing me closer to
him, it felt both soothing and invigorating. It felt a little bit
like jumping into Demeter's perennial magic spring had—
thoroughly healing, yet dangerously unpredictable. I worked
my hands around to the back of his head and ran them
through his crazy, wild, windblown hair. He groaned as my
fingers caught on some of the more snarled pieces and he
moved his hands down to my rear. Catching my upper lip
gently between his teeth, he quickly let go and then hoisted

me up onto the edge of the desk. I rested my hands on his shoulders and wrapped my legs around his waist.

Rafe's hands rested lightly on my thighs. I doubted he knew what effect his touch was having on me because he couldn't sense my emotions in my signature. In a way, it was freeing. But it also reminded me that I needed to work harder to make sure he knew how I felt. I ran my hands over his chest, surprised and pleased by how hard and defined his muscles felt, even underneath the bulky wool sweater he had on. Even better though was the look in Rafe's eyes as I did it. I realized then that describing Rafe's gaze as "slightly smoldering" was about as accurate as describing dynamite as "slightly charged."

I slipped my hands up underneath his sweater and the tunic he had on beneath it, but before my fingertips grazed anything more than the skin at his waistline, he grabbed my hands with his.

"Remember how I told you back in Maize that I didn't want anything unsaid between us? That I wanted to start off right and tell you everything in the beginning?"

I tensed and slid my hands out of his grip. He let me, but didn't move from where he was standing. His face lost its smoldering look and he replaced it with a more serious one I didn't care for. Seeing *serious* on Rafe's face made me nervous, especially after what we'd just been doing. I unclasped my legs from around his waist and leaned back on the desk, with my hands behind me now.

"And I told you I didn't care," I said. "About the memory you have of Ari's. Or that your brother was a drakon. Those things don't change how I feel."

He nodded, but the sinking feeling in my stomach told me those details were just the beginning. But Rafe didn't tell me the rest of the story. At least, not right away.

Instead, he took off his silver bracelet again. The one with the name "Bhereg" and the date "9-2-92" etched on its back. Rafe had been six years old when he'd accidentally tripped on his family's weathered pier and dropped his baby brother into the Lethe. Even though it was an accident, I knew Rafe blamed himself for Bhereg's death, as much as if he'd held Bhereg under the water to drown.

I looked up from the bracelet suddenly, meeting Rafe's gaze. *Oh, Luck. Is that what Rafe wanted to tell me? That his brother's drowning wasn't really an accident?* But my mind rejected that thought almost as soon as it had formed. While no Angel family would welcome a drakon in their midst, I couldn't imagine anyone intentionally drowning one at birth. And Rafe had only been six. He couldn't have done something like that.

Right?

With growing horror though, I remembered that Rafe had first taken an interest in me at a public execution last semester. At the time, he'd seemed obnoxiously obsessed with whether or not I could, or would, kill a demon in cold blood.

Ice started spreading through my veins. It felt as if someone had taken a hollow pin full of snow and plunged it deep into my heart. *Had the drowning been an accident or was that just how I'd chosen to interpret things?* I wanted to know now as desperately as I didn't.

Rafe's face was dark and unreadable. I'd never seen him look this way. As I'd done only a few minutes earlier, he placed his bracelet in the larger bowl on the Sanguine Scales.

"Four hundred and eighty grains, huh?"

Rafe picked up the weight I'd found before that nearly matched the weight of the bracelet. His voice had an edge to it that I hadn't heard in a long time—since the night I'd tried to give him the memory of Bhereg's funeral back. But Rafe's mercurial feelings about Bhereg and the way he'd died made no sense. If the drowning *hadn't* been an accident, why did Rafe wear a silver bracelet with Bhereg's name etched on it and the date he died? Rafe had even told me that he'd given his brother his name. That didn't sound like something a cold-blooded killer would do. But Rafe's expression made it clear that there was more to the story of Bhereg's death than I'd first understood.

"Unfortunately," Rafe said, pointing to the bracelet, "the memory attached to this weighs a lot more than four hundred and eighty grains."

He set the weight back in the tray and picked up the knife.

"Rafe, put the knife down. Just tell me what happened. You can't use the Sanguine Scales to weigh anything other than ordinary things. They won't work—or worse, they will and who knows what will happen?"

He gave me a sardonic smile, but I could tell his scorn was self-directed.

"I'm going to tell you about the memory I have. Because I want you to know *exactly* what led to that other memory of mine that *you* now have—the one of Bhereg's funeral."

He pricked his ring finger with the knife and a bright red spot of blood welled on his fingertip.

"Then you can let me know whether you're interested in granting more wishes or meting out justice."

He reached for my hand.

Part of me wanted to refuse to give it to him. I was terrified of what I was about to hear. And terrified of possibly invoking the aberrant magic of the Sanguine Scales. But looking away, or refusing to listen, would have been as impossible as refusing to hear my own judgment.

Rafe took my hand and wrapped it around his, squeezing. A few drops of his blood spilled into the bowl. I wrenched my hand free then, but not before I felt the magic of the scales gathering. Its rapacious hunger made my hair stand on end.

Rafe plucked the black feather out of the well. The hawk's feather. The one chosen by sinners who wanted to plead guilty. But seeing the black feather in Rafe's hand didn't look right. Whatever might have happened on the Sinclair pier nearly a quarter century ago, it wasn't fratricide. I knew it as surely as if my heart were the Sanguine Scales. I didn't need a damn copper bowl and a feather to judge how much honor Rafe had. He was a good person. I *knew* it.

I reached out, this time willingly, and placed my hand on Rafe's again.

"You chose the wrong feather," I whispered. "But neither feather is guaranteed to judge the accused fairly. The scales can't be trusted *or* used."

But Rafe shook my hand off, his jaw hardening. *Did he want to be punished? He seemed to have already judged himself.*

"You don't know what I did, Noon, although you must have some idea from the memory you have of mine."

"Some," I said. "But I don't need to hear the details of what happened to know it was an accident. You need to let your guilt go." Again, I tried to remove the black feather from his hand but he held fast.

"No," he said in a dead tone. "It *wasn't* an accident. That's just what Valda told everyone."

My hand stilled. Outside, the wind was more than whistling. In fact, it was starting to sound like the North-South Express was on its way here. Even this stone refuge seemed fragile under the onslaught of the increasing winds and threatening magic storm.

"I already told you Bhereg was a drakon," Rafe said. "Who knows which demon caused his spawning? My mother claimed it was Estes himself." He scoffed. "But how likely is that? More likely it was some other demon that Valda laid with in return for something of little value. The real value of whatever unholy union she'd gotten herself into was the resulting infant, but she only wanted to get rid of him, as quickly as possible. She told me if I didn't do it for her, she'd put me in the dunk tank or use the thumbscrews on me. I believed her.

"Even so, that's not what made me do it. I did it because, if I didn't, she would have. And if *she* did it, it would have been far less merciful and far more horrible."

"So you drowned Bhereg?" I said frowning, my tone clearly disbelieving. All of my focus was now on Rafe's confession, not the scales.

Rafe nodded. "And unlike the *rogare* demon you executed last semester in the Shallows, Bhereg had done nothing wrong. His only sin was being born."

Shocked, I let go of Rafe's hand. He moved it over toward the small bowl, holding the black feather suspended above it. I knew if he dropped the feather the magic of the scales would mete out whatever "justice" was due. I had myriad problems with what was happening, by far the most immediate was the fact that Rafe was about to invoke the spurious magic of the Sanguine Scales.

But before I could put a stop to his brinkmanship, Rafe said something even more shocking.

As before, when I'd learned something that should have been obvious to me sooner, I wondered how I'd missed it. How I had forgotten once again that, in Halja, Luck and life were more twisted than entwined. How Luck sometimes had a vicious sense of humor.

"I floated him out into the Lethe," Rafe said. "I put Bhereg in a reed basket, cast a spell over him, and pushed him out into the water from the edge of our pier. The last time I saw him he was heading northeast with the current, a small, dark, wriggling basket set against the shining brilliance of the rising sun on the Lethe. That's why I named him Bhereg. It means burnished, like gold—or silver. Bhereg was a brief 'shining brightness.'"

Rafe watched me closely. Waiting for a reaction. But my mind was skipping like a flat stone thrown across still water. My first coherent thought was that Rafe didn't want forgiveness. He wanted the opposite. He'd said grace was his specialty. He'd spent a lifetime punishing himself for his brother's death. And if Rafe had things his way, he'd spend the rest of his life punishing himself.

He held the black feather over the small bowl, twirling its end between his thumb and forefinger. All he had to do was drop it to get the punishment he thought he deserved.

Did he want me to argue with him? To try to convince him the drowning wasn't his fault? That he'd been forced to do it because his abusive and barbaric mother would have tortured him had he not? Did he want me to remind him that Valda would have done it regardless, and Bhereg's death then would have been far less kind? Maybe he did; maybe he didn't. But either way, it wouldn't matter. Rafe had judged his own actions a long time ago. He didn't need me or the Sanguine Scales to do it for him.

I guessed then that Rafe didn't intend to take our relationship beyond that first wished for kiss. Because anything beyond that would bring him too much joy, too much fulfillment. The joy and fulfillment that he believed he'd denied his drowned brother.

But it hadn't happened like that.

Rafe wasn't guilty. Not because he had an affirmative defense. But because the sin hadn't been committed. Bhereg hadn't died. He'd *lived*.

Rafe hadn't drowned his brother; he'd saved him.

How did I know? I nearly cursed Luck then and there. Because I knew that, through either Luck's guiding hand or Estes' divine intervention, Bhereg's reed basket hadn't sunk. Instead, it had traveled the width of the Lethe. Where it had been found by the one woman who had the will and magical makeup to raise a drakon child. A drakon she'd raised as a member of the Host. A drakon she'd raised as a hero among the Hyrkes he'd grown up with. A drakon who would later serve as executioner to the executive—and who would later fall in love with the executive's daughter.

Bhereg had lived and Joy Carmine had found him and named him Aristos.

Ari was the half brother that Rafe thought he'd drowned.

But before I could tell Rafe that Bhereg's reed basket hadn't sank as he'd always thought, he dropped the black feather. It floated toward the bowl, its leisurely pace in direct contrast with the severity of its effect should it reach its intended destination. If the Sanguine Scales worked like waerwater or any other trial by ordeal—or, Luck forbid, as Joy Carmine thought they might—I didn't want Rafe to be subjected to its judgment or punishment. That wasn't the justice he deserved.

My body and my magic acted simultaneously. I flexed my arm out, punching the base of the scales with the heel of my hand. At the same time I sent a bolt of waning magic toward the feather, singeing it midair. The feather was instantly incinerated but I watched in horror as a few ashes fell into the bowl just before my shove sent the scales crashing to the floor. *Were those ashes enough to trigger the scales' magic?*

After that, everything seemed to happen at once.

Copper weights scattered, drops of blood splattered, and ashes rained down over it all. It was the magic of the scales, I knew, but it was still a sight to behold when the blood, metal, and ashes started to multiply and magnify before our eyes. Outside, Telesto and Brisaya started howling. I'd never heard barghests howl before and the sound of it sent shivers racing up my spine. At the same time, I felt something I knew I'd feel on this trip—I'd just hoped it would be later—*rogare* demons.

Chapter 17

Inside, things looked as desperate as they sounded outside. The smashed bits of copper from the Sanguine Scales, Rafe's silver bracelet and blood, and the ashes from the incinerated hawk's feather each expanded like a balloon and then combined into one big magic meld, which grew still more and then morphed into a colossal metal monster right before our eyes. I'd been afraid the magic of the scales would work immediately. That Rafe would instantly be turned into one of the *mortem animae* by the unnatural perennial magic curse contained within the Sanguine Scales. But either the scales didn't work like that or I'd severely messed things up by shoving the scales onto the floor and smashing them. I might have saved Rafe's life, but it appeared as if my pardon would grant him (and anyone standing near him) minutes only.

The *monstrum metallum* (I could think of no better term for such an unnatural alloy of magic and metal) crouched before us. Its bulk was so big that it couldn't stand upright in the bailey gaol. Instead of a face, it had a copper helm with

a hawkish beak; instead of skin, it had copper armor streaked
with silver. In its hand was a sword that looked vaguely like
the one Justica had held in the statue I'd destroyed last semester, but this sword was longer than my leg and thicker
than Rafe's chest. The *monstrum* let out a mighty battle cry,
sounding like the North-South Express screeching to a violent and unscheduled stop. Its shrill squealing sent the barghests into a frenzy. A moment later, Telesto and Brisaya
burst through the door.

Telesto wasted no time in engaging the *monstrum* head-on.
The impact of their collision sent a piece of its shoulder flying
off. I ducked to avoid decapitation and fired up a war hammer.
Instantly, the arrow tip in my chest pulsed and then steadied
into a searing ache. Rafe murmured a series of rapidly spoken
spells under his breath and I felt a few slip in place. Likely
Impenetrable (for me), Damage Cascade (for my magic in
general), and possibly Amplify (for my war hammer in particular). Taking only enough time to ensure that my hammer
would hit the *monstrum*'s head and not Telesto's, I threw it
with as much force and speed as I could muster. I watched as
it sailed through the air, flipping end over end, its fire flickering and spitting until it made contact—dead center—right
between the *monstrum*'s eyes. The war hammer exploded in
a shower of fiery red sparks just as two blue bolts of Angel
light pierced the *monstrum*'s helm.

Telesto retreated and the *monstrum* staggered back, shaking its massive head, the grating, scraping sound of it giving
me brief hope that our magic missiles might have knocked
head from body . . . but no. An instant later the *monstrum*
regained its balance and raised itself to full height, smashing
a hole right through the bailey gaol's ceiling with the back of
its armored head, neck, and shoulders. It ground out another
wrenching shriek while pivoting its upper body, swinging its
metal fists, and battering huge swaths of the building.

Blocks of stone and sand descended upon us as ice-laced
wind blew through the newly created hole in the ceiling. It
lashed my cheeks and stung my eyes, temporarily blinding
me. I threw up a waning magic shield and raised my arm to

cover my face. By the time I lowered it, the hearth fire had spread to the shelves of tattered books, shredded paper, and dust. Needless to say, the ancient tinder ignited so quickly we barely had time to leap back from the billowing flames.

"Is your magic having any effect?" I yelled to Rafe. He was covered in soot and ash. He shook his head, never taking his eyes off the *monstrum metallum*, which seemed to be gaining sentience and mobility at an alarming rate.

The screeching, banging, and clanking sounds that had been emanating from it lessened, but somehow that only made it more frightening. The *monstrum*'s gaze locked on Rafe and I knew that somehow the magic of the scales had retained its original purpose. Worse though, was that our magic didn't seem capable of denting or destroying it. Worse *still* was the fact that the *rogare* signatures I'd sensed earlier were zeroing in on us.

"Outside!" I screamed. Together, by throwing untold amounts of waning magic and bolts of Angel light at it, we managed to avoid immediate pulverization, barely escaping from the bailey gaol.

Once outside, the blizzard's full effects hit us immediately. The wind now felt as if it were spiked with shaved bits of metal. Each and every one of them seemed to take aim at my face. I raised my hand to my forehead, to try to gain some cover for my eyes. Telesto and Brisaya circled us, snarling, clearly unsure of which direction the next threat might come from, only sensing that it would. Before I could form any more of a plan beyond *run*, the *monstrum metallum* rose up out of the now demolished bailey gaol and stepped toward us. There was no time to dig out the sledge or load up the supplies. We grabbed our packs and ran for the first available cover, a small outcropping of rocks about seventy yards from the bailey gaol. The *monstrum* may have been sentient, but it wasn't very smart, and we easily lost it in the near-whiteout conditions. We huddled together behind the rocks, too afraid to light our weapons for fear of being seen.

If we didn't find shelter soon, the cold would kill us as surely as that blasted metal beast. I *already* felt as if I were freezing to death. My cloak, hat, and mittens were buried under the now destroyed bailey gaol. I wrapped my arms around myself for warmth and allowed my waning magic to settle around me like a blanket, but my efforts to keep it controlled but unlit made the arrow tip in my chest feel like a hot coal embedded in my heart. I didn't know which would be worse . . . freezing to death from the outside or being burned alive from the inside.

The approaching waning magic signatures were unfamiliar to me, but Rafe had already risked a glance around the rocks to see what other, possibly greater dangers were coming.

"Winged ice basilisks," he shouted. "A whole swarm of them."

They appeared to be following the Old Trail, which seemed odd. *Why would winged demons follow an old road?*

I turned to Rafe, so that we could attempt to form some sort of coordinated battle strategy. We'd been in fights like this before—facing impending doom from one threat while awaiting attack by a pack of *rogare* demons hoping to take advantage of our weakened position. Unfortunately, I remembered all too clearly exactly how our last big *rogare* battle had ended.

I tried to remember the geography around Corterra.

Wasn't Briery Vale near here? Maybe we could lure the monstrum metallum *toward it and somehow maneuver it over the cliff wall?*

Before I could share my plan with Rafe though, he told me his.

"You need to make a run for it. No!—better yet, *ride*. Telesto is less likely to try to buck you off and he's stronger. Climb up on his back, use your magic to control him, and GO!" He roared that last bit and then tried to push me away from him.

As if! Last year I might have listened—maybe—but this year, uh-uh. No way.

I just laughed, although there was no real humor in it.

"It wants me, Noon," Rafe said, attempting to reason with me. He leaned close to my ear, his tone low and urgent. "Not you. I'm sorry. I never meant for *this*"—he swept his arm toward the *monstrum*, who had finally figured out that following our footprints in the snow was its best chance of catching us—"to happen. I didn't think the magic of the scales would work this way."

I grunted my agreement. "I don't think that metal monster was what Metatron had in mind when he ensorcelled the scales," I said. "I think *I* brought it to life when I knocked the scales over."

We only had a half second or so before we were hopelessly trapped between the *monstrum* and the basilisk swarm and I wanted to make sure Rafe didn't do anything wildly stupid when my back was turned.

The *monstrum* was only a few steps from the outcropping.

"You're more honorable than anyone I know," I said, placing my hands on Rafe's shoulders.

It was true. I thought of all the times last semester that Rafe had acted selflessly. And I recalled the much more recent revelation that, even as a six-year-old, Rafe had tried to save his demon half brother from their Angel mother's murderous intent. That fact alone proved Rafe's heart was beyond reproach. But I also knew it would take more than a simple sentence to convince him. For starters, it would take telling him the truth about what really happened to Bhereg, but doing so properly would take more time than we had and would certainly require a far less dangerous setting. So I settled on reminding him of his Guardian's oath.

"I'm holding you to your oath, Raphael Sinclair," I shouted into the wind. "I don't care how guilty you feel about what you confessed to earlier. If you ever try to invoke the judgment of a divination tool again, I will declare you an oath breaker. And if you try to shirk your duties toward me by surrendering yourself to that metal monster, *I will declare you an oath breaker.* Understood?"

His only answer was to throw his arms around me and shove me to the ground. I might have made the mistake of thinking it was romantic roughhousing but for the fact that

shortly thereafter I heard a grinding shriek of metal, the ex-
plosive sound of rocks being smashed into dust, and the light
patter of small bits of crushed stone raining down on Rafe's
back. The *monstrum* had found the outcropping we'd been
hiding behind and was doing its best to destroy it. Immediately, I wriggled out from under Rafe, making a mental note
to tell him later that I only expected him to shield me with
his spells, not his body, and fired up another war hammer.
This time, the pain in my chest was nearly as bad as when I'd
first felt the arrow pierce my chest. My war hammer flickered
and dimmed. Since my previously thrown hammer had had
little effect on the *monstrum*, I doubted this weaker weapon
would work any better. Which meant, if I didn't come up
with a plan soon, Rafe would be in bloodier pieces than the
monstrum.

Briery Vale was out. It was too far. We'd never be able to
outrun both the *monstrum* and the basilisk swarm. In fact, the
basilisk swarm was actually the worse threat because those
demons were smart, there were tons more of them, and they
wanted to kill all of us, not just one of us.

A feeling of hopelessness descended on me as if it were
more debris from the *monstrum*'s unstoppable metal sword
and fist. A memory suddenly came to me. One I remembered
I wanted to save for times just like this. Dark times. Hopeless
times. It was a single moving image in my mind: my mother,
standing amongst the pristine beauty of Demeter's winter
spring, stripping the white blossoms off a pear branch into
her palm, and then blowing them onto the pond's glassy surface. And then a new plan came to me. One that probably
wouldn't work, but was worth a chance because doing *something* was better than doing *nothing*.

I grabbed Rafe's hand and together we ran from behind
the outcropping. "The white feather," I screamed. My lungs
burned from running, my throat from yelling, my chest from
the red-hot arrow tip. "We need to find the white dove's
feather from the scale."

Rafe stopped abruptly in the middle of the Old Trail and,
because I was still holding his hand, reverse momentum sent

me crashing back into him. He held me upright. The look in his eyes told me he thought I was absolutely insane, but the corners of his mouth twitched.

"A feather?" he said, laughing. "Amidst all that?" He gestured to the pile of ruined debris that had once been Corterra's bailey gaol. "Only you, Onyx. *Only you*," he repeated, shaking his head.

"Come on!" I yelled. At least he hadn't actually said *needle in a haystack*.

After that everything happened so fast, I couldn't help but think that Luck was on our side. Sure, during those first few seconds while we were searching for the feather, it felt as if death would surely be the only outcome. So, in a way, each of those seconds felt like an hour. But luckily, I spotted the feather almost immediately in a pile of dust and rubble. It didn't look very white anymore; it was more of a dove gray. But nothing, in that moment, could have looked more beautiful to me.

The *monstrum* let out another mighty screech and raised its sword high in the sky above us. In the next moment, it would come down on our heads and I didn't think even the spell Impenetrable could save us then. But this feather might.

I knew, based on my own past experience, as well as my mother's and Fara's, that small unensorcelled objects could sometimes cause the most profound effects. A match. A book. A knife. And now, hopefully, a feather. My mother had said she thought perennial magic worked like a switch. *You turn it on; you turn it off . . .*

I placed the dove's feather gently in the palm of my hand and incinerated it, blowing the ashes toward the *monstrum*. I'd risked our lives on this theory. That the *monstrum* was never meant to be. That it had only been created because I'd destroyed the scale while it was still measuring, birthing some abysmal, heinous alloy of blood, metal, and ashes from a bird of war. I'd risked our lives on my hunch that the ashes of a bird of peace would neutralize this *monstrum*.

Was I right?

Luck intervened one final time because instead of blowing the ashes every which way, the wind blew them straight into the *monstrum*. The effects were immediate. The ashes did what our magic couldn't. It was almost like watching the *monstrum* being born in reverse. It shriveled up, twisting and untwisting, turning itself in, then out, finally breaking apart into its small, harmless building blocks: copper pieces from the smashed scale and Rafe's silver bracelet.

The ashes and the blood were gone.

I picked up the silver bracelet. Its etchings were still intact. I handed it to Rafe. After a moment's hesitation, he accepted it and put it back on.

Regardless of how bizarre this trial by ordeal had been, Rafe had won. Hopefully double jeopardy and Rafe's promise to me would prevent any future trials.

Now, if only ice basilisks could be defeated as easily . . .

Chapter 18

༆

Destroying the *monstrum metallum* with a puff of ashes invigorated Rafe and me. Our predicament was nearly as dire as before, what with the below freezing temperature, our lack of proper gear, the agonizing pain in my chest, my weakening magic, and a swarm of winged ice basilisks on its way to attack us, but there was no denying that eliminating at least one enemy had a heartening effect. That is until I felt a waning magic signature I recognized at the head of the swarm—Brunus Olivine.

Immediately, I felt even weaker and almost violently ill. It would be impossible to forget the rotten feel of Brunus' signature. And Brunus' presence meant that Peter Aster wouldn't be far behind. Well, that explained why the basilisks were following the Old Trail. They were following Brunus and Peter. But what I couldn't tell was whether Brunus and Peter were controlling them—or trying to outrun them.

With my heart in my throat and my eyes on the barely visible horizon, I yelled to Rafe. "It's not just the basilisks. Brunus and Peter are headed here too."

The sky was leaden, as if it were full of smoke, but I knew it was snow. Above the Old Trail, less than a mile away, was a dark spot of what looked like spilled oil. It writhed in the sky, black laced with the iridescent colors of a prism. The basilisks. And, beneath and ahead of them by a few hundred yards, were Brunus and Peter.

In many ways, they looked as Rafe and I had probably looked traveling that stretch of the Old Trail earlier today. They wore similar clothes: heavy cloaks, fur-lined hats, and dark spectacles raised above their eyes so they could see in the darkening twilight. They traveled on a sledge similar to ours and they too were battling wind, snow, and uneven terrain. But whereas we'd been racing *toward* something, I saw now that they were clearly running *away*. It was immediately obvious that Brunus and Peter weren't controlling the basilisk swarm; they were trying to outrun it. Which might have caused me to be the slightest bit sympathetic toward them but for the other difference. Instead of barghests, their sledge was being pulled by an exhausted, abused, and terrified yeti. Brunus was using magic to control it and—knowing Brunus and seeing the yeti's pitiful condition—I couldn't help but feel more sorry for the beast.

Under normal circumstances the yeti would have inspired a healthy dose of fear in me. What it lacked in magic, it made up for in size and ferocity. Nearly four times my height, it was covered with spiky white fur that stood up on end as if it had been electrocuted. Its light-colored fur made its mouth and eyes appear as if they were giant black holes, two windows and a door into the beast's dark misery. It roared and then snapped its jaws shut, clawing the air as it ran as if it were trying to gain traction from it as well as the ground.

As the basilisk swarm flew closer, its iridescent shimmer grew more pronounced and individual shapes could be discerned from the dusky snow blowing around it and within it. Winged ice basilisks look a bit like drakons but they are a lot smaller and lack the hind legs and lance-like shoulder bone extensions that give drakons their dangerous yet regal appearance. These creatures looked like tiny black-winged snakes.

But their diminutive size didn't fool me. If hornets, wasps, and scorpions were but a bit bigger and possessed deadly magic, they'd possibly be able to take on a swarm of neonate ice basilisks. But those weren't neonates headed toward us. They were full grown and full of lethal fire and poisonous spit.

Rafe turned to me with a grim look on his face. "What do you think about riding Telesto and Brisaya now?" he shouted.

I glanced at the yeti. Brunus was blasting it with a bolt of waning magic shaped like a whip.

Is that what it would take to control Telesto and Brisaya?

I couldn't imagine doing that to a beast that wasn't threatening me and didn't even have any magic to defend itself.

"Where would we go? They'll catch up to us eventually. Here, at least we've got partial cover and we're not exhausted from running."

I guess, under different circumstances it might have seemed adventurous or possibly even romantic. Like we were the hero and heroine of one of those ancient Haljan legends about two lovers facing impossible odds. Problem was those lovers were always *doomed*.

And they were lovers . . .

But my wayward thoughts gave me an idea. I just hoped our fate would be different than the two people who had inspired my most recent survival strategy.

"The jail cells," I shouted. "We can hide in there."

This time, there was no joke about me not doing things by halves. We both knew digging a path through the rubble of the destroyed bailey gaol to the stairwell would take more time than we had. And, having just narrowly escaped the *monstrum metallum*, we were both only too aware that we were treading on Luck's good grace to expect another such positive outcome so shortly after the first one.

Rafe and I started digging through the debris like dogs as Brunus, Peter, their abused yeti, and the ice basilisk swarm grew closer. Just as I was wondering if Brunus would even try to stop the yeti's crazed flight in order to make a stand at Corterra with us, their sledge caught a snag. It stopped

abruptly, sending them and all of their gear into the air. I
watched with mixed marvel and dismay as they sailed forty
feet or more into the air and then landed not ten feet or so
from where we'd been digging.

Brunus' fall must have severed his hold on the yeti. With
renewed fervor, it snapped the leather reins that had tied it to
the sledge and turned to face the incoming basilisk swarm.
Clenching its fists defiantly, it emitted a roar that sounded
almost demon-like. The rumbling feel of it in my feet and
ears galvanized me. I whistled to the barghests to help us dig.

Brunus and Peter survived their falls. They rose, shaken,
and joined us at the edge of the bailey gaol's pile of rubble.
Peter's gaze locked with mine and a look of shocked awe
crossed his face. In that moment, Peter's near-white coloring,
marble-sculpted features, and slight smile made him look
beautiful. But as his gaze took in my sweaty, sooty, unkempt
state, the blood under my fingernails, and the barghests and
other Angel at my back, his joyful look turned first peevish
and then angry.

I switched my gaze to Brunus, who was casually taking
our measure despite the fact that, behind him, a war raged
between one overgrown beast and several hundred winged
demons. His confidence had grown along with his magical
prowess.

"Nouiomo Onyx," he said, his voice as rough as the wind,
"we thought you were dead." It was obvious from his expression that he *wished* I were dead.

*Was his surprise and disappointment due to the fact that
he'd been told I was dead or because he'd been the one to try
to make it so? Had Brunus shot the cursed arrow tip toward
my heart that day at Kalisto's Crystal Palace? Or had it
been Vicious?*

*Or some other overzealous, law-breaking, would-be Lau-
reate?*

I quirked a smile at Brunus, not trusting him for a single
second.

"You'll be the one to die if you don't start digging," I
growled. Brunus glanced at the barghests and then the yeti

and the basilisks. I estimated that we had about fifteen seconds to find the stairwell's entrance before we found ourselves under direct attack.

"Help us find the bailey gaol's dungeon entrance," I shouted above the wind, "and I *might* let you in it."

Three heartbeats later, we were all trying to dig our way out of certain death. Once again on an assignment I found myself flanked by two Angels, but this time one of them definitely did not make me feel safe, which should have been odd since he'd been my closest friend for the first twenty-one years of my life.

"Guess you found a way to search for *Album Cor Iustitiae* after all," I said to Peter. He stared up at me with a stone block in his hands and a hateful look in his eyes. I hoped the look was for the basilisks and not me. I should have known better than to expect contrition from Peter Aster. I don't think I had ever—in my life—heard Peter say he was sorry or that he'd been wrong about something.

"At least Brunus is motivated for the right reasons," he spat out, as if I were the one responsible for getting him into this mess. "He knows who he is and what he wants."

"I know what I want, Peter. *You're* the one who thinks I should want something different."

He glared at me as he tossed the brick he'd been holding aside and reached for another. "You really want to become this year's Laureate so you can work for a Hyrke riverboat captain?"

"Well I sure as hell don't want to spend next year in places like *this* with people like *you*."

"Onyx," Rafe called, somehow managing to make his voice sound like a drawl even above the wind. "Fight with Aster later. Dig *now*."

But it was already too late. The war between the yeti and the basilisks was over. The basilisks had won and now they were zeroing in on their next target—*us*. Brunus turned toward the swarm and formed a fiery bow and arrow. With cold precision, he shot at least a dozen out of the sky before they were upon us.

It galled me to have to stand and fight beside someone like Brunus, but dying would serve no purpose. And while proverbs like *the enemy of my enemy is my friend* had always sounded stupid to me, ones like *there's strength in numbers* didn't. There were scores of basilisks and only six of us.

I fired up a sword but it soon became clear that, though my sword fighting had improved dramatically in the past twelve months, I was no match for the basilisks. And the effort of maintaining the sword's shape and strength made me feel as if someone had repeatedly stabbed me in the chest with an ice pick laced with lightning. In a pain-induced fugue, I experienced the next four minutes or so as a violent maelstrom of beating wings, lashing tails, razor-sharp claws, and poison-laced teeth.

I'd seen Brunus fight before and Rafe and I had fought side by side many times. But Peter and the barghests were new battle companions for me. I was relieved to see that Telesto and Brisaya were better fighters than the yeti had been. They lacked magic, but either Haljan evolution or Linnaea's breeding had turned their jaws into lethal basilisk traps. They managed to kill at least a dozen of the miniature winged beasts before being bitten themselves. Peter was, quite frankly, scary to behold. He seemed to take perverse pleasure in zapping the basilisks out of the sky. I knew we were under attack—and I knew it was kill or be killed—but it was disturbing to see how much he seemed to enjoy it.

How had I missed this side of him during childhood and adolescence?

For my part, I was doing badly.

I knew if I lived I'd hear hissing in my sleep for months. In fact, after this, I probably wouldn't be able to sleep. At all. Ever again. Each basilisk was like a small winged snake and the sky seemed to be full of hundreds of them. I'd no sooner cut one or two or four down and ten more would swarm me. Every scale on their skin was barbed so each time one of them grazed me, it slashed or scratched. Before long it felt like someone had scrubbed every inch of my exposed skin—my face, neck, and hands—with steel wool.

The pain in my chest was nearly intolerable and I wasn't sure how much longer I'd be able to stay on my feet. Rafe had found the entrance to the bailey gaol dungeon, but it looked like he needed a few more minutes to dig a hole big enough for us to squeeze through. It was a few minutes we didn't have.

Which is probably why Brunus and Peter decided not to make a last stand with us.

Ordinarily, I would have been relieved to be rid of them. Problem was, they'd had the same thought as Rafe had earlier— that riding the barghests might be the best way to escape this place. I watched in horror as Brunus leapt on Telesto's back. He reshaped his bow into a fiery whip and cracked it next to Telesto's ear. Telesto reared, snarled, and clawed at the air. Brunus held on by grabbing fistfuls of his hide and then rammed the butt of the whip into Telesto's rump, urging him to flee. This directive, no matter how forcefully issued, was so contrary to Telesto's natural instincts to stay and fight alongside Brisaya that he rolled his eyes back in his head and tried to shake Brunus off. But Brunus' patience had run out. He reshaped his magic yet again into a small knife. When I saw him raise it toward Telesto, I instinctively reshaped my own into a similar weapon and threw it toward him. He easily deflected it.

My breathing became labored. The cold outside seemed to seep inside my body. It felt like my blood was turning to ice—that it was now so thick and near solid that my heart was having trouble pumping it. I fell to my knees just as Brunus sliced one of Telesto's ears off. I opened my mouth to shout but no words came out. I could barely breathe. I coiled all of my hatred of Brunus and his brutality into a *dark* fireball and threw it at him.

I missed. It was cold comfort that the blast seared and blackened another handful of basilisks.

Brunus plunged the knife deep into Telesto's rump and, finally, after emitting a heart-wrenching bray, Telesto bolted south taking Brunus with him. I raised my arms to try to cover my face from the continuing onslaught of basilisk tails, teeth, and claws, but they went right for the exposed skin on the back of my neck. I felt a sharp, searing pain as one of them sank its teeth into me. The venom's effects were immediate. All of the things I'd been feeling previously—pain, cold, terror—multiplied. Just when I thought those feelings couldn't get any worse, I saw Peter riding Brisaya hell-for-leather after Brunus and Telesto. His hands were coated in eerie electric blue Angel light as he gripped the ruff of her neck. I didn't need to hear her squeals or see her hair standing up on end to know that whatever he was casting into her *hurt*. This time I shaped my magic into a razor-sharp, steely thin, platinum-strength shaft of *dark* magic and threw it straight toward Peter's chest.

Let him feel what I feel right now, I thought savagely. *And what* Brisaya *feels.* It enraged me that I had to expend energy and magic on two people who should have been fighting beside us, not abandoning us.

But instead of finding its way to Peter's heart, my dark javelin hit his shoulder. It hurt him, but not nearly enough to kill him or even unseat him. In a flurry of snow and ash, which I saw through a veil of beating tails and wings, Brunus, Peter, Telesto, and Brisaya were gone.

The basilisks remained, poised to overtake us. Rafe and I were now bleeding from countless festering wounds. If we couldn't fight our way into the bailey gaol dungeon soon, my fire would be out. Completely. Finally. And forever. I wanted—*needed*—a new weapon. Something that was more graceful, numerous, and organic than a flaming replica of some ground bound inflexible steel blade. Something that might even have its own sentience and mobility, as the *monstrum metallum* had had. And that's when I decided to try shaping my magic into hawks.

Not living hawks, but waning magic hawks, which would be as real as my weapons were. As real as the fiery frogs that I'd shaped for my mother in Demeter's spring. As real as the flaming dove that I'd shaped for Delgato, our training professor from last semester. But this time I wouldn't just shape one blazing bird of peace; I would shape a whole flock of fiery war birds.

I gathered my waning magic and volatile emotions around me like a burning cloak and then flexed my signature. It pulsed like a solar flare. It was the kind of indiscriminate blast that normally harmed everything but demons, which would have included Rafe. But just as Rafe started to cast a defensive shield, I willed my inchoate magic into dozens of reddish black firebirds. Those blazing raptors lit up the gray skies and the oily iridescent shine of the basilisk swarm. The basilisks emitted an angry collective hiss as my war birds took aim at them. Of course, the devastating, ironic beauty of my flaming creations was that they couldn't die. The moment a basilisk managed to get a choke hold on one or managed to bite one of their heads off, they just reformed. It would have been one of the most energizing, empowering moments of my life . . . if I didn't know that creating them had also, possibly irreversibly, pushed me on the path toward death. Throwing that blast and then reshaping it into the war birds pushed the cursed arrowhead right up against the beating wall of my heart.

I sank to the ground, my vision blackening, my hand grasping at the rubble, seeking purchase to hang on, not just to consciousness, but to life.

To me, it seemed like I sat there for hours while the battle around me still raged, but it couldn't have been more than a few seconds before I felt a few spells slip over me and Rafe's arms slip around me. He dragged me down into the now uncovered stairwell, the whole of whatever else was still going on up top unknown to me.

The last thing I saw before everything went black was the silver rectangle of dusk light at the top of the stairs full of ash and fire.

II

Uneasy lies the head that wears a crown.

—SHAKESPEARE, *HENRY IV, PART 2*

Chapter 19

❦

I awoke, hours later, still in Rafe's arms, feeling only marginally better—the effect of heavy spellcasting. We were slumped against the stone wall in the short hallway of the bailey gaol dungeon. Rafe was still sleeping. In some respects, it reminded me of our train trip down to Maize. But this time, the pain in my chest was more of a pressure. It felt like someone had coated my heart and lungs with tar. Just breathing was a struggle and I knew instinctively that trying to use my magic again without first removing the arrow tip would probably kill me.

The silver rectangle of dusk light had turned black. Nothing had crept in on us as we slept, however. My guess was that Rafe had cast Impenetrable over the top of the stairwell as well as an ordinary spell of warmth down here because despite the stone surroundings and our lack of fire, I wasn't cold. Up above, the hissing basilisks had been replaced by the whistling wind. I supposed the rest of the basilisks had either been killed or had left. My thoughts turned to Brunus, Peter, Telesto, and Brisaya.

Were they still alive? If so, where were they?

I was desperate to get back in the race myself, but I was equally aware that I wouldn't make it even a mile in my current condition. And Luck forbid we were attacked again. I'd likely die before I could shape a weapon to defend myself.

I shifted my weight, waking Rafe. He looked only slightly battle worn so I knew he must have healed most of our injuries earlier. It seemed the only remaining injury was the one I'd had *prior* to the battle with the *monstrum metallum* and the basilisks: the embedded arrow tip. I knew it would have to come out, one way or another, but before attempting something that could just as easily end my life as save it, there was something else I had to do.

Tell Rafe the truth about Ari.

"We're stuck down here for a while," Rafe said, stretching as his low voice echoed off the stone walls. He cast a small ball of Angel light, which he then enlarged and floated toward the back of the hall. At once the darkness retreated, replaced by shapes outlined in glowing shades of cerulean, cobalt, and indigo.

"Why's that?" I asked, sitting up. My head swam and I put my hand out to steady myself.

"Even I couldn't cast our way through that storm," Rafe said, pointing up.

Oh. It hadn't occurred to me that we might be trapped down here for reasons other than my need to dig the arrow tip out of my chest. At least, if they were still alive, Brunus and Peter were stranded wherever they'd found shelter as well.

"We'll have to dig out some food," I mumbled, trying to ignore the dull ache in my stomach, which was only slightly less distracting than the pressure in my chest.

"I went up about an hour ago. The sledge is destroyed but I managed to bring down most of the gear and food."

I noticed, for the first time, that he'd rescued my cloak. It was wrapped around me. I nodded, wincing.

Rafe frowned. "I thought you were completely healed. Where does it hurt?"

"It's not pain as much as pressure," I explained, glancing up at him. My voice sounded hollow and it wasn't just the echo. "It's the arrow tip."

Rafe looked confused. "I thought your swim through the spring with your mother removed any magic that the arrow tip may have had." But then he saw the look on my face and his confusion turned to anger. It was the first time I'd seen Rafe look angry with me. But his angry look soon softened to one of resignation.

"Onyx, why?"

"Why didn't I tell you the arrow tip was still cursed?"

Rafe just stared at me.

I chewed on my lip. A nervous habit I thought I'd banished.

"I guess . . . I thought . . . well, I didn't want you—or anyone else—trying to stop me from racing."

Rafe considered me for a while. It was his contemplative look times ten. Finally, he said, "You're right. I would have tried to talk you out of it. But that doesn't mean you shouldn't have told me. I'm your *Guardian*, Noon. How am I supposed to protect you if you don't even tell me when you're *cursed*?"

Rafe's irate look was back.

"I'm sorry," I said, clasping his hand. "It won't happen again. I promise."

Since Haljans weren't in the habit of making promises lightly, my words seemed to assuage his ire.

"It has to come out," I said a second later, letting go.

Rafe shook his head slowly. "Your brother said it was ensorcelled. Now that we know it's cursed, it's even more certain that trying to remove it could—"

"Kill me. I know." Maybe I was getting too used to these situations. But instead of feeling scared, I just felt determined. "The arrow tip's interfering with my magic. Removing it *might* kill me, but leaving it in definitely will."

Rafe started to look stubborn so I fast-forwarded to what we needed to talk about before attempting my plan.

"Rafe . . ." I began slowly, gathering my thoughts. Even though moving made it harder to breathe, I turned around and straddled his legs so that I could see him in the semi-darkness. I grabbed both of his hands with mine and shook them gently. I took a deep breath and looked toward the dungeon's stairwell. Toward the outside. Toward a land covered in snow and ice, one that had been beaten down by howling winds, and then tucked under a threadbare blanket made of empty nights and starless skies.

How was I supposed to tell Rafe that Aristos Carmine was the drakon half brother he thought he'd drowned all those years ago? It sounded preposterous even to me and I knew it was true.

"Bhereg didn't drown," I said. Sometimes, being blunt worked best.

Rafe stiffened and I squeezed his hands. "Before you start arguing, just listen. Joy Carmine found the basket that you floated into the Lethe. *Ari* is your brother." Rafe's warm expression cooled, hardened, and congealed, finally settling into a mask of confused horror. I continued in a rush of words, eager to tell him the whole truth before I lost his attention to the shock of hearing such an astonishing, implausible—yet undeniably accurate—story.

"I've heard the story of Joy's finding Ari floating on the Lethe at least a half dozen times by now. I've even seen a picture—of Joy holding Ari with the basket at her feet. And the timing matches. Perfectly." I pointed to Rafe's silver bracelet. "You put Bhereg in that basket twenty-two years ago during the month of Ciele. And Joy found Ari twenty-two years ago. During the month of Ciele."

Rafe became so still he could have been a statue. I suppose I should have expected it. What I'd just told him likely refuted his deepest, darkest self-belief—that he'd committed fratricide at the age of six. Still, I guess I'd naively thought he would look happier at the news. Instead, his eyes reflected the eerie electric blue of the Angel light and his normally cheerful expression appeared chiseled from granite.

"I would have told you sooner but I didn't know what happened. All this time I just assumed, from our discussions and the memory of Bhereg's funeral, that he drowned in the Lethe and that it was an accident. If I'd have known—"

"That it was no accident—"

"Stop it," I growled. The pressure in my chest was veering toward pain again. "You were trying to save his life."

"Bhereg might have seen it that way, but Aristos Carmine? Unlikely."

"You don't know that," I protested. "You should . . ." My voice trailed off as I considered where all of this might eventually lead.

We spent an untold amount of time after that, sitting in the dark, saying nothing. I knew it would take time for Rafe to process what this revelation really meant. After a while, he gave me a rueful smile.

"You think I should try and find him?" He barked out a laugh. "And what should I say if I do? Should I tell him I'm sorry the basket leaked? Should I tell him that I didn't *really* mean for him to drown?" He lowered the volume of his voice then, but not its intensity. "And what about how he's feeling now? Should I tell him I'm sorry he's miserable? Because I know he is. How? Because I've still got *his* memory. Of *you*. Ari's memory. *Bhereg's* memory. Of loving *you*."

Rafe pressed the heels of his hands to his eyes and made an angry, anguished sound. But he looked up a second later, his eyes dry and his expression bitter. "Ari is *never* going to get over you, Noon. I know because I *still* feel what he feels for you." A burst of something icy hot exploded in my stomach. I clenched my fists and turned away. But a moment later, Rafe gently turned my face toward him again.

"And when I meet with Ari," he whispered, "to tell him the truth . . . and suggest that we reconsider our relationship from a more fraternal perspective . . . should I tell him that I didn't mean to kiss you too? That kissing you was just another unintended 'accident'?"

I stared at Rafe, my gaze wandering across his thick, wavy, wheat-colored hair. In this light it looked like he'd rubbed charcoal into it. His eyes glowed like twin moons while his unsmiling features were half eclipsed by dark shadows. For once, he looked every bit the powerful spell-caster he was.

It suddenly occurred to me how emotionally inconvenient the truth was. I didn't want to be talking about Ari. I didn't want to be thinking about Ari. It wasn't fair, to either Rafe or me, to dwell on the consequences of finding out that Luck had played a cruel joke on us. On *all* of us.

I leaned toward Rafe.

"Ari lost his right to complain when he kept the truth from me," I said. "You, on the other hand, chose to be honest." I tensed as a new thought occurred to me. "There isn't anything else you haven't told me, is there?"

Rafe gave me a contemplative look. After a while, he reached up and tucked a stray strand of hair behind my ear. He let his hand rest against my cheek for a moment, but then let it drop.

"No . . . there's nothing else."

I nodded my head and swallowed. "Then it's time."

I scooted off him, stood up, and removed my cloak. I laid it on the ground like a blanket. I pulled off my sweater and started unlacing my tunic. My fingers were stiff and my heart was racing. I didn't want to change my mind. Rafe eyed me with a combination of humor, desire, and not a small amount of wariness. I fumbled with the last knot on my tunic, finally untied it, and lifted the shirt over my head. I stood before Rafe in my fur-lined leather leggings and bustier. Quickly, before I lost my nerve entirely, I shucked the bustier and flopped down on the ground in front of Rafe, faceup.

To his credit, he kept his eyes on my face and gave me a dubious look.

"Time for what exactly?"

"Time to remove the arrow tip, Rafe. It has to be done. Grab a knife from the kit and get ready to cast."

"No way, Onyx," he said, throwing his own cloak over me. "I watched your brother work on you the night we arrived in Maize. He knows what he's talking about."

"I'm not saying he doesn't. But Night's not here for a follow-up consultation. And the fact is, I'll never make it back to Maize if you don't help me take it out."

"How do you know?"

I could tell Rafe was just going through the motions of an argument. He was humoring me. He had no intention of helping me gouge a hole in my chest. I sighed. I'd known convincing Rafe wouldn't be easy.

"I can feel it, Rafe. Not just physically. But magically."

He frowned. And fell back on his earlier argument. "If we try to remove it, it might kill you."

"Maybe. But the alternative is *certain* death. Which would you choose? I know some people think of Maegesters as modern-day knights. And that most knights would rather die in battle. But do you really think *I* want to? Come on, Rafe. I don't want to go out in a blaze of glory during our next demon fight. You know me. I want to try and survive. Help me."

Rafe looked conflicted. And worried.

"Maybe I can cast a spell—"

"It needs to come out," I said in a steely voice. "That's why I told you about Ari. Not that I wouldn't have anyway," I said quickly. "But I wanted you to know . . . just in case . . ."

His worried look turned mutinous.

"Rafe, I'm going to cut it out one way or another," I said, sighing. "You can either heal me afterward. Or not. If you don't, I'll die so you won't even have to hear me call you an oath breaker."

He made a sound of disgust. "How can you say such things?"

He stood up and paced back and forth for a while, clearly conflicted about what he was about to do. I lay there, trying to remember if I'd told him everything he might need to know if . . . things didn't work out. His thoughts must have been following the same lines because he finally stopped pacing and said:

"I have one more thing to tell you."

Instantly, I stiffened but then he lowered his body so that

he was lying next to me. He propped his head up with one hand and reached around behind my head with the other one. He rubbed my cheek with his thumb for a moment. He was either trying to convince himself to do whatever it was he was going to do next, or he was trying to etch the scene before him into his memory forever.

Finally, he pulled me close.

His eyes gleamed with Angel light but his features reflected something much softer—an emotion I didn't dare name, even in my own mind. Facing my own death was scary enough. Having someone else . . . well, feel *that* way about me so soon after breaking it off with Ari frightened me even more.

Because if I lived, I'd have to acknowledge what I saw shining in Rafe's eyes. And it wasn't just Angel light.

But Rafe wasn't going to wait.

"I don't want to lose you," he said, cradling my head in his hand. "And it's not just because I swore an oath to protect you."

He brought his mouth down on mine, deepening his kiss almost immediately. I reached up and clasped my hands behind his neck, arching my back and pressing up against him. I realized I was long past the point when I should have realized that Rafe could, depending on the circumstances, elicit nearly every emotion from me: aggravation, amusement, safety, fear, and now, most unabashedly, lust and longing. My fingertips brushed the nape of his neck and then plunged into his lionish mane, grabbing whole fistfuls of it. It felt like Virtus' pelt, wild and rough on top, but with an undercoat that was soft as silk. Rafe groaned, broke off the kiss, and shifted his mouth so that it was near my ear.

"Noon, do you have any idea how *madly*"—he pressed his lips against the skin just behind my ear—"*deeply*"—I shivered as he moved his mouth slowly down my neck—"*fiercely*"—he kissed the spot on my throat where my pulse beat wildly—"*ridiculously* in love with you I am?"

I shook my head slowly. It was getting hard to breathe again, but somehow I didn't think it was the arrow tip next to my heart. I was pretty sure it was something much less tangible *inside* my heart.

A few minutes later, it occurred to me that Rafe might be trying to distract me from my original purpose. So, much as what we were doing was infinitely more pleasurable than what we needed to do next, *requisita ante desideria—needs before wants* and all that. I gave Rafe a last lingering kiss and stood up. Wrapping his cloak around me for warmth, I walked over to our pile of gear and rustled through it. After a few moments of poking around, I finally found what I was looking for: a long, sharp knife and a small pair of pincers. I held the knife up, examining it in the iridescent Angel light. Its edges sparked and its surface flashed, looking very much like the blade was made of sapphire instead of steel. It would do nicely. I held up the pincers next—and that's when I started to lose my nerve.

Imagining what I wanted Rafe to do with those pincers, and knowing that I wanted him to do it in the next five minutes, nearly undid me. I started to feel light-headed and weak. My legs started shaking and my breathing became even more difficult. I stumbled over to Rafe, nearly falling in his lap. I pressed the tools into his palm and rolled over onto my back, squeezing my eyes shut.

"Volo tecum vivere, volo autem tecum mori," I whispered. *I want to live with you, but I am willing to die with you.* "Please don't make me wait any longer."

I heard Rafe exhale sharply but he did as I asked. He lifted his cloak off me. I felt a rush of cool air, the soft touch of his hands and then the tip of the blade pressing against my chest. He murmured a series of unfamiliar words and the haze of a spell slipped over me. Just before I lost consciousness, I felt a searing sting as Rafe pierced my skin and thrust the knife straight toward my heart.

Chapter 20

ᕬ

The stone floor beneath Rafe's cloak felt like a block of ice. My body shook and my teeth chattered. I saw only darkness. I heard only breathing. I felt thirsty and tired, but somehow cleansed. I lit a fireball, looked down at my chest, and realized that *cleansed* probably wasn't the best choice of words. Dried blood was everywhere. It was impossible to tell if I still bore my old scar, a darker mark, or just a new wound because the whole area was splattered with what looked like black ink. But, for the first time in over a week, I felt like myself again.

I glanced at Rafe, who was sleeping on the floor next to me. Or at least, I hoped he was. For one panicked second, I had the most horrifying thought: that Rafe might have somehow traded his life for mine. My fireball flickered and went out. My hands reached for him in the renewed dark as I pressed my cheek to his chest and my finger to his pulse. He was alive, thank Luck and all his legions.

But what was wrong with him? Why didn't he wake?

I shook him again, this time more violently. His hand

slipped from his chest to the floor and his fingers uncurled. There, in the palm of his hand, was a tiny iron spur. *The arrow tip.*

It was instinct only, but suddenly I thought I knew why Rafe wasn't waking up. In all the time I'd worked with him, I'd never seen him lose his *potentia*. But I think pulling the arrow tip out of my chest without killing me had finally tapped all his reserves. And, if I had to guess, I'd say the cursed arrow tip was now preventing him from regaining his *potentia*, similar to the way it had leached waning magic from me.

Once again I walked over to our pile of gear, but this time I pulled out a small dagger. I walked back over to Rafe, crouched down beside him, and used the tip of the blade to push the arrowhead off his palm. It fell harmlessly to the floor and Rafe's hand twitched. A moment later he arched his back and gasped for air. I placed my hand on his forehead. His skin was warm and dry. His breathing became easier and, though it was hard to tell by the light of my flame, I thought his color had improved too. Hopefully, all he would need now was rest. I lowered my fireball closer to the arrow tip and squinted at it.

The words were so small, I could barely see them. But I was familiar enough with the saying to recognize it.

SUFFOCA IGNEM

Smother the fire.

Haljan legend said that, during the last moments of Armageddon, Lucifer's final battle strategy had been to pierce the Angel's front line with fire. But, midrally, he was struck down with the lance that killed him. His rallying cry? *Aduro Velum! Burn the veil!*

The Angels' response? *Suffoca Ignem!*

Since then the Angels' final battle cry had been infrequently used as a curse spell against waning magic users. Its use was considered highly illegal. Whoever had cast this spell into the arrow tip not only knew their history (which ruled out no one; every Angel knew their history) but they also were unafraid of using grand, arcane, unorthodox spells (which narrowed the list down to only one Angel that I knew of—Peter Aster).

I sank to the ground, rubbing the spot where the arrow had pierced my chest. In my other hand, my fireball glowed soft and steady. Peter had betrayed my trust two semesters ago by threatening me with Ari's death in exchange for my promise to marry him, but I'd *never*—even after seeing how livid Peter was during this semester's oath ceremony— thought he'd try to kill me. If the thought didn't make me so sad, I might have made a joke about Heaven having no rage like love turned to hatred or Halja having no fury like a man scorned.

But Peter hadn't really loved me. He'd loved my family connections. And he'd loved the idea that, if he could find a way to reverse my magic, it would be further evidence of his already considerable spellcasting skills. My throat hurt and I marveled that Peter of all people could still make me want to cry. This was just additional proof that I could spend an infinite amount of time perfecting my magical and physical strength, but I was still just as soft and weak on the inside as I was when I'd first enrolled at St. Luck's.

I swiped a hand across my wet cheek and then raised the dagger up and brought the blade crashing down on the arrow tip. There was a brief spark of violet light and a pop that sounded like a firecracker. An acrid, bitter smell filled the air as I lifted the blade. Beneath it, the arrow tip now had a hole in it. The words of the spell were marred but not completely obliterated.

I flexed my signature. It felt good—strong, healthy, and supple once again. I could detect no trace of the poisonous feel of the *Suffoca Ignem* curse in it. So I blasted the broken arrow tip with waning magic, smelting it into a shapeless blob of glowing iron. When it cooled, I would tuck it into my pocket—as a reminder that Luck offered no guarantees. That even old friends could become enemies.

I glanced over at Rafe then, struck by a sudden urge to

kiss him. To seal our friendship. To make it so that *we* might never end up as enemies.

If I kissed him, would he wake?

How many legends spoke of kissing cures for sleeping people? At least a few . . .

I pressed my lips against his, willing him to wake up, almost expecting it. But he slumbered on. Crae Ibeimorth's lover's cure came to mind next, but instead of convincing me to use a bucket of ice-cold water on Rafe, it convinced me to use one on myself. So I gathered up my bloody cloak and made my way out of the bailey gaol's tiny dungeon and over to the winding set of stairs leading farther down to the underground spring.

I had to duck and crouch the whole way down. At the bottom, I found an old wall sconce to set my fireball in and stepped over to the tub. Considering that it might have been used for torture instead of washing, I wasn't too disappointed to see that the spring's once forceful flow had, over the centuries, dwindled to a trickle. I doubted I could have settled in for a nice relaxing soak in an area that may have been used for dunking and trials by drowning.

The spring's manmade stone basin was nearly dry. But there was one spot near the back where a small stream of water burbled up before disappearing back down into the cracks of the basin once again.

Even though I'd said I never wanted to swim in a perennial healing spring again, I found myself feeling extraordinarily grateful to have the water from one available for washing up. I spent the next hour or so scrubbing the blood and muck off me and my clothes. All the while, I thought about what Rafe had said earlier—that he was "madly . . . deeply . . . fiercely . . . ridiculously" in love with me. It scared me, but maybe not quite as much as the first time someone had said that to me.

When Ari had first told me he loved me.

Ari's love for me had been nearly overpowering. Rafe's seemed safer. Maybe it was because he was my Guardian, so I associated him with safety instead of risk. I had a feeling that Rafe would try to protect me from all harm, both physical and emotional. In fact, he already seemed to be doing everything in his power to spare me emotional pain, from offering to stand aside if I chose to reconcile with Ari, to making sure he'd confessed to every dark secret he'd ever harbored that I could possibly object to. It seemed like every time Rafe thought of me in any sort of romantic way, he also thought of Ari though, which was disturbing on several levels. And it led me to wonder if Rafe really did love me. Or if his "madly, deeply, fiercely" feelings were simply the result of his possessing *Ari's* memory and feelings of falling in love with me.

I stopped scrubbing and stared at the bloody, burbling water. *Where* was *Ari now? Would we ever see him again? Did I want to?*

I shook my head and started scrubbing again. Only two things were certain: Ari wasn't in the Verge and I didn't have to decide until later whether I would seek him out.

My current feelings were clear enough. A part of my heart would always belong to Ari (he was, in many ways, my true "first"), but I'd done the right thing in breaking it off with him. I didn't trust him (even though I knew his lie by omission hadn't been made with the intention of betraying me) and I'd needed some distance from him (already I felt more independent; I'd only thought of him 907 times during this race already).

As for Rafe, I cared for him, quite deeply. And I didn't want to hurt him. I wondered if there would ever come a time when Rafe and I threw caution to the wind and stopped trying to protect each other from everything all the time, but maybe that wasn't how our relationship was destined to be.

By the time I finished scrubbing, my skin nearly glowed . . . except for the spot above my heart. My demon mark had returned, much darker than before. Previously, it had looked like a small drop of spilled tea. Now it looked like a big splotch of spilled ink. It reminded me of Ari's mark and I couldn't help wondering if the magic *signare* Ari had put there last year was still there or not.

Upstairs in the bailey gaol's dungeon hallway, I got dressed. I walked over to the now cooled lump of iron that had once been an arrow tip lodged next to my heart. The words from the spell were now entirely erased and the iron piece had a smooth and melted appearance, although it still had a hole in it. I realized then that it was the iron "coin" with the hole in it that I'd seen under the water in Maize. On impulse, I raised it to my eye and peered through the hole, but everything appeared exactly the same. I yanked a few strands of my hair out. Instead of tucking the iron bit into my pocket, I tied it around my neck.

Rafe was still sleeping so I pulled out the tin box of letters. I carried it over to where Rafe lay sleeping and curled up next to him, wishing I had electricity to reread them with instead of flickering fire. This time, I started with the last one first.

9th day of Ghrun, 991 AA
Septembhel

To my successor—

My mule died at Tartarus' gatehouse. The guards refused to lend me a mount, although it should have been no surprise to me that miners are not as generous as Mederies. So I am left to wonder if the Ophanim will overtake me tomorrow as I cross the Fiddleback on foot.

My plan is to offer Orcus a strong room unlike any he has seen before, which I will build myself, in exchange for his keeping the White Heart safe within it. If he agrees, I will construct the vault deep within his mine, not his keep.

There's a new building technique that Orcus will be very interested in—it disguises an opening, instead of using a conventional door that opens and shuts. After construction is complete, gaining access to the room will be very difficult.

I trust that Orcus will take me up on my offer. He is the most avaricious demon there is. And Metatron de-

signed a very special set of Sanguine Scales just for him,
which I also carry. What demon would refuse a person-
alized set of sacrificial scales if it meant he could become
Album Cor Iustitiae's *eternal keeper?*

KB

Postscript
27th day of Eis, 1002 AA

Eleven years in Tartarus building Orcus' strong room!
Many days I wished the Ophanim had caught me on the
Fiddleback before I'd been given sanctuary inside. For-
get Tartarus. Forget the White Heart. Let no one disturb
that final resting place. The sole reason I don't burn
these letters is that they are the thread that holds the
sword suspended . . .

At the bottom of the letter was a crudely drawn map. One
of the passages had a circle drawn around it with a slash
through it. I had to admit, if only to myself in the flickering
light of my own fire, that I now doubted for the first time
whether I was doing the right thing. But if I turned around
now, Friedrich might not allow me to work with a Guardian
again. And while Rafe might happily live life on the lam, I
couldn't. And I could never be the cause of his doing so. If I
turned around now, I wouldn't win the Laurel Crown or become this year's Laureate. I wouldn't get to choose where I
worked next semester. The Council could force me to work
for Adikia, the Patron Demon of Abuse, Injustice, and Oppression at the New Babylon Gaol. How long would I last in
a residency where I was expected to torture people? Execut-
ing vile sinners to save innocents was one thing. Torture?
Uh-uh. No way. Wouldn't do it. I actually would live life on
the lam on my own to avoid *that*. Finally, if I turned around
now, Brunus and Peter might find the White Heart. And
there's no way I'd want people like Brunus and Peter wield-

ing a sword with that kind of power. So, despite Bialas'
creepy warning, I still wanted to race.

Besides, Brunus and Peter had Telesto and Brisaya and I
wanted them back.

By the time I finished putting the letter away, Rafe was
awake.

Chapter 21

ک

"So what's the plan?" Rafe said, shouldering his immense pack and squinting against the sun's brightness on the new, unbroken snow. He straightened and glanced south along the Old Trail and then north toward Maize, Etincelle, and New Babylon. Even Rafe, who was usually game for almost anything, had to have been thinking it might be best to reverse course.

Earlier this morning, we'd pulled out the map and route notes and calculated that it would probably take us a day and a half to two days to reach Septembhel on foot. Then it would take another few hours, possibly a half day, to traverse a flat, low-lying plain in between Septembhel and Mount Iron called the Fiddleback—the one Bialas referred to in his third letter. If we still had the sledge and barghests, we might have been able to cover the distance in one long day, which meant that Brunus and Peter had a day's lead, possibly more. I knew Peter would have taken notes on the contents of Bialas' journal and probably even copied relevant sections outright.

Would the false trail left by Bialas be enough to keep

them busy at Tartarus while Rafe and I caught up to them? How long would they search for the sword before giving up? What would they do then? What if they found it anyway, despite the journal's erroneous clues? Were they treating Telesto and Brisaya as horribly as they had two nights ago? Were they feeding them or letting them hunt?

Utterly frustrated with the situation, I made a sound of disgust and picked up a piece of rubble from the pile of bailey gaol debris. I tossed it up into the air and blasted it with waning magic. The exercise was pointless and futile. It was simply a release of magic and emotion before I too shouldered my pack and started hiking south—because I wasn't giving up, no matter how far behind we were or how inferior our position might be now. Besides, I had a new motive for wanting to catch up with Brunus and Peter. I wanted to rescue Telesto and Brisaya. I was on the verge of scowling, cursing my magic's useless destructive nature, wishing it could help with problems such as the one we were facing, when the bits from my blasted rock flushed a small flock of snow falcons out from under their nesting place. As I stared at their startled flight, I was similarly startled by a spark of inspiration.

Night before last, I'd shaped my magic into small fiery war birds. And last semester, I'd shaped it into a medium-sized flaming dove. Maybe today I could shape it into something else. Something animated, but bigger than a hawk or a dove. *Why not?* I'd shaped my magic into amorphous blasts, deadly weapons, and winged birds. So there was no reason I couldn't try to shape it into another beastly form—like barghests. And if I could . . . well then, we might be able to ride them, right? After all, if I was able to *fight* with the weapons I made, why couldn't we *ride* them as well?

I told Rafe my plan. At first, he just stared at me. I couldn't see his expression because he had his snow goggles on and the wind was whipping his hair every which way. Then, very slowly, he started grinning.

"Finally, I get to ride a barghest," he said.

Well, I wasn't at all sure about that but I was determined to try.

Quickly, I funneled my emotions into my magic: my extreme desire for haste, my worries over Telesto and Brisaya,
my revulsion over Peter and Brunus' many hateful actions,
and my heartfelt wish to win the Laurel Crown so that I
could be in charge of my own destiny. My waning magic war
beasts sprang to life looking more like burning mounds of
clay than fiery creatures with well-defined limbs and features. But I sucked in a lungful of cleansing, fortifying southern Verge air and *willed* those fiery masses of magic into
something more defined. I tapped into my still present sense
of loss and longing for Ari, my deep affection and growing
feelings of attachment to Rafe, my fear that one day our fate
might be the same as the two skeletons we'd laid to rest in the
bailey gaol dungeon, and, finally and most somberly, my intense desire not to let the White Heart fall into the hands of
people like Brunus and Peter.

It didn't work.

Try as I might, after six aborted attempts, I could not get
two fiery barghests to light. But on my seventh attempt, I
tried for only one and succeeded.

My barghest flared to life, finally well-defined enough to
ride. In fact, except for a few wispy tendrils of fire at her ears,
mane, and tail, she looked almost indistinguishable from
Brisaya. But unlike Brisaya, this barghest was fully within
my control. I pulled myself up onto her back and Rafe
climbed up behind me. Before I could consider how odd it
might be to name a beast that wasn't truly real, I'd dubbed
her "Nova" and then fervently hoped she would "live" long
enough for us to catch up with Brunus and Peter.

Riding was unlike anything I'd ever experienced before.
I'd never ridden a horse. Not many New Babylonians had.
Within the city, we relied on motorized cabriolets and without, boats or trains. Horses were more often ridden by the
farmers of Sheol and the various outpost settlers. Even
though the Onyx estate had a stable, I'd never spent much
time in it. So I had no idea if what I was experiencing now
was anything like riding a horse. But I suspected that riding

a waning magic war beast was as similar to riding a saddle horse as riding the North-South Express was to walking.

South of Corterra, Halja's Verge grew steeper by the minute. The Old Trail snaked its way upward into the mountains through sloping fields of snow-frosted slate and sage-colored grasses. The trail itself was a mix of chalk, gravel, and rocks. Soon, I lost myself in the ride, my focus directed inward and outward simultaneously through my magic. I felt the ride through Nova's sheathed claws and paws—every rock that shifted under our weight, every stray blade of grass that blackened as we passed, Rafe's strong arms around my middle, and the clutching of my hands in Nova's fiery mane.

I'd never interacted with the world around me through my magic like this before. I wasn't even sure if *anyone* had ever done this before. I'd never heard of a waning magic user other than me who'd been able to shape their magic into something that ordinarily was alive.

I was well aware that Nova was *not* alive—and never would be. But the experience changed me, as surely as lighting my first bonfire with Ari had. I think it was the fact that I—and I alone—added emotion to my magic. It made my magic stronger and more capricious sometimes, but alive too, in its own way. Nova was an extension of me more than any weapon ever could be.

But, like an Angel casting spells with *potentia*, I could only throw, shape, and control my waning magic for so long. Fueling something as large and complicated as Nova (not to mention making sure she didn't burn either Rafe or me) depleted my magic quicker than I would have liked. All too soon, Rafe and I crashed to the ground. My hands and cheek hit the chalky dust of the trail, and various rocks and stones painfully pressed into my sides, hips, and thighs. I shook my head, trying to clear it. The fact that we'd managed to travel for this long and far on a beast that was really just smoke and fire was likely a Haljan magical feat akin to Lilith's legendary Armageddon ride.

I hauled myself to my feet to be swept off them a moment

later by Rafe who crushed me to him, lifted me off my feet, and then spun me around in dizzying circles. I knew if he had not been afraid of the echo and the attention it might attract, he would also have been shouting. His grin was as wide as the Verge when he finally set me down.

"Tell me you can repeat that trick," he said. His hair and beard, in that moment, were so windblown, he looked like a full-grown lion.

"I'm not sure," I said truthfully, "but it was fun while it lasted, huh?"

We stood in the middle of the Old Trail, grinning at each other, and holding hands. Then, ever aware of our need for haste, we turned south again and started hiking.

As Bialas had, I started to feel that the middle part of our journey was endless. That we might never reach our intended destination. We walked . . . and hiked . . . and walked . . . and hiked . . . The trail grew steeper and more twisted, narrower with more dangerous drop-offs on either side. I had a pack with some gear, but nothing that would aid us if we had to do any serious climbing. I just hoped we wouldn't have to. Until now, thirty-three story Empyr was the highest place I'd ever been. As my breathing became shallower, and my limbs became stiffer, I realized that heights were not my friend. I began to feel an irrational urge to flatten myself against the mountain slope like an insect. My stance became crouched and soon I was scrambling inartfully up the mountain on all fours.

Once again I found myself longing for the race to be over—and for me to be its declared winner. *Enough* already with the elements and out of doors! I wanted to work somewhere where I could sleep in a bed at night. Where I could eat at a table in the morning. Somewhere where I could keep my clothes in a closet and my books on a desk. Somewhere where light could be generated by electricty instead of magic. Somewhere where I might even see fresh flowers or produce (provided they were far away and/or on someone else's plate) and possibly even a *regulare* demon or two if it meant that I didn't have to live off the land, scale tall mountains, or worry about getting killed *every single day*. Kalisto's Crystal Palace warning sprang to mind:

The southern Verge is one of the most dangerous and forbidding places in all of Halja. One out of every two hunters who follow the Old Trail will not return. Read the risks below. If you are unprepared to face these dangers, turn back now.

But when we rounded the next bend and saw Septembhel's bell tower, I realized that Kalisto had left some of the deadliest enemies of all off her list: old friends and current classmates.

Septembhel's bell tower was an ancient structure, probably dating to the pre-Apocalyptic days. It was said there used to be bell towers all across Halja, in much the same way there are now bonfire frames scattered across the eastern Lethe. Most historians believe they may have been used in a similar way—as markers. Not just for space, but for time as well. Until the Apocalypse stopped them. Some say that the cry that started the Apocalypse—*Cavete! Angeli ad portas! Beware! Angels at the gates!* was immediately followed by the Host's destruction of the Angels' bells. Others say it was the Angels themselves who destroyed the bells when Micah died. Only one thing was certain. Halja's bell towers had been silent for over two thousand years.

As happens ofttimes when a structure survives for millennia, its original use changes. Most of Halja's bell towers had been swallowed up by time and the hinterlands, but Septembhel's bell tower had survived. It was a trail marker today, but in the past, when the Verge had been populated with Hyrkes, it had been used as a gatehouse for Tartarus and, later, as an illegal sacrifice site.

The bell tower's gallows were now gone, but there were several stocks, two pillories, dozens of pikes, and even a few skulls lying on the ground at the base of the tower. Of course, after last semester's assignment any discomfort, revulsion, or fear over skulls I may have had had been thoroughly scrubbed from me through complete and utter overexposure. So it wasn't those that bothered me.

No, it was the sight of Telesto and Brisaya's bloody bodies lying on the ground that nearly drove me to the brink of apoplectic fury.

I cried out, uncaring of who or what heard me, and ran over to them, dropping to my knees in front of them. By the time they'd reached this bell tower, Brunus had sliced more than just Telesto's ear off. And poor Brisaya, I could barely contemplate what her final moments must have been like. Whatever Peter had been casting into her must have eventually burned her from the inside out. The smell of their remains was absolutely, putrifyingly horrible, but I couldn't back away. I knelt there on the ground in front of them for what felt like an hour, bawling the whole time.

It wasn't as if I hadn't seen death before. I had. I'd even been the cause of it more than a few times now. But *never* had I seen anything as grisly and brutal and despicable as this.

Who could be so cruel?

If Brunus or Peter had been standing right there just then, and if I'd had any magic whatsoever left after creating Nova, I might have incinerated them on the spot. Brunus had proven yet again how hateful he really was. And Peter? Bile rose in my throat as I considered that I'd once called him a friend. I knew he was capable of betraying me, cursing me, and possibly even trying to kill me, but this was worse. Unlike me, Brisaya had done *nothing* to Peter to have deserved such shameful treatment.

After a while, Rafe pulled me back from the bodies. I let him and when we were a few yards back, I turned around and buried my face in his chest.

"I can't even cremate them," I said miserably. It would likely be hours before I was able to throw waning magic again. And I'd certainly have to be more judicious about creating large, animate creatures from my fire in the future.

"I can do it," Rafe said. His voice was rough and, even though he'd shed no tears, I could tell the sight of the barghests' dead bodies had deeply moved him.

As we had with the two skeletons we'd found in Corterra's bailey gaol, we said the Final Blessing, but this time Rafe used Angel light to burn them. There was no flicker, only a steady illumination that changed hues from indigo to azure to aquamarine and then finally to a white so bright it might have been starlight. I raised my hand to shield my eyes and just as Rafe and I were saying *requiescat in pace* together, I saw them.

The *mortem animae*.

They just materialized before our eyes. I didn't think I'd ever get over seeing that. I knew that some demons could travel through the ether, but the *mortem animae* weren't demons. They were supposed to be Hyrkes. Or they had been.

But now they were simply shadows, tragic and pitiable—but worse than lethal.

At least two dozen of them surrounded us. They were a lot less horrid than most of the other creatures we'd faced. Physically, they weren't very intimidating. Sure, they looked like walking corpses, and all of them had pasty white paper-thin skin that covered organs and arteries that were so loaded with iron they looked like they'd turned to solid metal centuries ago. (Only magic could make a creature look simultaneously denser than a black hole yet lighter than a thought.) But the *mortem animae* didn't have fangs or claws or tails. They weren't immensely big or strong. They didn't growl or grunt or bray. They wouldn't bite or sting or scratch. No, they would simply *touch* us. And then we'd be in Hell. Until someone found a way to release us, which to my knowledge, no one yet had.

Instinctively I tried to shape a weapon, but none appeared. My fire was out, which caused a painful zinging in my stomach. *Never* had I wanted my magic back as badly as I did then.

Rafe started murmuring the words to a spell. It wasn't one I recognized, but I was betting it was some sort of shielding spell. But I was also betting his faith-based spells wouldn't work against perennial magic. What had my mother said at the spring? That perennial magic was the magic of time and inanimate elements. That it was the oldest kind of magic there was.

Rafe and I stood back-to-back as the *mortem animae* amassed around us, silent as gagged Angels and deadly as demons. They weren't demons, but the thought made me think I might be able to offer them a bribe instead of a sacrifice.

Tartarus had been emptied of its underground riches long ago. Now it had infinitely more miners than metal. Did the *mortem animae* really want more of their own kind? Maybe they would accept iron in exchange for leaving us alone. I scrambled to remember what was in my pack that might be made of iron. There was the box of Bialas' letters from Joy. But that was made of tin. And there were the odd gardening tools from my mother. But they were made of steel.

"Rafe," I shouted, "what do you have that's made of iron?"

"Nothing."

One of them stepped forward, his arm extended, his hand reaching for me. I stiffened immediately, but instead of touching me, he merely pointed at my chest. My own hand raised up to touch the spot. And I felt it. What the *mortem animae* longed for almost as much as their prior lives. It was in their blood and their bodies. It ruled their minds and filled their hearts, yet they hadn't seen it in centuries.

Iron.

Resting against my chest was the hollow, smelted arrow tip that I'd tied around my neck.

I wondered what the lump looked like to them. Did it shine like a diamond? Was it brighter than the sun? Or did they feel it like I felt other waning magic users' signatures? With a yank, I pulled it free and dangled it in front of the one who'd stepped forward. He reached for it, but I snatched it back. Just so there was no misunderstanding, I said:

"A lump of iron in exchange for your oath to leave us alone."

He nodded once and held his hand out, palm up. I dropped the iron lump into it. He held it up, examining it as one might examine raskovnik or a four-leaf clover. Once he was satisfied with it, he opened his mouth and swallowed it. The bulge moved slowly down his throat, making him look like a giant, gray snake swallowing a rat. I grimaced. Soon, however, the iron that had once resided in me resided in him.

The *mortem animae* left soon after, going as they had come. They simply disappeared into the ether. It was disconcerting because it was disturbingly demon-like and because it underscored the fact that they could return at any time. But I'd learned to take Luck's blessing when I could get it.

Despite the late hour, we followed the Old Trail all the way down the southern slope of Septembhel. Our first view of Halja's southernmost dungeon came shortly after nightfall. It was every bit as dramatic as my imagination had led me to believe it would be. Even in the distance, across the Fiddleback, it looked like a bigger, more sinister bailey gaol. In the moonlight, Tartarus' spires rose up out of Mount Iron like pikes upon which drakons or giants could be impaled. There were no lights shining from it, not even the flickering light of fire. Which made me wonder what had happened to Peter and Brunus. *Were they inside? Or had they been touched by the* mortem animae*? Or killed by* rogares *hiding in the Fiddleback? Or had they simply slipped off the side of the mountain and broken their necks?*

One could hope . . .

Rafe and I stood, side by side, bent over, panting from our exertions, hats in our hands, the wind in our hair. For once, the frigid air felt delightfully chilly against my sweat-soaked skin. I glanced over at Rafe. He looked dark and brooding.

"Too bad Fara's not here," he said.

I nodded. She'd certainly proven her skills last semester, not to mention her bravery and loyalty. But Rafe was a more powerful spellcaster. I wondered what had brought her to mind.

"Too bad *Virtus* isn't here," I quipped. "I'll bet even the *mortem animae* wouldn't scare him."

"Cats can see in the dark, you know," he said. But the reply was automatic and his gaze was locked on Tartarus.

"Come on, you don't know a spell called Night Vision or Cat's Eye?" I teased.

He shrugged, then shook his head. He was acting fatalistic again. I recognized the signs. He was trying to pull back emotionally. He was trying not to care. Last semester, I called this look his carefully carefree look. But there was an edge to it now. Ever since the train ride down from New Babylon to Maize when Rafe had held me to this world with only the barest thread of magic, he hadn't been able to pull off that look as effortlessly as before.

"If I knew a spell like that, I would have told you before now."

This time, I shrugged. I put my hat back on. Rafe's sharp tone was uncharacteristic. But I knew why he had it.

He was anxious about the fact that we were about to break into Hell.

Chapter 22

ě

I realized a few minutes later, when Rafe cast a glamour over me, why he'd been thinking of Fara. Despite his fear of *becoming* one of the *mortem animae*, he had no fear of *pretending* to be one. The problem was, unlike Fara's glamours, Rafe's glamours were horrible. Instead of looking like victims of the *mortem animae* curse, we now looked like the victims of an exploding X-ray machine. The two of us crouched down, our booted feet crunching in the snow, our bodies glowing like two ape-shaped lightning bugs. I held my hand out, peering at its luminescent outline surrounded by darkness and then squeezed my eyes shut. *Terrific.* I now had zero magic, was temporarily blind, and I was shining brighter than the New Babylon port beacon. *Yep, right on schedule,* I thought. *Luck loved to test me, yes he did.*

"Rafe, how about a simple cloaking spell, huh? For you, me, and my signature, just in case my magic decides to reassert itself just as we breach the gates?"

Rafe gave me a lopsided grin and then cast me up. Our glowing outlines faded until I could barely see us against the stygian sky and the flat plain of permafrost in front of Tartarus. We now looked like shadows, the only evidence of our existence a slight blur and a stir in the air. We crept silently down the mountain and started crossing the plain, maintaining a steady pace toward the cheerless castle rising up in the distance.

Crossing the Fiddleback was eerie, and not just because I could hear us but not see us. About halfway across, I heard what sounded like music. It was just a few strains at first, which I dismissed as the wind possibly moving through an oddly shaped bit of rock. But as we moved closer, the sounds grew louder. *Halja did* not *have ghosts*, I told myself. *I was imagining the long, slow, low note that sounded as if a demon were drawing his bow across a violin string.* But I wasn't imagining it. The sounds became more fervent the closer we got. Piercing whines, staccato bursts, women wailing, children crying . . .

I slowed down to a walk as we approached Mount Iron. The hairs on the back of my neck stood up and I felt suddenly nauseous. There, at the base of the palisade, was a mound of debris taller than any building at St. Luck's. Nothing about it was natural, not how it had been made, nor what it had been made of.

The top of the mound, as well as several acres of area surrounding it, was littered with the broken parts of men and their machines. There were coils of uncut cable and hundreds, if not thousands, of counterweights, cylinders, pistons, valves, spools, cranks, skulls, and other bones scattered across the area. I gazed up at Tartarus with renewed revulsion. It was like gazing up at a metal hydra's head. And slithering out of its mouth was a forked iron tongue—the old railway line. It was broken and bent now, but at one time—when Tartarus was a fully operational mine—the railcars had come out of its northern facade on an elevated track, which then branched right toward East Blast and left toward West Blast. Jutting out from the castle's curtain wall were various planks—the "teeth of the beast" that rebellious miners (or their family members) were probably made to jump off.

Studying something in class, abstractly learning about a place of torture and what happened there, wasn't at all the same as seeing it in person. My throat closed up and my stomach clenched. There was absolutely nothing that could be done to right the wrongs that had occurred here. Thousands of innocent people had been killed here and nothing would ever bring them back or undo the pain of their deaths. I'd thought I'd developed an immunity to the horror of seeing skulls last semester, but this was so much worse.

The skulls that had adorned the watery bowels of the giant's keep in the Shallows last semester had a vague, unremembered history. Those skulls may have belonged to the giants' family members as much as their enemies. Their inclusion in the architecture of the Stone Pointe keep could have been as much for veneration as for intimidation. Either way, torture and a complete and utter lack of respect for the dead hadn't been a part of *that* ghastly display. *This*, however, *this* . . . mound or lump or tell wasn't created for any purpose. It was merely a method of discarding the unwanted. This site was simply Orcus' trash dump.

It was more than disgusting and awful.

It was evil.

I wanted to burn that pile more than I'd ever wanted to burn anything in my entire life. But I knew if I did it would not only possibly alert Brunus and Peter to our presence but also other *mortem animae*—and I had no iron left to bargain with. It was bad enough we were trying to sneak into Tartarus. I wasn't about to bang on the door and demand a fight too. So I turned my attention from the mound to the various entry points that were available to us. Unfortunately, blocking out the visual assault of the atrocious place proved easier than blocking out its unnerving audio assault. Up close, the grating musical notes sounded like someone pulling a metal bow across a violin strung with barbed wire. I gritted my teeth and tried to ignore the screeching, off-key melody.

As I saw it, we could enter Tartarus in one of two ways. We could hike up the mile-long, narrow, twisted, ill-maintained road that led to the castle's barbican, hope the portculis was either open or that we'd be able to raise it, and *then* hope we'd be able to successfully cross the ravine in between the barbican and the castle regardless of what perilous winged or tentacled creatures might still be lurking there. That option, obviously, held little appeal. Rafe and I dismissed it almost immediately. I'd jokingly told Joy I was going to storm the gates of Hell, but I hadn't meant it. Only a fool would say something like that and mean it.

Our second option was to climb up one of the elevated rail supports and make our way in through the rail line. Certainly that approach was the most direct. Whether it would be the easiest or not depended on how sturdy the old rail line was.

Needless to say, I asked Rafe if he knew a simple levitation spell. I tried not to be too disappointed when he said he didn't (Fara had, albeit it may have been capable of only raising us two feet off the ground). But then Rafe told me he knew something better.

"I know a trio of climbing spells called Vice Grip, Verticle Leap, and Dynamic."

I raised my eyebrows at him, but of course my face was blurred and obscured by the cloaking spell. He could tell I was in front of him, but he couldn't see my expression.

"What are you waiting for then?" I asked. "Cast us up!"

When I first started working with Rafe, his spells were so unusual, I was always wary. But now, not only had he proven his spellcasting skills, he obviously cared for me (he claimed to be in love with me), and he'd taken an oath to protect me. The glowing glamour miscalculation aside (glamours simply weren't Rafe's spellcasting strong suit), I knew he wouldn't botch a spell or cast something that could harm me.

The new spells felt strong and sticky and I wasted no time in trying them out. Just to be on the safe side though, I pulled some rope out of my pack. I tied it around both my waist and the support column I'd decided to climb. My plan was to climb up the way a lumberjack would. I'd only seen it done once, years ago, when my father had some of the woods on our estate cleared. Once I got started, I was absolutely certain that I *never* would have made it to the top but for Rafe's spells. Strong and sticky they were, but snow boots weren't made for scaling slippery smooth vertical surfaces (and neither were Maegesters-in-Training). The rope saved me from falling more than a few times. By the time I got to the top and dragged myself up over the edge of the rails, I didn't think I'd have the energy to stand up, let alone walk.

I lay on the tracks regaining my breath, my strength, and, hopefully, my magic. The wind was more than relentless. It was nearly skin flaying. Up here, on the old elevated rail line, we were level with Tartarus and the top of Septembhel, but we were now hundreds of feet above the Fiddleback. The light of the moon gave us just enough light to see the faint fiddleback shape of the mountain cove we'd just hiked across.

All around us were mountains. Not just Septembhel and Mount Iron, but others as well. Behind us, the rail line snaked its way east and west, through two different mountain passes. I knew the Old Justice Circuit lay beneath and beside the rail line. Regardless of which version of Metatron's history was true (whether he'd loved Justica or not; whether he'd died of angina or a broken heart), one thing was certain: he'd once traveled here in an oxcart. He'd traveled up and down and all through these mountains. It was an astonishing feat, even if he'd done it during a time in Halja's history when the trail might have been slightly more manageable.

As Rafe and I made our way across the rickety tracks toward Tartarus, my musings about Metatron were derailed by the renewed metallic screeching sounds. To maintain sanity, I decided to name them (as one might name a classical musical piece): "Serrated Bow Being Drawn Across Rusty Violin Strings." Maybe the jarring notes were part of the castle's defenses. There was no doubt the sounds set us on edge and made it even more difficult to think than it might have been otherwise. Although, admittedly, our entire situation was pretty unsettling. Here I was, hundreds of feet up in the air, suspended on tracks that were centuries old, navigating the broken portions amid gusts of wind that topped eighty miles an hour or more, wondering if my magic would return in time to fight (or preferably elude) anything that might be waiting for us inside.

As soon as we entered the mouth of Tartarus via the elevated railway, we lost the moonlight. Rafe cast Angel light and, after a moment's hesitation, I tried to light a fireball. My sigh of relief when it flared to life was audible. I'd have to think long and hard before I *ever* shaped my magic into such a large semi-sentient being like "Nova" again. Both our cloaking spells and the radioactive glamours had worn off so I could now see Rafe in his natural, adorably disheveled state.

The passage we were in wasn't built to be welcoming. It wasn't even supposed to be an entrance. It had been built to be an exit for the iron ore that had been mined here and then shipped east or west to one of the furnace towns to be smelted. So the whole passage was very utilitarian, which suited me just fine. Except for the warm, orange glow of my fire and the cool, soothing glow of Rafe's light, there was no color in the space. Everything was either charcoal, slate, stone, or smoke colored.

In addition to the rails we walked along, there were also broken iron pipes, dangling wires, twisted grates and fencing, piles of stone and debris, as well as several overturned railcars. A half-inch layer of grainy powder covered everything. We tried to keep our steps as light as possible, not just to avoid detection, but also to avoid breathing in centuries of dust and ash, but it was impossible. Soon, we were as covered in the nasty stuff as the place itself.

We emerged from the railcar loading docks into the castle's bailey. To our left was the keep, which was a high, square, stone tower. That's where the jarring, discordant violin music was coming from. To the right was the mining pit. It was a huge, deep, dark hole in the ground with a giant windlass over the top, which was now standing idle. Immediately in front of us was the courtyard, which made Septembhel's illegal sacrifice site seem like a charming roadside inn by comparison.

If the mound outside Tartarus held the consequences of

evil, then Tartarus' bailey was the cause of it. It was full of the same sort of standard torture equipment that, while barbaric, had been widely used all over the Verge during medieval times. There were the requisite stocks, pillories, and pikes, but there were also machines. It was all too easy to imagine what they'd been used for *because they were still being used*. By *mortem animae* on other *mortem animae*. It was almost too horrible to process.

I knew the *mortem animae* had been cursed, but until now, I'd just assumed the curse was only related to mining. Endless, everlasting mining. But apparently Orcus hadn't just mined iron ore here; the berserker demon lord had also mined psychological terror. In their minds, these victims were *still* suffering terrible atrocities. And they'd *been* suffering them for centuries upon centuries. And they would *continue* suffering them for time immemorial. Because there was no way to lift the curse. Except by possibly using the White Heart, which both my mother and Joy Carmine had warned me not to do. Still, seeing . . . *this* . . .

Well, I didn't know how I'd be able to walk away from this if a possible cure was in my hand.

The *mortem animae* noticed us then. They had enough sentience to stop their grisly work but they made no move to come toward us. I don't know if it was because we now had full use of our magic or if it was because the oath the Septembhel group had given me had broader application than I'd dare hope.

I only knew that I was dead wrong about one thing. I'd thought the *mortem animae* scared me. But that was *before*. When I thought they were only mindless miners. *Now*, I was absolutely terrified of them. The only reason I didn't change the shape of my magic into a more formidable weapon was because I didn't want to appear more threatening. There was zero chance we would be able to escape their touch if they chose to advance on us now. And this was the last place I'd want to be touched by one. I never thought I'd think it, but even digging aimlessly in the bowels of Mount Iron with no memory of anyone I had ever loved, liked, or lived with prior would be preferable to spending an eternity here in Tartarus' bailey reenacting the horrors being performed here.

Rafe and I slowly, cautiously, and ever so carefully made our way over to the windlass that was constructed over the top of the pit. Once we made it to the crank—and realized one of us would have to stay at the top and lower the other one down—our gazes locked. Both jobs were dangerous and ones I would rather have avoided under any circumstances. The person who operated the windlass would have to man the crank, among the hundreds of *mortem animae* gathered here, risking exposure to their curse by a chance graze or a full-on assault. The person who was lowered into the pit would have to brave a dark hole full of Luck knew what and hope that the person at the top wasn't attacked or otherwise pulled from their post before they made it back out.

There wasn't really a choice in who did which task though. Angels had some offensive capabilities, but their real value came from the spells they could cast that boosted their wards' capabilities. And besides, I was the one racing for the crown, not Rafe. I could hardly lower him down into that hole to retrieve my target for me. I did, however, nearly laugh out loud at what I was about to do. Once again I found myself facing a dark hidey-hole at the end of an assignment.

This time was different though. This go round, I wasn't searching for demons. I was hoping to avoid them. And I wouldn't be crawling in. No, this time I would be lowered down—with absolutely no way to get back up again if something should happen to Rafe at the top.

Rafe started turning the crank, drawing up the bucket, and I started mentally preparing myself. When the bucket was at the top, Rafe found a steel shepherd's hook and reached out with it to grab the rope, bringing the bucket close enough to the edge of the pit for me to be able to climb into it.

I turned to him. We'd survived all sorts of stuff together. Plenty of things that should have killed us but didn't. We'd battled water wraiths, hellcnights, ice basilisks, and the *monstrum metallum*. We'd drowned together once—only to be spit back out of our watery grave by Luck and magic. But

Rafe had saved me as many times as Luck had. He was the one who'd kept me alive after I'd been shot with the cursed arrow at Kalisto's Crystal Palace. And he was the one whose *potentia* had been strong enough to pull the iron tip out of my chest at Corterra. And, if I was being honest, he was also a large part of why I hadn't fallen to pieces after breaking it off with Ari last semester. Ever since we'd met, Rafe had been there for me. Mostly as a friend, but lately as something more.

Suddenly, I wanted to tell him how I felt. I wanted to *show* him how I felt. But there was no time. And *here* wasn't exactly the ideal place for declarations of love and commitment. So instead, I pressed my lips to his in a hard, parting kiss and jumped into the bucket.

"Volo tecum vivere . . ." I said as he let go of the rope. *I want to live with you . . .* The bucket swung out over the pit. *"Recuso mori sine te!"* And *I refuse to die without you!* After a few pendulum swings, the bucket came to a stop suspended over the center of the pit. Rafe pulled a knife out of his cloak and looked at me grimly.

"Just be quick," he said.

I wanted to joke around. To make some quip like *no kidding* or *ya think?* but my throat was too tight for me to say anything else.

Rafe put his knife between his teeth and started turning the crank. The bucket lurched as it lowered and I reached for the rope to steady myself, my gaze locked on Rafe's face. If I were going to die down here, I would take comfort in the fact that one of my last memories was of Rafe's rugged features, partially obscured by his frost-covered beard, his wavy, windblown mane of hair, and his unusual, unforgettable taupe-colored eyes.

His face finally faded into a silvery circular blur of light that grew smaller and smaller until it completely disappeared.

Chapter 23

ও

To keep sane, I tried reminding myself that *this was it*. This would hopefully be the last time I'd have to enter a dark hidey-hole. But the descent took longer than I wanted it to and so I found myself alone with only my fire and my thoughts for company. I began to think of all the things I regretted not doing or leaving half done. I began to think of all the things I might never do again . . . if I didn't make it out of this pit. It was a horrible thing to think about. It produced a fatalistic feeling of dread unlike anything I'd ever experienced before. And yet, I could not stop myself.

Perhaps it was natural, being in such a perilous situation, but I thought of my mother first. Sure, we had our differences. And it wasn't likely that we'd see eye to eye on everything in the future even if I did make it out of here, but if I didn't, one of the things I'd regret the most was that I couldn't have more days with her like the one we'd had at Demeter's perennial magic spring. To have actually practiced magic together—waxing and waning, mother and daughter—I'd never thought it possible before. If I didn't make it out of here, I'd miss the chance to see her smile more. To say "I'm sorry" for all the times I didn't, or refused to, see her side of things.

I thought of my father. He was gruff and unapproachable at times. We'd never been close, mostly because he'd never been around. But the more I saw of Halja—and what was in it—the more I understood why. Since no one was particularly interested in returning to the days of war, it fell to him and those who supported him—the *regulare* demons and his Maegesters—to keep the *rogares* in line and to keep Halja at peace. I realized miserably that if I died in this dark pit, I'd miss the chance to tell him I appreciated all of the sacrifices he'd made.

And I thought of Ari. How I missed him. Even though I still felt conflicted about the fact that he'd lied to me about being a demon, I couldn't help having the feelings I still had for him. But how could there be any future for us together? I knew it was impossible, but I still missed him. I missed Ari, my friend and confidante. Ari, my ally and field partner. I didn't miss Ari the drakon, but I found myself regretting how I handled our breakup. Maybe I'd been too unforgiving. Too harsh. I'm not sure what I would say to him again if I had the chance. But I couldn't help feeling we had unfinished business. I hated that feeling. Hated thinking I might never see him again, even if it was just to know that he was okay.

And then, because thinking of Ari seemed to open my emotional floodgates, the thoughts of all the things I'd miss—or never have a chance to do—if I died here just started pouring in. I'd never ride another fiery barghest or carve another snow demon. Night wouldn't have a chance to grow my tooth back. I'd never dig in my mother's blackened garden or eat Innkeeper's Pie or charred red snapper again.

I'd never have another glass of Empyr wine, never attend another festival in Timothy's Square. Never again be taunted by Sasha's barbed words or Gordy's Gorgon-like tendrils of deadly magic. I'd never fight, make love, laugh, light a bonfire, make a mistake, learn a lesson, spend a quiet afternoon in the stacks of Corpus Justica, prepare for another horrible assignment, see another outpost, puzzle out any more of Halja's convoluted and conflicting legends, confront another *rogare* demon—

The bucket hit the bottom of the pit with enough force to knock my remaining teeth together. Thoughts of things I'd done—or had not done and now might never do—fled. The only thing that mattered now was focusing on the task in front of me. I needed to find Orcus' strong room, figure out how to get into it, find the White Heart, and then get my butt back in this bucket.

Before stepping out, I took a quick look at my surroundings. The area was a rough circle that had been either carved or blasted out of the natural stone foundation that supported Tartarus on this cliff side of Mount Iron. There were some old rail carts and more broken tracks. They led away from here into the darkness through three separate passages. I pulled out Bialas' last letter and oriented myself, trying to ignore the fact that I was heading to the spot that had a big, black slash mark over it. *There*, to my right, was a narrower passage with no tracks. According to the map, that was the passage that would lead to the strong room.

I didn't sense any demons or the *mortem animae*, which was good, and, because of how the mine had been designed, I doubted there would be any natural beasts to worry about. So I stepped out of the bucket and onto the dusty stone floor.

My boots scuffled and echoed, making it sound as if there were three of me, which was unpleasant. I didn't like knowing I couldn't trust my own ears to warn me if something might be right behind me. I estimated that I was at least three hundred feet down, maybe more. I started following the narrower passage. After only a few moments, I passed through a rusty gate and then, after a few steps farther, I came to a dead end. I spun around slowly.

Was I standing in the strong room? Was this it?

The area didn't look like a place where Orcus would keep a treasure cache. It was merely a dead end. And the gate I'd passed through had looked more ornamental than useful. I peered at the map again. It showed an arrow pointing to this

passage and that big dark circle slash. But upon closer in-
spection, I noticed that the arrow wasn't pointing at the center of the circle. It was pointing to the end of the circled
passage. So I walked to the end until I was nearly against the
back wall.

And that's when I saw the opening.

There was a hinged grate flush with the floor, which covered a shallow depression that was at most a foot wide and
no more than eighteen inches deep. I knelt down, lifted the
grate, and put my fireball closer to the depression in the floor.
My fireball flickered a bit, but nothing else happened. I spent
a few more minutes searching for a hidden door catch. I
would've spent longer, but I was already worried about how
long I'd been down here—and how long Rafe had been up
top alone. Besides, Bialas' letter had said the door to the
strong room wasn't a conventional one that opened and shut.
So I lay down on my stomach and tried to peek into the small
depression at the end of the passage. All I could see was that
the shallow space continued past the point where my light
could reach. Ever so cautiously, I reached into the space,
bringing my fireball and my light with me.

With every passing second I expected the stone ceiling of
that small niche to come crashing down on my arm—breaking
it, crushing it, and trapping me forever down here. Or for a
spike to be driven through my wrist (producing the same effect). Or for a million spiders, snakes, or rats to come stream-
ing out of the hole. Or something worse. Like one of the
mortem animae . . . or a demon.

But nothing happened. When my arm was fully extended,
I saw that the shallow depression opened up on the other side
of the back wall of this passage. The entrance to the strong
room was a slip passage—easy enough for a demon to navi-
gate, but much more difficult for humans.

I swallowed, thinking about what I needed to do next. In
order to enter the strong room, I'd have to lay down, slide my
body into a less-than-eighteen-inches-deep stone ditch, and
scoot my way to the other side—the entire time thinking my
body might be subjected to the same things I'd just worried

my *arm* might be subjected to. *If only I were a barghest whelp,* I thought, *I could just wriggle under it like a whelp wriggles under a fence.* But of course I wasn't. I was over five and a half feet tall and, due to this semester's training in the Gridiron, I'd built up some substantial bulk.

I took some fortifying breaths. And reminded myself that—

This.

Was.

It.

If I was successful, this would be the last time I'd have to do something like this. And then I took a few more fortifying breaths.

Hadn't Rafe once said he knew a spell called Backbone? Why hadn't I thought to have him cast that *over me before I climbed into that damned bucket?*

I took off my cloak, sweater, and vest to make myself thinner. I stood before the back wall in nothing but leather leggings and my bustier. At least it was an outfit I was used to fighting in. I lowered myself to the floor again, this time laying on my back, and slowly slid myself into the ditch.

Things didn't get bad until I was about halfway in. At that point I'd been scooting inside in agonizingly small increments for what had seemed like hours (although, in fairness, it had probably only been about five minutes) when my bustier got stuck on something. And I couldn't move. Couldn't breathe. Suddenly, it felt as if the wall above my chest was lowering on me—that the crushing had already started. My breathing grew shallower and I began to panic. I was squeezed into this space so tightly, I couldn't even draw enough breath to scream. And, even if I did, who could help me? If Rafe came down to pull me out, no one would be up top to raise the bucket and get us out. Then we'd *both* die down here.

What, in the name of Luck, was I supposed to do now?

I closed my eyes.

I forced myself to relax. To think of something calming. The memory that came to mind surprised me. It was my study carrel at St. Luck's. I made myself remember all the books that I kept on the top shelf: *Manipulation: Modern-Day Control of the Demon Legions*, *A Maegester's Manifesto: How to Avoid Demon War*, the *Demon Register . . .*

My muscles relaxed and breathing became easier. I focused on moving different muscles than I had been before and whatever it was that had snagged my bustier loosened. I scooted the rest of the way into the strong room and got to my feet.

Immediately, I felt the presence of perennial magic. My body shivered and my signature shimmered in response. I allowed my fireball to grow larger so that I could see into all the dark corners of this place. There were as many corners, holes, and hiding spots in here as there were stars in the sky. For a moment, I completely forgot I was in a dark pit in the middle of Hell itself with some of my country's most feared magical creatures waiting just outside. It was a stunning collection. Everywhere I looked were scrolls, leather-bound books, ensorcelled paintings, charms, chests, and weapons. I might have worried about how I was going to find the White Heart among all this excess but in the center of the room was a locked chest with the words *Album Cor Iustitiae* carved into it.

On its top was a set of Sanguine Scales.

Ever aware of Rafe waiting at the top of the mine shaft for me, I squatted in front of the chest and wasted no time in trying to use waning magic to pick the lock. The instant my magic hit the lock, I was thrown back into the shelves behind me. Unfortunately, my head and back took the brunt of the blow. After being briefly showered with the lighter, looser stuff from the shelves, I got up—my head pounding and my body bruised—and walked over to try again. It had been a while since my magic hadn't cooperated for me but maybe I'd done something wrong.

Several more attempts with similar effects convinced me it wasn't me. Becoming increasingly agitated and impatient, I decided to try a different approach. I tried to move the Sanguine Scales off the top, thinking to just bypass the lock and blast my way into the chest, but the scales wouldn't budge from their position.

And that's when I knew. The Sanguine Scales were the real lock. Bialas' journal had said that a set of Sanguine Scales would measure the "amount of honor in a man's heart." And Bialas' last letter had said that Metatron had designed a "special set of Sanguine Scales" just for Orcus.

My guess was that the lock would open for those judged worthy by this set of Sanguine Scales.

Remembering the *monstrum metallum*, I stared at the scales. They looked just like the ones we'd seen at the Corterra bailey gaol—just before they turned into the metal monster that nearly killed us. These scales were green aged copper too, with two bowls, one large, one small, a set of weights, a knife, and two feathers, one white and one black.

I pulled the knife out of its well and made a shallow cut on my palm, letting a few drops of my blood drip into the smaller bowl. It was something I'd done countless times, but the rising magic of the scales gave me pause. The magic from the Sanguine Scales started melding with the magic that I could feel radiating from the chest. I guess that made sense since the White Heart and the scales had both been made by Metatron with perennial magic. If I'd had any doubts, however, about whether Metatron's reputation as a powerful alchemist was deserved, they were put to rest as I felt the gathering magic swirl around me.

I studied the feathers.

Black or white? Did I want to be judged as a hawk or a dove?

Choosing incorrectly would only cost me my life.

I hated to think these scales had anything to do with proving real guilt or innocence. To me, they were as trustworthy as any other trial by ordeal or trial by combat. I was generally and specifically against all forms of *Judicium Divinum*. But there had to be something that triggered the punishment if the "wrong" feather was picked. Maybe it was a matter of matching the blood in the bowl to the feather. I was an Onyx and a waning magic user, so maybe I should pick the black feather.

But if the choice was that easy, the trick to beating the Sanguine Scales would have been figured out long before now. So it had to be something more complicated. Or more subtle.

Or maybe something as simple as what I'd read in Bialas' journal—that the scales judged what was in one's heart. That is, how they felt about themselves. Hawk or dove? Sinner or saint? It was a better theory than any other I had and time was running out. I plucked the white feather out of its well.

I'd always wanted to be a dove, right?

I placed the feather in the bowl.

It was a mistake.

Chapter 24

ও

As the Sanguine Scales at Corterra had, these scales started morphing before my eyes. The copper weights, drops of blood, knife, and the white feather began to merge, grow, and shape themselves into something else—a demon berserker wearing ensorcelled armor and carrying the *mortem animae* curse.

It was Orcus, I thought breathlessly, *brought back to "life" like some horrid genie from the Sanguine Scales.*

Bialas' third letter and postscript now became all too clear. He'd said that Metatron had created a special set of Sanguine Scales just for Orcus. "What demon would refuse a personalized set of sacrificial scales if it meant he could become *Album Cor Iustitiae*'s eternal keeper?" he'd said. When I'd first read the letter I'd thought "eternal" was just Bialas' nod to the fact that, as a demon, Orcus would have lived for centuries after Bialas' death. And in his postscript, when Bialas had said, "Let no one disturb that final resting place," I'd thought he'd meant the final resting place for the White Heart. He'd also meant the final resting place for *Orcus*.

The personalized set of sacrificial scales that Metatron made for Orcus had cursed him and then tied him to the instrument of that curse, trapping him forever in his own strong room. It was elegantly efficient. In one fell swoop, Metatron had created an eternal, invincible guardian for the White Heart *and* took revenge on Orcus for his cruel treatment of the victims of the *mortem animae* curse—victims that Metatron had spent the latter half of his life trying to help.

But piecing together that ancient bit of mystery wasn't going to help me survive a fight with Orcus.

He was one of the largest, most fearsome demons I had ever seen. His build was as big as a barghest's, although he stood on two feet. He towered over me, his head nearly scraping the arched ceiling of the strong room. His face looked like a snake's, but he had a flatter nose and more prominent fangs, and he carried a scimitar that looked like a bigger version of the sacrificial knife I'd just used.

I stepped back in horror, only too aware that there was no quick exit from this room. My back hit the wall behind me and I glanced helplessly down at the slip passage I'd just squeezed through. Orcus advanced on me, not roaring as the *monstrum metallum* had, but instead croaking and clicking like a giant beetle. His gaze never left mine and I saw far more intelligence and cunning in his eyes than I'd ever seen in either the *monstrum metallum* or the *mortem animae*. He grinned evilly and I knew he wouldn't kill me quickly or touch me right away.

I shaped a matching scimitar and considered my options. Unlike the *mortem animae* at Septembhel, Orcus wouldn't be tempted to accept a lump of iron—if I had any—in return for leaving me alone. And even if he would, he wouldn't allow me to take the White Heart with me when I left.

Orcus came closer, emitting gentle croaks and clicks. The sounds gave me goose bumps. Slowly, I started stepping sideways, keeping the wall at my back and Orcus in front of me. But the distance between us lessened. I clamped down on my signature, not wanting to give Orcus any reason to change his behavior from the soft clicking to active attacking. I couldn't control my heartbeat though and it started to race. I swallowed and Orcus tipped his head back, snapped his jaws, and made a wet, snuffling sound. His waning magic rushed over me, which made me suddenly feel as if I'd been doused with boiling water and then shut in an iron maiden. I bit the inside of my cheek so I wouldn't cry out but a moment later Orcus skewered my upper left arm with his scimitar, pinning me to the wall.

I screamed. I couldn't help it. I knew instinctively that hearing me cry was exactly what he wanted. But there was no stopping my shriek as the fiery tip of his blade split my skin, sliced through bicep, brachialis, and bone, and then bore straight into the stone wall in back of me.

Why had I come in here? Was winning the Laurel Crown worth all this?

Probably not, but I couldn't turn back now. Luckily, my time in the Gridiron had prepared me for an automatic response. And, unlike the Gridiron, where I abstained from deadly force, I wasn't about to make that mistake here. I turned my shriek into a shout of rage as I swung my scimitar right at Orcus' neck. The anger and pain that I put into the blow was so great, I nearly chopped his head off. Almost a complete beheading on the first try. Not bad for someone who went out of her way not to step on ants.

But Orcus just righted his head on his neck and two seconds later it was as if the damage had never happened.

A spot of fear formed in my belly. It was small at first. After all, I wasn't completely inexperienced anymore. I'd gone up against all kinds of demons. And defeated them. I'd killed my fair share by now. I'd never lost a rank match in the Gridiron. And I was still my class's *Primoris*. My magic was strong and I had a will to live like no other.

But none of that mattered here. And so the spot of fear grew bigger and Orcus' grin grew wider. I fired up another scimitar and, even though the pain and loss of blood were causing me to feel faint, I tried to wrench my arm free of Orcus' fiery hold. I only succeeded in losing more blood.

Orcus fired up another sword. We parried a few times, but

my injury and vulnerable position made me weak and slow.
I was all too easily disarmed and I watched in dismay as my
weapon clattered to the floor, hissing and spitting like an
angry firecracker before finally burning out.

I stared at Orcus in the semi-darkness. The only light now
came from his swords—the one in my left arm and the other
one that was slowly moving toward my right arm. Was his
plan to pin me against the wall and use me for target practice?
I hardly thought this ruthless monster needed any more practice in being vile and evil. The only thing that saved me from
going completely insane was that he couldn't touch me without passing the *mortem animae* curse to me, which would
then prevent me from dying.

But then, of course, I realized the error of my thinking.
Because victims of the *mortem animae* curse could still feel.
They just couldn't die.

Orcus pointed the tip of his sword toward my right arm.

I started yelling then. As much from anger as pain. I was
well and truly pissed now. I didn't want to die—and I certainly didn't want to be tortured. I'd been overly confident
and way too blasé about the risks in coming here. I'd known
about the dangers, but only in an academic, theoretical, and
intellectual way. I'd *studied* about what it would be like to
attempt a trip to Hell and back, but I'd had no idea. No one
did. You had to *experience* it. And who in their right mind
would willingly experience Hell? Even if they thought they
could escape? It had been lunacy, mania, complete and utter
delirium to think I could do this.

But then I thought of the *mortem animae* up above me
who were still suffering in the bailey and I thought of Rafe
waiting up there for me, facing Luck knew what other
threats, and I knew I couldn't just give up. I needed to think
of a way to defeat Orcus no matter how impossible it seemed.

I narrowed my eyes at his copper helm, thinking how
ironic dove feathers looked on such a predatory, lethal being.
And that's when I remembered how we beat the *monstrum
metallum*. I'd incinerated the second feather and it had neu-
tralized its magic.

Would the same thing work again? Had it only worked before because the Corterra monstrum metallum had been birthed from a magical accident—the destruction of the Sanguine Scales when I'd kicked them off the table and they'd smashed to the floor? Or would it only work with the ashes from a dove's feather? Maybe I didn't want to see what this thing would be like if I added the ashes from a hawk's feather to it.

But it was the only plan I had. I gathered my feelings of revulsion and horror over this place, what had been done here, and what was still being done here. I gathered my feelings of pain and helplessness over my current situation, my feelings of worry and concern over Rafe, and my longing for us to be free of this damned place. And I harvested the hatred I had for Orcus and what he stood for. I laced my waning magic with all of those emotions and then shaped it into a big, angry storm of fiery ice basilisks.

It was a personal record. The waning magic war birds at Corterra had been impressive, and Nova even more so, but I outdid myself with my small army of winged demons. If I wasn't aware of how much they would cost me magically, I would have thought after that I was invincible.

But I knew it was my last-ditch effort to save myself. It was do, die, or become eternally cursed at this point.

My flaming basilisk swarm flew right into Orcus' face. It stunned him and gave me just enough time to wrench the scimitar out of my arm. My right hand burned as if I'd just squeezed a hot coal in my fist. Orcus' scimitar had been made with his waning magic not mine, so it burned me the same as it would anyone else.

I ducked underneath his flailing arms, careful not to touch him, and ran to the chest. I plucked the black feather out of the well of the still intact Sanguine Scales and incinerated it, blowing the ashes straight toward Orcus.

Nothing happened.

Nothing.

I wasn't sure how many more defeats I could take without giving up. As before on other assignments, I started to question whether Luck wanted me to die. But I'd resolved that question already (or so I thought). And the answer was a resounding "no." If he wanted me dead, I'd be dead. It was that simple.

So again I searched for a way out. Something I'd missed. And saw it in the most obvious place of all. Carved beneath the words *Album Cor Iustitiae* on the chest were the words:

"Tempus edax rerum."
Etiam eorum qui vivificarentur per magicas perennis.

I certainly wasn't as good at interpreting ancient languages as an Angel would have been but I was able to translate it quickly enough.

"Time devours all things."
Even those kept alive through perennial magic.

I had a feeling the first part wasn't just a truism.

It was a perennial magic spell. It was Orcus' "off switch." The only question was whether I'd be able to cast it. But there was no time to waste on worrying. In my loudest, most commanding voice, I shouted, *"Tempus edax rerum!"*

It worked. My relief was so palpable I sank to my knees as Orcus vanished into the ether. After that, everything happened pretty quickly. As Orcus' sword's light died with him, I found myself plunged into a blackness more intense than any I'd experienced before. It wasn't like closing my eyes. It was as if I were truly blind. There was simply no light down here except for what we brought. *Lucem in tenebras ferimus. Into the darkness we bring light, right?*

But had I just spent all my fire on that ice basilisk swarm? How long would I have to wait here for my magic to return?

I held my hand out, palm up and willed a fireball to form there. It should have been the most rudimentary, automatic act by now, something akin to covering my mouth when I yawned, and yet, it was as difficult as it had been for me when I'd first enrolled at St. Luck's. Finally, a fireball took shape. Frankly, part of me was surprised I was able to light anything so soon after shaping the ice basilisk swarm. But either I was getting better at shaping animate beasts out of waning magic or the swarm simply hadn't "lived" long enough to truly tax me. I relaxed and let my fireball enlarge and hover near my shoulder. As quickly as I could, I wrapped one of my leather belts around my arm to staunch the bleeding. It felt as if a barghest had chewed my arm off, but at least I was now only minutes away from one of Rafe's soothing healing spells. I flipped open the lid of the chest.

Inside was an exquisitely beautiful millennium-old gold scabbard, hand carved with hundreds of whorls, scrolls, and spirals and set with no less than a half dozen precious stones.

And the sword.

Album Cor Iustitiae lay in the chest beside its scabbard. It looked stunning and felt electrifying. Metatron *had* carved it out of an opal, I marveled, wondering where he'd managed to find a gemstone large enough. Clearly, however, after this experience, I would no longer question Metatron's ability to create awesome and terrifying magical objects.

I admit, even after defeating Orcus, which should have boosted my confidence enough for me to think I could single-handedly take on an entire *rogare* army, I was still afraid to touch it. But I didn't have the luxury of waiting for courage. With a trembling hand, I reached inside the chest and withdrew the sword.

Touching it was less electrifying than I'd feared, but still a shock. A zap of perennial magic lashed at my fingertips upon contact, raced up my arm, and popped in the air above my shoulder. I jumped but kept hold of the sword. I raised the White Heart up, tip to ceiling, twisting the blade so that I could see its glinting edges—one side razor sharp and the other dull as a butter knife—in the light of my flickering fireball. Gazing upon it was intoxicating, but a moment later I averted my eyes, grabbed the scabbard, sheathed the sword, and headed back to the grim task of scooting back under the slip passage.

I slid the White Heart under first and then I lay down on

the floor and squeezed back into that coffin-like ditch that led to the outside world. *If only I could emerge immediately up top next to Rafe!* I'd already decided I was going to give him the biggest, longest, sloppiest kiss ever.

Slipping out of the strong room seemed to take a lot less effort and time than slipping in. Maybe it's because I'd already done it. Or maybe it was because the hard part was over. Or maybe it was because I now knew that we were on the "and back" part of this race to Hell and back. Whatever. Didn't matter. The fact that I was on my way out buoyed my mood considerably.

Once out of the strong room, I scooped up the bulkier clothes I'd shucked in order to slip into it and ran back through the narrow passageway. I threw my clothes and the sword into the bucket and hopped in. I yanked on the rope, signaling to Rafe that he should start turning the crank and pulling me up out of this blasted pit. When the bucket lurched upward, I sighed with relief, thinking how glad I was that I'd never see this place again.

Chapter 25

❧

The trip up to the top of Tartarus' mining pit took forever. I was impatient and not nearly as fatalistic as when I'd been heading down. I craned my neck upward toward the growing gray circle the entire time. When I finally arrived at the top, my neck was aching and my arm felt like a rat had crawled inside and started to gnaw on it. *But I was free.*

As soon as the bucket rose above the mouth of the pit, my face was hit with millions of ice pellets. The wind was relentless. It felt like I was standing on the bow of a boat, but instead of the warm, sun sparkled spray of the Lethe, I was being sprayed with hail from a sky that looked like the dark billowing plume of an explosion. Faintly, beneath the roar of the wind, the out of tune violin played on. I wasn't sure which gave me greater chills, the wind or the discordant melody. I narrowed my eyes and raised a flat hand to my forehead so that I could see Rafe as he pulled me toward him with the shepherd's hook. But it wasn't Rafe.

It was Peter.

My relief turned to alarm. I spun around looking for Rafe.

His welcome face emerged out of the shadows. He looked relieved to see that I was out of the pit, but he also looked wary and angry—because Brunus was holding a knife to his throat. Rafe's hands were tied and he'd been gagged.

I scrambled to unhook the shepherd's hook from the rope that was holding the bucket. I didn't necessarily want to be suspended over this pit, but neither did I want Peter pulling me out. The bucket swung wildly from side to side. The pitching and rocking of the bucket, the jarring musical notes, and the swaying images of Peter scowling at me and Brunus holding a sharp, fiery blade to Rafe's throat, all combined into one big, dark, delusional nightmare. But I knew it was real.

Brunus stared at me with those mud brown eyes of his. Like Rafe, both he and Peter had grown beards. Brunus' beard was big and bushy, covering the entire lower portion of his face. But his eyes were all too visible. Even if I couldn't sense his signature, I would have known we were in trouble. Brunus' expression was deadly, vengeful, and tinted with dementia.

But his signature was worse. Brunus' magic had always smelled rotten to me, but tonight it felt noxious. It felt like radiation poisoning, pulsing with sickness, greed, jealousy, and hate. Like a concave mirror, it seemed to absorb all of my positive emotions and turn them upside down so that, when I felt Brunus' signature, all I felt was a hollowed out, twisted version of mine. His signature reflected, and amplified, all of my fear, hunger, and pain. My arm felt as if it had been sawed off. I realized I hadn't eaten anything in almost twelve hours. And I became almost paralyzed by my own vulnerability. Not just because I hung suspended over a three-hundred-foot pit with only a thin rope holding me in place, but because my Guardian Angel (whom I loved with my recently scarred heart) was being held captive by my heartless opponent.

"Nouiomo Onyx," Brunus sneered, "*Primoris* of the second year class at St. Luck's, daughter of the executive, ex-field partner of former classmate Aristos Carmine, and teacher's pet."

The bucket swung left, right . . . left, right . . . I realized, in this wind, it might never stop. I widened my stance and gripped the rim of the bucket with my left hand, leaving my right hand free to hold a weapon. But I held back lighting anything. I could sense in Brunus' signature that he wasn't just standing on a physical edge, he was on a psychological edge as well.

"I'm hardly the teacher's pet, Brunus." I thought of all the times Rochester's teaching methods had nearly killed me in Manipulation and how disappointed Glashia often was with my inartifice. But Brunus scoffed at me.

"From the start, you were favored. Seknecus gave you his Manipulation books to study from, Rochester arranged to have his old friend, Delgato, train you in unorthodox ways disallowed by the faculty, and now this semester, you were allowed to compete in the Laurel Crown Race even though your academic history is littered with the evidence of your weakness and inferiority."

Rafe shifted, twisted, and rammed his head back into Brunus' face. Brunus' nose started bleeding. He leaned in close to Rafe's ear and said something too low for me to hear. But Rafe looked at the rope and then me as he stood stiffly in front of Brunus. Brunus smiled and the temperature seemed to drop another ten degrees. Peter reached for the bucket with the shepherd's hook again and this time I let him. In hindsight, attempting to reason with two attempted murderers while swinging over a three-hundred-foot pit wasn't the soundest plan. As I came closer, Peter's gaze swept over every exposed inch of me, from my bloody arm to my leather bustier, from my bare décolletage to my newly blackened demon mark. His face registered equal parts surprise and disgust with just the slightest hint of hesitation.

Good, I thought. *He* should *be afraid of me.*

I neared the edge and Peter reached for the bucket and clamped it into its small dock. I started to hop out but Peter grabbed me by the arm. My left arm. I winced and wished immediately that I hadn't. I could almost hear Glashia's hiss of disapproval. I straightened my back and looked Peter squarely in the eyes. An odd moment passed between us. I remembered the countless hours we'd spent together as children, swimming together in Cocytus Creek, walking together along the Lemiscus, hanging out at the Etincelle docks. I remembered Peter throwing stones at my bedroom window, the messages he'd left for me on my bedroom mirror, the secret meetings in the Aster garden, and the night we found Lucifer's tomb—the night he'd first kissed me. Peter must have sensed the direction of my thoughts. His face softened and his grip on my arm loosened. I wasn't sure I wanted to hear his answer, but I had to ask.

"How could you have used the *Suffoca Ignem* curse against me? Did you really mean to kill me, Peter?"

For the span of a single heartbeat, I thought he'd beg my forgiveness or try to convince me he hadn't. The part of me that didn't want to be the victim of such a horrible betrayal wanted him to. But then his expression hardened and his grip tightened. Instead of my childhood friend, he became a stranger again. He became somebody who hated what I'd become.

"Brunus asked me for a curse that would take you out of the race. I meant for it kill your magic, not you," he said. "Now, where is it?"

Whether intentionally or not, Peter had laced his voice with bitter magic and it hurt to hear it. It was a blunt reminder of how powerful his spellcasting could be. And my own spellcaster was still incapacitated. I saw out of the corner of my eye that Rafe was starting to give Brunus trouble again, but he was at a severe disadvantage. I tried to step back from the edge of the pit, but Peter held me tight. I fired up a sword and held it low in my hand. Brunus hit Rafe on the back of the head with the butt of his blade. I knew the next time Brunus struck Rafe he wouldn't use the blunt end.

"Where is what?" I said, feigning ignorance and stalling for time.

"*Album Cor Iustitiae*, Noon. The White Heart." With each word, Peter's voice grew louder, angrier, and more laced with magic. "The sword Metatron made for Justica. I want it. *Now*." By the time Peter said the word *now*, it felt like he was driving a spike through my ear.

"I don't have it. It wasn't down there."

"Glashia gave you something, didn't he?" Brunus shouted. "Always the favorite, right, Onyx? He gave you a map. Or more clues. There's a reason you went down there." But instead of pointing into the pit, he moved Rafe closer to it.

I started to get scared. Rafe didn't know a levitation spell. We'd proven that much climbing our way in here. And if Brunus let go, there would be nothing, not even a thin rope to stop Rafe's fall.

"Glashia gave me nothing," I said, not caring that my voice now sounded desperate. Glashia wouldn't approve, but I didn't think pretending I wasn't afraid would help either.

"You're lying," Brunus said, pushing Rafe farther toward the edge. Rafe started struggling again and Brunus held the knife closer to his throat. A few drops of blood trickled down Rafe's neck.

"It wasn't Glashia," I said, talking quickly. "It was someone else. But you're right. I had a map. Orcus kept a strong room down in his mining pit. But the White Heart wasn't in it."

Peter leaned over the bucket's rim and peered inside. He stared at the White Heart, which was nestled amongst my clothes at the bottom of the bucket, for longer than he needed to in order to recognize what it was. *What was he thinking?* In an alternate version of my life—one in which Peter had not betrayed me—it might have been Peter and me trying to bluff our way out of this deadly situation. But that wasn't the version of my life I was living in. Peter raised his head up and met my gaze. His look was hard and then he turned to Brunus.

"She found it," was all he said.

With those words, I watched Brunus' next two moves in what seemed like slow motion. His grip on the knife tightened as he prepared to draw it across Rafe's throat and his body tensed as he prepared to shove him off the edge and into the pit.

I remembered all of the times that Brunus Olivine had

been the cause of my pain, discomfort, humiliation, or worse. The time he'd knocked my books over before that first class we'd had together, the rush of magic he sent up my legs when Rochester introduced us, the countless times he'd tried to kill me with his beloved nadziak, the broken noses, the burns, the blood—the time he'd tried to bludgeon Night at the Barrister's Ball. The fact that he'd killed Martius Einion during the rank matches. And more recently, Brunus' horrid and heart-wrenching treatment of Telesto. How he'd sliced him, stabbed him, and finally killed him when the poor beast no longer could or would serve as his mount. I remembered that Brunus had committed attempted murder when he'd shot an arrow that was laced with the *Suffoca Ignem* curse toward my heart.

Brunus Olivine was a vile and loathsome person. But that wasn't why I did what I did. No, in those last few moments, two other images came to mind that cinched my decision. The two skeletons at Corterra's bailey gaol and Kalisto's warning: *One out of every two hunters who follow the Old Trail will not return.*

It was simple really. I didn't want Rafe and me to be the ones who died.

After that, instead of in slow motion, everything seemed to happen at once. Brunus pressed his knife into Rafe's throat and stepped forward, Peter leaned into the bucket to retrieve the White Heart, and I threw the brightest, strongest, most densely controlled blast of waning magic I'd ever thrown right between Brunus' eyes. It was better and more brilliant than the diamond-strength shaft I'd thrown that had instantly killed Serafina, the first demon I'd ever killed. A second later I threw another blast—a rougher, cooler one that had more *push* than *penetrate* behind it—at Rafe's shoulder. Then I jammed the heel of my hand into Peter's nose, wrenched the White Heart free from his grasp, and shoved him backward.

I too stepped back from the edge of the mining pit, just in time to see Brunus' body tumble into it and Rafe fall backward onto the ground.

I unsheathed *Album Cor Iustitiae* and stood before Peter

likely looking like vengeance personified. I could feel my hair writhing in the wind as I raised the White Heart in the air. I felt its eerie magic gather, causing the hairs on the back of my neck to raise. In the predawn light, the White Heart glowed like white fire.

"Run, Peter," I said. "Run very far because if I ever see you again, I will kill you."

His wide, wild eyes narrowed as he glanced from me to the pit to Rafe and back to me again. He glared at my black mark and stared at the White Heart and then finally, he turned on his heel and left.

I watched him walk through Tartarus' bailey toward the barbican and portcullis. He never looked back. When he passed from sight, I lowered the White Heart and ran over to Rafe, crouching down next to him. *Still alive*, thank Luck! I ripped the gag out of his mouth.

"Fara warned me about you," he croaked, sitting up. My hands were shaking but I managed to untie his hands. "She told me not to play with fire, but I couldn't resist." I wrapped my arms around his neck and he reached up to rub his shoulder.

"Damn, Onyx, you throw one hell of a fiery punch."

He started murmuring the words to a healing spell and I fought not to burst into tears.

Chapter 26

Rafe had a slight nick on his neck and a dislocated shoulder, but overall his injuries were minor so it didn't take him long to heal himself. I grabbed my clothes from the bottom of the bucket and put on my long-necked sweater, down-filled vest, and heavy, hooded cloak. Just the act of bundling up against the wind and cold seemed to calm and comfort me. If it hadn't been for the discordant music and the ghastly sight of the *mortem animae* in Tartarus' courtyard, I would have felt lighter than air. Instead, I felt only moderately relieved, as if I still had more enemies to defeat, which was not a comfortable feeling.

I was just about to resheath the White Heart when I had an idea. Oh, it was a dangerous one, there was no doubt about that. But it was one I felt I couldn't disregard without some thought. How could I walk out of here as Peter had, leaving the *mortem animae* behind to suffer for another millennium, possibly more, or forever? Turning my back on them when I might hold the key to their salvation seemed like the most egregious sin imaginable. I glanced from the *mortem animae* to the White Heart.

My mother had warned me not to use perennial magic. Or at least not perennial magic that had been artificially placed in things. She seemed to think that it was unnatural and could only lead to *bad things*. Joy also had warned me against using the White Heart. Although her admonishment was slightly more specific. She'd said the sword might be able to "make someone who is absent, present again."

Think about what that means, Noon. If you had the power to bring someone back, would you?

But it was Joy's ancestor, Kaspar Bialas, who'd been the most direct. He'd said in his letters that he was hiding the White Heart because he believed it was a modern-day Sword of Damocles. Bialas had seemed to believe that the *threat* of the White Heart's use (versus its destruction or actual use) was what kept Halja properly balanced after Metatron introduced it to our world. Bialas too seemed to believe that the White Heart might be capable of far more than just curing the *mortem animae*, which was Metatron's original goal when he'd created it. Like Joy, Bialas had also believed that the White Heart might be able to make someone who is absent, present again. To bring them back, which he most emphatically stated in his letters he did not want. In fact, Bialas had spent eleven years in Tartarus building Orcus' strong room and then he'd imprisoned both Orcus and the sword within it before he left, to avoid the possibility of anyone either using or destroying the sword. Bialas couldn't have been clearer that his preference was an empty throne. I didn't have to pull his letters out again in order to remember his words.

I want my children and my children's children to rule themselves. And if that is a sin I will willingly burn for committing it.

And yet . . .

How could Bialas have turned a blind eye to the *mortem animae*'s cursed existence here at Tartarus? It would take more than a blindfold. It would take a heart made of stone. And besides, no one came back to life in Halja, right?

"Spill it, Onyx," Rafe said, putting on his hat and raising the hood of his cloak. "What are you thinking? You can't possibly be considering resting here before moving on. Are you worried about Aster ambushing us?"

I shook my head slowly and swallowed.

Was what I was considering really as grave as Aurelia, Joy, and Kaspar Bialas thought it was?

I only wanted to find a way to help the *mortem animae*, not bring back one of the lost lords of Armageddon. But I was also aware of that old adage, "The road to Hell is paved with good intentions."

Was the mortem animae's *continued suffering the price all Haljans paid for peace?*

I couldn't believe that. Didn't want to. But I also didn't have to make the decision alone. I told Rafe what I was thinking of doing. And I told him all about my spring side discussion with Aurelia and my backyard patio discussion with Joy, and I had Rafe read each of the letters from Kaspar Bialas.

All the while, in back of us, the *mortem animae* repeated the atrocious cycle of torture and abuse that they'd been repeating for almost a thousand years. It had to stop and I laid my case for ending it before Rafe. I didn't want him to be the sole judge of what happened here, but I did want his advice. After listening to what I had to say and reading the letters, he put them back in the box and said, "See? I knew you'd be interesting." It was one of the things he used to say when we first started working together—that I was like a jar of pickled hearts.

Rafe never told me why he agreed with me. Just that he did. Told me whatever happened as a result of my using *Album Cor Iustitiae* he'd stand by me. That it would take more than ancient magic for him to ever stop believing in *me*.

I nodded and swallowed and turned toward the *mortem animae*.

I didn't know how sentient they were. Enough to still feel pain, longing, and a vague sense of their surroundings at least and obviously a little bit more because when I turned toward them holding the White Heart in my hand, they turned toward me as well. One of them stepped forward. I recognized him. He was the one who had stepped forward at Septembhel. The one who'd eaten the iron "coin" with the hole in it. The coin that had once been a cursed arrow tip embedded in my chest.

The *mortem animae* knelt before me. I tensed. How was I supposed to use the White Heart to cure him? Lop his head off? Ugh. But then I remembered that, in medieval times, some outpost lords had "knighted" their Hyrke sheriffs by giving them an accolade—tapping them on the shoulder with the dull side of a sword blade. That seemed like a much kinder way to bestow the possible blessing of the White Heart upon him.

I met Rafe's gaze and then slowly lowered the White Heart's blade down onto the shoulder of the *mortem animae* who was kneeling in front of me.

What had I expected?

Best-case scenario? That he be cured, of course.

Worst case? That his body would explode and shower Rafe and me with its bits so that we too became infected and unable to help the other 999+ of them, including us.

Worst, worst case? That someone, or someones, who had died a very, very long time ago might be brought back to life, thus ushering in Armageddon II.

It didn't matter what I expected. Because nothing happened. Nothing. Nada. Zip. Zilch.

I raised the sword up and placed it on the shoulder of the *mortem animae* again. It was less of a tap this time and more of a smack. Then I placed it on his other shoulder. Then, after some deliberation with Rafe, I gave him first a ceremonial cut and then a full-fledged beheading. I was afraid it would be gruesome, but *nothing happened.*

Each time I tried to touch him with the White Heart, it passed through him as if he were made of smoke.

Finally, the *mortem animae* pointed. As he had back at Septembhel. But this time he pointed to my backpack.

I picked it up and started riffling through it, trying to

think of what might be in there that this cursed man would be interested in. I'd already given him the only bit of iron I had. The only metal I had left was the tin box full of letters and the bizarre burlap sack full of gardening tools.

I looked up. And pulled the burlap sack out of my pack. The sack hummed with perennial magic—*naturally imbued* perennial magic.

Of course, I thought. *Shoulda been obvious, right? I mean who doesn't use their gardening tools to remove curses?* I would have snorted and laughed out loud if the situation weren't so serious.

I resheathed the White Heart and took the scythe out of Aurelia's burlap sack. All it took was a nick from its blade and the *mortem animae* was gone in an explosion of light, heat, and sparks. *Huh,* I thought. *Perennial magic. You turn it on; you turn it off.* The iron coin I'd given the cursed man at Septembhel dropped to the ground in front of me. It was all that was left of him, but instead of mourning his passing, I celebrated it.

One by one, each of the *mortem animae* came up to be released from their curse. I knew that some of them had been guilty of the sins they'd been accused of when they'd been judged guilty by the Sanguine Scales, but many more had not been, and *all* had suffered enough by now.

It took until daylight to free them all. After the last one had been liberated, I picked the iron coin up off the ground and held it to my eye. It appeared that the world was the same. The only difference was that there were no more *mortem animae*. That could only be a good thing.

I yanked out a few more strands of my hair and tied the coin around my neck again. The world was so unchanged in fact that the damned discordant music was still playing.

We could have left. There was nothing to keep us in Tartarus. I'd found the White Heart and freed the *mortem animae* from their curse.

But we didn't leave.

It was the out of tune melody, tickling the back of my ear, crawling into my brain, poking around my subconscious, as if there was still unfinished business here.

Shouldn't ghostly, ghastly music stop once the villain is defeated and the victims saved?

Tartarus' courtyard appeared eerily empty now that the *mortem animae* were gone. We made our way past the bile-inducing torture devices and ascended the tower stairs of Orcus' old keep. This is where the false trail laid by Bialas' journal had led past White Heart hunters. Even though I felt a strong sense of foreboding, it was still amazing to know that I was treading on the same set of stairs that Graemite, Percevalus, and Jacindus had tread on. And it was even more amazing to know that I'd found what they hadn't. (Although I'd had help, of course.)

I realized, as we navigated our way up the spiral stair-case, that the inharmonious sounds were coming from above. At the top was a small room with arched windows that looked in every direction. To the north, I could see the Fiddleback and the remains of the old elevated rail line. To the east, low mountains in shades of copper and pine. To the south, taller mountains in shades of pitch, pearl, and blue. To the west, the mining pit I'd crawled out of earlier, the horrid metal structures in the courtyard below, and farther off, the ravine that served as the castle's moat and the barbican and portcullis that Peter had left through.

In the center of the room was an enormous metal frame. On one side was a wheel and, lying all over the scarred wooden floor, were the broken bits of whatever had hung on the frame.

It had been a bell. And the sound was coming from its pieces.

Apparently Tartarus' keep had been built around one of Halja's ancient pre-Apocalyptic bell towers. And pieces of the old bell were still here. It was remarkable.

But that isn't why I did what I did. I did it because I'd seen this broken bell before in Demeter's spring when I'd taken that healing swim with my mother. I realized that nearly all of the things I'd seen then were things that I'd seen before or during my trip to Tartarus: a bloody tooth, a bonfire, an arrow, a crossroads, a jail cell, a set of Sanguine Scales, the iron coin with a hole in it—which I now wore around my neck—and a white sword. There were only three things I hadn't yet seen: the huge, slobbering, grinning beast with a star on its forehead, although I'd seen a miniature version of it (Telesto and Brisaya's whelp, which we'd left behind in Maize), the dam with lightning in the sky above it, and the broken bell.

But in my vision the broken bell had been welded back together.

"I want to fix it," I said to Rafe.

"Why?"

I didn't answer him at first, just stared out of the window at the wreckage in Tartarus' courtyard and at the base of Tartarus in the Fiddleback. After a while, I said simply:

"Because I think I'm supposed to."

Rafe raised his eyebrows, staring at me, and then finally shrugged.

"How?"

I think lack of sleep was making him monosyllabic. I smiled at him.

"With waning magic. Let's gather up the pieces and I'll weld them back together again. Come on, let's ring the Angel's bell just once before we go."

Rafe looked skeptical about my plan but helped bring the pieces to me one by one. After I'd patched up all the holes and sealed all the edges back together, it looked like the version of it that I'd seen beneath the water in Maize.

Rafe walked over to the wheel and gave it a whirl. At that point, I think he just wanted to leave—to get away from Tartarus so that we could find somewhere safe to sleep. But, as with the first time I'd tried to use the White Heart, nothing happened.

"Wait!" I cried suddenly, laughing. "Where's the clapper?" After a few fruitless minutes of searching, we admitted defeat. Until Rafe reached forward and grabbed the iron coin

from around my neck and gently pulled. He held it up by the
few pieces of hair that I'd used to tie it around my neck and
dangled it in front of me.

We grinned at each other and then Rafe crawled under the
bell with it. I stood at the wheel for a moment, waiting for
Rafe to stand up. When he did, I spun the wheel. The bell
rang . . .

And everything changed.

At least it did for us, even if nothing changed for the rest
of the million or so people in Halja. The metallic *GONG*
sounded in the tiny stone room, much louder than it should
have been with only that small iron coin making the sound.
Clear and bright, it was the audio version of a shooting star.
It was the opposite of discordant in every way. I felt the
sound, acoustically, physically, and magically. Because it
wasn't just sound; it was perennial magic.

It knocked us right onto our butts.

And when we got up again, we weren't the same. Or
rather, we were exactly as we had been previously.

That feeling that I'd had last semester—when we'd passed
through Ebony's Elbow and my "anchor" memory had been
ripped out and replaced with Rafe's—was back. It felt like
someone had plucked a piece of hair from underneath my
scalp, not on top of it. And the memory I'd had of Rafe's
brother's funeral—of Bhereg's/Ari's *premature* funeral—
was gone. All I had left was the memory of having Rafe's
memory, not the memory itself. To say that the whole experience left me feeling disoriented and confused was an understatement.

I looked over at Rafe, who was also sitting on the floor. He
met my gaze with an unreadable expression on his face. I had
no idea what he was thinking.

When our heads cleared as much as they were going to
clear, I got up and ran to the windows. Outside, all was not
as it had been previously. Instead of the remains of men and
their machines, the courtyard and the Fiddleback were now
full of flowers. Hundreds of them. Thousands of them. They
were lilies and they shined like stars.

When I picked the White Heart up off the floor where it had fallen, it felt infinitely heavier. In fact, I could barely lift it. And its glow was gone. Now, it just looked like a dirty, dull blade. It could have been carved from an opal, marble, or concrete for all anyone could see under the coat of grime that was now on it.

The White Heart's magic was gone with our borrowed memories.

Perennial magic, I thought, gritting my teeth. *You turn it on; you turn it off.*

I ran over to the wheel and gave it another crank. Rafe stood at the north window, his back to me, legs wide, arms crossed in front of him.

The bell did not ring again.

I finally climbed beneath it to see what was stopping it.

The clapper—the iron coin with the hole in it—was gone.

Chapter 27

ॐ

Rafe and I said very little to each other as we retraced our steps across the Fiddleback. Mostly, it was that we were tired. Exhausted really, physically, emotionally, and magically. By the time we reached the southern base of Septembhel, we collapsed and crawled into our bedrolls without even pitching our tent. Luckily, the weather was cold but clear and our magic, though depleted, was strong enough to keep us warm while we slept. At some point that night, I woke up screaming—shouting someone's name, I think, although once awake, I couldn't remember who or what the dream had been about.

The next morning I awoke with Rafe's arm draped across my middle, but that was the last time he touched me that day. The next day was similar. Despite our having accomplished our objective (I'd found my target and we would likely make it back to New Babylon in a little under two weeks; I had a real shot at winning the Laurel Crown), things between us seemed strained. Rafe was detached and quiet, reserved and withdrawn. We reached Corterra by nightfall.

It was an odd, though not unpleasant, experience seeing the wreckage of Corterra's bailey gaol and the area where we'd made our stand against the *monstrum metallum* and the ice basilisks now that the worst part of our journey was over. Snow still covered the ground, but the sky was clear and the wind wasn't as punishing as it had been the last time we'd been here. Though the urge to press on was strong, we realized we'd have to sleep at some point. The trip was far too long to make without resting. In fact, without Telesto and Brisaya, we'd be lucky if the return trip north took only twice as long as the trip south had.

So we crawled back inside Corterra's bailey gaol to sleep for the night. As he'd done previously, Rafe cast Impenetrable over the top of the stairwell and then cast a spell of warmth below. The effect of being in such a comparatively warm and safe place would have been extraordinarily comforting but for Rafe's unusual silence.

After we lay down, I spread my cloak over both of us and he tensed immediately. I finally asked him what was wrong. He sighed, relaxed, and pulled me close. But he held off kissing me. He hadn't kissed me since we'd rang that blasted bell. Until now, I hadn't really thought about it because for the first twelve hours after that I'd slept, and for the next twelve, I'd hiked. But now that we'd stopped again, and we were in a relatively safe place and not quite as exhausted, it was time to address the loss of our borrowed memories and what that might mean.

"I've just been thinking about where we go from here, that's all, Onyx. If you win the Laurel Crown, is your plan still to work for the Jayneses on board the *Alliance* next semester?"

I stiffened. I didn't think Rafe was asking because he thought it odd I wanted to work for Hyrkes. Rafe was the last person who would care about social distinctions or civic ambitions. Rather, I feared he might be asking because *he* might be having second thoughts about next semester.

"Is there someone else you'd rather work for?" I asked. "Or someplace else you think would be a better fit for us?"

Us.

That word suddenly seemed to take shape and hover in the air. Was there still an "us" now that I'd rung the Angels' bell? Had Rafe's *madly, deeply, fiercely* feelings for me disappeared along with his borrowed memory of Ari's loving me that way?

Luck, I hoped not. How cruel, twisted, and unfair would that be?

But Rafe's hesitation in answering my questions told me something was wrong. That *something* had changed.

"Noon," he began slowly, looking away, unable to meet my gaze. "There's nothing more I'd rather do than spend next semester with you on the river . . . or anywhere else . . . battling *rogares* or doing whatever else you felt needed to be done . . ."

His voice trailed off. By then I was stiff as a board and barely breathing.

"But?" My voice sounded angrier than I intended. I think I was already starting to gird myself for whatever hurtful news I sensed was coming. I slipped out from under my cloak and stood up. I rubbed my arms and paced, trying to ignore the panic I was starting to feel. After a few moments, I stopped in front of Rafe and leaned on the wall behind me, looking down at him. Finally, he looked up, meeting my gaze once again.

That look. I'd never seen Rafe look so somber. Or so serious. I swallowed.

He stood up and leaned on the wall opposite me. We stared at each other in the bluish blackness.

"But . . ." he repeated, clasping his hands behind his back, almost as if he were afraid of what he might do with them if he kept them free. "I'm not sure I could live with myself if, in addition to almost drowning Bhereg, I kept you away from him too. Ari might not like me, but he's never wronged me either. How could I justify treating him so horribly not just once, but twice?"

Suddenly, I wanted to scream. There were so many things

wrong with what Rafe had just said but by far the biggest was: "*You're* not keeping me from Ari. I am."

I clenched my fists and looked away, worried about how revealing my words had been.

Why had I let this happen? Why had I given in to the temptation to kiss Rafe?

I'd raced this race partly for the privilege of continuing to work with him. Had I ruined our friendship and professional relationship by giving in to my nascent romantic feelings for him while still dealing with my latent feelings for Ari? Nascent romantic feelings I might have been able to ignore if it had not been for Rafe's gentle prodding. My eyes stung and I was unaccountably angry. With myself. With Rafe. With Ari. With Luck.

"Nouiomo," Rafe whispered. My head snapped back toward him. "You still love him, don't you?"

We stood there for so long, I'm pretty sure time stood still with us. I became numb. With cold and the desperate desire to *feel nothing*. Then I became hot—so hot I thought I'd burn the half-destroyed bailey gaol with us in it. Turn the area within which we were standing into one big crematorium. My feelings of love, loss, injustice, bitterness, and longing became overwhelming and nearly impossible to control. Throughout this endless expanse of time, Rafe just stood there. Looking at me. Waiting.

He either had more faith in me than I did or he was perfectly willing to burn to death with me.

"I'm going to train as one of the Ophanim knights when we get back," he finally said, transforming his face into a perfect mask of nonchalance, as if he was telling me what he was going to order at Empyr or the Black Onion for his first home-from-the-trail meal.

"Neither of us is sure anymore if my feelings for you are real. Right?" Rafe continued softly, "That's what you've been thinking about and wondering since the bell rang, isn't it? Well, this will give us a chance to sort things out."

"Sort things out apart, you mean."

"Were we ever really together?" His voice was almost a whisper now, as if he was just as afraid of asking the question as hearing the answer.

It hurt a lot more than I thought it would. I hadn't realized until that moment how much I truly cared for Rafe—as more than just a friend.

I turned my face so he couldn't see how upset I was. If he wanted to join the Ophanim, I wasn't going to stop him. If he wanted to use my feelings for Ari—feelings I often wished I didn't have—as a reason to leave, I wasn't going to beg him to stay. And if he wanted to suggest that the Angels' bell had taken away his feelings for me . . . Well, I wasn't going to argue.

Because it must have. Because no one could be strong enough to walk away from someone they loved that much.

Except that I had.

Thank Luck Rafe couldn't sense how upset I was by my signature. All I had to do to survive the rest of this night was get my emotions under control and make sure that my face reflected none of the anguish I was currently feeling when I turned back to face him.

It took more than a few minutes, but I did it. I dug a deep well inside of me. A well so deep Orcus would have been slack-jawed with envy. And then I dumped my sense of betrayal (which wasn't fair), my sense of loss (which was enormous), and my utter panic (I'd gotten used to having Raphael Sinclair in my life; thinking about his absence now caused my throat to seize) over its edge. Off they went, tumbling down into the darkness.

I turned back to Rafe, my face as nonchalant as his.

Glashia would have been proud.

I t took us almost nine days to reach Maize from Corterra. By that time I was so sick of auster hare meat, I thought I might become a vegetarian. I'd restrung my snowshoes a total of seven times, lost my snow goggles, and ironically become sunburned. But, due to our magic, Rafe and I were able to avoid some of the risks that are more dangerous to other hunters who come to the Old Trail. We were never in any serious danger of frostbite, exposure, or freezing to death, although we did have one run-in with a yeti. Luckily for both us and it, a few fireballs and a blast of Angel light convinced it that running was preferable to fighting.

As we neared Maize, it occurred to me that likely no one would be at the springhouse. That guest house was reserved for waning magic users and I doubted Demeter had many. So I asked Rafe to hike to the hospital to let the Mederies know we were back. It was early evening and the last train to New Babylon had left. We'd be spending the night regardless of how quickly we conducted our business here, so our ever-present sense of urgency to return to New Babylon was temporarily quelled.

I walked up the dirt path toward the barghest pen in a contemplative mood. My hood was down, my pack was light, and, while the White Heart still felt heavy to me, I'd gotten used to its weight in between my back and my pack. I rounded a bend in the trail, came out of the woods, and stepped into the clearing where the barghest pen was. And that's when I saw her.

The barghest with the white star on her forehead. She was full grown now. What had Linnaea said the night before we'd first come to this pen?

"I'm looking forward to it. And if the barghests knew you were coming, they would be too. If they had a motto it would be paratus sum. I am ready. *Barghests scoff at being 'born ready.' They are* conceived *ready. Conception to birth in less than twenty-four hours."*

And apparently, birth to full grown in a little over a month. Impressive.

As I came closer to the pen the no-longer-little whelp started wriggling and whining. Instantly, I felt a crushing sadness. *She was waiting for Telesto and Brisaya,* I thought, as my throat grew tight. The "whelp" glanced from me to the trail once before I entered the pen. She yipped and then let loose a full-fledged barghest howl. After that she came rushing toward me—a huge, slobbering, grinning beast with a star on its forehead and the most enormous canines I'd ever seen. It was the penultimate vision-come-true from the perennial magic spring here.

She bounded up to me and I sank to my knees. She plopped herself down in front of me, belly up, tongue lolling out of her mouth, her breath as disgusting as any barghest's breath I'd ever smelled. And yet it was the sweetest homecoming I'd ever had. I decided right then and there to take her with me when I left.

You want to do what?"

My brother looked at me as if I were that mythical barghest breeder's nightmare, Cerberus, the barghest with three heads. He and Linnaea exchanged a look that clearly questioned whether I'd lost my sanity off the Old Trail along with the poor whelp's parents and the sledge they'd loaned me.

"I want to pay Demeter for the lost sledge, barghests, and for this young one here. I want to take her with me."

"You want to take a *barghest* to *New Babylon*?" Linnaea repeated, still unconvinced of the soundness of my plan.

When Rafe had first brought Night and Linnaea back from the hospital where they'd both been working, Night had scooped me up in a great big bear hug. It was so amazingly demonstrative for Night that I realized he really had thought I wouldn't come back. In fact, he was quite choked up about my return—until he found out that Rafe had dug the cursed arrow tip out of my heart with a steel knife and magic and that Peter Aster had been the one who had cursed it. I think if Night had not already taken an oath to try and save lives, he would have sworn to kill Peter right then and there. And he was livid with Rafe for having performed such a risky surgery, in the bowels of a dirty dungeon no less, which raised Rafe's ruff, not a little bit, until I explained to Night in no uncertain terms that I would have cut it out myself, so Rafe had really *saved* my life, not risked it. And then, to make sure the topic was well and truly changed, I put forth my plan to adopt Telesto and Brisaya's whelp.

"Noon, where will you keep a barghest at St. Luck's?" Rafe asked. We stared at one another. The trail had aged Rafe. Or maybe it was the beard. Either way, he looked like a man in his midthirties now. I worried that I'd never see the carefree side of him again. That silly, ridiculous side. *Where was the spellcaster who'd created spells called Flame Resistant Blanket and Chillax? I guess that person was as gone as the girl who had needed them.*

"I won't be staying at St. Luck's for long. I'll be sailing on board the *Alliance* as its new sentry," I reminded him, partly to show Linnaea and Night I was serious about my intention to provide the whelp a good home, but partly because I was wondering what Rafe's response would be.

Was he really *going to abandon me so that he could become an Ophanim knight?*

But Rafe said nothing. I suppose he might have clenched his jaw. *How would anyone know with that beard?* If I were a more selfish person, or a less proud one, I might have made a mental note to grumble to him in private later about the fact that he'd said just a few weeks ago that *I* would be the one deciding whether we worked together next year or not. But of course I wouldn't. There was no way I was going to ask Rafe to stay with me if he didn't want to.

"So what are you going to name her?" Linnaea asked, finally capitulating.

"Nova," I said, grinning at the grinning beast who was now mine.

L ater that night in the Demeter springhouse surgery room, Night grew my tooth back. It was a dreadful experience. I guess I'd naively thought that since I'd survived the Old Trail, a *monstrum metallum*, a swarm of ice basilisks, the *Suffoca Ignem* curse, the *mortem animae*, Orcus, *and* Brunus Olivine, the classmate who'd been trying to kill me since last year, that having my loving, caring brother grow a single, solitary tooth back wouldn't hurt that bad. But Night explained before he started that neither Rafe nor any of the other Mederies would be able to use their magic to alleviate my pain during the event. Apparently, what Night was attempting was still relatively new territory for the Mederies.

In fact, no less than half a dozen of them showed up to observe him do it. Which meant that no less than half a dozen lady healers got to watch Nightshade's sister—this year's possible Laureate—scream like a kid and bawl like a baby when he started growing that itty, bitty thing back. I tried to stop him once, but Linnaea, good dental assistant that she was, slapped my hands away from my mouth. In the end, there was an embarrassingly little amount of blood.

Rafe came over after it was all over and leaned in close. Right before he started murmuring the words to a numbing spell, he whispered, "Luck, Onyx, you do make it hard to leave you." And then he laughed and the blissfully numb feeling in my mouth made it impossible to respond. So I narrowed my tear-filled eyes, lightly pinched his arm, and gave him a lopsided smile instead.

A few minutes before daybreak the next morning, we stood on the Maize train platform waiting for the North-South Express. Rafe and I were pretty much suited up as we had been for the past three weeks, with heavy cloaks and our backpacks, but Rafe's beard was gone, I carried the White Heart, and Nova now trotted at my heels. I'd be lying if I didn't say her menacing presence gave me the slightest bit of a confidence boost. I didn't know what everyone in New Babylon would think of her, but I was determined that, whatever the future held for us, I would take good care of her. Insult me, but don't insult my dog and all that. And besides I *dared* anyone to insult a would-be Laureate and her barghest.

With unbelievable ease, Rafe and I secured our own railcar and the three of us sprawled across the seats and floor in relative comfort for the next five hours or so that it took us to travel via train back to New Babylon. When I stepped out of the railcar onto the docks at the New Babylon train station the weirdest feeling passed over me.

Nothing would ever be the same again. And that damned bell wasn't responsible for all of it. I took a deep breath of city air, truly happy to be back and then—wasting no time because I had so very little of it if I was going to be the one to claim the top prize for twenty-two-year-old waning magic users in New Babylon—I asked Rafe to cast a cloaking spell over Nova and me. The last thing I needed as I raced to Timothy's Square was people stopping me because I had a huge, beastly dog in tow. I had the feeling it was the last cast Rafe would perform at my request but I refused to get teary-eyed at this point.

I asked Rafe if he wanted to accompany me to Timothy's Square. In his defense, he seemed genuinely torn, but then demurred, saying there was no way someone of my experience would be waylaid by anything this city had to offer up as resistance.

Part of me rejoiced at the fact that I was back in New Babylon. I couldn't wait to get a hot shower, eat real food, read a newspaper, have lunch with my friends—even see my parents. But there was another, tinier part of me that could admit now that New Babylon proper was . . . well, just a little bit boring.

I shook my head, amused by my own thoughts, as Nova and I sprinted up an empty alley on our way to Timothy's Square. Just before I got to the corner of Rickard Building and ran out into the square, I stopped. I held out my hand to stop Nova too and the two of us huddled in the alley between Rickard and an old warehouse building. This was the alley where I'd first let Ari touch my demon mark. It had caused a small explosion of waning magic but luckily no one else had been around to be hurt. It was deserted now as well.

I peeked around the corner.

Why the hell had I stopped? A painful zing started in my stomach and spread out to my chest, hands, and feet.

It was still there. No one had claimed it yet.

The gold leaf Laurel Crown was still hanging from the lamppost. I glanced around the square's perimeter and expanded my signature. There were two waning magic users in the square, but none that I recognized, and none that were agitated enough to be a potential Laureate.

That meant I was the first one back. I could walk right into the square and claim my prize. I could take that Laurel Crown off the lamppost and claim it as my own. I would no longer be a would-be Laureate. I would be *the* Laureate. I could choose my own residency next year. I could work for the Jayneses—or anyone else. I could work with any Guardian I wanted (except apparently Rafe, but I refused to let this moment be spoiled by that thought).

It should have been a moment of unbridled joy. A moment of pure, unadulterated bliss. A moment of complete and utter vindication.

But still I crouched behind the wall of Rickard, eyeing the prize instead of taking it.

Could I really walk away from the Maegester's life I'd trained for with my last assignment being the recovery of a sword?

Even if the White Heart was capable of reversing time, turning demons into Angels, or bringing people back from the dead, it was still just a sword. In fact, that's all it was now. I'd risked my life for a *sword*—a target, an object—not a person or an ideal. Crouching there unseen in the alley behind Rickard Building, I realized the Laurel Crown Race had given me very little satisfaction. And the things that had given me satisfaction during the race (like curing the *mortem animae*) had nothing to do with finding and retrieving my race target. Sure, I'd beat no less than seven different adversaries (a personal record) and I'd won the race. But I didn't want the rest of my life to be defined by the fact that I'd beaten everyone and won. I wanted it to be about making the right choices. And doing the right thing. I wanted it to be about helping those who needed it. As many of them as possible. I hated to admit it, but my father had probably been right. Working for the Jayneses would be wasteful and self-indulgent. They didn't need a Maegester's services. Even less an almost-Laureate's.

And then there was the problem of my Bounty Hunter's Oath—no small thing. I'd promised to use best efforts to find, retrieve, and deliver the White Heart into the hands of its *rightful owner*. Joy Carmine was the rightful owner of the White Heart. The letters of her ancestor, Kaspar Bialas, were convincing proof of that. Maybe it wasn't proof that would stand up in a court of law, but hadn't I said just last semester that I wanted my head and my heart to determine someone's fate?

Well, by not giving the White Heart to Friedrich, I was certainly determining my own fate. I may have thought I had no control over my future if I didn't win the Laurel Crown, but actually, I did. In choosing *not* to win, I was intentionally agreeing to go where the Demon Council needed me to go. Yes, I desperately hoped it wouldn't be the New Babylon Gaol, working for the horrid Adikia, Patron Demon of Abuse, Injustice, and Oppression, but I guess if that's where Karanos really needed me to go . . . well, I'd make the best of it and figure something out. After all, hadn't I figured it out with respect to the White Heart?

So, even before I felt the other racer approach, I'd made my decision. I wasn't going to collect the prize. I'd earned it, but someone else could have it. I didn't want it.

The second racer to make it to Timothy's Square was only minutes behind me—Tiberius Charnockite. From what I knew of him, he was good and honorable. If I had to lose to someone, he would do. I watched as Charnockite walked into the square from the southeast. On his arm was a woman with arresting beauty (wide-set eyes, high cheekbones, full lips, and an even fuller figure), semi-scandalous clothing (a rich-looking cobalt-colored robe draped over a jewel-adorned chemise paired with thigh-high satin boots and a whimsical three-cornered hat), and a haughty, almost amused look on her face. Her hands were tied behind her back and yet she walked into the square as if onto a stage.

Gou Nan Jounen An. Charnockite's target. Somehow he'd

managed to track down and capture the Hyrke double agent who had been on the Council's "Most Wanted" list since 1997.

When Charnockite reached the lamppost upon which the Laurel Crown had been hung, he jumped victoriously into the air and snatched it from its perch. Because he hadn't cloaked his signature, he was then immediately surrounded by a wave of other students alerted to his presence by the other two waning magic users in the square. Whoops and hollers, cheers and shouts erupted. I knew Nova and I would be discovered any minute. And I did not want to be discovered with the White Heart.

Very slowly, we crept back through the alley and away from the square. Just before I turned toward Bradbury in the distance, I felt an emotion in a signature I'd never felt before.

Tranquility.

Ari had once told me that waning magic users often experience tranquility in the presence of their family members. I looked around the alley.

Was Karanos here? I'd never felt his signature before, why now?

It didn't matter. I couldn't see him and I had to get away. The crowning of a new Laureate would mean a huge gathering in Timothy's Square tonight. The farther away I could get from here, the better.

Chapter 28

꙱

Ordinarily, I would have taken a cab from St. Luck's to Bradbury, but obviously Nova wouldn't fit in a cab, and even if she did, it would take too much time to find a cabdriver willing to take her. And it wasn't as if walking was foreign to me. That's all I'd been doing for the past two weeks or so. Luckily, Rafe's cloaking spell held out until midafternoon, which was when we finally arrived at the doorstep of the Carmine residence in Bradbury.

I hadn't been here since Beltane Break my first semester. At the time, I'd been brought in unconscious because my demon client had tried to kill me. After I'd recovered, I'd still been reluctant to use my magic in any way, even to light a celebratory bonfire. It was hard to imagine now.

I knocked on the door, hoping that Joy was home. I knew Steve, Ari's father, would be down at the docks, and Matt, his younger brother, would be away at school, but as conspicuous as Nova and I were now that Rafe's spell had worn off, I didn't relish hanging out on Joy's stoop waiting for her if she wasn't home. Thankfully, a few moments later, the door opened.

Joy stood there in canvas pants and an orange-, purple-, and red-striped sweater. Her white hair was tied back and small rubelite earrings dangled from her ears. Her gaze swept over my sunburned face, the sword between my pack and my back, and the barghest sitting on the sidewalk next to me. Nova's tongue hung out of her mouth as she panted beside me, her breath puffing in and out like smoke. She licked her lips, grimaced, and stood up. Anyone else not used to seeing such a beast surely would have fled.

"The barghest I did not *see*," Joy said with a slightly bemused look on her face. She glanced up and down the street to see if anyone else was watching. "Would she like to wait out back while we talk? I don't think she'll fit through the doorway."

I smiled my thanks and led Nova down the narrow sidewalk in between the Carmines' house and their neighbor's. Their backyard was smaller than the servant's dining room at the Onyx estate—Nova would take up at least a quarter of it—but it was a safe area for her to wait in while I went inside and spoke with Joy.

The Carmines' kitchen hadn't changed since I'd been here last. There was a scarred but polished wooden table in its center with matching benches and a cheerful table runner along its top. A cast-iron stove with all sorts of copper pots hanging above it stood in one corner, and in the opposite a desk surrounded by built-in shelves packed with recipe books. I tensed slightly upon entering the house, unconsciously preparing for Ari's presence. But the room was empty and I sensed the rest of the house was too.

Joy shut the back door and turned to me.

I stood stiffly before her, clad in everything I'd been traveling with—the heavy cloak, the pack, and the sword. It all felt beyond heavy now and I couldn't wait to be rid of it. I pulled the sword out from behind my back and laid it on the table. Joy walked over to it and stared.

"What's wrong with it?" she said.

"How do you know there's something wrong with it?" I asked. "I thought you didn't have any magic." *Well, except for that bit about being* immune *to magic and* seeing *things. But why mention that?*

"I don't have any magic," she said. "But that doesn't mean I can't feel magic. Or its absence."

Oh. I cleared my throat. I had intended to tell her the truth anyway. It was just that I thought I'd be able to lead up to the truth slowly. Apparently not.

"The White Heart's magic is gone. This is the sword that Kaspar Bialas hid, but it's no longer the famed *Album Cor Iustitiae.*"

I told Joy everything then. All of it. Except for the part about Rafe, which was none of her business anyway. I shed my cloak and my pack and slid onto a bench. Joy poured mugs of beer for us and then sat across from me, patiently listening as I told her the story of how I broke into Hell. She asked few questions, but expressed myriad emotions. And then she stopped me right after I'd told her I'd used Aurelia's gardening scythe to free the *mortem animae* from their curse. She was relieved to hear it but then said abruptly:

"I don't want to hear anymore."

I frowned. "Don't you want to know how the White Heart lost its magic?"

"No," she said emphatically. "I didn't see that and I don't want to hear about it either. It's safer that way. All that matters is that *you* know how the sword lost its magic. Because that means you can put it back."

I opened my mouth to argue—*aside from the fact that I never wanted to take a trip to Tartarus again, where would I get another iron arrow tip that had been: (1) cursed with the* Suffoca Ignem *curse; (2) shot almost directly into my heart; and then (3) removed by someone skilled enough to remove it without killing me?*—but the look on Joy's face prevented it.

She really did *not* want to know.

"Do you still have the box of letters from Kaspar Bialas?" she asked.

I nodded and pulled them out of my pack. Joy reached across the table, picked up the box, and took out the letters. When she only found three, she looked up at me, clearly questioning where the fourth letter—the one from Ari—was. I looked sheepish for a moment and then my expression hardened. Why should I feel guilty?

"I burned it."

Joy gave me an undecipherable look.

"Then you can burn these too."

"What?" I said, mildly alarmed. "Why would I do that?" I wasn't about to become an Angel archeologist but even I could appreciate the historical and sentimental value these letters had.

"Perennial magic works like a switch," she said.

Huh. Aurelia had said the same thing.

"Yeah, something like that," I agreed.

You turn it on; you turn it off.

"Read the last line of Kaspar's third letter again, Noon."

I unfolded the letters and found the line she was referring to.

The sole reason I don't burn these letters is that they are the thread that holds the sword suspended . . .

"If you don't burn them, I will," Joy threatened.

Luck below, had Joy Carmine and Aurelia Onyx been having lunch together while I was out battling metal monsters and fire-breathing ice demons?

I wasn't going to force her to get up and get a match. They were her letters. Hell, it was her sword. That's why I'd come back here. I shrugged and burned them. It was as easy for me as blinking. In less time than it took to say *red, orange, yellow* they were gone, ashes and all.

Joy smiled and then said:

"You *were* the White Heart hunter. Now you are its keeper. *You* are the thread that holds the sword suspended now."

I stared at Joy feeling all manner of emotions, although mostly I felt that I'd been tricked and that what Joy was asking me to take on was too weighty, too extreme, just too *everything*. But then she got up, unsheathed the White Heart, and set the scabbard on the table. She walked over to a small door in the hallway we'd walked down earlier and opened it. Behind the door was an ordinary closet. And then she slipped the sword into an umbrella stand.

An umbrella stand.

I glanced back and forth between her and the scabbard, getting angry.

"Was anything to do with the sword ever real?" I asked, my throat tight, my magic tighter, and my voice hoarse.

"All of it was. And is still. But since the White Heart's magic is absent, hiding it in plain sight will raise less suspicion here than building a strong room for it, don't you think?" When I didn't answer what was obviously a rhetorical question she said, "Take the scabbard and give it to the Divinity. They'll make a fuss, but believe me, most of them will back down when they see how valuable the treasure you've brought them is."

"Most of them? I'll bet I can guess who won't back down or stop searching for the sword this scabbard was made for." And, oddly, it wasn't Friedrich, the person who'd been the most incensed about my destroying the statue of Justica last semester. I had a feeling Friedrich would consider the scabbard fair reparations.

But Valda wouldn't.

"The Amanita and the Bialases have been at odds for centuries. And, if all goes well, we will continue to be at odds for centuries more."

"You're not really going to keep the sword in an umbrella stand, are you?"

"No, *you* are." And then she laughed and clinked mugs with me, looking as if all her cares in the world had been lifted, whereas I groaned inwardly, clinked mugs with her, and refused to be baited.

I left soon after. Before fetching Nova from the backyard, however, I did ask Joy one final question.

"Do you know where Ari is?"

She nodded and then told me.

"He's the new Demon Patron of Rockthorn Gorge."

* * *

In a way, I was glad Nova and I had to walk all the way back to St. Luck's. Because that gave me lots of time to think. *The Demon Patron of Rockthorn Gorge, huh?* So that meant that Ari was one of the demons who had offered me a residency position for next year. He was the one who was trying to build the hydroelectric dam—the one who wanted to meet with me before I accepted his offer so that he could outline the project particulars, the *rogare* threat, and *other matters that might affect my desire to accept his offer.*

I swear, if I didn't know how painful growing in a new tooth was, I would have cracked a molar right then and there. But by the time I made it back to Timothy's Square, I'd calmed down. Obviously, Ari had meant to tell me who he was and what he was up to before I accepted the position. That's why he'd made the offer conditional upon meeting me first. Karanos had said that, if I didn't win the Laurel Crown, I'd likely be placed in a residency with one of the two demon patrons who had made me an offer: Adikia, the Patron Demon of Abuse, Injustice, and Oppression, who'd wanted me to help her torture *rogare* prisoners at the New Babylon Gaol, and the heretofore unnamed Demon Patron of Rockthorn Gorge. So the only two questions now were:

1. Which residency would Karanos place me in next year?
2. If it was Rockthorn Gorge, what would I say?

The impromptu coronation celebration was well under way when Nova and I stepped into the square. As it had during the Festival of Frivolity, Timothy's Square now boasted numerous tents and vendor kiosks, as well as a large bonfire off to one side. The snow demons were missing though, although I couldn't say I was sorry about that. I'd had enough of snow and ice demons for a while. Lit up by the moon, the fire, and the lampposts, the gently falling snow served as a sparkling, silent backdrop for the denser, more boisterous human elements that were present in the square. At least a hundred students milled about, eating, drinking, shouting, and singing. Of course all of it stopped when I showed up with Nova in tow.

I had to admit, especially since I hadn't won and couldn't revel in any victor's glory, that it was more than a little satisfying when the crowds parted for me. I could tell from their faces that they were giving way out of respect, admiration, and possibly even awe, but not fear. These were my classmates. They knew me, if not personally, then at least by reputation. The fact that none of them ran when I brought a barghest with me into Timothy's Square was a huge compliment to me, and I suddenly wished I could buy them all a beer.

But first things first.

It wasn't hard to locate Karanos, Friedrich, and Valda. They were seated at a table on a raised dais overlooking the square, literally above it all. I walked up to the dais, snapped at Nova to indicate she should stay put, and then ascended the stairs. I gave my father a short bow and nodded at Friedrich and Valda, who sat to his right and left, respectively. I'd no sooner thought how odd it must look that I'd shown up without the Guardian I'd fought so hard for when Rafe bounded up the stairs and stood next to me. He too gave a short bow to Karanos, a nod to the Angels, and then grinned at me. I grinned back.

Karanos' signature was cloaked, and it wasn't as if his face was full of emotion, but he nodded back and his expression was tinged with approval, possibly even pride. I stepped forward and placed the scabbard on the table in front of him. Friedrich and Valda leaned toward it. Friedrich's eyes twinkled and Valda's narrowed.

"That's just a fancy scabbard," she said. "Where is the sword? Where is your target, *Album Cor Iustitiae*?"

"*Album Cor Iustitiae* is no more," I said with a clear conscience. I'd perfected the art of tempering the truth for good cause at the end of my last assignment, although I hoped it wouldn't become a habit for me. I then proceeded to tell them a shortened version of everything I'd just told Joy, including the fact that Brunus and Peter were the ones responsible for shooting me in the chest with the arrow that almost killed me—the arrow that had been cursed with a *Suffoca Ignem* curse. Their reactions to that were gratifying. Even Valda seemed surprised. And then I told them about the perennial magic spell I'd used to defeat Orcus. *Tempus edax rerum. Time devours all things. Etiam eorum qui vivificarentur per magicas perennis. Even those kept alive through perennial magic.* But I told them the White Heart disappeared along with Orcus and that all that was left was the scabbard. Valda seemed unconvinced.

"So the White Heart could reappear again at any moment?" she asked.

Our gazes locked as we each took the measure of the other. I stared into her taupe-colored eyes, so like Rafe's and yet so different. Her gaze was even more piercing tonight than it had been the first time she'd observed me—during my final Gridiron ranking match. I shrugged, breaking the tension on my end at least.

"I doubt it," I said. "You know what they say. Out of sight, out of mind."

"Why are you speaking in riddles, Noon?" Karanos said. "Speak plainly."

"Remember the ancient Sword of Damocles?" I said. "The one that hung suspended over a lord's throne by a single horse hair?" I could tell from their expressions that they remembered the story. "Do you think whoever ruled that country *saw* the sword hanging above him?"

"I thought that lord's chair was empty," Valda said.

"Exactly."

"*That* is your version of speaking plainly?" Karanos said. But instead of looking annoyed or displeased, he looked amused. Valda, of course, looked more than displeased, but Friedrich looked contemplative and friendlier than I'd seen him look toward me since I'd first met him.

I spoke directly to him.

"I know I haven't brought you the prize you asked me to retrieve for you," I said. "But I'm hoping you'll accept this scabbard as fair reparations for the statue I destroyed last semester. 'Metatron's Justica' may have been irreplaceable, but it's my hope that the commercial and historical value of this scabbard will in some small way make up for that destruction."

Friedrich reached for the scabbard, almost as if he were afraid to touch it. His face beamed with reverence. I recognized that look. I'd seen it on Peter's face when he looked at ancient objects. But it didn't mean that Friedrich would commit the sins Peter had. It only meant Friedrich was what he was—an Angel. They revered the past, pure and simple.

"Ms. Onyx, your debt to the Divinity is considered repaid," Friedrich said, picking up the scabbard and examining it further. Moonlight and firelight sparked from the facets of the embedded spinels, sapphires, and rubies. Gingerly, almost lovingly, Friedrich set the scabbard back on the table. I had a feeling I knew where I'd see it next—enshrined in the center of the House of Metatron over at the Joshua School, the place where the statue of Justica used to reside before I'd accidentally destroyed it.

"You may request the Guardian services of Mr. Sinclair for your residency next semester," Friedrich said, smiling at me. "And you will be most welcome at the Joshua School anytime you choose to visit."

I smiled back and then glanced at Rafe. *Had he told Valda of his plans to join the Ophanim? Maybe he'd changed his mind . . .*

"My son won't be accompanying Ms. Onyx to her residency position next year," Valda announced. Her gaze was sharp but not critical. She was too smart to continue a battle she'd lost.

Rafe turned to my father. "I've asked your daughter to release me from my oath so that I can join the Ophanim."

Karanos glanced at me (to gauge my reaction I suppose, which was bouncing around among grudging acquiesce, rueful resignation, and full-on unhappiness) and then nodded. I had no idea whether his nod meant he agreed with Rafe's decision or if he was just acknowledging that he'd heard him.

Our appearance before the "triumvirate of power" wrapped pretty quickly after that. Both Rafe and I would need to make an appearance before the Demon Council's court martial to make a statement about Brunus. The members of the court would have some questions for us but, considering Brunus' reputation, any "trial" would likely just be a formality convened for the sole purpose of gathering facts for the public record. My father told me he'd speak with me later about my residency assignment and then he encouraged me to pay my respects to Tiberius at the Laureate's tent. As I was turning to go, my father added:

"I imagine, Nouiomo, that *you* might have won this year's Laurel Crown if you'd only gotten to the square a few hours earlier." He gave me a knowing look.

Huh. Maybe it really had been Karanos' signature I'd sensed just before leaving to take the sword to Joy in Bradbury.

"Quandoque bonus dormitat discipulus," I replied. *Win some; lose some.*

"Indeed," he murmured.

Tiberius Charnockite's Laureate tent was not nearly as opulently furnished as Lord Lawless' tent had been, and the colors were much less garish, but there were just as many students inside of it, in just as many states of inebriation. Immediately upon entering, I heard three people call my name: Fara, Fitz, and Ivy, who were all waiting in line to congratulate the new Laureate. Ivy and Fitz were dressed in typical student garb: canvas pants, sweaters, and cloaks. But Fara, per her usual glamorous style and in keeping with the coronation theme, was dressed in a gown. The top of it was a leopard print bustier with black laces and light pink piping and the bottom was a billowing skirt made of pink, black, and brown ostrich feathers. Fara's usually platinum blond hair was streaked with low lights, piled high, and topped with a tiara. A huge tiger's-eye stone was nestled in the hollow of her throat. Which reminded me . . .

"Where's Virtus?"

"Prowling the alley in front of Marduk's." But she laughed when she saw my expression. "I left him sleeping in the Joshua School library. Where's Rafe?"

"He wandered off. Toward one of the drink kiosks, but I'm sure he'll be at the fire later." We both knew Rafe wasn't one for paying respects to false lords.

"I saw you got a dog," Fara said.

I bristled. "A barghest." *As if anyone would mistake a barghest for a dog* . . . I knew Fara was teasing though. She loved to try to get a rise out of me and I loved her for it. My mock frown turned into a grin, but quickly disappeared when both Ivy and Fitz started shouting at once. Ivy wanted to make it absolutely clear that she would *not, under any circumstances*, sleep next to a *barghest*. She'd just gotten used to *Virtus*, Fara's tiger, and now she was expected to live with a *barghest*?! Besides, no barghest would even *fit* in Room 112 of Megiddo. Where on earth was I going to keep it?

"Her, not it," I corrected. "Her name's Nova."

"Nova," Fara said, amused. "That's cute." She stepped forward. We were next in line to speak with Tiberius.

Fitz, on the other hand, just wanted to make it absolutely clear that I could *not, under any circumstances*, allow anyone else but him to dog sit.

"She's not a dog," I cried, groaning.

"I wonder how she'll get along with Virtus," Fitz said. We all looked at each other, eyebrows raised, considering—and then we burst out laughing. Their first meeting wouldn't be dull, that's for sure.

I let Fara, Fitz, and Ivy congratulate Tiberius on their own. I knew it would be quick and it was. Then they too left the Laureate's tent in the direction of drinks. Tiberius was another Maegester-in-Training at Lothario's Law School near Northbrook. His face was round, friendly, and freckled, his hair was so short it was practically nonexistent, and his build was strong and muscled. He called me up and before I could even congratulate him, he said:

"You took my prize!"

I knew I must have looked completely confused, because I felt that way. *I* took *his* prize?

"My top residency choice for next year was going to be working for the new Demon Patron of Rockthorn Gorge, but he said the only MIT he was interested in working with was *you*. Damn you, Onyx," Tiberius said, laughing as he clapped me hard on the shoulder. "And damn him too, daft loon." I swear it was only Glashia's training that kept my jaw from dropping at Tiberius' irreverence. I knew he was decent and fearless by reputation, but he must be half-crazy too, and apparently he valued that same trait in others. "The guy's out of his Luck-forsaken mind. A *demon* trying to get an electro-hydraulic dam built? In Rockthorn Gorge!" Tiberius hooted and slapped his knee. "That is going to be one *hell* of an assignment."

He seemed to realize that I hadn't yet said anything and he grinned even wider.

"Never mind," he said. "Congratulate me and I'll wish you Luck's blessing." So we exchanged well wishes and he called up the next person in line.

I'd already left the tent before I thought to ask . . . When had Tiberius spoken to the Demon Patron of Rockthorn Gorge?

Was Ari here in New Babylon?

Chapter 29

❦

When I walked over to the bonfire, only Fara, Ivy, and Fitz were there. My heart lurched. I knew Rafe wouldn't be sticking around now that he'd told everyone he was going to train with the Ophanim, but I thought he'd at least say good-bye. I turned in a circle, looking everywhere for him. I finally spotted him, leaning against the brick wall of Rickard Building. His back was to the bricks and one leg was bent, sole resting on the wall. His sandy blond hair fell in disorderly waves to his shoulders, partially obscuring his face. As I neared him, he raised his hand to his mouth and puffed on a cigarette. His silver bracelet caught the firelight, flashing brilliantly a second before the tip of his cigarette turned first fiery red, then grayish black, and then disintegrated completely.

It was like a repeat of one of the first times we ever spoke to one another. And it made me realize, whether I liked it or not, that Rafe and I had come full circle. Whether our lives would ever circle together again remained to be seen. But this chapter of our story was coming to a close and I would soon feel his absence, rather than his presence.

Rafe saw me and took a deep, deliberate puff. When he exhaled he blew the smoke in my direction, but right before it reached me, he turned it into a smoke simulacrum—a drakon. He'd done it once before. On the day he'd stopped smoking.

Light this and it will be the last one I smoke, he'd said to me.

Ever?

"Ever" is only as long as I'm working with you.

I stepped close to Rafe, but instead of lighting his cigarette, I leached oxygen from around its tip and extinguished it.

Rafe's carefully carefree look was back, but now it was even worse. Now he looked carelessly carefree. Recklessly carefree.

Hurt that he seemed so cavalier about the end of our partnership, I looked down, wondering what to say. A second later, his warm, dry palm cupped my cheek and gently lifted my head. My gaze met his. Reflecting the light of the fire, his taupe-colored eyes looked like flickering candlelight, at once both opaque and reflective. They glowed with an emotion that was both hidden and a mirror of my own. I looked down at his wrist as he twisted his silver bracelet off. I glanced up at him, surprised.

"Here," he said, his voice rough. "Take this to remember me by." I looked up at him, surprised. He shrugged.

"Bhereg didn't die, so I don't need to remember his death anymore."

I slipped the bracelet on.

"You should try to find Ari," he said.

I nodded slowly, thinking, and then said, "If I find him . . . what should I tell him about you?"

"The truth, firestarter. Tell him everything."

I moved closer to him.

Had he really only said he loved me because he'd had Ari's memory of falling in love with me? What would our lives have been like if I hadn't rung that bell? Maybe Rafe and I were supposed to have stayed together. Or maybe we

*were never supposed to have been together in the first place.
Magic! There were probably a million different lives for
each of us and all of them the "right" one.*

I stood on my tiptoes until my face was only inches from
his.

"And what should I give *you* to remember *me*?"

His gaze became even more opaque. The hand that had
rested against my cheek only moments ago was now buried
deep within the hair at the nape of my neck. His other hand
gripped my shoulder as if he were just about to pull me toward him. For a moment, he seemed torn. But then he gently
pressed me back. "I've got my own memories of you, Noon.
I don't need his—or anything else—to remember you by."
Then he kissed my forehead. "I will *miss* you, Nouiomo
Onyx." He cupped my chin for a moment and just as I was
raising my hand to hold it there—to hold him there—he was
gone. He dropped his hand, turned on his heel, and left.

Later that night, after we were all good and drunk, Fitz
asked me—since Rafe and I had just spent nearly a month
traveling in Metatron's footsteps and tracking down an artifact he'd allegedly created for his lover—if Metatron really
had loved Justica.

"Yes," I said unequivocally, staring into the fire, clutching
my cup.

Suddenly I wanted to believe that Metatron had loved
Justica . . . madly . . . deeply . . . fiercely . . . and ridiculously.

T he day after Tiberius' impromptu coronation celebration
was another, more formal, celebration—Bryde's Day. It
was a major holiday in Halja, honoring Bryde, the most powerful Mederi who'd ever lived. The holiday celebrated life
and those who make it. For obvious reasons, it had never
been a favorite holiday of mine. In years past, I'd dreaded
this day, and with each month, week, and day that it grew
closer on the calendar, I'd become more tense, more morose,
more unhappy. Not this year. This year I'd nearly forgotten
about it.

Last night, after saying good-bye to Rafe and trying un-successfully to obliterate him from my mind with good old-fashioned unensorcelled Hyrke beer, I'd stashed Nova in the cavernous lobby of Megiddo and stumbled up to room 112. Technically, my leave of absence from class was over, but I also knew no one would complain if I took one more day off before throwing myself into my studies and campus life once again, so I slept in.

I woke to find a note from Ivy, which made me smile.

Noon—

Went to Corpus Justica to study. If you get up in time for lunch, meet us at the Black Onion. Otherwise, we'll see you later at Lekai for this year's Bryde's Day feast. NO EXCUSES!

Ivy

p.s. Wear something dark and comfortable. There will be tons of food and possibly some ashes in the air after the MITs—that means you!—burn the Yule greens.

Much as I would have liked to have met Ivy and Fitz for lunch at the Black Onion, I had another place in mind for a midday meeting—the Office of the Executive. In all the time I'd been a student at St. Luck's, I'd never wandered over to my father's office, despite the fact that it was only blocks away from St. Luck's. I took a chance my father would be in and dressed conservatively: dark leggings and a velvet bus-tier worn over a gauzy undershirt that partially concealed my demon mark. Then I rescued Nova from the lobby, fed her, dropped by Marduk's, and ordered P.M. Grab Bags #3 and #6 (warm rarebit ham sandwich and cold turkey, lettuce, and tomato, respectively). After that, Nova and I set out to meet one of the most powerful people in all of Halja—Karanos Onyx.

The Office of the Executive was housed in a fairly nondescript one-story redbrick building to the northwest of the New Babylon train station. Looking at the building I couldn't imagine the Demon Council met inside of it. This building was much less lofty than any building at St. Luck's or the Joshua School. Scattered around the sidewalk outside of the building were a half dozen or so Hyrkes. They all had bicycles and map cases and wore suit jackets, flat caps, and trousers, so I figured they were document deliverers and messengers. Working for the Office of the Executive must have hardened them to seeing all manner of things because they merely stared when I walked up with Nova at my heels. Luckily there was an old horse trough near the entrance so I left her happily slurping as I walked inside.

The interior lobby was much busier than the outside. In here, no one was milling about waiting for orders. There were at least thirty other Maegesters, ranging in age from twenty-two to eighty-two, whose signatures assaulted me at once. It was impossible to process them all at the speed with which they washed over me, so I didn't bother trying. Instead I sent out the briefest ping of magic—my equivalent of a handshake and a shot across the bow—warning them to ratchet down.

Did they always greet new Maegesters that way? Or was everyone just so used to the decibel level that they automatically tuned each other out? Or maybe they all had magic tinnitus from overexposure to one another and they couldn't sense the overload.

Regardless, my ping had its desired effect. Everyone's signatures instinctively closed up. The rest of their senses turned toward me, however, and I suddenly knew how my father felt when he entered the Black Onion and everyone stopped talking and stared instead.

I walked over to the largest, most central desk. The man sitting there looked like he was in his late twenties. He had short straw-colored hair and gray eyes. On the thin side, with a signature that felt bouncy. Like rubber. *Interesting,* I thought.

"I'm Nouiomo Onyx," I said, warning myself not to feel

stupid for holding two paper bags if it turned out that Karanos either wasn't in or couldn't see me.

"I'm Faustus Flint," the man said, smiling. "I'm your father's intake clerk. It's great to meet you." Then he lowered his voice and said in a conspiratorial whisper, "You were my pick for Laureate in the office pool."

I'm quite sure my face registered the surprise I felt. For starters, it felt odd to meet someone who seemed to know me so well when I knew nothing about him, and secondly, *there'd been a betting pool about me? Here?* I couldn't help asking:

"Who did my father bet on?"

Then it was Faustus' turn to look surprised and, a second later, peevish. "The executive doesn't bet," he said rather stiffly.

"Of course not," I said hastily, and then added, "I'm sorry you lost."

He nodded and shrugged and told me that Karanos was out. I winced, but then decided to make the best of it. I took one of the sandwiches out of the bag, borrowed a pen, and left a note for my father on Grab Bag #6.

He found us in Timothy's Square not half an hour later. The wind was light, the sun was high, the air was crisp, and the sandwiches were gone. I'd eaten the turkey and Nova had inhaled the rarebit in one bite (who could blame her? It had to be infinitely better than the crow, vole, and lizard parts I'd fed her earlier). My father took a seat beside me.

"So you found the sword after all," he said without preamble.

It occurred to me to lie. Or to find some way to give him a vague nonanswer. That's what I'd done after my last assignment when Karanos had asked me if Ari had really disappeared in the Shallows. But there was no reason for my father not to know the truth this time. So I told him I'd found the White Heart, but that its magic was gone. He didn't ask me how or when that happened and I didn't elaborate. The only thing he wanted to know was whether I thought the sword that once was *Album Cor Iustitiae* was safe. I thought of the

White Heart standing upright in the umbrella stand inside the Carmines' coat closet. I didn't know whether to groan or laugh out loud. Glashia's training saved me from doing either.

"It's safe," I assured Karanos.

After a few minutes of awkward silence, I told Karanos I was willing to accept whichever residency position he placed me in—that I'd go where he needed me to go. In some respects, it was a silly declaration. Of course I'd go where he told me to go. That's how it worked. I wasn't the Laureate and regular MITs couldn't bow out or decline an assignment. But Karanos seemed to appreciate the sentiment behind my words. He seemed to understand that I wanted to share the burden of managing Halja and its many demons, both *regulare* and *rogare*.

"What about the Jayneses?" Karanos asked.

"I'm helping them interview sentry applicants later this week. Some of the candidates are actually overqualified. The *Alliance* will be in good hands next semester," I said.

He nodded, looking contemplative, but his gaze had already turned northwest toward the Office of the Executive. I knew his attention would soon return to all the myriad matters waiting for him back there. He pulled an envelope out of his cloak pocket.

"I could use you out at Rockthorn Gorge," he said. "There've been some . . . incidences there over the past year." I chuckled inwardly, both at Karanos' understated term and the fact that I'd heard him say something similar previously. *What a difference a year made!* The last time Karanos had spoken of *incidences* at Rockthorn Gorge, I hadn't wanted Ari to go up to deal with it, let alone me. Now Ari was Rockthorn Gorge's patron and my father was suggesting I become his consigliere.

"Two Maegesters and the former patron have been killed in the past year up there," Karanos continued. "So it's a position with some potential danger. But for an MIT who's been to Tartarus and back—not to mention one that could have been this year's Laureate—I think your skills will be well matched to the challenges you'll be facing. The new patron wants to meet you though. Said his residency offer was conditioned upon your accepting it." Karanos gave me a piercing look. "So I guess you get to choose after all."

I peered into his eerie, unreflective eyes.

"Father," I said cautiously, "have *you* met the new Patron Demon of Rockthorn Gorge?"

He frowned. "No," he said peremptorily, scoffing and standing, "That's what I'm asking *you* to do."

He pushed the envelope toward me. "Your meeting place and time. I'll be at Lekai tonight for the Bryde's Day feast. If you're going, you can give me your decision then."

I mumbled something—no idea what—and Karanos started walking out of the square. I stared at the crimson seal embossed with a waterfall. My mind was spinning and my throat was tight. I swallowed. Karanos had said I could let him know my decision *tonight*. That meant Ari was here in New Babylon. *Right now.* That he wanted to meet with me *today*.

I ripped open the envelope.

OFFICE OF THE PATRON DEMON
OF ROCKTHORN GORGE

Dear Ms. Onyx,

Our patron would like to meet. He'll be waiting for you at sundown on Bryde's Day in the tax and tithing section of Corpus Justica. If you are still interested in a fourth semester residency with us, please meet him there.

Nephemiah Zeffre
Foreman

I stayed at the top of the stairs for so long, I was afraid the desk clerk might come and ask me if anything was wrong. And I didn't want any attention on me. I was having a tougher time controlling my emotions than I would have liked. It felt like Fara's spell wasn't even working.

After my father had left Timothy's Square earlier today, I'd sought out Fara. She'd actually been on her way to see me. I asked her two things: (1) If I decided to accept a residency at Rockthorn Gorge for next year, would she agree to serve as my Guardian? and (2) Could she cast a cloaking spell over me that was strong enough to hide my emotions from even the strongest waning magic user? Then I confided to her that Ari was now the Demon Patron of Rockthorn Gorge and I was on my way to meet him.

She'd given me an unequivocal "yes" to my first question and admitted that she already knew why I'd asked the second question. That's why she'd been on her way to find me. Apparently, Ari had also sought out Fara's not insubstantial spellcasting skills for a similar emotional cloak to don for our meeting.

"And you agreed?" I'd said, my voice just the tiniest bit shrill. I mentally pinched myself and swore not to forget Glashia's teachings again. "Wasn't it you that said Angels were under no obligation to serve 'the demon horde rabble'?"

"We're not," Fara had said. "But I didn't think you'd want to meet him with *both* of you wearing your hearts on your sleeves."

I'd glared, but backed down. Fara had cast me up and here I stood, on the main stairwell of Corpus Justica, seemingly unable to ascend the stairs at a normal pace. The foreman's note had said sundown. It was now almost half an hour after dark.

I clutched the bannister, gritted my teeth, and pulled myself up the stairs.

I was afraid. Which was a ridiculous emotion to feel after all of the things I'd survived this semester.

But I was afraid of all of the other emotions I might feel. I knew my complicated feelings for Rafe didn't mean the ones I'd had previously for Ari had been erased. They'd been created naturally and I was stuck with them, even if I had to pretend I didn't have them in order to appear professional during the first meeting with my potential employer for next semester . . . *a demon patron who was having trouble at his outpost . . . A regulare demon who'd used the proper channels to request help from the Council for the unrest in his outpost . . . A demon who'd requested the services of a top-ranking MIT for his consigliere . . .*

A demon who'd made love to said potential consigliere countless times . . . A drakon who—

As viciously as if I were slicing off an opponent's hand with a waning magic sword, I slashed my thoughts, cauterizing them and sealing them forever in my memory vault. I refused to pull them out again.

Those memories could only be detrimental to me now. I needed a clean slate, and while I wasn't (yet) willing to let Fara create a memory-erasing spell to help me, I knew the secret to sanity lay in forgetting all of my past ties with my future employer.

So when I finally stepped into the unpopular tax and tithing section of Corpus Justica on Bryde's Day, with the whole of St. Luck's campus outside carrying candles that they wanted to share with loved ones, I was half worried that I might be greeted by candlelight.

Thank Luck I wasn't.

Ari was leaning against my study carrel. I think, because I was avoiding focusing on him too intently, the first thing I noticed was that I still had some unreturned books on the shelf. I'd need to return them before I started working for him.

The Demon Patron of Rockthorn Gorge.

Ari.

I looked up into his eyes. They looked the same, the color of black coffee with just the slightest hint of cranberry. I don't know what I expected to see there. Love perhaps. Pain maybe. Desire, longing, loss, sorrow—all the things I'd felt during the months in between now and when I'd seen him last. It was both more and less horrible that I didn't see any of those things.

"I saw Fara before this," he said by way of greeting. His

words seemed rushed. It was one of the only times I'd ever seen him struggle for composure.

"I know," I said. "I did too." I breathed an inward sigh of relief that my voice sounded steady, confident. I'd elected not to change. After carefully considering my choices, I figured the conservative leggings, bustier, and light shirt would be perfect for what we were all trying to pretend this was—a job interview. Besides, not changing had seemed like another way to try to convince myself that this meeting was *no big deal*.

Ari's chestnut-colored hair was cut short again and he was wearing a long leather cloak and boots. Something about the way his cloak hung on him looked odd and I spent a considerable amount of time studying the clasp, which was, in and of itself, unremarkable. But he never said a word. Maybe he was as content as I was to simply be in the same room. Although *content* wasn't exactly the word I would use to describe what I was feeling. And then I was angry with myself for having those thoughts. Ari's grimace was slight, but I caught it and frowned. Fara was almost as good an Angel as Rafe. Had she not cast me up as she'd said she had?

"Fara's an excellent Angel," Ari said, "but I think even she would have a hard time masking our feelings for one another."

I stepped back and Ari said quickly, "Please don't leave. I won't speak of it again."

As he had so many times previously, he let his gaze sweep over me. I knew that no detail of my appearance went unnoticed: not my bigger, blacker (and likely free of his *signare*) demon mark, visible as a dark shadow under the diaphanous material of my undershirt, not Rafe's silver bracelet, which I still wore (and which ironically bore Ari's real name), not my stiff stance, nor my hopefully expressionless face, nor my racing heartbeat, evidenced by the thrumming vein in my throat.

Unbidden the image of Ari shifting into a drakon inside of the Stone Pointe keep came to mind. But instead of feeling fear, I felt only compassion and forgiveness. *Six words,* I thought. It wasn't the Angel's bell that changed everything. It was six words:

You still love him, don't you?

Instead of wanting to run *from* Ari, I suddenly wanted to run *to* him. I wanted to run to him and press my cheek against his chest. I wanted to wrap my arms around his back and squeeze. Hard. I wanted to tell him how much I missed him, how much I . . .

Mentally, I cleared my throat. Well, how *worried* I was about the future. But not because I was scared of demons anymore. Because I was scared for them, or at least one of them. And what might happen to him when my father found out that Ari had deceived him.

And yet . . .

I knew continuing his deception wasn't the answer. I'd deceived everyone for the first twenty-one years of my life and I had no desire to return to a life of hiding. So Ari and I were both going to have to learn how to live, and get along, in a different way. We needed a new dynamic. He'd said it himself.

I never could decide whether to help you stand on your own two feet or sweep you off them. I realize now, it was never my choice to make.

If I went rushing back into Ari's arms now, all of the independence I'd worked so hard to achieve would be lost. And it would make it doubly hard to counsel Ari. To convince him to do things he might not want to do: admit he was wrong in deceiving us, apologize to my father, accept my forgiveness—and learn the truth about Rafe.

"Of course, I'll listen to what you have to say about what's going on up in Rockthorn Gorge," I said, "but I've already made my decision."

Ari's face fell and I was glad not to feel whatever emotion lay behind it.

"I'll do it."

We had things to work out, but the last thing I wanted was to make Ari suffer or manipulate his feelings. For whatever reason (likely some professional, some personal), he had asked if I was willing to come to Rockthorn Gorge. I was and I wasn't going to play games about my answer. But I would give him my terms.

"I'll spend my fourth semester residency in Rockthorn Gorge on three conditions," I said.

Ari's tense expression fled. His look softened and then he gave up pretending not to care that I'd just agreed to become his consigliere. His mouth quirked.

"What are they?" he asked.

"You need to tell Karanos the truth about what you are."

His look changed again but I honestly had no idea what this new one meant. It was undecipherable. He stared at me, his expression enigmatic. Finally, he nodded.

"Agreed," he said, "I'll tell him by the end of your fourth semester residency. What else?"

"I need two weeks off at the beginning of the semester to help train a new riverboat sentry."

"A riverboat sentry?" Ari frowned, clearly confused.

"Yes, for the Jayneses," I clarified. "For their flagship, the *Alliance*."

"But why are *you* training the Jayneses' new sentry?" He looked completely nonplussed now.

"Because they asked me to and I said I would," I said with just the slightest hint of irritation. *Was he going to start telling me how to prioritize my life again now that I'd told him I would spend next semester up north?*

"I'll also need another two weeks off during the month of Fyr to attend St. Luck's Fire Festival. There's a new skill I want to share with the first year MITs. And one of the weekends in—"

"*You're* performing at the Fire Festival?" he asked incredulously.

"Yes, Ari, *I'm* performing at the Fire Festival," I snapped and then I bit my lip, chagrined that I hadn't stuck to my own *show no emotion* rule, and then I nearly groaned out loud that I'd bitten my lip. *Where was my self-discipline?* Maybe

Glashia would agree to come with me. Because apparently being in Ari's presence made it extraordinarily difficult to keep my emotions to myself.

But Ari didn't seem to notice my inner turmoil.

"I thought you hated burning things."

I thought of all the responses I could make that would correct Ari's oversimplification and then decided maybe simple statements were best.

"People change, Ari."

His gaze slowly swept over me again. It was as if he were two different people: the contrite, apologetic fellow MIT that I'd known and loved, who'd lied to me and broken my heart, and the neophyte demon lord who was still stretching his wings, trying to build his fiefdom, and laying claim to what he thought was rightly his.

I narrowed my eyes and tilted my chin up. I reminded myself that, so long as I could control my emotions around him, I could control him. Maybe.

He narrowed his eyes at me and smiled. But it was a calculating smile.

I stepped toward him, so that I was only inches from him, intentionally provoking him with my nearer presence.

"I'm not the person you left behind in the Shallows," I said, my voice low and threatening. "Still want me as your consigliere now that you know that?"

"Yes," he said without hesitation, although his voice was as rough with unshed emotion as mine.

After a minute or so of neither of us backing down (it was like a kids' staring contest and I refused to blink), Ari finally said, "What's your third condition?"

I looked away and stepped back from him. "I'm going to need accommodations for a tiger . . . and a barghest."

Ari knew who would be bringing the tiger. He knew Fara and Virtus well, since Fara had once been his Guardian and we'd all traveled to the Shallows together last semester. But the barghest was news to him. Still, he chose to comment first on the beast that was more familiar to him.

"A tiger," he murmured, frowning and refocusing his gaze

on the silver bracelet I wore. He'd seen it on Rafe's wrist countless times last semester so he knew whose it was. "Did something happen to Rafe, Noon? Down in southern Halja?"

To his credit, Ari looked genuinely sorry. Which was why I was so quick to correct his misunderstanding.

"Lots of things happened," I said, grunting inwardly. *What an understatement,* I thought, although I knew now wasn't the time to tell Ari the *everything* that Rafe had suggested I tell him. "But Rafe didn't die. He decided to train with the Ophanim knights."

Ari continued to stare at the bracelet, his expression opaque and impossible to decipher. I'd tell Ari the truth, of course. Eventually. And he could have whatever reaction he was going to have. Maybe he wouldn't care. Although seeing him now, I knew that he would. But I'd done nothing wrong. And Rafe had done nothing wrong. Hopefully, with time, we'd all be able to forgive one another.

"And a barghest," Ari said finally. "Yours?"

I nodded. "Her name's Nova," I said then, suddenly grinning. At least there was *something* I could safely show my emotions about.

Ari stared long and hard at me, thinking of Nova and smiling at him. Then he said in a soft voice: "You know what Nova means, don't you, Noon?"

"A star that's a thousand times brighter than all the rest, although it eventually fades," I said, reciting a definition I'd learned long ago.

"Yes," Ari said, his voice softer still, "but every now and then, there's one that's a million times brighter—that *never* fades."

He struggled with some inner emotion. His hand twitched. I made no further move toward him. I wasn't ready to touch him. Or for him to touch me. Maybe I wouldn't ever be. He walked over to the window that overlooked Timothy's Square. I joined him and together we looked down at the Hyrkes in the square. They all carried lit candles. This evening, they were symbolic gifts of life and love.

Ari and I stood together, inches apart but not touching,

watching the revelers. I remembered that Ivy and Fitz, my father, and likely Fara too, were all over at Lekai. Suddenly, I wanted to join them. I said good night to Ari and started walking out. On impulse, I called back to him.

"I'll bring you a lit candle," I promised. "When I join you up in Rockthorn Gorge."

The look on his face was almost enough to have made everything—*everything*—we'd been through worth it.

Then I left the demon I loved in darkness and made my way toward the light.